A DISCOURSE *in* STEEL

"[Paul Kemp's] name should be mentioned along with not only RA Salvatore, but also with such luminaries as Neil Gaiman, George RR Martin, Terry Pratchett, and Tad Williams. His novels are a reminder that reading can be both entertainment and thought-provoking, all in the same breath."
Grasping for the Wind

"This rollicking tale hooked me from the get-go. Told with zest and humor, this is everything that is good and golden about classic old-school fantasy yarns. It joins my precious bedside shelf of favorite re-reads, 'comfort food' books I turn to again and again. Egil and Nix might not be the safest guys to go adventuring with, but they're sure good company. I'll be waiting for a sequel. Impatiently."
Ed Greenwood, bestselling creator of Forgotten Realms

"Did I mention how much fun Egil and Nix are? So. Much. Damn. Fun… I loved it. No, seriously, I really did. *The Hammer and the Blade* is about as sword and sorcery as it gets."
Tor.com

"Kemp delivers sword and sorcery at its rollicking best, after the fashion of Fritz Leiber's Fafhrd and the Gray Mouser."
Library Journal

PAUL S KEMP

A Discourse in Steel

A Tale of Egil & Nix

ANGRY
ROBOT

ANGRY ROBOT
A member of the Osprey Group

Lace Market House,   43-01 21st Street, Suite 220B
54-56 High Pavement,   Long Island City
Nottingham NG1 1HW   NY 11101
UK   USA

www.angryrobotbooks.com
Secrets and lies

An Angry Robot paperback original 2013

Cover art by Lee Gibbons
Set in Meridien by EpubServices

Distributed in the United States by Random House, Inc., New York

ISBN: 978 0 85766 253 8
Ebook ISBN: 978 0 85766 254 5

Printed in the United States of America

9 8 7 6 5 4 3 2 1

For Jen, Roarke, Riordan, Lady D, and #4

CHAPTER ONE

Ool's clock rang two bells, the deep gongs of the mad mage's spire filling the quiet of the small hours. The streets were empty and the city felt like a tomb, haunted by memories of vice and violence. A cold rain fell, the heavy drops thudding like sling bullets against Nix's drawn hood. The wind screamed through the narrow night-shrouded streets, drove the rain into horizontal sheets. Nix drew his cloak tighter about him. As always when he walked the Warrens, he dropped a copper common or silver tern every now and again, leaving them in the road for anyone to find, little seeds of hope and relief for the stricken.

He had his falchion drawn, and Egil had a hammer in each fist, though the precaution appeared unnecessary. Only fools walked the streets of Dur Follin on this night, at this hour, and the denizens of the Warrens were desperate, but not fools.

When the clock of Ool rings three bells,
And Minnear glows full and dire.
Walk not the streets, but fear the Hells,

Or lose your life entire.
'Ware the alley that comes in black.
For souls once lost, ne'er come back.

Nix recalled the rhyme from childhood, probably everyone in Dur Follin did. He thought he'd actually seen Blackalley once, as a boy. It had been just after the third hour, deep in the night, and he'd marked a fat teamster for a purse lift. The man had staggered through the dark streets singing a mournful, drink-slurred dirge. Nix had followed, waiting for the right moment, and then... he'd felt something, a deepening in the air is how he thought about it in hindsight, and a wash of profound sadness. The teamster's song had died and Nix had seen the man standing before the mouth of a narrow alley, an alley so dark Nix could not see even a step into it. The teamster mumbled something – Nix thought he might have been crying – and stepped into the alley. Nix had blinked, just once, and the deepening of the air, the sadness, the teamster, and the darkness were gone. He'd run back to Mamabird's home after that and had never ventured into the streets at that hour again.

Until tonight.

He shook his head and put the memory from his mind.

"We should look in on Mamabird," Egil said.

Mamabird, obese, ancient, and lovely, had been taking in groups of urchins for decades, feeding them, housing them, loving them. She'd saved Nix from a short, brutal life on the street, and he loved her as if she were his mother. Egil did, too. Everyone did.

"Tomorrow," Nix said, and left unsaid what he knew both of them were thinking.

If we have a tomorrow.

The rain and damp raised the stink of the Warrens and the blowing wind did nothing to clear it. The cool air carried the foul reek of decay from the Deadmire, the vast swamp to the south, carried too, the pungent, wretched smell of mold and garbage and shite and hopelessness that permeated the Warrens. Nix was well acquainted with the odiferous air from a youth spent scrounging in the Warrens.

"Smells like wet dog," Nix said, just to say something.

"Bah," Egil said, and raised his hammers as if he could smite the offending stink with them. "It smells like a diseased dog that bathed in the Deadmire and then rolled in its own shite. I'd breathe deep the smell of a merely wet dog."

"No doubt," Nix said, unable to resist. "Your people are said to have a… well, let's call it a *fondness* for their herd dogs."

Egil stomped his boot in the muck, splashing Nix with mud.

"These are new trousers!" Nix protested.

"My people are likewise said to be impatient with sharp words from small men with dull minds."

"A dull mind?" Nix said, his pride pricked. "Me?"

Egil shrugged under a wet cloak that hugged his mountainous form. "If it's apt. And by *small*, I spoke of girth, of course."

"*What*?" Nix stopped in the street and turned to face his friend, pointing at Egil's broad nosed face, barely visible under the cloak hood. "Small you say? Me?"

"Lacking in girth, I said. And I made only a general observation." The priest waved a hammer noncommittally and started walking again, the mud of the street audibly sucking at his boots. Over his shoulder he said, "But again, if you think it apt…"

Nix ran after him, further splashing his trousers with mud. "I don't."

"Ah," Egil said insincerely. "Well enough, then."

"Well enough what?"

"It's inapt. So you say."

"*So I say?* There's not a woman in Dur Follin who'd attest to your claim of small girth. Kiir only the most recent. And as for the rest, I was enrolled in the Conclave before I'd seen twenty winters. No one of dull mind could have done so. And, I'll add, only a hillman of infinitesimally small mind would think otherwise."

"Infinitesimally," Egil said, his tone carrying a smile. "Nice. But you quit the Conclave, Nix."

"Now I know you're just trying to be irritating. You know well that I was expelled."

"So you say."

"So I say?" Nix stomped his own boot in the muck, trying to splash Egil, but instead spattering himself with mud. He cursed and the priest ignored him.

"So I say? That's what you say?"

"So. You. Say. That's what I say."

They both stopped, turned, and stared at one another a long moment. The rain beat down. Thunder rumbled. Each broke into a grin at the same moment.

"You did call my people fakkers of dogs," Egil said.

"I meant nothing," Nix said with a tilt of his head. "Trying to distract myself. And it warranted a rebuttal, I concede. But small of prick *and* dull of mind? One or the other would be fair, but both? That's bringing a blade to a fist fight."

Egil nodded. "A fair point. Apologies. I meant neither, of course."

"Apologies likewise," Nix said. He checked the sky, their surroundings. "Let's just get this over with."

He walked on and Egil fell in beside him.

"Aye," the priest said. "What is it that we're looking for?"

"A good spot."

"There's under an hour remaining."

"I know."

Nix ticked away the moments in his mind as he sought a likely intersection, searching for promising alleys. Egil hung one of his hammers from a loop on his belt, took out a pair of dice from a beltpouch, and shook them as he walked, the sound barely audible above the beat of the rain.

Kulven's light was visible low on the horizon, though the cloud cover turned it into a shapeless silver smear. Minnear, the smaller, green moon of mages, would rise within the hour. Nix had to have everything prepared before that.

"Fakking rain," Egil said from the depths of his cloak. "This is a night for Gadd's ale and fish stew."

"It is," Nix agreed absently, eyeing the surroundings. "I blame you for my lack of drunkenness and the empty belly."

"Me?"

"Of course *you*," Nix said. "You've never been able to say no to a lady."

Egil stopped and turned to face him. "Wait a moment, now..."

"Here," Nix said, looking past Egil. "Right here."

They stood on a narrow, muddy road in the Warrens, at the intersection of two streets. Nix could see the dark rise of the Heap above the sagging roofs of the nearby buildings. Beyond that, backlit by Kulven's dim light, rose the great spire of Ool's clock.

Dilapidated buildings lined the street, creaking in the wind, leaning against one another for support like drunks. A shutter banged now and again in the wind. Alleys opened in the narrow gaps between the buildings, four of them. Just what Nix had been seeking.

Egil threw back his hood, blinking against the rain, and looked around. He ran his hand over the tattoo that covered his bald pate – the eye of Ebenor the Momentary God, aflame in a sunburst, a divinity that had lived and died in the span of a moment. To Nix's knowledge, Egil was Ebenor's only worshipper. And *worship* perhaps stretched the word into unrecognizable form.

"Nervous?" Nix asked.

Egil shook his head slowly, the way he did when thoughtful. "No, but this feels different than our usual."

"Agreed. Not too late to turn back," Nix offered, knowing what his friend's response would be.

"We gave our word," Egil said.

Nix nodded, threw back his hood, and unslung his satchel of needful things, both magical and mundane.

"*You* gave it, at least," Egil continued, "You wouldn't even take payment." Egil pocketed his dice and retrieved his second hammer from its thong.

"Sometimes you have to do the right thing, Nix."

"No harm in getting paid for doing it, though," Nix said. He glanced over at Egil and winked. "You were charmed by the lovely professor, yeah?"

Egil would not look him in the face. "Bah! I simply think one of us has to bring a conscience to this partnership."

Nix smiled and pressed no further. "Best that be you, I suppose."

"Best indeed," Egil said with a harrumph, and shifted on his boots. "She *was* lovely, though."

An old instructor of Nix's from the Conclave, Professor Enora Fenstin, had sought out Nix at the Slick Tunnel. Professor Fenstin – tall and shapely, her long dark hair marked with a single, striking band of gray – drew the eyes of all in the Tunnel the moment she walked in, including Egil's. In hindsight, Nix realized that the priest had been smitten from the moment he'd seen her.

Enora, obviously uncomfortable amidst the smoke and drink and bawdiness of the Slick Tunnel, had explained that her colleague, Professor Reen Drugal, had disappeared while doing research on the mysterious phenomenon everyone called Blackalley.

Nix and Egil had cursed as one.

"I thought the High Magister banned further research on Blackalley." Nix said.

Enora did not make eye contact, studied the table as if it were interesting. "He did."

Nix understood. "Drugal's work was unsanctioned by the Conclave, then?"

Enora nodded once, brushed the waves of her hair out of her face. "The Magister refused him an exception. But Reen went ahead anyway."

Nix shook his head. Drugal had taught Portals and Translocation and Nix had liked him immensely. "That's ill news. I was fond of Drugal. He was good to me during my tuition at the Conclave. Many others were not."

Enora licked her lips and leaned forward. "That's why I'm here, Nix. No one knows I've come. No one even knows that Drugal is missing."

"Yet," Nix said. "That can't hold."

"Yet," Enora acknowledged. She sighed and leaned back in her chair.

Nix saw the shape of things. "You helped him, I take it? And you stand to lose your appointment to the Conclave if this becomes a scandal?"

She didn't bother to deny it or protest. "Yes."

Nix took a draw of his ale. "You could just stay quiet. People disappear all the time in Dur Follin. There's no call for a scandal. Perhaps Drugal took a lover, wandered off."

"Nix…" Egil said, but Nix held up a hand. He needed to get at Enora's motivation.

"I can't leave him in Blackalley," she said, and looked started by her own earnestness. "He's a friend, Nix. I can't just leave him there."

Nix accepted that. "There may not be a 'there'. No one knows what Blackalley is. And no one comes out, once in."

She swallowed, for a moment looking entirely lost. "I know. But Reen spoke of you often, followed your… adventures. Both of you. He thought highly of you. And with your reputation, I thought perhaps…"

She trailed off and let the silence ask the question.

"You thought we could find Blackalley, go in, get Professor Drugal, and come back out?"

She nodded, visibly tensed in anticipation of a refusal.

Nix put his face in his ale cup, chuckling and shaking his head. He tried out the words to a polite rejection but Egil jumped in before he could offer it.

"We'll do it," the priest said. "We'll get him out."

Nix dropped his ale cup on the table. "What? I mean, what my friend means…"

Egil gave Nix a hard look. "I *meant* exactly as I said. We'll find it and get him out."

"We will?" Nix asked.

"We will," Egil said with a firm nod, Ebenor's eye on his bald head, like a wink.

"How much have you had to drink?"

"We can do it," Egil said.

"Really? How?"

A long moment passed before Egil shrugged and said, "We'll figure something out."

"This is Blackalley, Egil."

The priest spoke slowly, meaningfully, his eyes on Enora. "We'll figure something out."

Nix swallowed, licked his lips, shook his head, and called for another round of Gadd's ale. He sat back in his chair and looked across the table at Enora. "It appears we'll get him back."

Relief softened her face. Her eyes welled with gratitude, making her look lovelier still. She leaned forward and reached across the table and touched Egil's hand.

"My gratitude to you, to both of you. I will owe you much."

"Speaking of that," Nix said. "I presume the payment for this…"

Egil held up his hand and shook his bucket head. "No payment is necessary."

Nix tried not to look appalled, probably failed. "It's not?"

"It's not," Egil affirmed. He placed his huge hand over Enora's. She colored.

"You are drunk, aren't you?" Nix asked him.

Egil smiled. "No. You've spoken often about assaying Blackalley, Nix. Now we've got a good reason."

"Gods, man, you said 'assay'."

Egil just stared at him.

Nix knew from the priest's expression and tone of voice that an argument would be fruitless. He surrendered to the moment and raised his beer in a half-hearted toast.

"To good reasons, then." He tapped his temple. "Though I fear we've lost our reason. I'll need something of Drugal's."

"I can give you one of his journals," Enora said.

"That'd be perfect," Nix said unenthusiastically.

Egil thumped him on the shoulder, nearly dislodging him from his chair. "All will be well, Nix. You'll see."

Nix put his face in his ale, his thoughts already turning to the problem. He'd been intrigued by Blackalley for years. It was legend in Dur Follin, a dark doorway to a netherworld that appeared at random around the city, but always around the same hour. On a dark night a person might not even see it before it was too late, and everyone said they knew someone who knew someone who had a distant relation who'd disappeared forever into Blackalley while making their way home after a night of revelry.

Some thought it the open mouth of some incomprehensible otherworldly being. But Nix had trained for a year at the Conclave, where he'd been taught that Blackalley was most likely a wandering portal, probably some sorcerous flotsam left behind by the civilization that had built the Archbridge.

"We think it's a portal," Enora had said, as if reading his thoughts.

"Maybe," Nix said, sipping his ale.

Many had sought it over the decades: explorers hired by a city desperate to be rid of it, wizards of the Conclave in search of fame ere the High Magister's ban, adventurers with an itch to solve the mystery and whatever treasure Blackalley might yield. Most gave up without ever seeing it. Some presumably did see it, but no one could be certain, for they disappeared and were not seen again.

"Why your interest in Blackalley?" Enora asked Nix.

"*Interest* overstates things," Nix said. "I saw it once, as a boy."

"It's terrible," Enora said.

"Aye." Nix looked up and smiled. "I have some thoughts on it, that's all. Besides, no one has ever gone in and come back out."

"And that's the draw," Egil said, nodding.

She looked from one to the other, a question in her delicately furrowed brow. "I'm afraid I don't understand, gentlemen."

"Ha!" Egil said. "*Gentlemen* overstates things, too."

She smiled at Egil and now it was the priest's turn to color.

Nix tried to explain what Egil meant. "Milady, some men were put on Ellerth to write poetry, or discover lost lands, or start new religions, or do whatever it is that their gift impels. Egil and me, we were made more simply than that. We were put here to get in and out of places and situations people say can't be gotten in and out of."

Egil nodded again as the two friends tapped mugs, put back a slug.

"And that's your gift? Your purpose?" She smiled. "I admit I like that."

"Gift, purpose, both seem a bit much, don't they? All I know is that we've managed to keeps things lively."

"I should think," she said. "May I have one of those ales, also?"

While Nix called for an ale, Egil cleared his throat nervously and eyed Enora. "May I ask after your relationship with Drugal? You said a dear friend and I wondered...?"

"And speaking of getting into interesting places," Nix murmured, but the priest and professor ignored him.

Enora smiled at Egil without shyness. "Just a friend and a colleague. Nothing more."

Egil exhaled and leaned back in his chair, the wood groaning under his bulk. His eyes never left Enora's face.

"In that case, I'd be pleased to have your company for the evening."

"Listen to *you*," Nix said. "So polite."

"That sounds delightful, Egil," Enora answered.

Nix had slammed back his ale, excused himself, and left them to it.

The rain fell so hard it felt as if it would drive Nix into the mud. He crouched down, shielded his satchel with his body, and rifled through it. The sky rumbled, a hungry thunder.

"For souls once lost, ne'er come back," he said.

"What's that, now?" Egil asked.

"Just saying I hope we don't get lost," Nix answered.

"Aye."

"Take a look around, would you? Just make sure things are clear. I don't want anyone else getting caught up in this by accident."

"All know your spells never go awry," Egil teased.

"Fak you," Nix answered, smiling.

While Nix took the few things he needed from his satchel and ran through the steps of his plan, Egil stalked around the intersection, poking into alleys to ensure there were no drunks passed out nearby.

"No one about," Egil said when he returned.

The rain, having spent itself, abated to a stubborn drizzle. The wind, too, died, and sudden calm felt ominous. A thin mist rose from the muddy earth. The stink, of course, remained. Minnear had risen.

Nix took six of the finger-length sticks of magically-treated tallow and pitch from the satchel and handed three to Egil.

"Candles?" the priest asked.

"Not candles. And don't smell them."

Of course the priest sniffed one and immediately recoiled. "Gods! What's in these?"

"Didn't I say not to sniff them? They're made from something awful. You don't want to know."

"If I didn't want to know, I wouldn't have asked."

"Fine, then. They're made from pitch, a binding agent, and the rendered fat from the corpse of a man who died in regret."

Egil stared at Nix for a long moment, his eyes heavy, his expression unreadable. "Regrets?"

Nix nodded and said nothing, knowing "regret" cut close to the bone for Egil.

The priest spit into the mud. "Fakkin' gewgaws."

"Aye, and speaking of," Nix said, and pulled from the satchel an ivory wand and a fist-sized egg of polished black volcanic glass etched with a single closed eye. The latent magic in both caused the hairs on his arms to tingle. He rummaged for the special matchsticks he'd need, and soon found them.

"Dying with regrets seems a bad way to go out of the world," Egil said, his tone thoughtful.

"They're all bad," Nix said. He closed his satchel, looped it over his shoulder as he stood. "So let's avoid it for a while yet, yeah?"

Egil's gaze fell on the items Nix had in hand: the shining eye, the matchsticks, the shafts of tallow, the wand, which had a bestial mouth meticulously carved into one end. A boom of thunder rattled the Warrens.

"No more rain," Nix said to the sky.

"Let's get on with this," Egil said.

"Aye."

Egil followed Nix to the mouth of one of the intersection's alleys.

"Use those tallow sticks and scribe a line down the sides of the buildings on either side of the alley mouth," Nix said. "Like this."

He dragged the tallow stick vertically down the corner of the building, starting at about the height of a door. It left a thick, black line caked on the wood.

"Just lines? They need to be straight or…?"

"Just lines. They don't need to be perfect, just continuous from about door height to the ground. And make them thick. We need them to burn for a while. We'll need sigils, too, but that's what the scribing wand's for."

"Wait, we're going to burn the lines?"

"Aye."

"You'll burn down the Warrens, Nix."

"It's all right." He held up the matchsticks. "They don't burn with normal flames. They'll consume only the lines. Couldn't burn wood if I wanted them to."

Egil looked at the matchsticks, the lines, back to Nix. "And you think this will summon it? Blackalley?"

"We'll see," Nix said.

They moved from alley to alley, lining the sides of the alley mouths with borders of corpse fat and pitch. Nix followed up with the scribing wand. He spoke a word in the Language of Creation to activate its power, and felt it grow warm in his hand. He stood in the center of the first alley, aimed it at the wet earth, and spoke another word of power.

A tongue of green flame formed in the wand's carved mouth. With it, Nix wrote glowing green sigils that hovered in the air, the magical script stretching across the alley mouth between the tallow lines he and Egil had drawn. He scribed one set of summoning sigils across the alley at the top of the lines, and one set at the bottom, just off the ground. When he was done, the lines and the sigils formed a rectangle, a doorway. He stepped back regarded his handiwork.

"None too bad, I'd say."

Egil grunted.

"You still stuck on regrets and death?" Nix asked his friend, trying to make light of it, but Egil made no answer.

Nix checked the sky. He could no longer see Kulven's light through the clouds, but Minnear put a faint, viridian blotch on the clouds. Had to be getting close to third hour.

"We fire the lines now?" Egil asked.

"Not yet," Nix said, putting the wand and remaining shafts of tallow back in his satchel. "Now we wait."

"For what?"

"For Ool's clock to ring three bells. *Then* we light them."

"Three bells," Egil said absently. "Walk not the streets but fear the Hells."

"Aye," Nix said. He held his blade in one hand, the matchsticks and smooth oval of the shining eye in the other. He handed a few of the matchsticks to Egil.

After a moment Egil cleared his throat and asked, "How do you know he died in regret?"

Nix was focused on the hour and at first didn't take Egil's meaning. "Who?"

Egil held up the stub of the tallow stick. "The man whose fat is in this. How do you know he died in regret?"

"Hells, Egil," Nix said. "Who doesn't die in regret?"

"Truth," Egil said softly. "Some more than others, I suppose."

Nix could imagine the line of Egil's thoughts – his wife and daughter and their death – but he said nothing. Speaking of it only picked at the scab of his friend's pain, so he just stood beside him in silence.

The summoning sigils cast an eerie light on the intersection. Time seemed to slow. Nix pushed his wet hair off his brow and moved to the nearest of the alley mouths.

"When the clock sounds, we light them. The smoke should help draw it, as should the sigils." He thought back on the night he'd seen Blackalley, thought of the sudden, inexplicable sorrow he'd felt, thought of the way the mournful teamster had wept. "I think it's attracted in some way to sorrow or hopelessness."

"Ergo, the tallow sticks of regret," Egil said.

"Aye. And that's why I think it shows up in the Warrens more than anywhere else."

Egil glanced around. "Hopelessness and regret aplenty. Nasty bit of business, this Blackalley."

"That it is."

Egil tested the weight of his hammers in each hand. "Any idea what we'll find inside?"

"None. But when has that ever stopped us?"

Egil ran his hand over the tattoo of Ebenor. "Never."

"Right. Besides, my concern isn't getting in or what we'll find inside, but getting out."

"You said you had a theory about that, though."

"I do." Nix shrugged. "But it's just a theory."

"A theory's more than we usually have."

"Truth." Nix looked askance at the sky. "The threat of rain bothers, though. The lines, once lit, are to show our way back. I don't want the rain putting them out."

Egil looked up at the sky. "I think the worst of it's already fallen."

"So you say," Nix said. "We could wait a night, I suppose."

"We could, but how long can the professor survive in there?"

Nix shrugged. "No one has ever come out. He could already be dead. We don't even know that there's a *there* there. We could just… die the moment we cross."

"But you don't think so."

"No, I don't think so. I think it's a portal."

"Then so do I.

Nix hoped his friend's faith was not misplaced. "You light those two alleys and I'll light those. Light the left line at its top, the right line at its bottom. Got it?"

"Got it."

Nix shifted on his feet. "You know, the more we talk about this, the more ill-advised it seems."

"Aye," Egil said.

Ool's clock started to chime three bells, the gong of the great timepiece booming over the city.

"Remember," Nix said. "Left line at the top. Right line at the bottom. And don't hit the sigils with your body."

"Fakkin' gewgaws!" Egil called over his shoulder, as he stalked toward the nearest alley.

Nix did the same, and struck his matchstick with his thumb, and it flared to life, a green flame dancing on its end. He put the magical flame to the lines in the manner he'd described. The line did not catch fire all at once. Instead only a small flame burned on the end of each line, emitting a steady column of stinking black smoke that trailed back down the alley.

As Nix watched, the flame moved incrementally down the left line and up the right, just a blade width, as if the lines were a pyrotechnic fuse. Satisfied, he ran to the next alleyway and repeated the process. Soon all eight lines were lit and the chime of Ool's clock was nothing more than an echo in the heavy air.

The two comrades retreated to the center of the intersection.

"Those lines will burn for about an hour at that rate," Egil said.

"Aye," Nix agreed.

They'd have to be in and out of Blackalley by then.

Nix ran his forefinger over the etching on the shining eye he held in his hand. He took out Drugal's small journal, given him by Enora, and sprinkled a compound of enspelled pyrite on it. He spoke a word of power and the powder flared and was consumed. He tucked the book back into his tunic, close to his chest.

"Nothing to do now but watch and wait."

The two men stood back to back in the eldritch glow of green magefire and sorcerous sigils and the mage's moon, eyeing the alleys, waiting to walk through a sorcerous door that everyone else tried to avoid.

Nix watched the green flames move along the tallow lines, not sure if he was relieved or disappointed that Blackalley hadn't yet appeared.

The rain picked up. The magefire sizzled and danced in the drops as it burned its way through the tallow.

"Fakking rain," Nix said.

"Nix," Egil said.

"What?"

"Look."

Egil's tone pulled him around and there it was: Blackalley. It looked much as Nix remembered it. Darkness as thick as spilled ink filled one of the alleys, a black wall that stretched between the lines they'd drawn. Nix's sigils floated in the air before it, their light illuminating nothing. The journal in his tunic warmed, meaning they were closer to Drugal.

Nix felt as if he was looking into a hole that went on forever, and he felt a disconcerting lurch, as if he were sinking, falling into the hole, into the dark, lost forever. His thoughts took an abrupt turn. He flashed on himself as a boy, knifing an old man as they fought over bread. The shame of that murder reared up in him, overwhelmed him. He realized he was weeping, just like the teamster. Just like the teamster. The teamster.

"Shite."

He shook his head, came back to himself, grabbed Egil by the shoulder and shook him.

"Egil!"

Egil stared into Blackalley, his expression pained, haunted.

Nix grabbed him by the face and pulled him around.

"Egil! Keep yourself! Egil!"

The priest's eyes cleared. He shook his head, focused on Nix.

"Fak. That's… disconcerting."

"Aye." Nix stared into Egil's blunt-featured face. "We still going?"

"Nix, if he's still alive in there…"

Nix nodded, patted the journal through his cloak. "We can't leave him to that. Fine. Good. Well enough."

Nix spoke a word of power to activate the shining eye in his palm. Sparkles of light formed in its depths. He tapped the etched eye on its surface.

"Wake up. And go bright."

The eye opened and emitted a beam of white light. For the nonce, Nix aimed it at the ground.

"Ready?" Nix asked Egil.

Egil nodded. "Aye."

"Isn't this one of the moments you're always talking about?" Nix said to him. "Shouldn't you pray or chant or something?"

"My whole life's a prayer. Let's do it."

"Well enough," Nix said, as they turned in unison to face Blackalley.

The black wall shimmered. Nix aimed the light from his crystal and the beam illuminated nothing, was merely swallowed by the dark.

"Shite," Nix said. "It'll weigh down on you. Don't let it."

"Aye," Egil said. "Link up."

They locked arms as they walked toward Blackalley.

The clamor of the Low Bazaar leaked through the tent's dyed canvas: the beat of drums, the ring of a distant gong, the thrum of conversation, raucous laughter, an occasional shout, the music of buskers, and the occasional outbreak of applause.

Merelda smiled. She'd spent the first twenty two years of her life imprisoned by her own brother, her life made artificially tiny, her experience of the world trivial. She loved the Low Bazaar so much because it felt so wild, big, and unpredictable. In that regard she supposed it reminded her of Egil. He, too, made her smile, though she sensed the sadness in him.

She and Rose had adapted to their new lives quickly. Egil and Nix had been helpful, even solicitous – allowing them to room in the Slick Tunnel for as long as they needed, providing them with coin when necessary – but Rusilla insisted they not come to rely on the two adventurers.

"We make our own way," Rusilla always said.

And they were. They'd rented a stall on the outer fringe of the Low Bazaar, a smokeleaf stall on one side, and a seller of wool to the other. They dressed themselves in ornate but cheap jewelry, robes, and headwear, and told fortunes for silver terns.

Patrons came in for a reading and a shallow read of their minds told Rusilla and Merelda what they wanted to hear. The patron left pleased and Rose and Mere dropped another tern or three into the small coffer that held what they earned.

"For a home, in time," Rose always said when she deposited the coins.

At first, in order to get paying patrons, they'd had to busk the customers of the smoke leaf and wool stalls. But their reputation had grown quickly – quickly enough that they soon had a score or more customers per day, and many regulars who returned weekly. In fact, the "seeing sisters" had gotten well-known enough that they'd cut into the custom of the four Narascene readers elsewhere in the Bazaar, the oldest and wrinkliest of whom gave Merelda and Rose the Witch's Eye whenever they crossed paths. So far things hadn't gone any further than that, but Merelda worried they might.

She pushed back her chair and stood back from the cloth covered table, wincing at the headache that had rooted in her temples. She rolled her head from side to side, dabbed her nose to check for blood.

None, thankfully.

She stretched, her movements constrained by the gauzy, layered robe she wore. She bumped her headdress on a candelabrum and cursed. She spent most of each day covered in beads and cheap crystals and grease make-up and heavy cloth and she was well and truly tired of it. She imagined she felt a bit – just a bit – like the girls who worked for Tesha in the Tunnel. They, too, layered on clothes and makeup and false emotions and pretended to be someone else while they worked.

She reached out for her sister's mind. *Have you talked anymore with Tesha about us buying half her interest in the Tunnel?*

The mental projection deepened her headache.

Rose's mental voice carried from behind the wooden screen that separated a third of the tent from the rest. They kept a moth-eaten divan and table back there, as well as their coin coffer, and they used the tent's back flap to come and go unobserved. Merelda imagined Rose lying on the divan, resting.

Don't use the mindmagic casually, Mere, Rusilla projected, then said aloud, "You know better. And I'm trying to rest."

Merelda massaged her temples. "Did you, though?"

"Not in a while. We don't have the coin right now and I'm not sure she wants to sell a part interest. I can't push her, Mere. And I'm not sure it's right for us."

Merelda nodded. Tesha was not one to be pushed around. "I think it is and I'd wager we could buy from the boys."

A long silence. "Let's see how things go, Mere."

"Let's see how things go usually means no."

"Let's just see, all right? I don't like owing them anything more than we already do."

Merelda stayed on her side of the screen. She didn't want to see Rose's impatient expression.

"They're nice to us, Rose. And they don't expect anything."

In fact, both Egil and Nix seemed so solicitous of the sisters that Merelda sometimes teasingly reminded them that she and Rose weren't made of glass.

"Not yet," Rose said. "But they will. That's how men think."

"That's how our brother thought," Merelda said. "But he wasn't all men."

She could imagine the roll of Rose's eyes.

"We'll see, Mere," Rose said.

Mere rolled her own eyes and pulled off the headdress she wore. She set it down beside the incense burners, small gong, and various crystals that decorated the table they used for readings. The smell of cooking meat cut through the smell of incense that always lingered in the tent. Merelda realized she was hungry.

She poked her head around the screen and found Rose just as she expected – reclined on the divan, her long red hair spilling over the arm, her pale skin made even paler by the makeup they wore.

"I have a headache," Merelda said. "You take the next one, all right?"

"A headache?" Rose asked, concern in her pale face. She sat up. "Are you all right?"

"Just fatigue, I think," Merelda said.

Rose stood, came to her side, and put her hand on Merelda's brow.

"I'm not sick, Rose," Merelda said. "Just tired."

Rose dropped her hand and hugged Merelda. "I know. The readings are taxing, even the shallow ones. But it's worked and the coin is coming in steady now." She held

Merelda at arm's length. "We're not going to do this forever. Just till we save enough to start something real."

"Talk to Tesha again," Merelda said. "And if she's not interested, then talk to the boys. Owning part of the Tunnel would be a good thing." She laughed. "Pits, we could even rename it."

"It *is* a tasteless name," Rose said. "Fine, I'll talk with them. And I'll take the next few readings, too, but you fetch some lunch, then, yeah? Maybe some of Orgul's sweetbreads? I can smell them all the way in here."

"Me, too."

As Rose donned her costume, Merelda shed hers, removing the outer robes and the gaudy jewelry. Mere took five commons from the coffer they kept hidden under the divan and winked at Rose.

"Be back shortly."

Before she hurried out the back flap of the tent, the small bells that lined the front flap chimed as someone entered. Rose smiled her crooked smile, fell into character, and stepped out from behind the screen.

"You've come for a reading on a matter of trust," Rose said to the patron. "Sit here, across from me..."

Smiling, Merelda ducked out and into the narrow way between their tent and the thin, slatboard walls of Veraal's smoke leaf stall beside them. She stepped out into the din and press of the Low Bazaar, turned for Orgul's stall, and ran headlong into a thin, balding man wrapped in a brown cloak.

"Sorry, milady, sorry," the man mumbled, not making eye contact. He sounded drunk.

Merelda grabbed the man by the cloak and with her other hand checked her pocket to ensure the copper commons were still there. They were, so she released the man.

"No harm done," she said, and let the man go.

A crowd thronged the wool stall, everyone jostling and barking bids for bales of wool. A smaller crowd lingered before Veraal's smoke leaf stall, examining bunches of his leaf. Veraal, his thin gray hair crowning a face that looked made from old leather, pulled the pipe from his smoke-stained teeth, blew out a cloud of smoke, and smiled at Merelda.

"I'll bring you a bite!" she called to him, and he saluted her with his pipe.

She swam through the sea of colors, sounds, and smells, following her nose to Orgul's stall one row over, where four braziers sizzled with small cuts of organ meat.

CHAPTER TWO

Blackalley hung in the air before them. As they approached it, Nix felt its darkness pulling at the reservoirs of regret and sorrow that filled the lonely, late-night places inside him, but he forced his mind to focus on brighter things: Mamabird, the joy the urchins must have felt when they found one of the coins he left scattered about the Warrens; he thought of the sisters, Rusilla and Merelda Norristru, whom he and Egil had saved from a dark fate.

Everything went black and silent the moment they walked into the swirl. Nix could see nothing. He felt stretched thin, a piece of parchment about to be torn. The darkness was oppressive, heavy, and seemed to cling to him, as greasy as lamp oil. He found it hard to breathe. He lost his sense of direction. Nausea twisted his guts. Things forgotten churned up from the muddy bottom of his memories, sins small and large, petty things he'd done, spiteful things, all the things he wished he had never done, that he wished could undo. He wanted only to curl up on the ground and forget everything, just go to sleep and forget.

It'll weigh down on you. Don't let it.

He flashed on Mamabird, her smile, and came back to himself.

"All right? Egil, are you all right?"

"What?" Egil said, his voice muted. "Yes."

"Keep walking and think of happy things," Nix said. He had an idea of the dark memories Blackalley would dredge up for Egil. "Only happy things, priest."

"Right," Egil said, though without conviction.

Nix looked behind him, saw the faint green lights of his burning magefire, and it gave him hope. He thought of the moments he'd spent laughing with Egil, Kiir's long hair flowing down her back, her smile, Mamabird. He thought of Mamabird's laugh, her stew, her hugs. Mamabird. Mamabird.

The darkness around them thinned and the silence gave way to weeping, wailing, not from them, but from others. The sound was so plaintive, so hopeless, that Nix wondered if the portal had taken them into one of the Eleven Hells, where the evil were reborn only to suffer.

He realized that the crystal's light was faintly penetrating a few paces into the black. The dark earth felt spongy underfoot, organic, like walking on flesh.

Warmth in his cloak. The journal! They were getting closer to Drugal.

"We're getting closer," he said, but Egil appeared not to hear him.

"Who's out there?" Egil shouted, startling Nix.

"Gods, prie–"

"Hulda? Asa?"

Nix hadn't heard his friend say the names of his wife and daughter in many years. He cursed, pointed the crystal at Egil. The priest's shadowed face showed wide, unfocused eyes.

"Egil?" Nix shook him. "Egil?"

The priest looked past him, nearly shoved him aside. "Asa where are you? Hulda? I should never have left. I'm sorry."

The priest's speech was slurred when he said "sorry", as if he were half-asleep. He started off through the darkness, trying to shake Nix loose as he went.

Weeping sounded on all sides of them, forlorn, bereft. Nix lost track of the direction they were moving. The journal in his cloak went cold.

"Egil! Godsdammit, Egil!"

He tried to pull Egil to a halt, but the priest was a mountain of muscle and Nix could barely slow him down.

"Hulda! Hulda!"

"Dammit, Egil! Your wife and daughter are not here! Egil!"

Nix glanced over his shoulder and saw the twin points of his magefire growing fainter, like distant, dying stars.

"We won't be able to get out!" he said, grunting against Egil's pull.

But Egil didn't hear him and dragged him onward and soon the darkness had swallowed the magefire entirely.

"Shite!" Nix cursed, and tried to plant his feet. "Stop, Egil! Stop!"

"Asa!" the priest said, his voice breaking with tears. "Asa, I'm sorry. I'm so sorry."

The journal against Nix's chest warmed.

Egil slumped to the spongy earth, weeping. "Asa. Asa."

The darkness around them deepened, perhaps fed by Egil's thoughts. Nix fought it with thoughts of sun and laughter and love. A presence manifested off in the black.

To Nix it felt like a door had opened and something big and dark and terrible was looking through. Nix sensed the weight of an alien regard as it settled on him. His teeth chattered. A breeze picked up, warm and damp, like the breath of something unimaginably huge.

Nix's mind roiled, memories assaulting him, hateful things, matters he regretted, things that made him loathe himself. The darkness grew more profound. He could barely see. The light of his crystal was dying. He wanted to cry, to curl up and cry. He ran his finger over his falchion's edge, drew blood, and hissed at the pain.

"Keep yourself, keep yourself, keep yourself," he said over and over. He dug a fingernail into the cut on his thumb and the pain gave him focus. The darkness relented a bit. But something was coming, something dark and spiteful and beyond Nix.

"Asa," Egil pleaded, sobbing. "Oh, Asa."

Nix kneeled over the priest and smacked him hard, once, twice, a third time.

"Egil! Egil!"

The priest bled from his nose and Nix hit him again and again.

"Egil! There's something in here, something that feeds on sorrow and hate and regret it's coming for us now and we have to get out! Get up! Get up!"

"What?" the priest's eyes gained focus. He daubed at his nose. "What? Oh gods, Nix."

With the priest freed from the cage of his thoughts, the darkness lifted still more. Nix thought he heard a slithering out in the black, something huge and serpentine sliding over the spongy earth.

"Come on!" he said, and they staggered through the

dark, nearly blind, both terrified, as something awful squirmed after them.

The journal in Nix's chest went from warm to hot. He wanted to ignore it, but he couldn't.

"Wait, wait! He's close, Egil."

"I know!"

"No, I mean Drugal! Professor Drugal! Quiet."

They fell silent and tried to listen over the sounds of their own beating hearts and gasps. Sobs from the left.

"There," Nix said, and pulled Egil along behind him. He pointed with the light, its beam a faint, diffuse glow, and saw Drugal. The professor lay on the ground on his side, half submerged in the dark, spongy earth. Tendrils of it snaked up his arms and face like black veins, like roots. It was as if he were being slowly absorbed by the ground. He had his hands over his eyes and his body shook with sobs. He murmured something unintelligible.

"Gods," Nix said. He kneeled and put his hand on the professor's shoulder. "Professor Drugal!"

The presence grew closer, stronger, darker.

"Nix!" Egil warned.

"I know." Nix shook Drugal. "Drugal!"

Nix tried to roll the professor over but he was stuck. Nix tried harder, heard a wet ripping sound, and the professor screamed with agony. Nix put the crystal eye right up to the professor's body and almost puked.

The earth – or whatever it was – had merged with his flesh, the spongy, black substance growing into his skin and into his body. Nix pried one of the professor's hands from his face. His eyes were gone, replaced by a nest of black, scaly tendrils that presumably snaked up into his brain. Much of his body must have been filled by the writhing appendages.

Nix thought of himself and Egil going out that way and the idea nearly overwhelmed him, but he pushed it away.

"Nix, it's coming," Egil said.

"I can't leave him like this," Nix said.

"So don't," Egil said meaningfully. "Don't."

Nix took his point.

"Sorry," he said to his old professor. He stood and stabbed Drugal through the chest. The professor's entire body spasmed, and black ichor rather than blood oozed from the wound. But at least the weeping stopped. Nix hoped he found peace.

Nix looked back into the darkness where lurked a horror. He saw nothing, but he sensed it there, awesome and terrible and sinister.

"Come on," he said to Egil.

Together, they hurried off but Nix quickly realized he had no idea where his magefire beacons were. He didn't know which direction they were heading. They could've been going in circles.

"Nix," Egil said, tension thick in his voice.

"I know."

"We have to go."

"I know."

"Which way?" Egil said. "Which way?"

"I don't know! I can't see the damned lights! I need to think!"

The presence closed on them. Another warm breeze blew over them, the exhalation of reified terror. Nix fought down thoughts that bubbled from the dark parts of himself.

"Then think on the run!" Egil said, and grabbed him and pulled him along. They staggered and stumbled along in the darkness, the lurker looming large in their thoughts.

"I don't see any lights!" Egil said.

"We don't need the lights," Nix said, and stopped.

"What?"

"It feeds on sorrow, on self-loathing, regret. We're going to give it the opposite."

"What? You're not making sense."

"Yes I am. Turn around. Face it. And shove everything pleasing and happy back into its face."

"What do you mean?"

"We're going to make it spit us out, Egil."

"The fak?"

"Do it."

As one, they stopped, turned around and faced the emptiness, faced the fact that they'd done things and thought things that shamed them.

The darkness was utter, a black curtain, and cold, and coming, and the something that lurked within it was terrible and old and hateful, the embodiment and sum of the regrets and spite and shame of who knew how many poor souls trapped within.

Nix realized all that, realized the force of the creature he faced, held his ground, and smiled. He turned his thoughts mostly to Mamabird, but he thought too of friends he'd known and loved and with whom he'd laughed, he thought of Kiir's smile, of Tesha's well-intentioned anger, he thought of a stray dog he'd befriended in adolescence, of lives he'd saved over the years. He thought of Egil, of a friendship that had weathered the worst the world could do and endured.

The darkness howled at him, a deep rumble that carried a city's worth of spite in its bass tone. It came closer, closer, picking up speed. Nix imagined a great mouth, filled with fangs and hate and rage.

"Don't move, Egil. Think of the day your daughter was born, her first smile, think of the first girl you loved, your first kiss, the day you married your wife, think of that time we got over on that one eyed sorcerer and his familiar, think of Lis when she touched your arm at the Tunnel…"

The darkness streaked toward them, a howling, shrieking black wind that cloaked them in cold and night. They screamed in answer, braced against its onslaught, shielding their faces and blinking in the ink and Nix heard something in the shriek, a plaintive wail that sounded like…

The gong of Ool's clock.

A cool drizzle fell. He looked around, startled, the echo of Blackalley's howl still in his ears. He stood at the mouth of an alley, but not the alley in the Warrens. He grabbed Egil by his bicep.

"We're out! You did it! You all right?"

Egil shook his huge head, looked around as if he'd just awakened from a three day drunk. "Yeah. Maybe. I don't know. Where are we? Not in the Warrens."

"No." Nix searched the skyline for Ool's clock, for the Archbridge. He could smell the Meander in the wind, fish and sewage.

"Near the Dock Ward, I think."

"What happened?"

"I guess it spat us out." Nix answered.

"It's a good thing you taste like shite," Egil said.

"You're not the first to say that."

The sun was up, though hidden by a blanket of rain clouds. It was early morning. How long had they been trapped in Blackalley? It had seemed less than an hour, yet many hours had passed.

"Gods," Egil said and ran his hand over his tattoo. "Gods."

"Thirded," Nix said.

Egil gathered himself. "Well done, my friend."

Nix nodded, pleased with the ordinarily stoic priest's praise.

Egil blew out a breath, dusted himself off. "Who's going to tell Enora about Drugal?"

"You are."

"Why me?"

Nix dropped his voice an octave to imitate Egil's deeper voice. "Because sometimes you have to do the right thing, Nix."

Egil sagged. "Shite. All right."

"But first a drink, yeah."

"Aye," Egil said.

"Then a visit to Mamabird, yeah?"

"Yeah. Be more than good to see her."

As they walked away, Nix couldn't help but glance back at the alley: shadowed but not black, not Blackalley. He thought of the sound he'd heard in Blackalley's shriek, the plaintive words that had come not from those trapped inside but from Blackalley itself.

Free us.

He shivered and blamed the rain. Seemed better that way. He pulled his cloak tight about him and they made their way to the Slick Tunnel.

●●●●

Rusk lingered among the crowd and watched the fortune teller – Merelda was her name, the younger of the two faytors – disappear into the swirl of color and noise. She'd just made his work easier and for that he tossed a pray at Aster, god of the guild. Wasting no time, he ducked down the narrow opening between the fortune teller's tent and the adjacent smoke leaf stall.

Through the rear entrance to the tent he could make the other fortune teller's voice, together with that of the Upright Man himself. He smiled, thinking of the jest he'd been making since the guildseers had given them auspicious omens and he and Channis had gone forward with the click.

Gonna turn the Upright Man into a dustman.

He glanced back the way he'd come to ensure he was unobserved, then drew his crossbow from where it hung behind his back. He took a boiled leather bottle from his belt pouch and unwound the tie that kept it closed. The acridity of the bloodleaf paste within stung his nostrils and made his eyes water but he blinked it away and swallowed a curse. He drew a single bolt from the low capacity quiver on his thigh and dipped the tip into the bottle. Then he laid the poisoned bolt in its groove in the crossbow and placed the crossbow on the ground. He retied the bottle and placed it back in his belt pouch. Couldn't be too careful with bloodleaf.

Ready, he nodded at a shadowy corner between the tent and stall, held his hands before him, palms out, and threw a pray to the Lord of Stealth.

"Fly true," he whispered, then, to ensure the assassination went right. "And don't queer the click, yeah?"

His eyes fell on the holy sigil on the back of his hand: five blades sticking out at different angles from a central circle that looked like a coin. He grinned, thinking how the Committee's tats would shift after today, the ink, once changed, showing a new hierarchy.

He pulled up the hood of his cloak, hiding his features, picked up the crossbow, and crept into the tent.

The man who sat across from Rusilla wore a loose green cloak over fitted leathers. The thin blade of a gentleman hung from a snakeskin scabbard at his belt. He wore a silver chain from which hung a tarnished silver charm – a stiletto with a coin balanced on its tip, the symbol of Aster, god of merchants and thieves. Grey whiskers dotted the man's sharp-featured face and his small dark eyes seemed to miss little. He immediately struck Rusilla as coiled, tense.

"Word is you're a genuine faytor, not a zany like these others in the bazaar."

The man's manner of speech took her aback. He didn't speak at all like a gentleman, despite his attire.

"You mean 'seer'?" she asked.

"Ain't that what I said?" He smiled. One of his teeth front teeth was chipped. "So or not?"

"Yes," Rusilla lied, and reminded herself to be careful with this hard-speaking man with a wealthy man's weapons. He was not what he appeared.

The man leaned forward and put his gloved hands on the table and interlaced his fingers, a gesture Rusilla found vaguely threatening.

"'Cause I'll pay for the genuine thing. Fact is, I'll give you a lot of work if what you say happens, right? We can always use a true seer."

"We?" she asked.

He ignored the question, reached into an inner pocket of his cloak, removed a gold crown, and laid it on the table next to the gong. Rusilla was born to a noble family – albeit a cursed one – and had seen more than a fair share of gold coins, so the reveal of a crown perhaps didn't have the effect the man had hoped. He leaned back in his chair, brow furrowed.

"You see this is gold, yeah? It ain't 'feit. Bite it, if you need."

"That's very generous, but a silver tern is all that's required. Or two if you find the reading particularly useful."

He looked baffled at her response.

"Ain't I in the Low Bazaar? You a queen slummin' with your subjects?"

She smiled tightly. "Shall we begin?"

"Right, then," he said. "Right."

Rusilla rang the small gong once, waved incense smoke into her face and then into his. She reached across the table and took his gloved hands in hers while she extended her mental fingers and gently sifted the surface thoughts of the man.

He was worried.

"You are concerned about someone close to you."

His expression remained neutral, his eyes fixed on her, studying her.

She closed her eyes and furrowed her brow, part of the routine she used to impress patrons. She reached deeper into his thoughts.

"You question the loyalty of those close to you."

He tried to hide it, but she felt him tense.

"You fear they plot against you." She opened her eyes. "You're right to fear. They do."

He stared into her face and she stared back. Finally he gave a forced smile.

"You're good, yeah? But maybe I get to ask a question now? Ain't that how it works?"

She nodded, kept her delicate hold on his thoughts. If she were to reach deeper into his mind, she'd need to distract him. "Let me have your palms. Without the gloves."

He hesitated and she saw in his thoughts why: He had a tattoo on his hands, a tattoo that was special somehow, and that looked like a compass rose, eight blades sticking out from a central circle. It was significant somehow, magical.

"The tattoo needn't concern you," she said, to further amaze him.

He surprised her by seizing her hands in hands. His expression went hard.

"How do you know about that?" He looked around the tent as if enemies might be closing in. He shook her hands, shaking the table, nearly toppling a clay incense burner. "Who are you?"

She kept her voice calm. "I'm the seer you came to see. And I'm *seeing*."

He stared at her a long while, some kind of calculation going on behind his dead, cold eyes. She tried to see it but couldn't. He was practiced as a matter of course at keeping thoughts from his face, which had the effect of compartmentalizing them in his thoughts. And she didn't want to pry too far. She needed to cut this reading short.

"Release my hands," she said.

He stared at her a moment longer then opened his fingers, releasing his grip.

"Ain't you a gimcrack."

She cleared her throat. "I think I'm not the seer for you. And this is not a good day. It's inauspicious. We should end it now."

"That ain't happenin'," he said, and peeled off his gloves, staring into her face the while. "You read, and you tell me what I want to hear, yeah?"

"I don't–"

"*Yeah?*"

With his gloves off, she could see the tattoo on the back of his hand, the tattoo that she'd seen moments before in his thoughts. He noticed her looking at it, held his hands before his face acted as if he were playing peekaboo with a child.

"Boo," he said, with a mean grin.

The tattoo had no more effect on her than had the gold crown – she didn't know what it meant – and once more he seemed surprised at her lack of reaction.

"You don't know who I am, do you?" he asked.

"I don't need to for a reading. In fact it can get in the way."

He shrugged, seemed to accept that. He stared at the tattoo. "It moves about, see. The sigil. It's on my hand today, which usually means... well, it usually means I'll be using my hands for a certain kind of work. Tomorrow it might be somewhere else on my skin."

She nodded as if she cared and held out her hands once more.

"Shall we continue?"

"Yeah," he said, and allowed her to take his hands in hers. With her thumbs, she traced the lines of his hands, to distract his mind from her mental intrusion.

"Ask your question," she said.

"Right, then." He cleared his throat, tried to gesture with his hands as he spoke, but she held them tight. "I have men, see, lieutenants you might say, and a couple of them I think might intend me ill." He chuckled as if at some private joke.

She saw in his thoughts the faces of the men he meant, each with a tattoo similar to his own but slightly different. She squeezed his hands and snuck further into his thoughts, beyond some of the barriers he'd unconsciously erected. She saw the man he worried after most, a whip-thin, hard-eyed man with long dark hair and a face so scarred they looked like an old man's wrinkles. He had a tattoo with seven pointed blades sticking out of a central circle.

"The scarred man," she said, pulling out his thoughts and holding them up for him to see. "And seven points."

"Aye, him. And others. So if they intend something, I need to know. I'll need to do them ill first, you follow? And I can't trust the guild seers no more."

She nodded, digging deeper than she should into his twisting, paranoid thoughts, looking for the bricks she'd use to build a plausible answer to whatever he asked.

"So what I need to know," he said, "is when and where they–"

His eyes went wide and he gagged on his words as his throat sprouted the feathered end of a crossbow bolt. Blood spattered Rusilla's face, the table, warm crimson dots. The man wheezed, flailed, gurgled, and toppled back in his chair, his hands clutching at the air as if to pull himself back up.

His dying thoughts rushed into Rusilla, a lightning storm of images, feelings, regrets, faces, deeds, friends, enemies. She lurched up, toppling her own chair and slamming her knee into the table. The gong, crystals, and incense burners scattered to the floor. She screamed, stumbled back a step, bumped into the wooden screen, clutching her head and trying to pull her mind back from his. But the rush of his thoughts and emotions and memories held her, caught her up in its current, forced her to see, to know. The expiring man's thoughts exploded out of him like a wild blunderbuss shot, spraying her own mind, bits and pieces of his past and present lodging in her consciousness.

She lost her footing on something – a crystal – and fell and hit the floor hard. She was certain that her head would explode. It had to; it was filling too fast. She screamed out some of the images flooding her mind, calling out names and places, trying to expiate the memories and thoughts and feelings by giving them voice, but her shouted words soon turned to nothing but a long wail of pain.

She was dimly aware of smoke rising from somewhere in the tent, collecting near the billowing ceiling. She heard movement behind her but could not turn her head. Snot and blood poured out of her nose, ran down her cheeks. Her skull was going to crack open to let her swollen brain leak out. Her vision reduced down to a tunnel, narrowing, narrowing, narrowing...

CHAPTER THREE

Rusk cursed, backed off a step, and with his free hand signed against sorcery. The fortune teller was shouting things she couldn't possibly know, names and places and jobs and payments – *guild business*. But she did know somehow. Sorcery. Had to be. "Shite," he whispered.

He turned to bolt but she fell silent and he held for a moment behind the wooden screen, uncertain. He could smell smoke rising and Bazaar slubber's would smell it, too, and come. He needed to clear the tent, but the fortune teller *knew* guild business…

He made up his mind, hung his crossbow, drew his pig poker, and peeked around the screen. Two small fires burned, started by the overturned incense burners. The flames caught a blanket and a tasseled pillow. The whole tent would go up soon…

The Upright Man lay on his back in a pool of crimson, his legs tangled with the fallen chair, as much a dustman as a man could be. The faytor crumpled on her side near the screen, dead or unconscious. Rusk couldn't be sure.

But he could pick one and make it sure. And he should, given what she seemed to know.

He took a half step forward, blade at his side, when the tiny bells on the flap of the tent chimed as someone parted them. Rusk darted back behind the screen.

"Here!" said a male voice, shouting back into the Bazaar. "In here! There's fire! Rose! Are you all right? Rose!"

More shouts and exclamations from outside. A crowd must have been gathering.

Rusk stood on the other side of the wooden screen, mentally cursing.

"Gods! A man's dead in here! Rose, where are you?"

Another voice: "Check the back!"

Rusk cursed and dashed out the rear of the tent, sheathing his blade as he went. As he slid out from between the smoking tent and smoke leaf stall, he pulled up his hood, slowed his pace, and mingled with the crowd. People thronged the area near the tent, pushing and shoving, standing on tiptoes to get a better view. Lots of shouting from the front.

"What happened?" Rusk asked a veiled Narascene woman in a bright blue robe.

She shook her head, her loop earrings swinging. "Fire, I think."

"Awful," Rusk said, and swam against the current of the crowd.

As soon as he broke loose of it, he cut right and headed out of the Low Bazaar. Now and again as he walked, he eyed his hand, waiting for the tat to change.

That was the swag that he wanted out of this click, the only thing that made the murder worth the effort: a sixth blade on his skin.

"Come on, dammit," he said.

••••

Merelda's smile and light mood faltered when she saw the plume of smoke and the gathered crowd near their tent. If it had been pyrotechnics, there would have been applause and smiles. Instead, the ordinary sounds of bazaar life were gone, replaced by muted conversation, sagging shoulders, shared whispers, and an expectant hush. She hurried forward, concerned, and when she saw that the smoke was actually leaking from the top and front flaps of her and Rusilla's tent, her concern turned to alarm. She dropped the sweetbreads she was carrying and ran.

Rose? Rose?

Unable to feel the reciprocal touch of her sister's mind, she shoved frantically through the wall of people.

"Out of my way! Get out of the way! That's my tent! Get out of the way!"

Her voice sounded panicked, even to herself.

Rose? Please answer, Rose!

She burst through the front edge of the crowd and stopped, her hand to her mouth, as Veraal came through the tent flaps, coughing, stumbling, carrying Rose in his arms, his wooden pipe still clamped between his teeth.

Rose hung limp in his grasp, her long red hair brushing the ground, and Merelda's legs went weak under her. She stopped in her steps. She couldn't breathe. She'd only been gone a few moments, only a few moments.

Veraal lowered Rose down on the packed earth. People edged closer.

"Get some water!" he shouted to them. "Afore the fire spreads!"

Everyone with a stall or tent kept full buckets and barrels near to hand, both for drinking and for the inevitable small fires that bred in the Bazaar.

Merelda hurried forward, shouting at some of the men and women gathered around Veraal.

"There's a half-barrel of water behind the screen! In the tent!"

Veraal looked up at the sound of her voice, and his heavy expression did nothing to put her mind at ease. A man and two women darted into the tent, presumably to get at the water.

"What happened? How is she?" Merelda said, sagging to the ground beside her sister. "Is she?"

"She's breathin'," Veraal said around his pipe.

Mere's eyes welled with relief.

"Rose," she said, and touched her sister's hand, tapped her cheek. "Rose."

"I think she might've fainted," Veraal said. "Smoke and fire didn't harm her none. I got in there fast. Heard her shouting and ran over."

"Shouting?"

Veraal nodded. "She was shouting something."

Merelda cradled one of Rose's hands between hers. "Thank you, Veraal. We owe you."

He waved it away. "Nothing to it, little sister." Over his shoulder, he shouted, "How's that fire now?"

"Out," came the answering shout. "Not much damage."

Some scattered applause from onlookers.

"It was just a couple small ones," Veraal said to Merelda. "Lotta smoke. Not much flame." He shouted again over his shoulder. "Don't move that body none!"

"Body?" Merelda asked.

"Dead man in there," Veraal said, nodding. He took his pipe from his mouth and put the mouthpiece to his neck. "Shot through the throat. Very clean. Professional, looks to me."

"Dead man? You mean the one she was reading?" Merelda asked.

Veraal shrugged. "He was dead on the other side of the table, so probably. Looked like he got shot by someone from behind that wood screen. I didn't see anyone go in, though, but I was occupied. Like I said, probably Rose saw the click and fainted. Shocking sometimes, seeing someone clicked."

Merelda's hold on Rose's hand tightened, and her alarm redoubled. If Rose had been reading the man when he died...

Rose? Rose?

"You gotta matchstick?" Veraal asked, feeling around in his tunic. "Never mind."

He found a matchstick in an inner pocket of his tunic, struck it with his thumb, and lit his pipe.

Rose? Can you hear me?

No response. She could have fainted, though that seemed unlike Rose. Merelda considered reaching into her sister's mind, but out in the open Bazaar seemed hardly the place. Besides, if she had been reading the man as he died, when he died, her mind could be damaged. Merelda could worsen things by forcibly poking around.

"I need to get her home, Veraal," Merelda said. "Right now. Can you... handle the Watch?"

He exhaled a cloud of pipesmoke and grinned. "How long you been here, little sister? Shite, ain't nothing *to* handle. Gotta have at least three dead regular folk or one dead rich one to get the Watch interested in what happens in the Bazaar. If there ain't neither of those, we're on our own. And that man in there," he jerked a thumb over his shoulder. "He's only one body and he ain't rich, though he don't look poor neither. The Watch'll be along to get the body before Ool rings another hour, maybe two, but that's about it. They'll ask a question or three and be on their way with the corpse. You take your sister on home. I'll get you a wagon or carriage or something. Where you headin'?"

Merelda stared down at her sister's wan, slack face. "The Slick Tunnel."

"The Tunnel? You know the two slubbers who own that now? Egil and Nix? Big man and little one?"

"Yes, I know them. You do, too?"

"Aye." He smiled at some memory. "Well, you tell them Veraal says hello. You tell them if they need something, or if you do, they know where to find me."

"Uh, all right. I will."

"You be back tomorrow?"

She smoothed Rose's hair back from her face. "I... don't know."

He nodded, drew on his pipe. "I'll watch your tent and things while you're gone. Remember: you need something, you let me know."

The man and the two women came out of the tent, all three smoke smudged, the man still carrying a bucket of water.

"All out, dear," the heavier and older of the two women said to Merelda. "Your stuff is fine, 'cept the one chair." She nodded at Rose. "She all right?"

"I think so," she said. "Thank you." And then, to Veraal, "And thank *you*."

She hugged him close and he stuttered in surprise. He smelled of smoke and sweat and was all sinew and gristle and she wondered what he'd done before vending smoke leaf in the Low Bazaar. She'd have to ask Egil.

The crowd was already dispersing, the regular sounds of the Low Bazaar returning. Still no sign of the Watch. She wondered if they'd come at all.

"Take care of your sister," Veraal said. "I'll take care of all this till you come back."

Rusk dodged Watch patrols as he crossed the city, more out of habit than real concern. The Watch wouldn't be looking for him. Killings were as common as a common in the Low Bazaar. No one would know the murdered man had been the Upright Man. The tat would've disappeared with his death, and few knew his face. The former leader of Dur Follin's thieves' guild was just another nameless body tossed up by the swirl of the Bazaar.

Rusk checked his own tat obsessively as he walked, trying to will it into adding a blade. He must've looked a fool, eyeing the back of his hand every few steps, but he couldn't help it. He didn't even want to consider the possibility that he'd taken the risk he'd taken and not earned the score he expected.

He threw a pray at Aster, muttering under his breath, asking for the blessing he'd earned.

He highstepped piles of horse manure, slid through gatherings of laborers, peddlers, and teamsters, dodged wagons and mules, and checked the damned tat again and again.

Still no change.

As he moved north and east Dur Follin's buildings grew taller and less decrepit. Wood and mud-brick buildings gave way to baked brick and mortared stone. The streets became wider, paved with rough cobblestone, and carriages and horses filled them rather than open-top wagons pulled by mules and ponies. Merchants with oiled moustaches seemed everywhere, eyeing various goods while their bodyguards eyed passersby.

He moved past and through it all, as unobtrusive as a ghost.

Behind him, Ool's clock chimed another hour gone. The toll of the clock always summoned memories. He'd grown up in the shadow of the clock spire, not quite in the Warrens, but not too far removed. His father had gone dusty before Rusk had seen six winters, and his mother, who'd been a gimcrack, had provided for them afterward by doing odd jobs. He'd spent much of his childhood hungry. By ten he'd been nimming to eat, cutting buttons in the market, filching cloaks. By fifteen he'd been filching and pommeling nobs because it made things easier, not because he enjoyed it. His mother had gone dusty in a redsmoke den when he was sixteen. He hadn't even known she'd been a user. By twenty he'd clicked his first man – another non-guild thief who'd double-crossed him on a job – and by twenty-two he'd wormed his way into the guild. At thirty-two he'd earned a spot on the Committee. And now, at forty-five, he was Fifth Blade and looking to move up to Sixth, two steps removed from Channis, whom he presumed was the new Upright Man. He came around the corner of Mandin's Way, showing a fak-finger to an oncoming carriage that almost hit him.

Mandin's Way, a wide street lined with two-story shops and inns and club halls, followed the Meander's winding bank and ended in the Dur Follin Fish Market, a tent-and-stall-city in the shadow of the Archbridge. Street vendors hawked smoked fish and the ubiquitous river eel. He could hear their calls three block away.

The rise of Mandin's way allowed him to see over the low, stone ride of the dock wall to the small fishing boats that bobbed near the river's edge. The faint sound of drums and chanting carried from the high arc of the Archbridge, the sounds like voices coming down from the Seven Heavens. Pipe smoke carried from somewhere, the aroma of roasting meat.

Ahead and to his right he saw the familiar low stone wall and hodgepodge structure of the guild house. Channis would be waiting for him there in his private wing.

A century earlier the guild house had been a public inn called the Squid, a three-story, brick and wood affair complete with a wall, stable, and terrace that overlooked the Meander. Then, it had been the haunt of ferrymen and fishermen and others who made their living on the river.

The guild had started as a small group of rogues running an extortion operation that milked fishermen. The operation had grown quickly and the group soon formalized their relationship, and sealed the deal with religion. The very first Committee, worshippers of Aster all, had founded the guild in the common room of the Squid, each taking Aster's sigil while they swore the oaths and threw the prays.

Later, they'd bought the inn and converted it to a private club for their ever-growing criminal operation.

Today everyone called the founders the Arch Rogues and the eight of them had been buried in honor in the catacombs under the guild house. Their decision to form the guild, to make it a religious as well as criminal enterprise, had made a lot of men rich over the years, and a lot of other men dead. Rusk was angling for the former.

Now the Squid was known simply as the guild house. And both guild and house had grown bigger and stronger every year. Rusk figured one day the Committee would put their own man in the office of Lord High Mayor and the city would be theirs.

Meanwhile the guild's operations were a maze, and so too was the house, complete with underground tunnels and secret passages and deadfalls. Only the Upright Man was said to know all the building's secrets, and then only because the knowledge came to him when his tat showed the Eighth Blade.

Rusk checked his tat. Nothing. Shite.

As the Fifth Blade on the Committee, Rusk managed the guild's business in a large piece of the city in and around the Low Bazaar. If Aster threw him the sixth blade, he'd take over the Dock Ward and the Archbridge.

Warehousing and religion. That's where the real coin was.

The current Sixth Blade, Trelgin, would move to Seventh Blade and become the Upright Man's right hand. Trelgin deserved it, prick that he was.

Shite job, Seventh Blade. Much status, little coin.

A Seventh Blade ran nothing on his own, had no independent stream of coin. A Seventh Blade served the Upright Man and depended on his largesse for a cut of guild proceeds. He was a handmaid, nothing more, and the constant hope of a Seventh Blade was to become the new Upright Man, either through death or retirement of the current Upright Man. Where the Seventh Blade was shite, the Eighth Blade was gold. Lots of status, lots of coin. But also lots of threats and lots of murder attempts. And sometimes those attempts succeeded, as Rusk well knew.

No, Sixth Blade was the perch and Rusk wanted to be the bird.

A block from the guild house, he felt his tat start to change and almost hooted with joy. He felt it first as a tingle on his skin, but the tingle soon grew to a slight burning. His heart jumped. He darted across the street and stood in the shadow of a cloth merchant, his back to the passersby. He'd handle the bridge and warehouses better than Trelgin, with a more forceful hand, and in the process he'd get very rich. And once he was very rich, he'd build a manse on the Shelf and scandalize the old noble families that lived there. He'd keep a harem of women around, like a Jafari Sultan, and eat well and get fat and be done with guild life.

Wincing at the pain but excited, he watched the tat squirm on his flesh, Aster's will drawn in ink on the skin of one of his stealing priests. The tat sprouted another blade and he clenched his fist in glee to help contain his shout. But the burning did not stop, nor had the tat stopped changing. He stared in dumbfounded disbelief as it grew a seventh blade.

"Shite," he said, his jaw clenched so tightly that words could barely get between his teeth. He rubbed at the magical ink. "No, no, no. Shite, shite, shite."

He hadn't earned enough as a Fifth Blade to skip the Sixth and go right to the Seventh. He'd be as broke as an ugly whore. He'd never get out of the life. He'd be stuck serving Channis for a decade. If he ever became the Upright Man himself, he'd be too old to enjoy the coin.

"Gods dammit, no! Trelgin is supposed to be Seventh Blade! Trelgin!"

But no matter how much he rubbed, there it was: a seventh blade. He'd be the right hand to Channis, whom he presumed to be the new Upright Man. Aster had spoken through his ink, and he'd told a bad joke in the process.

"Fak, fakkin', fak!"

"You all right, goodsir?" said a passerby, a thirty-something merchant in a fur-lined tailored cloak and polished boots.

Rusk whirled on the man. The fakker's oiled moustache irked him. Everything irked him. He shoved the prick to the muddy ground, kicked him once, and spat at his feet.

"Worry after your own business, bunghole!"

The man scurried back crabwise, wide-eyed, and almost got trampled by a passing horse.

"I meant nothing," the man said. "Apologies. Apologies."

Other onlookers gave them a wide berth, though Rusk heard a woman say to her companion that someone should summon the Watch.

He wanted no part of the Watch, not at the moment. He was the gods damned Seventh Blade. He couldn't have a run-in with the Watch.

"If you mean nothing, then say nothing, fakker," he said to the merchant, and the man nodded fearfully.

Rusk stepped past the man, seething, and stalked down Mandin's Way. Channis was neither generous nor forgiving. And worse, he wasn't careless. Seventh to Channis was a shite job even by the measure of shite jobs.

"Fak!"

He was so preoccupied with Aster's little jest that he almost forgot to give the hand signs as he walked through the low, outer wall of the guild house. The snipers in the gatehouse probably would have recognized him and held their fire, but maybe not. As it was he remembered at the last moment and made the intricate symbols with his fingers.

"I already got shot in the arse once today. What's another few to me?"

He tried to get himself under control as he approached the raised porch and front double doors of the guild house, still painted with the image of a black squid and marked "members only". He wondered if word of the Upright Man's death had beaten him back.

He opened the reinforced metal-banded doors – every door in the guild house was reinforced and with its own lock – and nodded at Kherne and Dool, the muscle on duty. They were Channis's men.

"The Man wants to see you," Kherne said, his lazy eye looking off to Rusk's left.

"The Man does?" Rusk said, not wanting to tip his knowledge.

"Channis," Kherne said.

Dool nodded a head as large as a slop bucket. "Committee got reordered today."

Channis must have let out word that he'd sprouted an Eighth Blade. The rogues would be moving, trying to figure out who was who and what was what.

"I know," Rusk said, nodding at his tat.

"What about you, then?" Kherne asked, trying to see Rusk's tattoo. "You move up to Sixth?"

"No," Rusk said and walked off.

"You're not Sixth Blade?" Dool called after him.

"No," Rusk muttered, as he made his way through the labyrinthine corridors and stairways of the guild house. "I'm fakked is what I am."

CHAPTER FOUR

Egil and Nix sat alone at the Tunnel's bar, the stink of Gadd's pipesmoke in their noses, the memory of Blackalley on their minds. Tankards of ale sat on the time-scarred bar before them, untouched. Nix could not shake what he'd seen and felt, the old man he'd killed for bread, the pettiness he'd been reminded of, the spite. The words he'd heard as Blackalley spat them out haunted him still.

Free us.

He wasn't even sure anymore that he hadn't said the words himself. He tapped his fingers on the bar, agitated. Gadd's smoke agitated him. The stink of the Tunnel agitated him, being, as it was, all sweat and sex and smoke. Everything agitated him.

Behind them a few laborers and merchants sat at the tables, talking and laughing. The men and women who sold their bodies in the Tunnel lingered on the staircase – their tight, revealing clothing an open invitation.

"So," Nix said, turning his back to the bar and drumming his fingers.

"So," Egil agreed.

"You're irritable."

Egil stared up at the picture of Lord Mayor Hyram Mung. "I haven't said anything."

"It's your silence that shows your irritability."

Egil glanced over at him. "You make no sense."

"See!" Nix said and pointed a finger at his friend. "Irritable."

Egil shook his head and took the virginity of his ale.

"Didn't I tell Gadd to take down that thrice-damned picture of Mung?" Nix said. "He looks like a sow. And his beady eyes annoy me."

Nix drew one of the many throwing daggers he kept secreted on his person and threw. The blade pierced Mung's eye.

"Better," Nix muttered.

"Who's irritable again?" Egil asked.

Nix glared at the priest. "You're just trying to irk me, aren't you?"

Egil shrugged. "You seem irked already."

"Me? No! If I were irked I'd..." He trailed off, took a drink of his own ale, set the tankard back down hard enough to slosh some over the edge. "All right, aye. I'm irked."

"It's Blackalley," Egil said.

"It is!" Nix said, raising his arms and nearly leaping from his seat. "What *was* that? Regrets and sorrow and..."

Egil shook his head and took another pull of ale. "A fakkin' horror is what it was. Bleak."

The words Nix had been holding back came rushing out of him. "Making us see everything we've done and didn't do and should've done? No one should have to face that. I been running from that my whole life. Everyone does. The past is the past. I don't want to live inside my own head."

"None'd blame you for that," Egil said. "Empty place, likely."

"Now you're funny?"

"No. Apologies. But the past isn't the past, Nix. The past is us. It's the series of moments that led up to who we are right now." He jabbed a finger on the bar. "Everything that went before led up to this moment."

"Gods, man! Getting all priestly, now, are we? Why would you do that?" He shook his head. "Fak."

Egil ran his palm over the Eye of Ebenor.

Nix couldn't let it go. He picked up his ale, put it back down, fiddling with the handle. "You telling me we can't leave the past behind us? 'Cause there are some moments I'd rather forget. Lots of them, really."

"You can forget them, but they're still you. Everything you've done and seen and felt, it all sums to you, it adds up to this moment. It doesn't matter if you can remember the individual moments that lead up to it. Because they're all in you right now."

"Stop that," Nix said.

"Stop what?"

"I don't know, saying profound things. They irritate. They irk."

Egil sighed. "Well enough."

Nix sighed, too. "I say we get drunk and forget Blackalley."

Egil started to speak, probably to once more say something about how it wouldn't matter if they forgot it because it was in them now.

Nix held up a hand. "Don't you say it!"

Egil stared at Nix. "Right, then. Drunk it is."

Having said the words, Egil set to making them true. He slammed his ale in one long pull. Nix matched him and they sat there for a time in silence, empty tankards before them.

"Everything we've done, Egil. All those… moments. Fakking moments. And what do we have to show for it? This place and some coin. That's it."

"This is what you wanted. When we left the tomb of Abn Thuset, you said you wanted this."

"I did. I do. But there's gotta be something else, something more."

Egil smiled but it was half-hearted. "Now who's saying profound things? And you're right. They do irritate. Irk, too."

"I don't know what I want. It's always the next thing, something I don't have. What do you want, Egil?"

Egil's expression fell. He stared into his empty tankard. "I want to forget, Nix. That's what I want."

Nix flashed on Egil's weeping face in Blackalley, his teary apologies to his daughter and wife. There was nothing Nix could say so he put his hand on his friend's shoulder, just for a moment.

"So, drunk, then," Nix said, trying to lighten the mood. "Where's Gadd? Gadd!"

Egil sat up and exhaled, as though exorcising a ghost. He thumped his fist on the bar and called into the taproom in the back. "Return to your altar, priest. Bring forth libations."

"Libations?" Nix said, and tapped Egil's tankard with his own. "Nice."

Gadd hurried out of the taproom, his eyes wide, white, and alarmed in his narrow face, hawkish face.

Egil and Nix were on their feet at once.

"What is it?" Nix asked.

Gadd rushed forward and grabbed them by their wrists. "Come! Rose hurt!"

At first the words didn't register with Nix. "Rose? Our Rose?"

"Where's Merelda?" Egil said, and grabbed Gadd by his thin, tattooed arm. "Speak, man."

"She's with Rose," Gadd said, and shook himself loose.

Egil and Nix both leaped over the bar. Nix grabbed his dagger out of Hyram Mung's eye as he ran by. They hurried through the taproom, the storeroom, and out into the fenced area in the back of Tunnel, littered with old barrels, a bucket, an old door, and the weekly rubbish pile. The wooden gate was open to the street, where sat a rickety, open topped, straw-filled wagon. Rose lay in the straw propped against a bale, still dressed in the elaborate green robes and costume jewelry she wore when performing readings in the Low Bazaar. Her eyes were closed and her head drooped and she looked to Nix like a broken flower. The sight of her so vulnerable hurt his heart.

Mere sat on her knees beside her sister, cradling Rose's hand between her own. Mere looked over at them, her eyes swollen and red.

"Help us, Egil," she said.

Nix, Egil, and Gadd rushed to the wagon, leaped in it

"Rose," Nix said, touching her cheek. It was warm, thankfully. "Rose."

She opened her eyes but they drifted in her sockets, unable to focus. They closed again and her head lolled.

He bounded into the wagon, took her face in his palms.

"What happened?" Egil said.

"Rose?" Nix said, his heart in his throat. "Rose?"

He flashed on how she'd looked months earlier when her brother had kept her drugged. He lifted her arms, checked her for wounds, saw none.

"She smells like smoke," Nix said to Mere.

"What happened?" Egil asked again.

"At the Low Bazaar," Mere said. "She was reading and…"

Her eyes welled again. Egil drew her close, covering her in his embrace.

"It's going to be all right," the priest said to her.

"Let's get her inside," Nix said. He tossed a silver to Gadd. "Pay the driver, Gadd. No, wait. I'll pay the driver. You go clear the bar. Tell Tesha what happened."

But Tesha was already there. She must have seen Egil and Nix leap the bar and come out to investigate. In her embroidered green dress, she stood with her hand on her hip near the gate, her dark eyes concerned.

"I'll handle the bar. Is she going to be all right?"

Nix looked at Rose, at Mere, back at Tesha. "I don't know."

"She's been in and out, Nix," Mere said. "She's been talking the whole ride back. Sometimes she seems herself, others times not."

Nix tossed a silver tern to the old, grizzled man who drove the wagon.

"Obliged, granther."

Nix put his arms under Rose and lifted her from the wagon. Egil offered his aid, but Nix shook it off.

"I've got her."

"Aye," Egil said.

Nix stepped down out of the wagon, grunting with exertion. He looked down at Rose and her green eyes were open and focused, looking up at him. She looked wan, her eyes pained, furrows in her brow.

Nix swallowed, said softly, "How do you feel?"

"Bad," Rose said. "My head is just…"

Mere was at their side, brushing her sister's hair from her brow. "You need to rest, Rose."

Rose nodded, but winced at the pain even that small motion caused her.

Together, they took her inside, carried her through a now empty bar while Tesha looked on.

"I'll bring up some warm broth," Tesha said.

"Thank you, Tesha," Mere said.

Tesha's men and women had retreated to their rooms – presumably at her orders – and Nix carried Rose to the small bedroom on the second floor that she and Mere shared. After laying her down on the bed, Nix kissed her on the brow. She seemed asleep, so he covered her in a blanket, closed the door behind him, and gathered in the hallway with Mere and Egil.

"So what happened?" Nix asked her.

"She was reading someone as he died," Mere said, as though that were an explanation.

Nix looked first at Egil, then back at her, not understanding. "And?"

Heads poked out of doors down the long hallway, Tesha's workers giving in to curiosity. Nix waved them back into the rooms.

Mere said, "And that's why she's like that. It's dangerous to be in the mind of someone as they die."

"Dangerous how?" Egil asked.

Mere shook her head. Her short, dark hair was mussed and the makeup she wore to tell fortunes was smeared by tears. She looked lost. Nix wondered how she'd fare in the world if she lost her sister. Probably much as Nix would fare if he lost Egil.

"I don't know for sure," she said. "I've never had it happen before. Neither of us have. We've just heard that it's... bad."

Egil stood behind her and placed his hands gently on her shoulders. His touch seemed to calm her. She took a deep breath.

"Sorry," she said.

Nix waved it off. "In theory, then, dangerous how?"

She put her hand on Egil's. "A dying person's mind... explodes. Things can get jumbled."

Nix had some experience with the sisters' mindmagic. "Jumbled? Thoughts get mixed up?"

She nodded. "Thoughts, memories, feelings. Everything. It can overwhelm because it all comes at once. You can become... not yourself."

Nix flashed on Egil's words earlier about the sum of past moments making people who they were in the present. Rose had just inherited moments that weren't her own. What would that do to her? To Mere, he said,

"Maybe you could use your mindmagic to help her? Remove what's not hers?"

Mere shook her head and looked back at the door to Rose's room. "I can't. It would take a real mindmage. I can do what I can do because of... lineage."

"The only real mindmages are in Oremal," Egil said. "And we're a long way from there."

"We are," Nix agreed. He knew of another mindmage, though, or at least the rumor of one. But he had no desire to walk that path unless absolutely necessary.

"It could fix itself," Mere said, a flash of hope in her eyes. "I think we just need to let her rest."

"Aye," Nix said, nodding slowly as his thoughts turned. "Let us know if there's anything we can do."

"I will."

She turned to go back into the room and tend Rusilla but Egil first asked her, "How'd he die? The man she was reading."

"He was shot. Veraal–"

"Veraal was shot?" Nix said, thinking of their old friend.

"No," she said.

"Veraal shot someone?"

"No," she said. "Veraal said the dead man was shot through the throat. A professional job, he said."

"Uncle Veraal," Nix said, shaking his head and smiling. He hadn't had dealings with Veraal in years. "What's he doing there? In the Bazaar."

"He sells smoke leaf. Next to our tent. He said he knew you two, but he didn't say he was your uncle."

"He's not," Egil said. "An uncle is… He was our fence for a long time."

"Oh." She looked surprised, her lips pursing. "Well, he was nice."

"He's all right," Nix said.

"Selling leaf?" Egil said, and looked to Nix and both of them said at the same time, "Cover for his coin."

Mere looked confused. "What?"

"The leaf stall is just cover for his fencing operation," Nix said. "It covers his coin, should the Lord Mayor's taxman come knocking."

"She doesn't need to know all this," Egil said.

"I'm not a child, Egil," she said, hands on her hips.

Egil's ears colored under her reprimand. He ran his palm over his head. "That's not what I meant, Mere."

"Yes it is."

Nix changed the subject. "Tell me more about the dead man. If Veraal said it was a pro click, then it was a pro click. Maybe someone we knew."

"I didn't see. I wasn't in the tent and don't know any more about him. Rose was babbling in the wagon on the way from the Bazaar. She was talking about coin and clicks and naming places. A committee. And eight of something? And she said something about a tattoo, blades and a circle."

Nix looked sharply at Egil. "Committee?"

"Describe the tattoo in detail," Egil said.

"Was it on the back of his hand?" Nix asked.

"Doesn't have to be there," Egil said. "They move around, I hear."

Mere looked from one to the other, trying to follow their conversation. When they stopped, she said. "Rose said it was an eight-pointed figure. Like a compass rose you'd see on a map. That's what she said. Like a rose, like her name."

"Shite," Nix said, disbelieving. "You're sure she said that? Eight points?"

Mere nodded, a question in her eyes.

"And it had a circle in the center?" Nix pressed. "Like a coin."

"She just said a circle and I didn't see it so–"

"Shite," Egil said, and ran his hand over Ebenor's eye. "Gotta be."

Merelda's expression was growing alarmed. She looked very much like the young girl she denied being. "What is it? What's wrong?"

"Maybe a little, maybe a lot," Nix said.

"What's the tattoo mean?" she asked.

"It's a badge of office," Egil said.

"And it's more magical sigil than tattoo," Nix added. "It shows membership in the Committee."

"And that is?" she asked.

Nix remembered that Mere wouldn't know the power groups in the city. She'd been imprisoned in a manse outside Dur Follin most of her life.

"The Committee is the group of eight Archthieves who run the Dur Follin Thieves' Guild."

"Nasty slubbers, all," Egil said.

Merelda blinked. "So the man who was killed was a member of this Committee?"

Egil chuckled, but there was no mirth in it.

"No," Nix said. "Each member of the Committee has a different sigil that shows their rank. The lowest ranking has one blade pointing up from the central coin. The highest has eight."

"The Upright Man," Egil said. "Eight blades means the head of the guild."

Merelda's mouth hung open for a moment. "The head of the thieves' guild was murdered in our tent?"

"So it seems," Nix said.

"Shite," Merelda said.

"Well said," Egil said.

"What was he doing there?" Mere asked.

Nix shrugged. "You didn't see the assassin? And Rusilla didn't either?"

"I didn't. I don't think she did."

Nix stared at Egil. The priest said, "If they wanted no witnesses, she'd have been dead in the tent."

Nix thought it through, nodded. "Right. Whoever clicked him didn't mind witnesses, maybe even wanted it visible enough so that those with eyes could see."

"A power play, probably," Egil said. "Another one of the Committee."

"Aye," Nix said. "Probably none of our concern, then."

Mere said, "So one member of the Committee killed this Upright Man, who leads the Committee? Is Rose in danger?"

"I don't think so," Nix said. "All's game in guild business, is what they say, but the trick is that you click or cross another Committeeman, you can't get pinned with it. If you do…"

"You die ugly," Egil said.

"That's why we never joined," Nix said. "Among other reasons."

Egil harrumphed. "If we'd have joined, we'd be running that crew of slubbers by now."

"Truth," Nix said.

"None of that makes any damned sense," Merelda said.

"It's religion, is why," Egil said.

Nix added, "A guildthief isn't just a thief, Mere. He's a member of a religious order and their organization and rules makes about as much sense as any other order of zealots. They worship a nasty aspect of Aster. They're like priests, but priests who steal and kill, even from each other, provided they don't get caught."

Egil snorted contemptuously. "Priests! Dolts the lot."

Merelda's eyes went to the tattoo on Egil's head and her face crinkled with a question, but she kept the words behind her teeth.

"I'm a different kind of priest," he said, inferring her question.

"Egil's god is dead," Nix said. "Gives the doctrine a certain fluidity."

Egil chuckled.

Mere's gaze went the door of Rose's room, back to Egil.

"She shouldn't be in any danger," Egil said again. "If they'd wanted to hurt her, they'd have done it then. Ill place, ill time, is all it sounds like."

Tesha came up the stairs, a wooden bowl of broth in her hands. Despite himself, Nix smiled. He had never expected to see Tesha, with her form-fitting, beaded and embroidered dress, coiffed hair, and meticulous makeup, carrying a bowl of soup. She caught his look.

"What?"

"What what?"

"I can take this to her or you can wear it. Which do you prefer, Nix Fall?"

"I wouldn't look good in soup," he said with a wink.

She harrumphed and walked past him. "I sent for a saint of Orella. We'll split the expense."

"Aye," he said, still smiling.

Mere opened the door to Rose's room for her.

"See to your sister, Mere," Nix said. "We'll be downstairs if you need anything. Maybe the saint can do something."

Mere looked doubtful but nodded, and she and Tesha disappeared behind the door.

"We need to talk," Nix said to Egil.

"Aye," the priest said.

"Downstairs."

"Yeah."

Nix called down the hallway, "We're opening back up. Everybody out of your rooms. Come drink and eat and copulate, preferably as separate activities."

"Copulate," Egil said. "Nice."

Nix gave a little bow. "Come on! Out, out!"

As the doors started to open down the hallway, the two friends headed downstairs to the bar, where Gadd already had foaming tankards waiting for them.

"You're my kind of priest," Egil said to the tapkeep.

Gadd smiled, showing his sharpened fangs.

"Rose all right?" Gadd asked.

"Not sure," Nix said. "We hope so."

Gadd nodded. After sticking his pipe between his teeth, the easterner turned away to give Egil and Nix privacy, tending to his tankards and cups and plates the way a priest tended relics.

"It's this jumble bit that bothers," Egil said, taking a long pull on his ale. "This is good, Gadd," he said. "Very good."

Gadd glanced over his shoulder, nodded.

"My thoughts ran the same way," Nix said. "But how would they even know about that? The assassin probably shot, saw it sink, and bolted. To him, Rose and Mere are just common buskers. He'd have no reason to suspect anything else."

"Truth," Egil acceded, then, "But if they did." He left the thought unfinished, then said, "Guild slubbers."

"Aye, that."

"You ever really think of joining?" Egil asked.

Nix guffawed. "The only priests I want to associate with are bald, tattooed, and stubborn, yeah?"

"Stubborn?"

"A mule looks on you with envy, Egil. Stubborn."

"Fair enough," the priest acknowledged.

"Besides," Nix added. "Those guild slubbers aren't square in the head for the most part."

"That's truth."

They drank in silence for a time while the Tunnel refilled behind them.

"New Upright Man and shifts in the Committee," Nix said. "Should make things interesting for a while."

"We'll see," Egil said.

Rusk passed five bodyguards, hard-eyed and bristling with steel, on his way to see Channis. Rusk found the new Upright Man in a well-appointed waiting room in the southwest wing of the guild house, along with two more bodyguards. Rusk didn't even know their names, but their eyes never left his hands. Channis must have prepared for his rise for a long time. Rusk reminded himself never to underestimate Channis. He also cursed his lot as Seventh Blade.

"Lot of muscle," Rusk said.

"Prudence pays," Channis said.

A throat wound from years earlier had made the Upright Man's voice as coarse as gravel. Channis was said to have more scars than even the most holy of Millenor's self-mortifying priests. Rusk had heard many fellow guild men say over the years that Channis could not be killed. Too mean. Too thick a hide.

"Like coming to see a king in his court," Rusk said, irritated at himself for the nervous twinge in his voice.

"Is it?" Channis said, and Rusk heard a smile in his tone.

The new Upright Man stood before a window that overlooked the guarded grounds that abutted the slow, murky waters of the Meander. The sun fell behind the Archbridge and the huge structure painted a shadow across the guild house and the river. Channis, tall and blocky even in his fitted cloak, admired the tat on the back of his hand the way Rusk might admire a woman's thigh. A short, wide blade hung from Channis's hip. A few daggers hung from his belt, too, like the bastard children of the short sword.

Channis turned and dismissed the bodyguards in the room with a wave of his hand. They closed the doors behind them.

"He's down," Rusk said. "But you already knew that."

Channis smiled and approached him. Scars lined his face, a script of past battles, and he wore his long hair pulled back in a horse's knot. For a moment Rusk flashed on the idea of clicking Channis, driving a blade into his chest, testing just how tough was his hide, but put the idea out of his mind. Clicking a Committeeman – much less the Upright Man – had to be done without witnesses and with a great deal of discretion. Suspicion of clicking a Committeeman was one thing. Evidence of doing so was something else again, and got one sent to the tunnels below the guild house for a visit with Zren the Blade and his many pointy metal objects.

"Did he suffer?" Channis asked.

"One shot and down. He gurgled some."

"That's a job done well, Rusky. And now let's have a little talk."

He gestured Rusk over to one of the chairs that sat before the window. Rusk walked with him, but did not sit. Neither did Channis.

"So there are two men, and only two, who are in on this, yeah? And they're both standing in this room."

Rusk flashed on the faytor, the words she'd shouted, but he said only, "Yeah."

"So if there was ever a loose tongue about this here, well, then the person without the loose tongue would know it was the other of the two was yapping, yeah?"

"I don't yap, Channis. And even if I did…"

"Even if you did," Channis said, his voice like a blade over a whetstone. "I'd deny everything and there's no evidence and you'd go visit with Zren for… discipline."

"Right."

"Right, then." Channis put one of his huge hands on Rusk's shoulder, squeezed, then turned and walked away. "That's clear as good glass, then. We can help each other, you and me. I'll be calling the Committee together later, then we'll have chapel down below, say thanks to Aster, throw a few prays. I'm just waiting for Trelgin to show. He shoulda sprouted a seventh blade by now. He's not going to be happy how this goes for him."

Rusk winced. "About that…"

Channis turned to face him, his right-eye half closed due to scarring, and so stuck in a perpetual glare.

"There was a problem," Rusk said, and shifted on his feet. "Well, two. Though one is not so much a problem as a surprise."

Channis took a couple steps toward him, stopped, and stared. "Keep on."

"The faytor in the tent–"

Another step toward him and the other eye joined the first in the glare. "She *saw* you?"

Rusk shook his head. "No, no. But she... went down when he went down."

"You clicked her, too? So?"

"No, I didn't. She just went down, grabbing at her head, shouting things." He looked meaningfully at Channis.

Channis's voice was a low rumble. "What kind of things?"

Rusk swallowed. "Things she shouldn't know. Guild things. Things only the Upright Man – the old Upright Man – should have known. It was like it poured out of his head and into her."

Channis stared at him a long, uncomfortable while. "Why didn't you click her?"

"I couldn't. It happened fast and by the time I made sense of her words, the Bazaar slubbers were coming."

"So maybe she knows guild business but she didn't see you?"

"She definitely didn't see me. I had some of our streeters follow her out of the Bazaar. She was unconscious, taken in a wagon with the other faytor. They went to a joint called the Slick Tunnel. Live there, I think."

Channis visibly relaxed and Rusk let himself breathe. "That don't sound like a problem. That sounds like a nuisance. What's the surprise?"

"What?"

"You said you had a problem and a surprise. The problem we discussed. The surprise?"

Rusk could think of no good way to say what he needed to say, so he just said it. "I'm, uh, not Sixth Blade."

Channis's eyebrows rose in surprise, at least as far as the scars allowed. "No?"

Rusk held up his hand, showing Channis his tat. "No."

Channis's eyes lingered on Rusk's tat and its seven blades for a while before returning to Rusk's face.

"I guess Trelgin's not coming then," Channis said.

"I guess not."

Channis smiled, a predatory look. "I ever tell you how I came by all these scars?"

Rusk shook his head.

"These have come from men trying to do me ill, sometimes during a regular scrum, sometimes during guild business. All those men have a home in the ground, now, Rusky. You follow? You clear?"

Rusk kept his face expressionless. "I ken the game, Channis. I'm a loyal guildsman. And you're the Upright Man."

"What's loyalty got to do with it? Seventh Blade's a shite job, and I oughta know."

To that, Rusk said nothing.

Channis donned a softer smile, about as a genuine as a whore's moans of pleasure. He came to Rusk's side. The man had a smell about him, an animal stink. He took Rusk by the arm, put it beside his own so the tats on the backs of their hands were side-by-side.

"Aster's a funny bastard, ain't he, Rusky?"

Funny wasn't the word Rusk would've used. "Aye."

Channis released Rusk's arm.

"Gonna stay a shite job. I got plans for the guild and making the Seventh Blade happy ain't part of 'em. I thought it'd be Trelgin, but it looks like ol' Aster sent it your way. So be it. I ain't the forgiving sort, Rusk, but you know that already."

"Yeah, I know that."

"Good. You be a good boy now, Rusky. A *loyal* boy, like you said. And we'll see how things go, yeah?"

Rusk swallowed bile. "Yeah."

"Now here are the first couple things you're going to do, Seventh Blade. Get the Committee together so I can let them know how things are gonna be. And the second thing is, you're gonna send a group of men to go to that inn. They can pull from the guild's store of enchanted gear, if you think it's necessary. Anyway, they're to burn it down with that faytor in it. She knows guild business–"

"Maybe knows," Rusk said.

"Maybe's all I need. You questioning me already, Rusky?"

"No."

"Good."

Rusk nodded. "I heard that place is part-owned by some hard fellows, though."

Channis said, "They ain't hard enough. Get it burnt. Clear?"

"Clear," said Rusk.

He had some men in mind, and he didn't think they'd need to pull on the guild's store of enchanted items. Rusk disliked relying on sorcerous shite.

CHAPTER FIVE

Egil and Nix spent the evening worshipping at the altar of Gadd, while the tattooed easterner tended his congregation of hogsheads, taps, tankards, cups, and drunks. The buzz of the Tunnel went on behind them, laughter, conversation, occasional whoops and shouts. They checked on Rose from time to time, but there was no change.

Serving girls weaved deftly through the crowd and smoke, tankards and platters clutched in their hands. Tesha's men and women lingered flirtatiously on the sweeping central stair until patrons purchased their time and bodies, and they disappeared into the rooms upstairs. Kiir and Lis spent some time at the bar – both lovely in their bodices and flowing dresses – but Nix and Egil made such sullen company that they soon drifted away. By the eleventh hour, Nix and Egil sat at the bar alone, their only company Gadd and his pipe. Hyram Mung and his chins stared down at them from the portrait behind the bar. Nix toyed with the idea of putting another dagger in Mung's face, but resisted, and instead went upstairs again to check on Rose. He ignored the sounds of sex coming from many of the rooms, and adamantly refused to think of Kiir in any of them.

He knocked on Rose's door, entered, and found Merelda and Tesha sitting at Rose's bedside, daubing her forehead with a damp cloth.

"She's still asleep," Merelda said to him softly. "We'll know more when she wakes."

"How're things downstairs?" Tesha asked.

"Same as always," he answered. "Can I bring anything?"

"Thank you, no," Mere said. "Tesha's taking care of everything."

Nix smiled at Tesha. "I think Tesha could take of all of us, had she a mind."

Mere smiled. She looked back at her sister, asked almost coyly, "Where's Egil?"

Tesha shot Nix a meaningful look and he took the substance of it.

"At the bar," he answered. "He has… things on his mind."

"I see. Well, tell him to come up and check on Rose. If he wants, of course."

Nix shared a look with Tesha, said he would, and went back downstairs, sidestepping out of the way for Lis and a short laborer as they came upstairs, she with a professional smile, he with a face and expression flush with excitement. Lis rolled her eyes as she passed Nix.

He returned to Egil's side at the bar. Gadd had refilled his tankard.

"You know Mere fancies you, yeah? Though not even the gods themselves know why."

"Bah," Egil said. "She's just a girl, Nix. She's like a…"

He trailed off, his expression falling, and put his face in his tankard.

"She's not a girl. She's a young woman, and she most surely doesn't think of herself as your daughter. She fancies you and that's through no fault of yours, but you'll hurt her if you don't take care. Yeah?"

"I'd never hurt her, Nix."

Egil's eyes welled at some memory. Nix pretended not to notice.

"Not on purpose, I know." He put a hand on Egil's mountainous shoulder. "Just have a care, yeah? It'll probably pass, but be mindful so you don't encourage it."

Egil nodded. Nix said nothing for a time, giving Egil time to gather himself and divert his thoughts from his lost wife and daughter.

Nix asked, "Did you have a chance yet to talk to Enora? How'd she take the news about Drugal?"

"As well as she could."

"I suspect she'll get disciplined by the High Magister."

"Aye."

"She ask about Blackalley?"

Egil nodded.

"What'd you tell her?"

"I didn't tell her anything. Just that Drugal was already dead."

Nix flashed on Drugal's black eyes, on the way he'd been stuck to the ground, as if being absorbed or slowly devoured. He cleared his throat and his mind.

"Anything there? Between you and Enora?"

"Not anymore," Egil said, and left it at that.

They drank another tankard apiece before Nix said, "I don't remember us being such a somber pair of slubbers. How'd that happen?"

Egil grunted.

"Maybe we're more amusing when we're drunk?"

"Probably."

Nix planted a fist on the bar. "Then I say, that we *aren't* drunk is an unpardonable transgression. Gadd, you're the priest of this temple. You've failed us."

The easterner looked a question at him, smiled tentatively.

"But the failure can be rectified, by the gods," Nix said. "Drinks, Gadd, and quickly, that we might exorcise with spirits the spirit of sober reflection that vexes us currently."

Nix eyed Egil. Not so much as a grin.

"You've got to play along here, priest."

Egil offered a rueful smile. "I know what you're doing. It's appreciated. I'm fine, though."

Nix wasn't so sure. He thumped Egil on the shoulder. "I'm serious about the drinking, though. But that's the only thing I want to be serious about. Yeah?"

"Yeah."

"Seen enough shite in the last few days. We deserve a drink."

They tapped mugs and set to it.

Nix awoke later, head down at the bar, his face buried in his crossed arms. He blinked away the film coating his eyelids, glanced blearily around. Egil sat on the stool beside him, his huge arms thrown over the bar as if embracing it, the side of his face to the wood, snoring heavily, a small pool of drool collecting under his cheek. A single clay lamp flickered on the bar and dying embers glowed in the large central hearth. Nix had no idea of the time, though the hours had to be small. The common room was empty.

He smacked his lips, mouth dry, head muzzy. He needed a drink of something. Ale probably. He slid off the stool, wobbled, looked around for a hogshead. Nothing. From his portrait behind the bar, Mung smiled down at him. Nix offered the Lord Mayor's image a fak-you finger.

He reached over and shook Egil. It wouldn't do to sleep the whole night at the bar. He could imagine Tesha's frown.

"Egil. Egil."

A grunt, more snores, a clumsy attempt to push Nix's hand away.

"Egil. Go upstairs to your room."

The priest sat up, looked at Nix, blinked, grumbled something unintelligible, and put his head back down, face turned away.

Nix regarded him for a moment and shrugged. "As you will."

He turned to regard the central stairway. It didn't usually seem so far away or so high. He stared at it for a time, shaky on his legs, trying to work up the confidence to ascend it. He decided it was too much work. He slid back onto his stool and rested his head on the bar.

Sometime later a scraping sound from the rear the inn, behind the bar, pulled him back to alertness. He sat up, cursed, listened, blinking, but it did not recur. A dog or cat must have gotten inside the fence. Or a rat, maybe. He put his head back down.

He heard a similar sound, but this time from the front doors of the inn, and it pulled him fully to wakefulness. He turned on his stool, head cocked. He heard whispers from behind the door.

"The fak?" he muttered.

He rose from the stool, in the process toppling it. It hit the floor with a crash that sounded loud in the silence. Egil stirred, lifted his head.

"What's this, now?"

Nix ignored him and picked his way through the tables, past the fireplace, to the front double doors. He stood there a moment, listened, thought he heard the soft sound of stealthy movement on the other side.

"What is it?" Egil called from the bar.

Nix held up a hand for silence, slid the bar out of the doors, and tried to jerk them open. But the doors gave only a finger's width and he jarred his shoulder in the effort. Something had been wound through the two handles on the other side – a chain or rope – preventing them from opening it.

He heard a soft, menacing chuckle from the other side of the doors and put everything together in a rush. The sound he'd heard coming from the back hadn't been an animal. It'd been someone barring that door, too. And he knew of only reason to seal people into a building. Adrenaline flushed the drunk from his system.

"Fak! Everyone up!" he shouted. "Up! Up!"

Egil was on his feet, a bit wobbly but a hammer in each hand. "What is it?"

"We're locked in."

Egil's eyes widened. He understood the danger, too. "Fak!" In his deep, booming voice, he shouted, "Up! Tesha, get everyone up! Now! Right now!"

Nix's eyes went to the metal frame windows. The Tunnel had once been the house of a noble before the rich had moved across the Meander to the west side of Dur Follin, so it featured tall, narrow, leaded glass windows. They'd provide egress only to brooms.

Glass shattered in one of the windows facing Shoddy Way. Another broke on the other side of the common room. Nix saw movement and a dancing flame through the greasy, murky glass of the remaining panes.

He drew and flung his hand axe through the broken pane of one of the windows, just as the man outside tried to toss a bottle of what Nix presumed to be alchemist's oil into the Tunnel.

The throw was off and Nix's axe shattered another pane, but it sprayed the man with glass and he shouted, staggered back, fumbled the bottle and leaked oil all over himself. Instantly he burst into flame, screaming in agony, staggering, flailing. The stink of burning flesh poured through the broken window.

Through the other window came a second bottle of alchemist's fire and this one made it inside. It hit a table and shattered, the oil spraying table, floor, and nearby chairs, bursting into flames.

"I got the doors!" Egil shouted. "Get everyone out!"

Without waiting for a reply, Egil sprinted across the common room toward the front doors, chin tucked, shoulder braced for impact. He hit one of the double doors like a battering ram. Wood splintered and metal shrieked as the impact cracked the door, the frame, and pulled the hinges out of the jambs. The door and priest slammed into a man on the other side of it and all went down in a jumble.

Egil punched the man in the face, as good as a hammer blow, and the man went still. Nix supposed they could kill him later.

"Go!" Egil shouted back at Nix, as he scrambled to his feet, kicking the downed man as he rose. "I'll get water!"

Nix nodded and bounded up the stairs. Already several of the working men and women had their doors open and stood sleepily in the doorway. Smoke was leaking up from the common room, fogging the corridor.

"Fire!" Nix said. "Get out!"

Nix words spurred them into motion and most of them hurried directly downstairs in their night clothes, wide eyes and muttering in alarm. Some turned as if to go back into their room.

"No!" Nix said. "There's no time to grab anything!"

Nix sprinted down the hall, slamming his fist on doors, shouting.

Kiir and Lis and Tesha came out of their rooms in their nightdresses, coughing, hair mussed.

"Fire!" Nix said, to head off questions.

"Gods!" Kiir said. She clutched the small harp charm of Lyrra she always wore on a chain around her neck.

"Get out!" Nix said. "Right now!"

Kiir and Lis ran past him, Kiir brushing his hand with hers as she went.

"I've got to check the rooms," Tesha said. "Make sure everyone is out."

"Hurry," Nix said.

While Tesha started throwing open doors and shouting into the rooms, Nix ran to Merelda and Rusilla's room. Before he reached it, the door opened and Merelda emerged into the hall, her eyes frantic. She saw Nix and her shoulders sagged with relief.

"I can't lift her, Nix!"

"Aye."

Nix ran past her and into the sisters' room. He scooped Rose out of the bed, and carried her out. He came out into the hall to find Tesha still checking rooms.

"Tesha!"

"A few more," she said. Sweat pasted her dark curls to her forehead.

"I'll help her," Mere said. "Get Rose out. Go."

Nix hesitated, but went. He couldn't do much with Rose in his arms and he couldn't put her safely down. Smoke rolled up the stairway. The common room glowed orange with flames. He heard shouts and exclamations from below. Coughing, he staggered down the stairs.

He reached the bottom just in time to see Egil bull his way through the front doors, each of his arms wrapped around a catch barrel of water. Lis and Kiir and one of the working men whose name Nix didn't know lurched out from behind the bar, each holding a sloshing hogshead of ale.

The fire had consumed two tables and chairs but hadn't yet spread all that much. Egil tossed one barrel of water onto the blaze, then the other. Flames hissed and died. Smoke filled the room. Kiir, Lis, and their co-worker heaved their hogsheads onto the flames, killing even more of the fire.

"Keep it up!" Tesha shouted from up the stairway behind Nix.

She and Mere stood halfway down the stairs, their faces and clothes sooty.

Kiir and Lis and Egil and the second man made for the bar for more of Gadd's brew. Nix could see they'd have the fire out soon. Wanting to get Rose out of the smoke, he carried her toward the front door.

He saw the man Egil had flattened rise to all fours under the remains of the door. He looked around, eyes wide, and clambered to his feet.

"Shite! Egil!"

The priest turned and saw the same thing Nix did. He reached for a hammer, but had neither on his belt. Nix ran for the door, still carrying Rose, and Egil came after.

"Stop him!" Nix shouted. "That man! Stop him!"

He reached the door to see the man shove one of the girls to the ground and sprint off down an alley off Shoddy Way. He laid Rose on the ground.

"Watch her," he said to one of the men nearby.

Egil grabbed his hammers from the wreckage of the door. He must have dropped them after breaking it down. Nix looked back into the Tunnel, caught Tesha's eye. The fire still burned, but it would soon be out. They'd been fortunate.

"You all right?" Nix called to her.

She nodded. "Go! Go!"

Nix and Egil pelted off down Shoddy Way, pushing through a few late night tavern-goers who'd wandered near to see what was the tumult. As they rounded the alley, Nix saw nothing. He cursed, but motion drew his eye up. He saw the man clamber over the top of the roof of a two story building.

"Fakker's using the Highway," Nix said.

Egil had a hammer in each hand and an angry furrow connecting his eyes via the bridge of his nose. "I got the ground."

"Aye," Nix said. "Going up then. Been too long since I ran the Highway anyway."

Nix put his hands to the wall of the nearest building, found purchase, and scrambled up. Fingers, toes, grip, weight on the legs. He'd done it hundreds of times and the wall presented him no challenge. He was up on the roof in moments.

Before him stretched the Thieves' Highway: the irregular lines and rise and fall of pitched eaves, flat roofs, and alleys and streets narrow and wide. It was like another world. A gibbous Minnear painted the way in greens and grays. The spire of Ool's clock to his right jutted skyward, rising like a giant's finger from the sea of Dur Follin's buildings. In the distance rose the Archbridge, its soaring arc and twin support pillars ghostly in the moonlight.

"See him?" Egil called from down below.

Nix caught movement in Minnear's light: the man scrambling over the roof two buildings away.

"Got him."

Nix darted across the roof, leaped a gap to the next roof and sprinted after the man. As he ran he whistled every now and again so Egil could track him. Clutching eaves and leaping alleys, with roof tiles crunching underfoot, he dashed across Dur Follin's skyline. He lost sight of the man from time to time, but kept moving and eventually spotted him again. The man knew he was being trailed from Nix's whistles. Nix tried to use the cover of dormers and spires and the occasional rain cistern as he ran, concerned the man might have a crossbow or sling.

The man moved slowly – he might have been wounded when Egil knocked the door into him – and Nix gained ground quickly. He caught sight of him ahead, leaped a gap and for the first time was on the same roof. The man was at the peak and Nix at the eave. The man threw something down. Nix couldn't dodge but it was only a roof tile. It nicked his shoulder but did little damage.

Nix gave a whistle and scrambled up as the man disappeared over the peak. On the other side, the roof flattened a bit between two dormers overlooking a narrow street. The man was gathering his nerve and strength to leap it. He looked back and saw Nix. Nix slid down the roof and ran after just as the man sprinted into motion.

The man leaped across the gap and Nix leaped after him. They collided in mid-air and the impact ruined both their leaps. They slammed into the side of a shop, cracking shutters, falling earthward in a spinning tangle. The muddy road spared Nix a broken back but slamming into even soft ground drove the breath from this lungs, caused him to see sparks, and sent a shooting pain along one arm.

The man recovered first, rolled away and lifted himself on wobbly legs. Nix rolled over and lunged after him, hooking a few fingers on his mud-soaked cloak. The man whirled, swinging wildly with a dagger he'd produced from somewhere. Nix caught it on the forearm, cursed as it opened a gash. He lurched back awkwardly and reached for his handaxe, but it was gone. He'd thrown it. Turned out to be just as well as the man wanted no part of a street fight. He staggered off down the street. Nix cursed, stood, and stumbled after him, whistling for Egil as best he could.

From around the corner he heard a shout of alarm and a deep, fierce exclamation that could only be from the priest. He put his hands on his knees and tried to catch his breath.

"You got him?" he called.

Egil came around the corner, a hammer in one hand, the limp form of the man held aloft in the other like a neck-wrung goose. "I got him. You all right?"

"Mud covered and blooded, but all right." He stood up straight and grinned. "Still pretty though, yeah?"

"It's dark, so I'm going to say yes. But don't hold me to it."

"Fak you, priest," Nix said, cradling his wounded arm.

"You'd like that, I know. Let's get this bunghole back to the Tunnel."

"Gadd's cellar," Nix said.

"Aye, that," Egil said, giving the unconscious man an ominous shake. Nix stripped the man of a dagger, a purse and a boot knife. He hefted the coinpurse.

"Eight commons and six terns, or within one of each. Wager?"

"My half."

Nix dumped the contents into his palm. "Nine commons, six terns, and the single shiny disc of a gold royal.

"Shite. A slubber like this with a royal. This is a night for surprises."

He tossed the purse to Egil, who caught it, pocketed it, then heaved the man over his shoulder and carried him as he might a bag of grain.

By the time they returned to the Tunnel, many of the workers had drifted back to their rooms. Someone had carried the charred tables and chairs outside the building and piled them near Shoddy Way. They would eventually find their way to the Heap. The charred body was gone and Nix saw no sign of any Watchmen. Gadd, in a nicely cut shirt and pants embroidered with images of dragons, was trying to prop the broken front door in front of the open doorway.

"When did he get back here?" Nix asked.

"Did he leave?" Egil asked.

Nix shrugged.

Gadd saw them approaching and removed the door to allow them passage. As they passed, he showed his pointed teeth and barked something in his elaborate native tongue.

"Seconded," Nix said to him, nodding. "Whatever it was."

"What happened to the body?" Egil asked Gadd, nodding to the area on the porch.

"Pigs," Gadd said.

"Pigs?" Egil asked.

"Pigs," Gadd said with a nod. He grinned and returned to work on the door. Egil and Nix shared a look and sneaked through the dark common room. The floorboards in one corner, and the wall near the window on Shoddy Way, were charred and the whole of it smelled like smoke and spilled beer. Tesha would be airing out the inn for days.

"Stinks," Egil said.

"Stink gives character," Nix said. "Or so I tell everyone about you."

Before they reached the bar, Tesha's voice called down from up the stairs.

"What are you two doing?"

They turned to see her and Merelda seated side by side in the dark, halfway up the staircase. Nix nodded at the unconscious man.

"We're buying this one a drink. Oh, and also we're going to hurt him."

Merelda's eyes widened. Tesha nodded, her eyes hard. She took something resting beside her on the stair – a long wooden pipe of all things – and inhaled deeply. The glow of the bowl made her eyes look shadowed.

"I didn't know you smoked," Nix said.

"There's much about me you don't know, Nix Fall."

He smiled. "If I wasn't about to do bad things, I think I'd drop to my knees and ask to wed you."

"What kind of bad things?" Merelda asked in a small voice.

Egil changed the subject. "Everybody back in their rooms? How's Rose?"

"She's the same," Merelda said.

Tesha took another draw on her pipe. "Everyone's back in their rooms. Not asleep, I'm sure. What happened? Why would someone try to burn the inn?"

"That's what we're going to find out," Egil said, shaking the man he held.

Tesha drew on her pipe, exhaled, eyeing the prisoner. "I'll make sure no one comes down."

Merelda looked at Tesha, at Egil. "What kind of things are you going to do? Egil?"

"Only what we need to," Egil said. "No more."

"But no less," Nix added.

"Not helpful," Egil said.

Tesha stood. "Come on, Mere. We'll check on Rose."

"Mere," Egil said. "We may need you."

"For what? I can't–"

Egil was already shaking his head. "Nothing like that, Mere. But we may need you. Well enough? If this is what we think, we'll need you. All right?"

She nodded and she and Tesha went upstairs.

"We're going to use your cellar, Gadd," Nix called back to the easterner.

But if Gadd heard them he gave no sign. He was working to reattach the door.

Nix lit a lamp and he and Egil carried the man behind the bar and down into Gadd's large root cellar. Clay jars and leather bags filled the shelves. Glass jars filled with liquids of various colors gleamed in the lamplight. Herbs and other shapeless things floated in some of them. Hundreds of herbs hung from twine hooked to the ceiling or lay in bunches here or there. A bale of limbs from some kind of aromatic tree lay in one corner. Nix recognized mandrake, roseslip, and variety of other herbs, most of them with medicinal or magical uses, but many he did not recognize at all. Brew barrels and various items Gadd used in the fermenting process lined one wall.

"What in the Eleven Hells does the man do down here?"

"Much more here than he needs for cooking and brewing," Egil said.

"We're going to have to figure out his story one day," Nix said. "But not today."

"Aye," Egil said, and dropped the unconscious man to the floor. The man groaned. "Not today."

Nix took a length of thin, strong rope from his satchel of needful things – he always carried several lengths of the best line he could buy – and bound the man's hands and ankles. Then he went back up to the bar, half-filled a tankard with ale, returned to the cellar and threw it in the man's face. The man sputtered and blinked awake. He had small eyes, too close together, a large nose and a narrow chin specked with a day's growth of whiskers.

He eyed Nix, Egil, the cellar, swallowed hard. Nix could see thoughts moving behind his eyes.

"Yeah, you're in a bit of it," Nix said. "I've been there."

"It was just a burn job," the man said, his voice nasally. "I do it, I get paid, and I don't know nothing more than that."

Egil harrumphed and Nix tsked.

"Burn jobs don't call for barring doors, now do they?"

The man colored but his expression remained defiant.

A symbol hung from a leather lanyard around the man's neck. Nix grabbed it, yanked it off, and eyed the charm: a stiletto with a coin balanced on the tip. Aster's symbol. Nix shared a knowing look with Egil.

"This here's a guild boy, Egil."

"Fakkin' sneak priests and fools," Egil said.

"I don't know nothing about a guild," the man said.

Nix tossed the charm at the man and hit him in his overlarge nose. "Not too smart, are you?"

"That's just something I found," the man said, pointing with his chin at the charm. He looked up at Egil's head, at the Eye of Ebenor. "But speakin' of fools and priests."

"He's a funny one," Egil said, and glared. "I don't like funny ones."

"And speaking of tattoos," Nix said. He pushed the man prone, rolled him over, checked the man's hands, his arms, cut off his shirt to bare his chest.

"You at least gonna buy me a drink first?" the man said. "You don't even know my name."

"Your name's slubber, and that's clear enough," Nix said, and pulled him back into a sitting position.

"No magic ink, which makes you too dumb for the Committee, yeah?"

"The what?" the man said, all innocence.

"Who gave the order?"

"Order? I was offered coin. That's it. I don't even know the names of them others I was with."

Egil said, "The one burned alive on the street is named 'pig meat'."

"Hard way to go," the man said, shaking his head.

"There are harder ways," Egil said, his tone ominous.

"I'd ask you why you put a flame to the inn–" Nix said.

"*Our* inn," Egil said.

"Our inn," Nix corrected. "But I already know."

The man sneered. "Let me tell you something, slubbers. This ain't no inn. This is a shop for running slags and all-fours-boys."

Nix cuffed him on the head, hard. "Mind your tongue, prick. You're already on the blade's edge."

The man glared up at Nix, his rat nose twitching.

"What do we need from this slubber?" Nix asked Egil.

"Ask him where the guild house is," Egil said.

The man guffawed.

Nix faced the guild man. "You heard the big, intimidating, ill-tempered man. Where's the guild house?"

"I don't nothing about a guild house." The man's rat face turned sly. "But I wager that's not something safe to know 'less you're supposed to. I wager knowing something like that when you shouldn't might, I don't know, get your place burned down. Lot o' things like that."

Nix grabbed the man by his hair. "I find it best not to anger the priest."

The man glared and seemed inclined to keep talking, so Nix released him.

"As you will, then."

"I hear the guild," the man said. "They keep coming and coming until things finish up like they want them finished. And they come back for those that hurt their men. That's why I hear."

"Nobody's coming for you," Egil said.

The man jutted out his chin. "We'll see."

Egil approached the man and despite his superficial insouciance, the man quailed at the priest's approach. But Egil only turned him roughly around so that his back was to the door. Nix looked a question at him. Egil mouthed the word "Mere" and Nix understood. He nodded and Egil exited the cellar to get Mere.

After he left, Nix said, "I always heard guild boys were competent. Then I see a cock-up like this and have to wonder."

"Fak you. You got lucky."

"Tell you something else," Nix said, his tone serious. He grabbed the man by the hair, jerked his head back, put his lips to his ear. "There were twenty people in this inn and I care about all of them. You and your crew will answer for that."

"You have no idea what you're doing here, bungholes."

Nix punched him in the head, knocking him on his side. He struggled to keep his voice under control. "I know exactly what I'm doing. The guild is shite to me."

The man winced at the pain, blinked, licked his lips. "We'll see."

"There's only one thing saving you, slubber, and that's that I've had enough of regrets in recent days. Hard to say with the priest, though. He's not as forgiving as me. Strange in a priest, don't you think."

The man grinned. "No. I know a few priests just like that."

The cellar door creaked open and Egil walked in, Merelda small behind him. Nix eyed Egil, who nodded, then Merelda, who eyed the prisoner. Nix gave her a nod of encouragement. Egil came around to face the guild man.

"Where's the guildhouse?" Egil asked.

The man spit. "That again? I told you–"

Merelda closed her eyes, furrowed her brow. Nix imagined her reaching into the guild man's mind.

"What is this?" the man said, blinking rapidly. "What is–"

"Where is the guildhouse?" Egil said. "Tell us."

"I don't–" The man's words slurred. His eyes rolled. "I can't–"

Mere put a hand to her temple. Nix imagined her reaching in his mind, grabbing at his thoughts, unspooling them like weaver's thread.

Egil leaned over him. "Where. Is. The. Guildhouse?"

The man screamed, shook his head, rocked back and forth.

Merelda took a step closer to him, her pale face wrinkled in concentration. A drop of blood leaked from one of her nostrils but she seemed not to notice.

"No, no, no!" said the man.

"It's on Mandin Way," Mere said, her voice cold, her eyes still closed, her face still twisted up with effort. "Used to be an inn called the Squid. I can... see the layout."

"I know it," Nix said.

"Who is that?" the man said, trying to look over his shoulder. "Is that the bitch faytor?"

Merelda took another step toward the man. Blood flowed from both her nostrils.

The man fell to his side and shrieked, long and loud, and Nix hoped there were no Watch patrols on the street outside.

"There are many guards there, always. There are two levels under it, a chapel, training rooms, safe rooms, a torture chamber, cells. The sewers near Mandin Way and a guarded tunnel in the bank of the Meander give access to the lower levels."

She took another step closer to the man, who now moaned and writhed on the ground, blood coming from his own nose. Merelda's nosebleed worsened but she showed no sign of stopping.

Nix put a hand on her arm. "That's enough."

She whirled on him, projected, *He tried to kill us*!

He winced at the anger in her mental voice. "I know. You're hurting yourself, though. We have what we need. That's enough. That's enough."

Egil took her by the arm. "It's all right. You did good."

She stared at them, blinking, her eyes welling with tears. She looked down at the man, who moaned and muttered in a puddle of snot and blood and spit.

"Fak him," she said, tears falling down her cheeks.

"Aye, that," Egil said softly, and led her to the cellar door. He closed it behind her and he and Nix shared a look. Nix nodded, went to the guild man and pulled him up and around. Blood smeared his face below his nose.

"You don't look half as amused as you did. Huh."

The guildsman's eyes twisted into a glare. "Fak you. You don't know what you done here. Fak you."

Nix sighed. "You'd think more people would fak me. I do have a certain charm. Alas, the world is unfair."

The man spit snot and blood. "You keep on with this and it's gonna get more unfair for and yours real quick-like. You hear? Now let me go."

Nix looked over to Egil, eyebrows raised. "He's an arrogant prick, isn't he? Even bound and bleeding and after what just happened and he still can't shut his hole. Is this what it's like to talk to me?"

Egil shrugged and grunted, his hard eyes fixed on the guildsman.

Nix looked back at the guildsman. "Usually I'm on the other end of this, hands bound, bloody, wondering what's going to happen next. I like this better."

"You won't for long," the guildsman said.

"This really is no time get all cocky, yeah? Makes me irritable. And I'm not even easily irritated. My friend there, though, the big priest, he *is* easily irritated. He looks downright irritable this very moment. Irked, even. So." Nix considered, made up his mind, and stood. "He's going to beat you now."

The man's eyes went to Egil's hulking form, the priest's ham fists, and his arrogance crumbled. "What's that now?"

"Parts of you are gonna bleed," Nix said. "Probably that nose again. Other parts will probably break. But unfair is the world, yeah? Woe and alack."

"Wait, now. Wait," the man said, struggling against his bonds as Egil stepped toward him. "That ain't necessary, is it? We could–"

"Oh, but it is necessary," Nix said, his voice the soft, cold sound of a blade slipping its scabbard. "And I'm going to tell you why – because you fakkin' *deserve* it for what you did, you slubber prick bunghole."

"There's no need for torture, now!"

Nix grabbed the man by his shirt and gave him a shake.

"This isn't torture, slubber. We already know what we need to know. This is *punishment*." He stepped aside to make room for Egil, then put his hands on his hips and glared contempt at the guildsman. "Make it hurt bad, Egil."

"They'll come for you! Both of you for this! And everyone else in this fakkin' inn."

"No, they won't," Egil said, grabbing the man by his shirt and jerking him to his feet. "Because we're coming for them. You boys fakked up, crossing us."

The man grinned darkly, his teeth stained with blood. "You go at the guildhouse, you die. You won't come back from that."

Nix said, "I was just telling someone the other day that our lot in life seems to be to go where others say we shouldn't."

Egil's first punch put a few teeth and a lot of blood on the cellar floor. His second cracked ribs and left the guildsman crumpled on the floor, moaning.

Nix watched the rest of it unfold, knowing they were both giving themselves more to regret, more they'd someday have to look back on and face squarely.

He thought of what could have happened – Rose and Tesha and Mere and Kiir burned in a fire – and decided he could live with it.

CHAPTER SIX ·

"Pigs?" Gadd asked, when they brought the broken, bloodied form of the guild man out of the cellar.

Instead Egil and Nix armed Gadd with enough silver terns to make a suitable donation then had him drop the unconscious guildsman at the temple of Orella. Nix figured if the healer saints of Orella asked any questions, they'd get about as clear an answer out of Gadd as Nix usually got. And the beaten guildsman wouldn't be talking for at least a day, maybe two, if he lived. Egil hadn't been gentle. They'd earned themselves some time, but not much.

He and Egil sat the bar, the smell of the fire still heavy in the air. Egil rattled his bone dice in his fist. Both of them understood the weight of their situation.

"The sun'll be up soon," Nix said, for no reason in particular.

"Aye."

"They must think Rose saw something. Or maybe they know she read the clicked Upright's mind. Either way..."

"Either way," Egil said, nodding. "The guild'll keep coming. Especially now. They got one burned dead and one in the temple."

"Aye," Nix agreed. "Limits our play. We could try a sit-down with the new Upright Man. Explain the situation. Get them to back off."

Egil was already shaking his head. "They tried to burn down the inn, Nix. There were twenty people in here, including Kiir and Rose and Mere and Lis. And they won't let up on Rose if they think she knows guild business."

Tesha came down the stairs and they fell silent. She wore a nightdress and no makeup and her hair was mussed and she looked more vulnerable than Nix ever wanted to see her again. She slipped onto the stool between them.

"How are you doing?" Nix asked her.

"Fine," she said. "Merelda finally fell asleep. Will we have trouble with the Watch?"

Nix shrugged. "Doubtful. No bodies and a fire that was quickly contained. They'll come tomorrow. Maybe. If so, just tell them it was an accident."

She nodded, ran a hand through her thick black hair. She looked like she wished she had her pipe. "What do we do now?"

"Huh? We have the damage repaired. It's not that bad. Then we–"

"That's not what I mean, Nix."

"Ah," Nix said. "I forgot I was talking to you. Well, Egil and I were just talking about that."

"Mere said this was the guild."

"It was."

"That's not good. They won't come back tonight?"

"Not how they are," Nix said. "Word won't even get back until the morning probably. They'll plan, consider, then come again."

"Shite," she said. "And that man you two brought in?"

Nix nodded. "Guild."

"Shite," she said again.

"We have two days," Egil said. "Maybe three."

"They want Rose?" Tesha asked.

Nix nodded.

"I'm not even going to ask why," she said. "But they can't have her."

"Aye, that," Nix said.

For a time the three of them sat at the bar in silence. Nix knew what they had to do, but he didn't want to say it aloud.

"We'll have to go at the guild house," Egil said, saying it for him. "Tonight, I'd say. This new Upright Man must have ordered the burn and click. For that, we kill him and anyone else we find there. Maybe the next Upright Man gets reasonable about things. They want a fight, we give them all they can handle."

"Attacking the guild?" Tesha asked. "Is that wise?"

"You're asking that of us?" Nix said, grinning. "*Us*?"

Egil said, "They come at ours. We go harder at theirs. That's all they understand. We put a bunch of them in the ground and maybe they see that coming at us is bad business. But they've got to be taught that lesson with steel. Not even Nix can talk us out of this one."

"I've talked us out of worse," Nix protested.

"You've talked us *into* worse, too," Egil said, smiling.

"This is so," Nix conceded. To Tesha, he said, "You ought to send everyone away from the Tunnel, until things are resolved."

Her mouth formed a hard line and she shook her head. "I don't run. And even if I did, I don't have anywhere else to go. I think the same's true of Rose and Mere.

Gadd will stay, too. I'll send the rest off somewhere for a time. They won't like it, though."

"We ought to get some men here in the meanwhile," Egil said to Nix.

Nix nodded, and both of them spoke a name at the same time.

"Veraal."

"Veraal?" Tesha said.

"He'll have some men he can trust," Nix said.

"But how do you know you can trust him?" Tesha asked. "Who is he?"

"Veraal? He's an old colleague. And uncle. And he owes us one."

"Or several," Egil added.

Nix nodded. "Or several. And he has no love for the guild. They're the reason he runs out of the Low Bazaar."

"We'll need armor, too," Egil said. "Chain shirts, anyway."

"He can help us there, too."

"What do you have in that satchel?" Egil asked Nix, nodding at Nix's bag of needful things. "A few miracles, I trust?"

"Favor my gewgaws now, do you?" Nix said.

"I favor anything that puts my hands around the throat of Upright Man. Put the flame to my inn? My friends? That demands recompense."

Nix leaned back in his stool. "Recompense? You've been reading again, haven't you?"

Egil chuckled.

Nix turned to Tesha. "If by some unbelievable chance we don't come back from this by dawn tomorrow, Rose and Mere need to get out of the city. Veraal can help with that. Then you and everyone here just lay low. You're all in the cross shot. The guild will lay off if we're dead and Rose is gone."

She bit her lip. "This is that serious?"

"It is," Egil said.

"Bah," Nix said, imitating Egil. He stood, stretched, and hit Egil on the shoulder, "This is fun. We'll be laughing about it two days from now, yeah?"

"Yeah."

"We go in through the sewers, I think."

"Yeah," Egil said.

"That's it, then," Nix said, and turned to face Tesha. "So… this would be the time to declare your secret love for me. You might not get another chance."

She stared at him, expressionless, and he told himself she was trying to hold back a smile.

"Secret lust, at least?"

Her smile won through at last.

"That'll do fine," he said, and winked at her. To Egil he said, "I'll head out now. They'll get eyes on the inn by sun up. I want to be gone before that."

"Plan?" Egil asked.

"I'll go to the Bazaar and try to buy a few miracles. I'll get Veraal in motion, too. You stay here in case something happens during the day. Then tonight we sneak into the guild house and kill everyone that gets between us and the Upright Man."

"That's a good plan."

"That's not a plan," Tesha said.

"That's as good as our plans get," Egil said.

"You," Nix said to Tesha. "If something happens during the day, you keep everyone near Egil. The man's a tree and I haven't seen an axeman yet that can fell him."

"Nix…" she said.

"Say it," he prompted, smiling. "Come on. Say it."

She smiled again. "Be careful."

"Damn," he said, and snapped his fingers. "Almost had it."

"See you soon," Egil said to him.

"Aye."

Dool sidled up to Rusk just before morning chapel. Rusk could tell something had gone hinky from the slump of Dool's shoulders, the way he avoided eye contact.

"It was a cock-up," Dool said, finding his boots interesting.

"A cock-up?" Rusk said. "You telling me you fakked a simple burn job?"

Dool lifted his huge head, which melded seamlessly with his thick neck. "There were complications, Seventh Blade."

"Spill it," Rusk said, and his jaw got tighter and tighter as Dool related events in his slow monotone. They had one man down, burned to death, body's whereabouts unknown, and another missing altogether.

Dool looked into Rusk's face and licked his lips. "I can take a team back there today, right now. Walk in there and click the faytor and those two fakkers."

"No," Rusk said, his mind working on the problem. "The Watch will be looking into things today. And maybe tomorrow, too. Keep eyes on the inn and keep me informed, but otherwise stay clear."

"Seventh Blade, they clicked Lenil–"

Rusk stuck his face in Dool's. "Lenil's dust because he was an incompetent member of an incompetent team that can't even put a match to an unguarded building."

Dool swallowed hard and looked away.

Rusk put a hand on his shoulder. "They owe us a debt, yeah? And we'll collect, Dool. But it ain't gonna be today or tonight. Because now it's not just about the faytor."

"Now it's about those two fakkers," Dool said.

"Aye."

Rusk had told Channis that Egil and Nix were players, but all Channis would hear was that the job had gone wrong and that the faytor still lived. Not a good start to Rusk's run as Seventh Blade.

"They know it was guild work?" he asked.

Dool shrugged. "I don't know how they could."

Rusk had a missing man and a faytor with knowledge of the guild, so he thought it best to assume Egil and Nix knew the torch job was guild-ordered and that they knew why.

"They may try to sneak the faytor out. You have your eyes let me know right away if things look like that."

Dool nodded. "Sorry, Seventh Blade."

Rusk nodded. "Just keep it to yourself until I spill it to the Upright Man. We can fix this. Go on, now."

Dool nodded and went into the chapel. Rusk stood alone in the corridor, thinking of how to present things to Channis.

In the end, there was no way to pretty things up. They'd had a cock-up. They'd just have to clean it. Rusk's knot to untie was that Channis didn't like messes, and would like them even less when they occurred just after he took the position as Upright Man.

Rusk held the news until after chapel, throwing prays at Aster throughout that the Upright Man would be reasonable. He met him in his wing of the guild house in the late morning. As usual, Channis had his back to him as he entered. The Upright Man stared out at the slow current of the Meander, the boats, the swoop of the river gulls around and under the Archbridge.

Rusk could tell from the visible tension in Channis's posture that he already knew. But he was going to make Rusk say it and own it, which made Channis a bunghole. Rusk decided he might as well jump in.

"The torch job went wrong."

Channis turned to regard him across the expanse of wood floor. "Wrong how?"

"Went cock-up is how. Lenil was killed and his body's missing. Feegas is missing and no one knows what happened to him."

Channis walked toward him, that predatory stride, his hands crossed behind his back. "And?"

"And the place didn't light. The girl, that faytor, is still alive."

Channis came in close and circled him and Rusk could do nothing but stand there, as still as a sculpture. He felt like a condemned slubber at the scragging post.

"You chose that team, didn't you, Seventh Blade?"

Rusk nodded and did not give in to the temptation to tell Channis that three of the men on the team were part of Channis's personal crew before he'd become the Upright Man.

"Didn't lead it yourself, though?"

Rusk shook his head, resisting the impulse to tell the Upright Man that the Seventh Blade did not traditionally perform street work.

A punch to the stomach sent Rusk to his knees, gasping.

"Why the fak not?" Channis asked. He still hadn't raised his voice.

Rusk knew there was no right answer, so he held his tongue and shook his head. Let Channis interpret that as he would.

He interpreted it the way he interpreted everything else, and loosed a kick to Rusk's side. The impact drove Rusk sideways onto his back and the pain made him gasp. For a moment he couldn't breathe and he lay there, staring up at the cracked plaster ceiling and the emotionless oval of Channis's scarred face.

"When I order something done, you get it done. Clear?"

Rusk nodded.

"I can't hear you."

"Clear," Rusk said between gasps.

Channis reached down and pulled him to his feet. Rusk refused to wince in anticipation of another blow, and stared into Channis's face.

"You got eyes on that inn?" Channis asked.

"They'll be there as of sun up, yeah. Good ones."

"Can't move on it for a day or two."

"'Cause the Watch'll make it too hot."

"Yeah. But I want that faytor dead and I want them two pricks dead and I want it done within the week. They know the score, you think?"

"I think maybe."

Channis nodded. "If they're smart, they'll run. But if they run, we run them down. Can't have a member going down and unavenged after I first become the Man, yeah?"

"Yeah."

Channis smiled his fake smile, took Rusk by the shoulders, dusted off his shirt.

"I told you Seventh Blade to my Eighth is a shite job, and now you know it certain. That ain't gonna change. But you and me, we're all right. But don't bring me any more cock-ups, yeah?"

Rusk swallowed, nodded.

"Committee meeting tonight at midnight. Double the usual guards outside, but you see to it the house is cleared except for one personal bodyguard for each Committeeman. All but you. You go solo. Kherne will be my muscle. And you. Clear?"

Rusk nodded.

"That's it, then. Get it done."

Rusk left the room, cursing Aster for putting seven points on his tat and a bunghole in charge of the guild.

The great water clock of Ool the Mad rang the sixth hour. Nix exited through the front door of the Tunnel before the sun rose and walked Shoddy Way. The streets were empty of everything except Nix and the breeze. Charcoal embers burned fitfully in street torches lit by the city's linkboys hours earlier. Nix meandered through the streets, following the wind, wasting time, circling back and stopping now and again to determine if he'd been followed. It was unlikely the guild had put eyes on the Tunnel so quickly after the botched torch job, but he wanted to be certain.

After satisfying himself that he wasn't tailed, he let himself relax, shedding the mask and emotional armor he habitually wore. Even a liar had to be honest with himself sometimes.

His boots carried him in the direction of the Warrens, where he'd been born to a mother he didn't remember. The pre-dawn breeze carried the rotten stink of the Heap, the rotten stink of Nix's past. He thought of Mamabird, thought of his childhood, most of it spent hungry and scrounging the Heap for food and coin. He thought of his adulthood, most of it spent drunk, scrounging ancient tombs for treasure. Funny how the man hadn't left the boy too far behind.

He allowed that for a man who'd done so much, he'd accomplished amazingly little. He supposed that was another regret he'd have to carry. Of course he'd had a good time while accomplishing not much. In the end, maybe that was enough. And maybe it wasn't. He smiled, knowing he was trying to sell himself shite, lying to himself as always.

Mamabird had accomplished more with her life than Nix could ever hope to, and she'd never left the Warrens and saw less coin in a month than Nix and Egil spent on one night's decent drunk. Possibly that's why he loved her so much. He decided he shouldn't be walking the streets alone before sun up. Too much thinking got done.

Eventually dawn lightened the night sky to gray and he tried to let it lighten his mood. He knew why he'd turned maudlin. Taking on the guild was dangerous work. Likely they'd die, and fear of dying turned men sentimental.

The dung sweepers took to the streets, piles of stink stacked high in their mule-pulled wagons. He walked alongside the Poor Wall, the low, crumbling stone barrier that separated the Warrens from the rest of Dur Follin. The rising sun put its light on the desperate hovels of the poor, the bulky, irregular lines of the Heap. The mountain of Dur Follin's waste grew more every year, the scat of an entire city. Nix imagined the city collapsing, disappearing forever, and leaving no sign of its existence but the Heap and the Archbridge. Gulls swooped and wheeled around and on the trash. The desperate poor were already picking through the piles, looking for anything they could eat, use, or sell. Nix knew the life well.

The streets and the shops came back to life, too, resurrected by the dawn. Shutters and doors opened. Morning coughs and calls from neighbor to neighbor cut the silence. Wagons and mules and ponies appeared on the road and soon the streets were alive with activity. Nix donned his mask – Nix the Quick, Nix the Unflappable, always with a ready word and a ready blade – and headed back for the Low Bazaar as Ool's clock sounded the turn of a new hour.

To his right, high above the monumental stone sweep of Archbridge, a fusillade of pyrotechnics exploded in the air, expanding flowers of white and green sparks, beautiful but temporary, like everything beautiful. The day must have been holy to some cult or another. He stared at the smoke after the sparks had gone, and reminded himself to get some pyrotechnics, if possible.

He heard and smelled the Low Bazaar before he saw it. The wind carried the slow beat of drums, the ring of a tambourine, the smell of cooking fires and sizzling meat. The streets grew more crowded as he neared it, the walkways populated with a fringe of vendors who didn't have a stall in the Bazaar but wanted the benefit of the traffic. Nix fell in with the murmuring crowd, a river of people and animals. They turned a corner and there it was.

The Low Bazaar straddled a vast, rectangular grassy plaza between Shoddy Way and Endel's Ride. Like the Warrens, it was its own mini-town, a part of Dur Follin, but separate from it. A low, wooden fence surrounded the entire plaza, the equivalent of the Poor Wall, but no one paid it any heed. Young and old alike sat on it or climbed over it to get into the Bazaar. Tents of all sizes blanketed the plaza, a dizzying quilt of colors. Ponies and goats and sheep grazed in the grass, some in makeshift pens, some ranging free. Smoke rose from scores of braziers and fire pits. A veritable cloud of incense hung over the plaza, the smells often exotic but sometimes offensive. The Low Bazaar collected the odd, the exotic, and those who didn't fit squarely into any other place in Dur Follin – mostly foreigners like the Narascene, but also recent arrivals to the city, and all manner of entertainers, from musicians and acrobats to deformed freaks and sword swallowers.

Despite the early hour, scores of people, noble and common and poor, already thronged the worn footpaths between the tents and stalls. The shouts of vendors filled the air, hawking this or that.

"Every day is market day at the Low Bazaar!" called a tall, horse-faced man with a scraggly moustache who minded the gate. He wore a ratty, collared cape and used it to play hide-and-find with passing children. He collected a copper common from anyone who brought in a wagon or cart and dropped it in the strongbox upon which he sat.

Nix nodded at the man and picked his way through the smoky throng. He asked a few vendors for the location of Veraal's stall and soon had it. He cut through a circle of tents surrounding a fire pit over which hung a spit pig, already roasting, and soon found Veraal, tending his sturdy stall.

Veraal, thinner and grayer than Nix remembered, but no doubt still as tough as old leather, had his back to Nix. He placed tied bunches of smoke leaf on the table that fronted his stall. A long wooden pipe dangled from his mouth, leaking an unbroken line of smoke that looked to tether Veraal to something invisible in the air above him. Nix's experienced eye noted the blades secreted on Veraal's person: left boot, small of the back, each wrist.

A few locals eyed his wares and Veraal chatted them up with a smile. He exhaled smoke as he talked, like some kind of amiable dragon. Nix approached and put a hand on his shoulder.

Veraal whirled at the touch, a hand going for the blade behind his back.

"I don't remember you being such a smoker," Nix said.

Veraal's eyes flashed recognition and he stopped himself before drawing. His smile deepened the wrinkles on his weathered face. "An old man is allowed his vices." To the two customers, he said, "Pardon me, goodfolks."

He pulled Nix to the side. "You get yourself cut grabbing a man like that."

"Doubtful," Nix said, grinning. Veraal grinned in turn, his teeth stained yellow from smoke leaf.

"How you been, Nixxy?"

"Well enough," Nix said. He made a show of eyeing Veraal's stall, which looked like a small cabin. "I'm hoping smoking's not your only vice these days, yeah?"

Veraal chuckled. "Like the stall? Looks legit, don't it?"

"It does," Nix said, noting the bags of leaf inside. "Swag goes in and out in bags of leaf. Can't be moving much, though, yeah?"

Veraal puffed his pipe. "I'm more selective these days. Work only with folks I know and like. I do some legit work, too, and it ain't bad. You ought to try it."

"One day, maybe," Nix said. "Listen, I'm gonna need to call in a marker."

Veraal's face grew serious. He drew on his pipe. "Shite, man, those are some old markers. Have to do with those nice girls from the tent there? The murder?" He nodded at the colorful tent beside his stall. "Merelda said she knew you."

"It does, aye," Nix said. Nix had never actually been to Mere and Rose's tent. They'd done it up well: painted the dyed yellow canvas with nonsense but arcane looking sigils, the all-seeing eye, the flame of truth, and so forth.

"They're in trouble, then?" Veraal asked.

"Aye, and it looks serious," Nix said.

Veraal nodded. "Well, I'll help if I can. I like those girls. They're too nice for the likes of you."

"Truth," Nix said.

"And I owe you and Egil. How is that brute of a priest, anyway? Somber as always?"

"Better than when you saw him last."

Egil had been heavier into his alecups when last they'd had dealings with Veraal.

Veraal pointed at Nix with his pipe. "That I'm glad to hear. That man's got some pain in him."

Nix thought of Blackalley, of Egil's sobs. "Aye."

Veraal asked, "I take it that hit was guild work?"

They fell silent for a moment as a nobleman shopped Veraal's wares. Nix made as though he were considering some leaf while Veraal made his pitch. The nobleman left two terns lighter and several bunches of smoke leaf heavier.

Nix and Veraal stood side by side, facing the ever changing crowd of passersby. A pair of drummers strode by, an acrobat flipping and dancing to their rhythm. Pedestrians stopped and applauded, dropped commons into the open containers the drummers wore on belts at their waists.

"It was guild work, yeah," Nix said, picking up the conversation. "So you're going to need some men."

"Men?" Veraal removed his pipe from his mouth, uncorking his thoughts. "What do you have in mind? I trust it's reasonable?"

"It is," Nix said. "All I need you to do is sit on the Tunnel. That's it. Make sure no harm comes to it."

Veraal drew on his pipe. "Rose and Mere are at the Tunnel?"

"And others. Guild tried to torch it last night."

Veraal sniffed. "Caught 'em, did you? You and Egil?"

Nix nodded. "One burned by his own fuel. Pig food. One... questioned by Egil."

Veraal whistled. "That would not be fun."

"No," Nix agreed. "But deserved. Well?"

"I'm there for you, Nixxy," Veraal said. He drew on the pipe, exhaled through his nose. "Got some men I can use."

"Appreciated, Veraal," Nix said. "Only going to need you for tonight. I don't think anything will go down that fast. And after tonight this'll be resolved one way or another."

Veraal studied him over the length of his pipe as if taking aim. "You and Egil doing something stupid?"

Nix shrugged, tossed a common to a dancing girl who strode by playing finger symbols. "Stupid's where the fun is."

"If you say so."

"Listen, if it goes bad and we don't come back, I'd be grateful if you'd get Rose and Mere out of Dur Follin. Maybe set them up in New Dineen."

Veraal nodded. "Don't believe I've ever heard you talk about not getting clear of a scrape. But yeah, I can do that. Or take a pass on whatever you're planning and take them yourself. Just run. Shite, Dur Follin's just a city, Nix. It'll get along fine without you and Egil."

"We both know that's a filthy lie," Nix said, and smiled. "Besides, Egil's got his ire up, and you know how he gets. And we don't run, especially from guild slubbers."

"Figured," Veraal said, nodded. "Share a smoke, then? Ain't that customary for a condemned man?"

"No time. There'll be eyes on the Tunnel by now, so bring your men in piecemeal, yeah? Like you're just patrons coming for a drink. I don't want them to know we're wise to them. Everybody in before dark, too."

Veraal put a hand on Nix's shoulder. "It's done. Think no more on it."

Nix tossed a tern to Veraal, who snatched it out of mid-air. "Bring some of that leaf to the madam who runs the Tunnel. Tesha's her name. She appreciates a good smoke. Oh, and I need chain shirts for Egil and me. Can you do that?"

"Maybe you'd like me to rub your feet, too?"

Nix grinned. "You'd like that. See you this eve."

Veraal called after him. "You get the shirts only if you swear to bring them back, yeah?"

"We'll do what we can," Nix said.

After Nix left Veraal, he grabbed some sweetmeats from Orgul and walked to the Narascene portion of the bazaar, a world within a world where everyone wore colored robes and veils, incense smoked the air like a spring fog, and gongs and chimes made a continuous ring. He was known there, and nodded to familiar faces.

He soon found the tent of the hunched, yellow-robed harridan from whom he routinely purchased some of his gewgaws. He never knew what she'd have for him – sometimes she had nothing – but he figured the fun was in finding out. The beaded curtain gave way to an interior filled with stacked jars of pickled creatures, bunches of dried roots, piles of crystals, and various other items of arcane significance. Most were junk for the hobs, but not all.

She must have heard him enter for she emerged from the rear of the tent, hobbling on a bad hip, smelling of incense and sweat. She cackled when she saw him, and spoke in heavily accented Narascene.

"Always you come to me when in danger."

"And you always protect me, lovely lady," he said, and bowed.

She cackled at that and the cackling turned to a phlegmy cough. He waited for it to subside before asking,

"Do you have anything new?"

She looked at him with soft eyes – he always charmed her.

"I have something for you, small man," she said. "Cost is twenty terns."

He knew better than to haggle with her. He dug the coins out of his purse and placed them in her wrinkled, veiny hand. She secreted them in her robes, went to a shelf, and removed two amulets on leather lanyards. Tiny amethysts, four on each amulet, glittered in plain silver settings. When she handed them to him, the enchantments in them caused the hairs on his arms to stand on end.

"Protective," he observed.

Up close, the pores in her nose looked like they'd been dug out with a shovel. "Your schooling not tell you from what?"

He shook his head.

"That's because you quit too soon."

"I was expelled," he corrected.

"If you hadn't quit," she said, ignoring his correction, "then you'd know enchanted amethyst protects from venom, stomach gas, piles of the arse, and ugly girls."

She cackled at her own joke.

"I've never in my life met an ugly girl, milady," Nix said, slipping the amulets into one of the many pockets in his satchel. "And never once in this tent."

She colored, murmured something, and turned away.

He smiled and turned to go, but her voice froze him in the bead curtain.

"Small man! What you're doing? It will end with you swimming among the dead."

Nix knew the crone was a legitimate seer. Her words reached through his mask and crashed his false cheer. His expression fell but he rallied quickly.

"A surprising number of my days end just so, milady."

And with that he left her. Her words troubled him though, and he sought only half-heartedly for the cloaked, vacant-eyed, sexless agent of Kerfallen the Grey.

The wizard's servant maintained no tent or stall, merely walked the bazaar, seemingly at random, vending his master's gewgaws to those in the know.

Nix spotted him or her or it, jogged to catch up, and stepped directly in front of it. It stopped, staring at him with wide, unblinking eyes. The androgynous, hairless face did not change expression. Nix recited the required greeting in a whisper, trying not to roll his eyes at the silliness of wizards.

"The magery of Kerfallen is without peer in the Seven Cities of the Meander. I offer coin for his boon."

The agent held forth a hand.

Nix hefted a pouch holding a handful of terns and a few royals, placed it in the agent's palm. The creature tucked the pouch into its clothing, studied Nix's face for a time, as if reading something in his expression, then reached into its satchel and withdrew a bronze skeleton key as long as Nix's hand. The bit that hung from the end of the key's hollow blade was shaped like a tiny fanged mouth.

"I already have lots of keys," Nix said. "Another will–"

The mouth at the end of the key spoke in a tiny voice. "Give us a bite of apple. We lock and unlock for eats. Give us some apple."

"Burn me," Nix said, eyeing the mouth. He looked up to tell the agent he'd take the key, but it had already moved on, continuing its wanderings through the bazaar.

"Apple!" the key said.

"Patience," Nix said, and tucked the key into his satchel. He quickly found a fruit seller, traded a copper for a half dozen red apples, and put one of them in his satchel with the magic key. The key munched away on the feast.

Nix lifted the satchel's flap. "You earn the next one."

The Narascene seer's words bounced around his skull, resurrecting his melancholy. He retraced his actions of the last couple hours – evaluating his life, walking the Poor Wall, visiting the Low Bazaar, the Narascene seer, Kerfallen's agent, all of it a long goodbye.

"Should've had that smoke with Veraal, after all," he said with a rueful smile.

On his way out of the Bazaar, he spotted a wagon full of pyrotechnics – tubes made from a special paper, small balls of clay, rods coated in some kind of metallic substance, all of them made by Vathari alchemists, the methods unknown even to the wizards of the Conclave. The short, long-haired, well-dressed Vathari merchant who vended them probably sold them most often to the various cults and philosophical movements that squatted on the Archbridge, and indeed the shaven-head cultists of some god or other milled round the wagon. For his part, Nix always figured that if pyrotechnics impressed a person's god, the person needed a better god. Nix, however, could imagine a few uses beyond impressing country hobs.

He nodded and smiled his way through the bald zealots. The Vathari took in his blades but never lost his smile, false as it was.

"You don't strike me as the religious sort, young sir."

"I'm neither religious nor a sir. I worship good ale, which I find answers prayers about as well as any god, and have coin that spends as well as any priest's. Suffice?"

The cultists overheard him, shot him glares. He ignored them.

The man gave a slight bow. "Your faith is appealing to many and well known to me."

"Excellent," Nix said, taking a liking to the man already. "I'd like a few of your... gewgaws." He smiled. It felt good to hear the word used in reference to something other than the contents of his satchel. "Not the ones for the sky, mind, but something that I can use indoors, maybe smoke up a room."

"Indoors?" the man asked, raising his manicured eyebrows.

"An open area outside is what I meant," Nix said. "Maybe some loud things and... I don't know, spark shooters or something? You have something like that? Whatever it is needs to travel well. I'll keep it here." He indicated his satchel.

"Hmm," the man said, and circled his wagon while rubbing his chin and eyeing his wares. "Hmm. How much you spending?"

Nix showed him two gold royals. "This do?"

"Hmm. Hmmm."

Eventually the man provided Nix with several smoke balls, a few of the metal rods coated in a silver substance, and three tubes that the man called "boomsparks". Nix put them in his satchel but in one of the side pockets, to prevent the magic key from trying to eat them.

"A question, if I could," he said.

The man nodded for him to proceed.

Nix peeled back his lips and pointed at his eye teeth. "Filed teeth? And tattoos of magical creatures all up and down the arms? Do you know what those mean because–?"

The man's eyes showed their whites and he backed off a step.

Nix held out his hands. "Wait, wait, I didn't mean–"

The man used a finger to draw some kind of protective sigil in the air then waved Nix away. "You go! Go now! Now! Now!"

The man's outburst was attracting the attention of passersby, so Nix did not press. He turned and walked away, reminding himself once again that he had to figure out Gadd's story one of these days. Assuming, of course, he had more than a day remaining to him.

He headed back to the Tunnel. The guild would have eyes on it by then, and once he got back there'd be no leaving again without a tail. That suited him fine.

CHAPTER SEVEN

Shoddy Way looked as it always did in late morning –
a muddy ribbon filled with pedestrians making their
way to and from the Low Bazaar, a handful of wagons
and carts, a few too many wolf-eyed hangers-on, a few
urchins, and a few beggars. Nix had no doubt some of
them were guild men. He deliberately kept his eyes from
the rooftops. They'd have a man or two up there.

He felt eyes on him as he walked under the Tunnel's
sign, swinging in the breeze. The broken door was
reattached, hanging askew in the jamb, but working.
Gadd had done good work.

A handful of patrons sat the tables, nursing morning
ales with day old bread and cheese – the laborer's
breakfast. The interior smelled more of Gadd's stew than
it did of fire, but the blackened floor and the wall around
the burned window announced the attempted arson
well enough.

The Tunnel was more tavern than brothel before
evening, and Nix didn't see Gadd or Tesha. The alekeep
would be at the market, buying the day's supplies.
Probably Tesha must have been tending to Rose. Egil sat

alone in a corner, all three eyes on the door, his hammers close to hand, a bowl of stew before him. Nix joined him.

"How'd it go?" Egil asked.

"Veraal's in. He'll be along with his men."

"A good man, Veraal."

"Aye," Nix said. He patted his satchel. "I've got my miracles. I think we're ready."

"Eyes on this place," Egil said. "See them?"

"I didn't make 'em, but I felt them. They're out there."

Egil said, "We'll clear them before we head to the guild house."

"You talk to Mere? Get all the details she pulled out of that guild slubber's head?"

Egil tapped his bald head. "Got 'em. As good as a map."

"Good," Nix said. He fiddled with his thumb ring before asking, "Sun's up. This still seem like a good idea?"

Egil regarded him across the table, his brow furrowed. "You see another option?"

Nix didn't look at him but offered Veraal's advice. "We could leave. Take the girls. Head to New Dineen. Start over."

Egil scoffed, and that was about as Nix expected.

"You know we're going to have to leave a lot of bodies behind us, yeah?" Nix said. "Ideally not ours, but... is that going to leave a bad taste in your mouth? You've been rather priestly lately."

Egil sniffed and leaned back in his chair. A bit too casual, Nix thought.

"Doesn't bother me with these whoresons, Nix. They tried to burn our girls. That's a question needs the right kind of answer. You don't hurt ours. You don't even try."

"Aye," Nix said and nothing else.

He knew that men who harmed women earned Egil's rage like little else. Nix imagined that every time Egil saw a man hurting a women he relived the loss of his wife and daughter. Over the years countless men had paid vicariously for the death of Hulda and Asa, and countless more would, but Egil would never forgive himself, and the actual wrongdoers would never pay. Blood could only expiate so much. Egil just had to bear it.

Nix flashed on his friend walking the darkness of Blackalley, calling for his lost daughter and wife, the pain of self-blame in his voice. Nix pondered the pain Egil must live with; it made his chest feel tight. He looked away, cleared his throat.

"I'm more worried about *you*, anyway," Egil said, leaning forward, the chair protesting the shift of his weight. "Unless you got hard-edged while you were out this morning, leaving lots of dead men in your wake isn't your way either."

"No," Nix said, still fiddling with his ring. "But I'm with you on this. A torch job? Civilians and women? That ain't the game. And it's just bad form. I can put steel in slubbers who'd do that and not think twice. So fak them and their tattoos and their religion."

"As long as you're firm of purpose," Egil said, spooning some stew into his mouth.

"The only people who get to tell me to be firm of purpose are lovely women with parted legs," Nix said. He pushed back his chair and stood. "I'm going to go check on Rose."

"I'll come," Egil said.

Upstairs many of the doors in the hallway were open, the working women and men inside preparing for the day's work: splashing themselves with perfumed water, brushing hair, applying kohl. They traversed the hall and knocked on Rose's door. Tesha opened it a sliver and peeked out, circles under her dark eyes, her hair still hanging loose and unbrushed. She saw it was them, ushered them in, and closed the door behind them.

Rose was sitting up on the side of her bed, her face pale and pained, her breathing rapid. Merelda sat beside her, her tear-streaked face bunched up in concern. She looked very much a young girl.

Nix and Egil asked Tesha a question with their eyes. She shook her head and shrugged. Nix frowned, approached the bed, and kneeled before Rose. He had the urge to take her hands in his but resisted.

"Rose?" Nix said.

She looked up at him sharply, as if she'd just noticed he was in the room. Her eyes swam in their sockets, the focus coming and going.

"He's in here," Rose said, tapping herself roughly on the side of the head. "Croaking over and over again. I can't get him out!"

"Croaking?" Nix said.

"Dying," she said. "Dying, Nix. Going dusty."

He knew what the word meant, but the word choice struck him as out of place for Rose.

Nix looked to Merelda. "Is there anything you can do?"

She glared at him, her tone of voice betraying the tension she bore. "If there was, I would have already done it. Don't you think I'd have already done it?"

Her raised voice aggravated Rose, who winced and moaned.

"Put a bridle on that doxy," she muttered, then cradled her head in her hands and rocked back and forth on the edge of the bed. Mere rubbed her back, a helpless expression on her face.

"Get him out, get out! It hurts, Mere! It hurts!"

Nix stood and backed off, bumping into Egil. They stood in the center of the room, beside Tesha, the two of them useful for nothing but revenge.

"It's like I'm haunted," Rose said, her voice muffled by her hands. "He's a ghost, but I can't get him out. I hear him, I feel him, all the things he knew…"

She shook her head and her body vibrated with sobs. Mere sobbed, too, hugged her sister.

"Maybe Gadd could get drugs to soothe her when he comes back," Tesha offered.

As one, Nix, Egil, and Mere said, "No."

Tesha went wide-eyed at the vehemence of their reply. Egil explained.

"Her brother used to keep her drugged. To keep her controlled. And then he… hurt her."

"Apologies," Tesha said, and her expression hardened. "No drugs, then. And I hope that fakker's dead."

"Worse," Nix said, but explained no further. He signaled to Mere with his eyes that he wanted to speak with her off to the side. Reluctantly she left Rose on the bed and met with Nix near the door for a whispered conversation. Egil and Tesha joined them.

"She seems worse," Nix said.

Mere nodded, her eyes too drained for more tears. Egil raised a hand to put on her shoulder, hesitated, then did it anyway. She leaned into him, lost and small against his massive frame.

"Is there anything we can do?" Egil asked.

Nix almost made the offer he'd been holding in his head, but it was so desperate that he hesitated and the moment passed.

Mere shook her head. "She just has to rest. She has to clean it up herself, but she's just not able to yet. If not…"

She trailed off and Nix did not press. He could well imagine what came after the "if not".

Egil's lost, helpless expression mirrored Nix's thinking. There was no treasure to obtain, no information to extract from some slubber, no mystery to solve. They were useless. All they could do is give payback. That'd have to be enough.

"Let us know if we can do anything," Nix said. He cleared his throat. "Listen, we're going to be gone tonight. Some men are coming, though, men we trust and–"

Rose groaned, rolled into a ball on the bed.

"Tesha told me everything," Merelda said. She looked at Nix, at Egil. "And she told me why. But I want you to stay here. Don't do it. I don't want either of you to die. I lost my head in the cellar and…"

Nix was shaking his head and about to speak, but Egil took Mere by the shoulders and gently turned her around to face him.

"You have a gentle heart, Mere. Despite everything, you do. But listen to me. If we don't go to them, they'll come here for Rose and for us." He held up a hand to cut off her reply. "They think she knows their business and it looks like she might. Every other thing she says she's talking like a guild man."

Mere shook her head. "But she can't make sense of it all. It's a jumble. She–"

"Doesn't matter," Egil said softly. "Not only does she know guild business, but now we left one of theirs dead and one… badly hurt."

Mere blanched at the memory of the guild man in the cellar. Egil continued:

"This is the only way, Mere, the only thing they'll understand. And I, for one, have no intention of dying. Nix?"

Nix sniffed. "I'm too pretty to die. Everybody knows that."

"You see?" Egil said. "We'll do what needs done, come back, and we'll all three see Rose through this."

"Four," Tcsha said. "All four of us."

"Four," Egil corrected, nodding at Tesha. "Well enough?"

Mere stared into his face and nodded slowly.

He leaned in and kissed her on the forehead. She colored.

Nix cleared his throat, uncomfortable as always with genuine shows of emotion. "Well. Yes. Then. So. We'll be downstairs waiting for Veraal and keeping an eye on things. Our part of this little excursion starts around two bells. We'll be back in the morning, good as new. Well enough?"

Mere and Tesha nodded.

Nix asked Mere, "You told Egil everything you took out of the guild man's head about the layout of the guild house? Everything?"

She nodded.

"Good," Nix said. He stepped forward and gave her arm a squeeze. "That's it then."

Outside the room, Nix said, "You're not helping by making cow-eyes at that girl."

Egil looked back at the door, his expression thoughtful. "As you said, she's not a girl."

"She's seen twenty two winters, if that," Nix said, as they started walking the hall.

Egil shrugged. "I embraced her, Nix, that's all. I'm fond of her. I think."

As they descended the stairs, Nix brushed his fingers over Kiir's. She looked lovely in her tight black dress and he refused to let himself think about her with any other man.

"We're both getting domesticated. This ain't good. How fond?"

Egil shrugged. "I don't know yet."

"You're… hurting right now, Egil. Don't try to stop it the wrong way. You'll hurt her in the process."

Egil nodded, put a hand on Nix's shoulder, and steered him to the bar. Gadd put tankards before them.

"Tell me about your teeth and tattoos, Gadd," Nix said.

Gadd grinned at him, showing the filed eye teeth. "Teeth, yes. Sharp. You want different drink?"

Nix smiled back, but snatched Gadd's wrist as he tried to turn away. Gadd's eyes narrowed and his other hand twitched, as if he might strike Nix or draw a blade from somewhere.

"You want to keep some secrets?" Nix said. "Fair enough. Egil and I, we've got some, too."

Egil snorted at that. Nix went on:

"So you tell us if keeping your secrets ever puts this place or anyone in it at risk, yeah?"

Gadd lost his smile and lost the vacant look in his eye. The man looked downright cunning as he held Nix's gaze. "Clear."

"I'm good to my friends, Gadd. But I'm an unforgiving fakker to anyone faks me or mine. With me?"

Gadd said nothing, merely stared.

Nix let Gadd's wrist go and the easterner went back to his tankards and plates and beer.

"What was that?" Egil asked.

"Just making a point with the man," Nix said. "A Vathari merchant acted strange in the bazaar when I described the teeth and tats. Seemed frightened."

"Gadd seems right to me. And makes the gods' ale."

"Seems right to me, too. But right sometimes goes wrong. It needed said."

"Well enough."

They both swirled their drinks, but neither drank, which struck Nix as a terrible waste of Gadd's ale. They waited and watched. Egil shook his dice, rolled them on the bar. Nix checked and rechecked his gear, the contents of his satchel, stocked it with various items from Gadd's cellar so he could feed the magic key. He gave one of the amethyst amulets he'd bought in the bazaar to Egil.

"It'll protect you," he explained to the priest.

"From what?"

"Venom, among other things," he said, then started their routine. "It won't fix your lack of charisma, alas."

Egil put the lanyard over his thick neck. "I'm wearing it only in hopes it protects me from annoying small men."

"Annoying?"

"Also small."

"I'm small only when compared to a certain lumbering oaf whose company I endure only – *only* – in hopes that one day some small amount of my charm and wit might transfer to him, thereby rendering him only half-a-dolt."

"You neglect 'annoying'?"

Nix tilted his head. "Annoying I concede. And thanks. I needed that."

"Aye."

Over the course of the day Tesha moved the Tunnel's workers out in pairs or threes, usually mingling with exiting patrons so as not to arouse suspicion. Veraal's men started to come in around the fifth hour – all of them armed and armored, in at least leather jacks – and by the tenth, most of the Tunnel's workers were gone and the only 'patrons' were Veraal and his six men.

"I got two more with crossbows right outside," Veraal said, puffing on his pipe, his eyes hard in the nest of his wrinkles. He had a large sack that held two chain shirts and a large bunch of smoke leaf. "Best I could do for mail on short notice. Lady'll like the leaf, though."

Nix examined the used mail. His shirt looked too big and Egil's too small, but they'd have to do. Nix gave both of them to Egil to carry in his pack. They'd put them on before entering the sewers. Nix introduced Veraal to Tesha, who thanked him for the leaf, and Gadd, who flashed his pointed teeth. Kiir and Lis had remained behind, too. Nix turned to Kiir.

"You should go," Nix said to her. "It might not be safe here."

Kiir smiled, her hair falling over her face. "I want to be here when you come back."

"As do I," Lis said. She had her long dark hair pulled back in a horse's tail.

Nix was touched. Kiir leaned forward and kissed him on the mouth. Lis kissed Egil's cheek. The priest put a

hand on her hip and smiled at her, but Nix could see
Egil's mind was elsewhere.

"Mere and Rose are upstairs, fifth room on the
right," Egil said to Veraal. "You'll want to put a couple
men on the door and one inside, in case Mere needs
something."

"Of course," Veraal said.

Nix and Egil shook his hand.

"You boys certain about this?" Veraal asked. "Real
certain?"

"Certain," Egil said.

Nix shrugged and smiled.

"Good luck, then," Veraal said.

Egil snorted. "When have we ever had that?"

Nix and Egil exited the Tunnel, cold sober, a bit before
Ool's clock sounded the second hour past midnight.
The last time they'd been on the streets at that hour
they'd been hunting Blackalley. Now they'd be the
hunted.

As then, the streets were emptied but for the occasional
drunk slouched in a doorway. The sound of laughter,
conversation, and the clink of tankards sounded through
the shutters of taverns they passed. They moved quickly
in the direction of the Warrens, hunched in their cloaks,
looking over their shoulders from time to time as if
fearful of being followed.

"Make anyone yet?" Egil whispered.

"Not yet–"

Motion drew Nix's eye, about a block away, dark
shadows crossing the flickering light of the street lamps.

"And there they are."

"How many?" Egil asked.

"Two," Nix said. "One on each of side of the street. About a block back."

Egil put a fist in one of his palms. "Let's find a spot."

"Aye."

They continued on toward the Poor Wall and their tail crept closer.

"Ballsy," Egil said.

"Sloppy," Nix answered. "With them this close, you're going to have to move fast."

"I can move fast."

"I guess we'll see."

They eyed the alleys as they walked along, looking for a likely spot. Ool struck two, summoning bad memories for both of them.

"Fakkin' alleys don't look the same at this hour anymore, do they?" Nix said.

"Truth," Egil said.

"Minnear's full again tonight, too."

Egil grunted. "Well, you're not planning to grease up any alleys with corpse tallow, are you? Then let's not worry about it." The priest indicated an alley to their left. "This goes through to Crooked Way. It'll do."

"Aye."

They ducked down the wide, unlit alley that separated a two-story draper's shop and a cordwainer's store. Neither building had windows or doors that opened onto the alley. Barrels, some scrap wood, and piles of compost and rubbish lay at intervals along the alley's length, which went on for thirty paces before opening onto Crooked Way.

"Run along, priest," Nix said, and shoved his big friend

deeper into the alley. "They'll be along quick. You don't want me to have all the fun."

Egil sprinted toward Crooked Way, the tread of his boots like hammer blows on the cobblestone. Meanwhile Nix crouched behind the barrels near one wall, falchion drawn.

He didn't have to wait long. The streetlamps painted the shadows of their pursuers across the road in front of the alley. They were hustling, but slowed at the alley mouth and peeked around the corner, wary. Seeing no one, they stepped into the alley mouth, peering into the darkness.

"Shite," one said. "No doors. We lose 'em?"

"We go round to Crooked Way," the other one whispered. "Pick them up there."

As they turned to leave, Nix intentionally bumped a barrel. The sound caused both men to whirl around and draw their swords, the blades short and wide.

The moment they did, Nix bolted. He feigned a stumble as he pelted down the alley.

They cursed and gave chase, as he'd known they would.

"Check the barrels for the big one!" one of them said to the other.

"Not there!" said the other, barely slowing.

Halfway down the alley, Nix whirled and filled his off hand with the haft of his hand axe. The two men skidded to a stop, one bumping into the other, the leader nearly falling. Both breathing hard.

Behind the men, Nix saw Egil's shadow reaching across the alley mouth. Nix backed off from the men, as if frightened.

"What do you want?" he said, letting his voice quaver. "Why're you following me?

Behind them Egil slid down the alley, as quiet as a spider.

The men shared a look and the shorter one with the beard nodded.

"No one said we couldn't kill 'em," he said.

Nix backed off another step. "Kill me? What is that now?"

The men put on hard faces and spaced themselves in an arc before Nix, blades at the ready.

"What is this now?" Nix said.

"You cross the guild, you pay in blood," the taller of them said, and lunged forward, stabbing for Nix's abdomen.

Egil and Nix burst into motion at the same instant. Nix sidestepped the stab, stepped forward, and slammed the back of his hand axe into the man's temple, sending him to ground with a groan. The other man bounded forward, stabbing at Nix's chest, but Egil snatched a fistful of the man's shirt, then the seat of his trousers.

Surprise raised the man's voice an octave. "What in the–"

The priest spun and slammed the man headfirst into the alley wall. A meaty thud and he went limp. The priest threw him atop his fallen guild brother, their limbs an awkward tangle.

"I think they're in love," Nix said.

Egil checked the one he'd dropped.

"Dead?" Nix asked.

"No," Egil said, and looked up at Nix with raised eyebrows.

Nix frowned. "No point in killing the slubbers if we don't have to. They're down, so we're clear of eyes. Putting the Upright Man down is how we send the right message."

"Aye," Egil said. He stood, kicking one of the guild men for good measure.

"You're lucky slubbers tonight," Nix said to the two downed guild men.

Egil said, "Some of your boys won't be getting off so easy."

"You were as loud as a cart ox coming down that alley," Nix said.

"It's well that your blather drowned out my approach then."

"Blather? I thought it more a ballyhoo. I was acting."

"I'm staying with blather."

"Really?" One of the guild men groaned so Nix kicked him in the head. The men went quiet. "Fair enough. Blather it is, then."

They drew their hoods and walked quickly through Dur Follin's streets, violence on their minds. They saw other pedestrians now and again as they moved west, very brave or very foolish souls with no fear of Blackalley, but they avoided them. Their path took them under the smooth, sharp-cornered limestone spire of Ool's clock, the tallest structure in Dur Follin save the Archbridge. The sound of the perpetual cascade that powered the clock's inner workings sounded like a gently snoring giant. Graffiti covered the limestone. Some of the vulgarity was creative enough to make Nix smile.

Egil led them, knowing from his discussion with Merelda where they should enter the sewers, which

weren't proper sewers at all, but an Undercity, a
honeycomb of underground chambers and passageways
dug by the ancient civilization upon whose bones Dur
Follin had been built. Some of the passages had been
expanded and put to use by the city as sewers, aqueducts,
or storage, but many had been commandeered by
whatever squatter could take and hold them. Nix knew
firsthand that certain vile cults used the Undercity to
build shrines to gods whose worship was illegal even
among the otherwise tolerant citizenry of Dur Follin.
Nix had never seen a convincing map of the Undercity,
wasn't sure that one could be drawn. Rumor said the
layout of the Undercity changed from time to time
when the sorcery used to build it ran amok. Rooms
and halls disappeared, shrunk, or expanded, or new
ones materialized where before there'd been none. No
one even knew how deep the passages actually went.
Some said they connected under the Meander with
secret tunnels that that led down from the Archbridge's
monumental pylons. Some said they extended down
deep and then expanded east under the Deadmire. The
foolish said they extended down to the center of the
world, where demons of the earth plotted the fall of men.

Nix figured he and Egil would explore them in detail
one day, provided they lived to see sunrise.

Egil led them down Broadstreet, which ran roughly
parallel to Mandin's Way. Several grated openings dotted
the wide avenue, all of them grated and locked, all of
them leading down to the Undercity. Egil led them to the
nearest, in a part of the street ill-lit by the street lamps.
Dark shops with closed shutters rose on either side. The
street was empty but for them. Not even the Watch.

"Right here," Egil said.

Stink rose from the grated hole, the reek of old rot and new sewage. Graffiti decorated the cobblestone near the rusted, hinged grate, much of it worn away by the weather, but some still visible.

I pissed down this grate.

Dark down there. But not as dark as my heart.

Jherek is a bunghole.

A large padlock fastened one side of the grate to a u-shaped bar set into the stone of the street. Nix could've picked it, of course, but it would've taken longer than they could spare. Besides, he wanted to try out his new toy.

He reached into his bag, withdrew the magical key and an apple, then whispered a word in the Language of Creation. The key warmed in his hand and the bit yawned. Nix held the apple before the key's mouth.

"Give us a carrot," said the key.

"A what?"

Egil snorted.

Muttering, Nix shoved the apple back into his satchel and pulled out a carrot he'd taken from Gadd's cellar. The key took a bite and chewed.

"Doesn't it shite in your satchel?" Egil asked.

"No it does not. The magic of the key consumes what it eats. The food partially powers the magic. All of which you'd know if you weren't a simple hillman of limited faculties."

"At least I don't have a key shitting in my pack."

"Didn't I just say it doesn't shit in there? And it's not a pack. It's a satchel."

"So you say."

Smiling, Nix stuck the sated key into the padlock. He felt it vibrate as it squirmed itself into shape, then gave it a turn. Tumblers fell and the lock opened with a satisfying click. Nix looked back, holding up a finger, waiting for it, waiting...

"Gewgaws," Egil harrumphed.

Nix grinned and tried to pull up the gate. He stopped trying before he ripped something.

"Maybe I'll just get the lock," he said and detached the padlock.

"Grates are for simple hillmen, I guess," said Egil.

Nix stepped aside and the priest bent down and grabbed the grate. With only a mild grunt of exertion, he lifted it out of its seating. The screech of metal on stone broke the quiet of the night. Nix glanced around in alarm, but the street remained deserted. He put the key back in his satchel, took one of the silvered rods from his pack, and lit it with a matchstick, taking care not to confuse his ordinary matchsticks with the magical ones he'd used while summoning Blackalley.

The tip took the flame, glowed a soft red and softly shot off a spark now and then. He dropped it down the shaft and it hit dry stone twenty rods down, lighting a passageway that went off in two directions.

"Have a piece of chalk in that pack?" Egil asked.

"Satchel," Nix corrected, but handed over a piece of chalk.

Egil quickly scratched his own graffiti on the cobblestone near the grate.

Egil and Nix were here.

Nix nodded, smiled. "Why not, by the Gods?"

With that, Nix lowered himself into the shaft, pressing the soles of his feet against one side and pushing his back against the other, slowly walking himself down. After he'd gone about five rods, Egil followed him in, sliding the grate back into place and placing the padlock back in its place. He didn't lock it, but a Watchman would have to examine it closely to know it was unlocked.

When they reached the bottom, Nix took his falchion in one hand and the glow rod in the other, while Egil put the haft of a hammer in each fist. A small scattering of rocks and other debris lay on the smooth stone floor, probably bits of junk dropped down the grate by children. The air crowded them, a stale cloak, and it smelled moldy and vaguely of piss. Light from the glow rod illuminated less than a candle. At four paces Egil looked like a hill of muscle and hammers and anger. But Nix figured the dim red light would be harder to spot and wouldn't betray them as readily as a torch. The sound of their breathing bounced off the walls. A narrow corridor of cut stone stretched off before them.

Egil took the mail shirts from his large pack, handed the smaller to Nix, and they both worked them on over their tunics, both of them cursing to the sound of ringing links.

"I feel like a stuffed sausage in this," Egil said.

"Aye," Nix agreed, testing his range of motion. "How's a man supposed to kill someone in this nonsense?"

"Let's go find out," Egil said, and they headed off in the direction of the guild house, walking dark, musty corridors in a bubble of dim red light. The sound of dripping water came from somewhere and their breath and the soft ring of their mail seemed loud in the quiet. Between the weight of the armor and the close air, Nix was sweating before they'd covered two hundred paces.

"This keeps up and these slubbers will *smell* me coming."

Egil led them on, turning here and there, through corridors wide and narrow, but always moving in a generally southwest direction. Nix didn't question him about the route. A decade of robbing tombs all across Ellerth had given both of them a head for maps and a keen sense of direction, even underground.

From ahead a slow current of air carried the pungent stink of sewage.

"That's not me," Nix whispered.

Egil grinned as the narrow hall was bisected by a wide corridor. Walkways flanked a sunken channel of still water that stretched off into the darkness left and right. Filth floated on the surface of the water, shapeless patties of stink. The odor made Nix's eyes water.

"Leads out to the Meander," Egil said, pointing with his chin to the west.

A heavy rain or winter melt would raise the Meander and rinse the channel, but otherwise the water sat there, stagnant, a stew of shite and trash.

"City needs better engineers," Nix said.

Minding their step on the slimed walkway, they leaped the sewer channel to the other side.

Nix smelled himself and winced at the reek. "If I'd known this little excursion was going to put such a stink in my clothes. I might've let these guild boys slide. But now that I smell like a turd, we might as well kill a few of them."

"Or more than a few," Egil said. The priest stopped and visibly consulted the map in his mind. "We follow this for bit. Then right down a side channel, then we're under Mandin's Way and close."

After they'd walked for a time, Nix said, "Walking through sewers is less fun than I imagined."

"Imagined yourself walking through sewage often, have you?"

"Given the shite you're prone to utter, I don't have to *imagine* it at all."

Egil smiled, seemed about to say something in response, but stopped and held up a hand. He whispered, "Things are about to get more fun, I think. Listen."

From somewhere ahead, Nix heard someone clear his throat, then a soft cough. The sound bounced off the masonry, carried down the corridor. Nix used his hand to shield the meager light from the glow rod. They stood there still for a time, listening, wondering if they'd been heard. Nothing from ahead.

"That about where they should be?" Nix whispered.

Egil nodded. "From there, there's a concealed door to a stair that heads into the rooms under the guild house."

"And once we're in?"

"Fun's in finding out," Egil said.

Nix frowned and stared at his friend, eyebrows raised.

"I'm not to say that?" Egil asked.

"That's mine to say."

"I see."

"It sounds ridiculous when you say it."

"It sounds ridiculous when you say it, too."

"It does not. Wait... does it?"

Egil ignored the question. "Once we're in we'll have to search for the Upright Man. Or get lucky. Possibly we could have planned this better."

"Where's the fun in that?" Nix said. "Eh, did that sound ridiculous, too?"

Egil grinned. "Kill the glow rod. They'll have their own light."

Nix dropped the glow rod in the sewage channel, extinguishing it. Darkness enveloped them but it wasn't entire. A glow came from ahead, the soft flickering glow of torches.

Hugging the wall, weapons bare, the two crept forward in silence. The corridor and sewer channel split into a Y-shaped intersection. They followed the glow along the left hand wall and crept to the corner. Nix crouched and peeked around.

Ten paces down, four guild men sat on barrels to one side of the sewer sluice. One toyed with a dagger, two sat close, holding a whispered conversation, and one, heavyset, had his hands crossed over his ample stomach and his back against the wall, snoring. Two torches burned in makeshift sconces attached to the wall. All wore leather jacks and sharp steel. None looked alert. Nix imagined guard duty in the sewers was more punishment than posting.

He leaned back from the corner and put his mouth to Egil's ear. "Four men. This side. Ten paces. Slubbers, the lot." He put his hand axe in its belt thong, drew a throwing dagger, and showed it to Egil. "I take the sleeper."

Egil nodded, hefted a hammer in his throwing hand. "I take whoever I feel like killing."

Nix counted down from three with his fingers and when he reached zero they ran around the corner, leaped the channel, and charged, hurling their weapons as they went.

Egil's hammer hummed as it spun toward the guild man with the unsheathed dagger. The man looked up in shock for a only a moment before Egil's hammer slammed into his head, pulped his face, spraying the wall in blood and knocking him from his barrel.

Nix's dagger knifed neatly into the throat of sleeping man. He woke only to die, grabbing at the dagger's hilt, eyes wide, blood spurting around the shaft of steel. He rose, staggered, gasped, and fell face down on the floor, the upper half of his body in the sewer channel.

The two survivors, wide-eyed with surprise, cursed, drew blades, and shouted for aid. One of them went to the wall between the torch sconces and frantically worked some kind of mechanism. He pulled open a door concealed to look like the wall but before he could get through it Egil, roaring, hit the half-open door at a full run. The man, caught between door and jamb, squealed with pain. Bones audibly broke and he spat a mouthful of blood while he stabbed weakly at Egil. The blade caught the priest but scraped along the outside of Egil's mail.

Meanwhile Nix drew his hand axe in his off hand and bounded at the other man, who backed away, short sword and dagger drawn. Nix crosscut at the man's throat with his falchion, but the man parried with his dagger and returned a stab at Nix's stomach with his short sword.

Nix anticipated the counter and slipped sideways, avoiding the stab, then chopped down on the man's arm with his hand axe. The edge sank to the bone and blood sprayed. The man shouted with pain, recoiled, his fearful eyes already seeing his end. Nix lunged in close and stabbed the man through the stomach, feeling his falchion scrape spine.

The man's eyes went wide, his mouth opened in a silent wail of pain. He dropped his sword so Nix withdrew his blade and kicked him backward into the sewer channel. He hit the water in splash of stink and floated there with the rest of the grime, unmoving.

"See how you like that shite on your clothes," Nix said.

He turned to see Egil slam the door into the other man again, leaving him a broken, unmoving heap in the doorway.

"Door won't close," Egil said.

"Look at you with the jests now," Nix said.

Nix wiped his blade on the fallen guild man, stepped into the doorway, and held up a hand up for quiet. A set of stone stairs extended up to a landing, turned left, and then continued higher. He heard nothing.

"Nothing," he whispered.

He and Egil recovered their weapons and heaved the bodies of the dead guild men into the sewage channel.

"You want to say a prayer or something?" Nix asked Egil.

Egil stared down at the floating corpses. "That's what you get for trying to harm our girls and burn our inn. Fak you all."

"Well said," Nix said. He thumped Egil on the shoulder. "Now let's go find the fakker we came for."

"Aye."

They crept up the stairs, keeping close to the wall, listening for any indication of alarm. When they reached the landing, they saw that another flight of stairs ascended up to a reinforced wooden door with a latch and an elaborate key lock. Egil took Nix by the elbow and pulled him back down the stairs a ways, where they had a hushed conversation.

"It'll be locked and they'll have a coded knock," Egil whispered.

"A merry jig, no doubt," Nix said. "They'll probably have it barred, too.

"I'll handle that," Egil said.

"No doubt of that either," Nix said. "I'll handle the lock with the key, but swear you won't say 'gewgaws'."

Egil looked pained. "I always say 'gewgaws'. The world will end if I don't. You know that."

"All right then, say it but don't so smug about it, yeah?"

"Fair enough."

Nix took out the magic key, wrapped its mouth with his hand, and spoke a word in the Mage's Tongue. It came to life and nipped him on the finger, but he kept his curse in his mind rather than on his lips. He unwrapped his fingers slowly.

"Give us a turnip," it said.

"Fakking key," he muttered, and dug a small turnip out of his satchel. It was a good thing Gadd had a well-stocked cellar and that Nix had a magic satchel with so many pockets. To the key, he said, "Take two bites then open the door up there. And be quiet about it."

After the key took its bites, Nix and Egil sneaked back up the stairs. Nix slowly inserted the key into the door, wincing at the soft grate of metal on metal. The key squirmed gently in his hand, fitting itself to the mechanism. When it stopped moving, Nix back looked at Egil.

"Got it. Ready?"

Egil stared at him, eyebrows raised.

"Fak's sake," Nix whispered with a sigh. "Say it. I said say it."

"Gewgaws," Egil whispered.

Nix turned the key, the lock opened, and Egil slammed his shoulder into the door. Wood splintered, metal screamed, something snapped, and the door flew open to reveal a small room with no one in it. A table sat in the center, two tankards atop it, chairs set around it in orderly fashion.

"Shite. A bit anticlimactic, no?" Nix said.

One of the two doors in the room flew open to reveal a pot-bellied, horse-faced guild man in a chain shirt.

"What is going on—"

Egil's hammer flew, hit the man in the chest, shattered ribs, and sent him careening backward and down.

"Now that's more like it," Nix said.

Shouts from the room beyond sounded like another half-dozen guild men.

Nix and Egil darted for the door, Egil scooping up a chair in one hand as he crossed the room. The moment Nix filled the doorway, stepping on the man Egil had downed, two crossbow bolts thudded into his chest, knocking him sideways against the jambs. His mail turned the points but the impact still left him gasping.

"Fakkers," he hissed. Three guildmen stood in the hallway to his right, two with leveled crossbows.

Egil bulled past him and hurled the chair at the guild men. It crashed into the two crossbowmen, knocking one prone. Egil followed up and rushed the mass of them, taking his one hammer in both hands. A downward smash crushed the head of the prone guild man and Egil bulled past the second. The third man managed to get his blade drawn and stab at the priest's chest, but the blade skipped off Egil's mail. A backhand swing from Egil's hammer crushed the man's chest and sent him into the wall, his dying gasps the squeal of a broken bellows.

By then Nix had recovered and he hurled his dagger into one of the crossbowmen who'd shot him. The blade took the man in the arm and he cried out, dropping his crossbow. Egil wheeled around, swinging his hammer, and head hit the side of the man's head with a sound like a dropped melon.

Nix picked up the hammer Egil had thrown and handed it to the priest. "Which way?"

Egil looked back and forth, thought, pointed. "That way?"

Nix started off.

"Wait," Egil said.

"Wait?"

"Wait."

"Gonna be more along soon, priest."

Egil looked unsure. He shook his head. "All right, this way. As I said. Fairly sure."

Voices from the other direction carried down the hall, shouts. A lot of shouts.

"I concur," Nix said hurriedly. "That way. But first..."

"Now you with the waiting?"

Nix dug into his satchel, found two of the smoke balls and one of the boomsparks, a matchstick, and lit all three. The fuses sizzled and Nix tossed all three down the hall in the direction of the voices.

"Come on," Egil said, pulling at his arm.

"Wait, wait."

In moment the smoke balls boomed and filled the corridor with thick green smoke, and the boomspark went off, shrieking and shooting colored sparks in all directions. A steady stream of curses and shouts of alarm bounced off the walls.

"Come now!" Nix said, grinning. "That was worth seeing, no?"

"It was," Egil conceded. "But now *move*."

And move they did, pelting down corridors lit by hanging lanterns.

"We need to get up into the guild house itself," Egil said, looking back for pursuers. "Stairs are this way."

From ahead came shouts and the sound of men running.

"Getting interesting now," Nix said, and tightened his grip on his weapons.

He and Egil didn't so much as slow. Moving at a fast jog, they came around a corner and found themselves face to face with three guild men. Nix had time only to register the look of surprise on their faces, the glint of steel in their fists, before Egil shouldered into the first, driving him up against the wall. The priest took the man's face in his huge hand and slammed his head into the stone. Eyes rolled and he fell.

Meanwhile Nix slapped aside a clumsy, surprised stab from a short, thin guild man, then split his skull with a downward chop of his hand axe. The axe stuck in the skull like it'd had found a warm home and while Nix tried to pull it free the third man, shouting for aid, lunged at Nix, blade stabbing for his gut.

Cursing, Nix left his axe in the skull and bounded back, but he was too slow and the blade caught his stomach, sending a few mail links chiming to the floor. The man followed up quickly and stabbed at Nix's chest.

Nix backed into the wall hard and managed a sloppy parry with his falchion and the short sword rang on the stone of the wall. Nix loosed a kick into the man's balls and he went wide eyed, purple faced, and down on his knees. Nix drove his falchion through the man's face and out the back of his head, sending teeth to the floor to mingle with the chain links.

"All right?" Egil said to him.

"Fine, though we owe Veraal," Nix said, fingering the gap in his mail shirt.

More voices and shouting from behind them. Nix rocked his axe from the skull of the other dead guild man.

"Let's live long enough to pay the debt, eh?" Egil said.

"Is that a plan?" Nix asked. "I think we may have a plan at last."

Gore spattered the priest's face and thick, hairy arms. "Every guild man in this house is going to come down on us soon. We can leave thirty on the ground behind us but it won't matter if one of them isn't the Upright Man."

"Let's get moving, then," Nix said, and shoved his big friend forward.

Doors dotted the corridors at intervals. Nix kept a wary eye on them, waiting for them to open and puke up some guild men, but they stayed closed. When one did finally open to Nix's left, Nix was ready. The guild man who stood in it had a question on his face. For answer Nix drew a dagger from his belt and drove through the underside of his jaw, up into the brain case. The man fell

and Nix left the blade in its bloody home. Daggers he
could spare, just not his axe.

Another door opened, this one to their right, and a
skinny, brown-haired boy of maybe fifteen winters stood
there, mouth agape. Nix stopped the down stroke of his
axe a finger's width from the top of the boy's head. The
boy stood there in stunned silence, eyes wide, as rooted
to the ground as a tree. He didn't even wear a blade.

"Shite," Nix said, and dropped his axe to his side.

Shouts and the sound of running men behind them.
The boy's eyes darted back and forth between Egil and
Nix and the sounds of their pursuers.

"Don't kill me," the boy said.

Egil growled and grabbed him by his tunic. With one
hand he lifted him from his feet and pulled him close.
"How old are you?"

The shouts from behind drew closer.

"Egil…" Nix said.

"Thirteen winters… sir," the boy said.

A urine stain darkened the front of the boy's trousers.

Egil saw it, glanced at Nix, back at the boy, and tossed
him back into the room. The boy landed on his arse, face
pale.

"Don't open this door again," Egil commanded.

"N-n-never?" the boy said.

Nix rolled his eyes. "No, not never, boy. Just stay out
of the way, yeah?"

With that, he closed the door. The shouts from behind
faded some. Their pursuers must have taken a wrong
turn.

Nix glanced at Egil and the reality of the situation
settled on him. Blood spattered both of them, wet

weapons hung from their fists, a dozen dead men lay behind them, and a terrified boy trembled on the other side of the door.

"Not half as fun as robbing tombs, is it?" he asked.

"No," Egil said. The priest's expression fell but only for a moment before hardening. "But everybody in the inn would've burned. Rose. Mere. Kiir. Lis. Tesha. And every one of the guild men in this house would've happily struck the matchstick. And they would've come at us again, even if we hadn't come at them. Let's remember that."

Nix knew Egil was right. Some discussions were best had with edged steel.

"We tossed in our ante," he said. "Let's play out the hand."

The voices from behind grew louder again. The pursuers must have realized their mistake.

Egil turned to go but Nix grabbed him by the arm. "Wait."

Egil harrumphed. "Again with the waiting."

Nix threw open the door to the room with the boy. The frightened youth hadn't moved. He still sat on his arse in the center of the room. Seeing Nix, he backed off crabwise, his expression fearful.

"Where's the Upright Man, boy? Quick now."

"The who?"

"I won't ask again."

"You mean Channis? He's on the first floor, I think. In the grand room. A meeting, I heard."

"You know where the grand room is?" Nix asked Egil over his shoulder.

"Aye."

"Don't come out and don't tell anyone what you told us," Nix said. "They'll kill you if you do. And we'll kill you if they don't."

The boy paled and Nix closed the door.

"I think he took my point."

"Aye," Egil said.

Many voices sounded from behind them, the tread of many boots, a dozen or more. The guild men had gathered into a larger group.

"Tell me the grand room isn't that way," Nix said, nodding at the noise.

"Other way," Egil said. "Come on."

CHAPTER EIGHT

With Egil leading, they sprinted through lantern-lit, door-lined halls, through a dining hall, an armory, training rooms, what looked like quarters for the guild men, the occasional shrine to Aster. Any time they passed or ran through the latter, Nix made sure to throw the god an obscene gesture.

"Where is everyone?" Egil said.

"There aren't enough behind us?"

"I'd think there'd be a lot more men than this. Odd, is what I'm saying."

"Something to do with that meeting the boy mentioned, maybe," Nix observed.

"Here," Egil said, and turned down a long hall with no doors. Halfway down, Egil's pace slowed. Nix disliked the way the priest's brow furrowed.

"What?" Nix asked.

The priest pursed his lips, stopped. He looked forward, back the way they'd come. "I think we're going the wrong way."

"The wrong way? Shite, Egil, not a lot of room for error here."

The priest nodded. "No, no, this is right. Come on. Keep going."

The hallway terminated in a large archway, the thick wooden door thrown open. They rushed through and found themselves in a large, roughly circular chamber. No door led out. Torches hung in sconces and cast flickering light on various hooks, tongs, pokers, and blades that hung from mounts on the wall. A chain dangled from a ceiling-mounted winch, a leather loop tied to one end of the chain. A thick wooden table, like a butcher's block, sat in the center of the table, stained brown with blood, ghosts of pain hovering in the air around it.

For a moment, the two of them stood there in silence.

"The fak?" Nix finally said.

Egil ran his hand over Ebenor's eye. "Must be for discipline, punishment, interrogation, and whatever else. These slubbers are zealots. Anyway, this *is* the wrong way. We need to go back."

"Shite," Nix said. "We best hurry–"

A huge form barreled out of the dark corner to their left. The man, taller and broader then Egil, but more fat than muscle, plowed through Nix and knocked him flat, driving the air from his lungs. The man continued right through, bulled into Egil, and drove him up against the wall. Taken by surprise, Egil dropped his hammers and they hit the floor with a clang.

A sweat-stained tunic, leather jack, and blood-stained pantaloons wrapped the mountain of the man. He punched Egil in the ribs and the back, the mail ringing under the impact, the blows coming fast, all while Nix lay on the ground, gasping.

Egil grunted under the onslaught, wincing with pain, but dropped an elbow on the man's spine. The man grunted but loosed another punch into Egil, another. Egil crouched to protect his side, tried to maneuver his feet to get off the wall, all while grabbing at the man's wrist.

The man landed another two punches in Egil's side, the sound heavy and meaty, before Egil finally got a grip on the wrist. At that point the man roared, spraying spit, and reared back and slammed Egil into the wall once, twice.

To Nix, the two men looked like vying titans. He rose to all fours, still unable to breathe. He tried to pull himself up, to help his friend, but his body would not uncurl until he could recover his breath.

Egil slammed another elbow into the man's back, another. The man barked with pain and Egil leaned over him, wrapped his arms around the man's fat midsection, and lifted him just enough to de-anchor him from the ground. He whirled the man around and slammed him sideways into the wall.

The man snarled through his thick beard and kneed at Egil's groin, but the priest slid his hips sideways and instead took the knee on the thigh and punched the man in the jaw, wobbling him.

Growling, Egil grabbed him by his leather jack and slammed the top of his head, Ebenor's eye, into the man's nose. His wide nose audibly broke and exploded in blood. The man's eyes rolled. He staggered and would have fallen but Egil held him up, bashed his head into the man's face a second time. Nix couldn't tell if the man was still conscious.

The priest swung the stunned man around and walked him to the center of the room. He grabbed the chain, fixed the leather loop around the man's throat, grabbed the other end of the chain and hoisted. While the man gagged and kicked, Egil looped the chain around a leg of the table.

The man's tiny, pig eyes widened to white; his mouth opened, his tongue lolled, but not even a gag emerged. His legs kicked once more, he shat himself, and it was over.

"Fakkin' torturer," Egil said.

Nix stared at his huge friend. He could only imagine the bruising the punches would summon in Egil's side. Blood and snot, the dead man's, covered Ebenor's eye.

Egil touched his nose with his fingers, then looked at them, frowning. "Is my nose bleeding?"

Nix had not yet recovered his breath and could only shake his head.

"You all right?" Egil said. The priest stepped to his side and lifted him to his feet.

Nix nodded, his breath still coming hard as he struggled to refill his lungs. "Lost my breath is all. Are you all right?"

Egil looked at him in surprise. "Me? I'm fine."

"Shite, Egil," Nix said. He nodded at the hanged man. "Big, he was."

Egil picked up his hammers. "Not so big. Come on. Back this way."

They sped back down the hallway they'd come, concerned they'd get boxed into the corridor and have to fight their way out, but they reached the intersection without seeing any guild men. Shouts seemed to come from every direction, though. Without warning crossbow bolts hissed out of the darkness further down the corridor and slammed into the wall.

"Shite," Nix said, making himself small against the wall. He shouted down the hall. "That's not very sporting, you fakkers!"

"Come on!" Egil said.

Nix fell in behind him. "You sure you know where we're going? I mean, maybe there's some other big torturer fakker you need to stop and kill?"

"No, I think I'm good," Egil said. "Now keep moving!"

The tread of boots fell in behind them as they pelted down a long corridor. Crossbow bolts whistled past them from time to time, each one summoning a curse from Nix. Two hit him square in the back and only Veraal's mail saved his life.

The corridor ended at a wide set of ascending stone stairs.

"This is it!" Egil said.

Without slowing they took the stairs two at time, harried from below by the sounds of their pursuers. A large, reinforced wooden door topped the stairs. Nix pushed down on the latch and breathed easy when he found it wasn't locked.

Crossbow bolts whistled out of the darkness behind and below them. Two thunked into the wood of the door and quivered there, another slammed into Nix's back, the mail shirt once more saving his life.

"Here!" called a voice from below. "They're over here! Going up!"

Nix shoved the door open and he and Egil piled through and slammed the door closed behind them.

They surprised three guild men seated at a table, in the midst of a card game. Commons and few terns lay piled on a table and each of the men held playing plaques.

"What's this now?" said one of the men, his narrow face and long hair reminding Nix of a wolf.

"A bit of a misunderstanding," Nix began, but saw the truth of the situation reach the men as they took in Nix and Egil's bared weapons, the priest's blood spattered arms and face and pate.

"Shite," one of them said, and all three lurched to their feet, bumping the table, scattering coins.

"Yours for now," Nix said to Egil.

Egil charged the three men and they answered with shouts and curses. Wood splintered, coins chimed to the floor. Nix looked around for a bar for the door, saw nothing.

"How do you slubbers have all these damned locks but not simple bars?"

He pulled the magic key from his satchel, hearing behind him the spill of a chair, the meaty thud of Egil's hammer against flesh, an abortive wail of pain, the crush of bone. A word in Mage's Tongue animated the key and it gave its demand.

"Give us some meat."

"Meat, now? Fak." He didn't bring any thrice-damned meat.

Another thud from behind him, a cry of pain abruptly cut short as Egil's hammer reaped another guild man. The priest growled and more wood splintered. One of the men cursed and Nix imagined him backing up in a panic.

A jarring impact on the door knocked Nix away from it. It started to open. Nix cursed and threw his shoulder back into it, slamming it closed once more. Someone howled with pain on the other side. The door must have caught his fingers or hand. An idea struck Nix.

"I need one of those bodies, Egil!" Nix called, leaning into the door as the men on the other side pressed against it. "Hurry!"

A corpse flew in from behind, hit the door, and lay in a bloody heap beside Nix. The dead man's skull was concave from a blow of Egil's hammer. Nix shoved the key's bit into the dead man's cheek.

"Meat," he said, and the key bit a chunk and chewed.

Another impact on the door, another, another, each one pushing the door open an increment. Nix fumbled with the key and nearly dropped it, his feet scrabbling on the floor with the effort to reclosed the door.

"You fakkers are dead!" came a shout from the other side of the door.

"Egil!" Nix called. "Egil!"

The priest hit the door at a run and slammed it closed, eliciting curses from the other side. Nix shoved the key into the lock, felt it warm, and gave it a turn. Once it locked, he pulled out the key and shoved the blade of a punch dagger into the keyhole, hoping to foul the mechanism. He turned his back to the door and sagged to the floor. Egil did the same. The guild men on the other side continued to beat against the door, but they'd need a lot of time to get through the reinforced wooden slab.

"They have to have an axe somewhere," Egil said.

"Aye," said Nix. "Has to be another way up from the under chambers, too. Even so, I'm going to say this hasn't gone half bad so far."

"Agreed," Egil said, grinning.

The gaming table had lost a leg in the combat and sat slanted on the floor. All of the chairs had been overturned. The other two guild men, their bodies broken by Egil's hammers, limbs at grotesque angles, lay on the floor among the scattered coins and playing plaques.

"You fouled their game," Nix said. He picked up a plaque and showed it to Egil – The Knave of Blades.

"They weren't very good players," the priest said.

"How many is that now?"

"Guild men?" Egil asked. "I lost count."

The pounding on the door behind them ceased and the silence struck them as more ominous than the attempts to break through.

"Probably should move," Egil said.

"Aye, that," Nix said with a sigh. He stood. "To the grand room with us."

Egil indicated which door they should take, Nix listened at it and heard nothing to alarm him. He opened it and peeked out.

It was like looking into another world. They emerged from the dank chambers beneath the guild house to a long carpeted hallway appointed with cushioned chairs and wall art.

"Seems these guild boys do all right," Nix said, as they hustled down the hall.

Egil grunted.

They moved quickly through the guild house, Egil navigating its halls and stairs and rooms by way of the mental map Merelda had given him. They still saw no one, and it seemed that word of their attack had not yet reached beyond the underground chambers. But that was mere good fortune and they knew they had only a short time before someone raised a general alarm. They needed to get to the Upright Man before that.

"Place is a maze," Nix said.

Egil nodded, his mind obviously on the layout in his head.

"It's also emptied out," Nix said. The rooms and halls they walked were empty of guild men. "The Upright Man might not even be here."

"He's here," Egil said. "That boy said there was a meeting. That's where they all are."

As they moved, hugging walls, staying quiet, peeking ahead, Egil softly told Nix what he needed to know about the grand room.

"It's a big rectangular room. Double doors on all four sides. Big triangular table in the center, chairs around. Upright Man sits at the top point of the triangle. Lots of guards within. Outside, usually pairs of guards at the doors. That's all the usual, anyway."

"Mere pulled all that out of that slubber's head?"

Egil nodded.

"Get me to the doors opposite the Upright Man's spot at the table," Nix said. "I'll distract. You go in the other way and snatch him."

"Aye."

Nix shrugged. "Of course if he's not in there, we're fakked. We may be fakked anyway. Bit off a big piece of meat here, my friend. Makes for a hard chew. But it's now or not. We have minutes at best, before those slubbers from the rooms below get word up here. We move fast enough, we may yet take them by surprise.

"They feel safe here," Egil said.

"They should," Nix said, thinking of the reinforced doors and locks.

Egil nodded. "Take the two stupidest slubbers in Dur Follin to attack the guild house."

"Ballsiest is what you mean," Nix said. "I can barely walk I'm swinging so low."

Egil grinned and they hustled through empty rooms and corridors, making their way to the grand room. Presently Egil put up a hand to stop them.

"Right around this corner," he said softly.

Nix peeked around the corner and saw two guards. They looked more bored than alert. Word of the attack hadn't yet reached them. Nix pulled back.

"Two men, as you said," he said to Egil.

Egil pointed. "This hallway goes around to the other side, to the doors near Channis."

"Channis?"

"The Upright Man's name. The boy said it."

"Right. Aye," Nix said, then, "I'll take these two then get inside the room and draw eyes. You go around to the other doors, kill the guards there quick, and stand ready. When you hear the commotion inside, you get in and grab this Channis. I'll meet you over there."

"Good," Egil said. "Then what?"

"What do you mean, 'then what?'"

"We get him," Egil said. "We tell him why he's dying and do it. Then how do we get clear?"

"Why're you asking me?"

I thought you'd have a plan."

"Why would you think that? I'm making this up as we go. You're the one with the map of the place in your head."

Egil shrugged. "Hmm. I guess we'll figure something out."

Nix looked at him a long moment. "Shite, man. I guess we will. Here I go."

Nix sheathed his falchion, palmed a throwing dagger in each hand, and adopted a look of concern as he stepped out into the hall. He walked rapidly toward the guards, looking behind him from time to time, as if watching for pursuit.

"What're you about, git?" one of the guards asked. Both of them were hard looking men with scraggly beards and unforgiving eyes. They tensed and put hands to sword hilts. "House is to be empty 'cept for them with business at the meeting."

"Aye, aye," Nix said. "But there's something going on back there." He was counting the paces between him and the men, closing the distance. "I heard shouts and such, We need to let 'em know."

"Let who know?" said the other guard. "Who you with?"

"Me?" Nix said, and whipped the two daggers in rapid succession. The first took the larger of the two guards in the throat and he fell to the floor, writhing, gasping, spurting blood. The second hit the other guard in the shoulder and sank deep. He grunted, shouted, and started to pull his blade with his wounded arm. Before he'd cleared half the scabbard, Nix had his falchion drawn and drove it through the man's chest. The man died staring into Nix's face, a bubble of blood forming and popping between his lips.

"I'm with Egil," Nix said to him. "I don't think you know him."

Nix freed his blade, let the man fall, and pulled two smokeballs and the last boomspark from his satchel. He struck a matchstick, lit all three, took a breath, and loudly threw open the doors of the grand room.

Wall-mounted torches and a ceiling-mounted chandelier cast the grand room in bright, flickering light. Nix took it in at a glance.

Seven men sat around a triangular polished wooden table, its surface inlaid with Aster's symbol, the stiletto and the coin. Three men sat on one side of the triangle, three on the other, all of them in ceremonial black robes embroidered with Aster's symbol, with the number of coins embroidered around the symbol presumably denoting their rank. A pair of guards stood along the wall behind each of them.

Their personal muscle, Nix supposed.

One man, hulking and scarred, was at the table's apex: the Upright Man, Channis. His hand was raised, fist clenched, scarred face pinched in anger. Nix had interrupted him in mid-tirade, it appeared. A solitary man stood behind and to the Upright Man's left, also in ceremonial robes, rounding out the Committee.

"What is this?" Channis. His deep voice sounded like grating stone. He glanced back at the man standing near him.

An accusatory look, Nix thought.

Nix bowed. "Good evening, members of the Committee, you motley fakking collection of miscreants, slubbers, and bungholes. I've something to tell you."

Murmurs of surprise ran through the assembly. The guards along the wall drew steel. Several members of the

Committee, including Channis, pushed back their chairs and stood.

"And it is this," Nix said, and paused for effect. "Fak you all."

He doffed an imaginary cap and gave a bow.

"Someone snatch this little pissdrip," Channis said. "I want him sent to Zren."

Nix rolled the lit smoke balls into the room and tossed the boomspark onto the table, right on Aster's stiletto. Everyone around the table scrambled back, unsure what to make of the boomspark.

The rope holding the ceiling mounted chandelier was anchored to the wall near Nix. He cut it with a backhand slash of his falchion and the chandelier crashed down on the table. Hot wax splashed as the candles fell. Everyone leaped up from their seats, cursing.

Nix gave a bow as the guards along the wall rushed toward him. "Goodeve, bungholes!"

The smokeballs exploded, instantly fogging the room in green. At that everything turned chaotic: men shouted, coughed, accusations flew, members of the Committee barked orders, but the smoke was so thick Nix could scarcely see who was who.

He admired his handiwork for a moment, watching the far doors through the swirl of smoke, trying to see if Egil had come through. Just as things seemed to be settling, the boomspark went off, firing colored sparks in all directions, emitting a prolonged whistle that sounded like a scream.

Men ducked, exclaimed, shouted. Someone slipped and fell right at Nix's feet. Almost casually, Nix stabbed him through the back. Drapes along one wall caught fire.

Through the smoke Nix caught sight of the doors opposite him bursting open, the doorway filling with a huge barrel shape that could only be Egil, his hammers spinning through the smoke.

That was all Nix needed to see. He turned and dashed out of the room.

"Stop, fakker!" someone shouted from behind.

Nix glanced back to see two guards staggering out of the smoke-filled room behind him, blades drawn. They stumbled after him, shouting, and he quickly put distance between him and them.

He turned the corner and dashed up toward the hallway where he was supposed to meet Egil. Halfway down the hall, a door burst open ahead and to his left, expelling green smoke, a coughing member of the Committee and his bodyguard. Nix stabbed the bodyguard through the chest, punched the Committeeman in the jaw – the man had a droopy face, as if suffering from a palsy. The blow floored him and Nix kept running.

"They're here!" the droopy faced Committeeman said, coughing. "Over here, lads!"

"I should've stabbed you, too, bunghole!" Nix barked over his shoulder.

He came around the end of the hall to see Egil backing out of the double doors, a choke hold around the throat of Channis, a muscular, short-haired man with so many scars on his face that his cheeks looked like a map. Egil had disarmed him of visible weapons. The two guards Egil had killed to get entrance to the room lay in crumpled, bloodstained heaps on the floor.

Channis dragged his feet and clawed at Egil's arm, but Nix had never seen anyone dislodge the priest's hold once he'd set it. Nix put a blade to Channis's scarred face.

"You wanna keep breathing, pick up your damned feet."

The thump of the guards coming up the hall sounded louder. From another hall perpendicular to them came shouts, lots of shouts.

Egil and Nix shared a resigned look. They'd spent their entire time in the guild house running from one crowd of men or other.

As if to emphasize the point, a group of a dozen men came around the corner and stormed down the hallway, probably the men who'd pursued them in the tunnels under the house.

"There they are!" shouted the man in the lead, a towering blonde man with a scarred eye.

Several of the men stopped and leveled crossbows. Nix made himself small behind a stuffed chair while Egil shielded himself behind Channis. A bolt whistled past Nix's ear, taking a tuft of hair with it.

"We'll kill him if you come closer!" Nix shouted to them, jumping up and putting his blade to Channis's throat.

That was enough to buy them a moment. The men hesitated. The guards from the grand room came around the corner, too, and they also halted, seeing a sharp edge at Channis's throat.

"Bring him," Nix said to Egil, backing away.

Egil looked a question at him.

"He's the only thing keeping us alive right now. You wanted me to think of something to get us out of here, well I'm thinking of something. Bring him."

Nix eyed the guild men, a collection of blades, crossbows, and hard eyes. They reminded him of a wolf pack.

"Follow us and he's dead."

They backed more quickly down the hallway. The men hesitated, eyed one another, unsure of what to do.

"Move, move," Nix hissed to Egil.

A few of the men inched forward. One of the Committeemen appeared among the crowd, the droop faced man with six coins surrounding the stiletto on his robes. He glanced up the hall, saw Egil and Nix.

"What the fak are you doing?" he shouted, spraying spit from his misaligned mouth. "Get them!"

Nix and Egil turned and ran. Egil had Channis's head tucked under his armpit and dragged him along like a sack. The stamp of feet and the chorus of shouts behind them was like a roll of thunder.

"We need a room," Nix said.

"What kind of room?"

"A good godsdamned room!" Nix said.

They burst through a door and Nix slammed it shut behind them. Crossbow bolts thudded into it, at least half a dozen. Another hallway extended before them. They hustled down it, dragging the grunting guild master, who resisted as best he could. Nix was looking for a reinforced door with a key lock.

"No, no, no," he said, running past several doors that wouldn't do.

The hall door behind them burst open and men and crossbow bolts poured through. Once hit Nix in the shoulder, but deflected off his mail.

"You're going to hit your guild master, you stupid fakkers!"

They darted right through a pair of double doors and into a large lounge of some kind. Divans and chairs and a desk stood here and there on the carpeted floor, and a barred window overlooked the grounds outside.

"Bars?" Nix said. "Bars! Shite."

They couldn't get out through the window with the bars or Nix might have killed the Upright Man, broken through the window, and made a run for the river. Green light from Minnear filtered in through the glass, and beyond the grassy grounds and shrubbery the slow waters of the Meander glistened in the moonlight. Nix pulled off his weapon's belt and hurriedly wrapped it around and through the handles on the double doors, just as someone on the other side ran into it. It held but it might not for long. He grabbed a divan and dragged it before the door for good measure.

"Keep going!" he said Egil.

"To where?"

"I don't know! Somewhere!" Several doors led out of the lounge. "That door, there. I need a moment to think!" Nix shouted at the door, "You come after us and we kill him!"

"You're dead," Channis gasped, freeing himself enough from Egil's grasp to mouth some words. "Both of you."

"Then so are you," Nix promised him, and cuffed him on the head. "Egil? You've got the map in your head. We need a way out. A big window maybe. Which way?"

"This way," Egil said, tightening his grip on Channis and dragging the Upright Man along. They hurried through a door that opened onto another long hallway, then headed up a flight of stairs to the second floor.

Before them was a long hallway with doors along its length.

Voices sounded below them, men calling to one another. Channis worked his throat free enough to utter a hoarse call.

"Here, lads!"

Nix punched him in the face, silencing him, but the damage had been done.

The men below must have heard him, for the voices closed in on them. To Nix they sounded like they were right at the bottom of the stairs.

"Shite. Where, Egil?"

"I don't know," Egil said and hustled down the hall, pulling the gagging Upright Man along with him. "Pick a damned room! That slubber Mere read must not have known this area of the house very well."

Nix threw open a thick, reinforced wooden door to reveal a large chamber, maybe a reading room. Channis resisted entering the room, grabbing the door jambs as Egil backed in. Down the hall, a crowd of men thundered up the stairs.

"There!" one of them shouted. "Got them! Here, men!"

"Keep coming and he dies!" Nix shouted at them, but wasn't sure if they heard or cared.

"Don't let them take me from the house!" Channis shouted, his voice hoarse due to Egil's choke. "You heard me–!"

Egil choked off any further words and they pushed into the room and slammed the door behind them. Egil backed up against it.

"The key, Nix. Lock it."

"Aye," Nix said. He dropped his satchel, rifled it, and pulled out the magic key. He awakened it with a word of power.

"Give us a potato," the key said.

"A potato now!" Egil said, as bodies thudded into the thick wooden door. "How does a thrice-damned key have a sophisticated palette?"

"Sophisticated *and* palette?" Nix said, pulling a potato out of his satchel and shoving it at the key. "You've been reading."

"Fak you," Egil said.

The key took its price as the men on the other side of the room hammered at the door. Nix shoved the key into the lock. It warmed, changed form to make itself fit, and Nix locked it down. They backed off a step, staring at the door, satisfying themselves that it would hold for a moment. Nix shoved the last of his punch daggers into the lock so the men, had they a key, couldn't unlock it from their side.

"They'll find axes," Egil said.

"Aye," Nix agreed.

CHAPTER NINE

Nix turned and took stock of the room. The only other door in the room opened onto a small storage closet. As before, a barred window looked out on the grounds. There was only one way in, but there was also only way out.

"This ain't good," Nix said.

Egil took stock of the room too, jerking Channis around roughly. "Shite."

Nix bent over to look Channis in the eye. "Locks, barred windows, and reinforced doors throughout. You guild boys don't trust each other much, eh? That or you're gearing up for a siege."

Channis just stared at him.

"Not the chatty type. Fair enough."

Couches lined the walls. High backed chairs sat before a stone hearth. A desk featured in one corner. Abstract paintings hung on the wall.

"What in the Eleven Hells kind of guild house *is* this?" Nix asked.

He'd expected to find sparsely furnished quarters, filthy drinking halls, rooms with training dummies, maybe a run-down shrine to Aster, and instead they'd found an organization that had parlayed religion and crime into enormous wealth.

"Maybe we should have joined these slubbers, after all?" Nix said.

"Bah," Egil said, and shook Channis. "They're murderous bungholes, the lot."

Channis tried to say something but it only came out as a gagged grunt.

"I think he said he agrees with you," Nix said. He bent over to look Channis in the eye again. "It's good that you understand your faults."

Channis squirmed in Egil's grasp, legs kicking.

Egil flexed his arm, tightened the choke. Channis's eyes rolled. "I'm tired of holding this bunghole. Bind him, would you?"

"You can cooperate or I can cut you," Nix said.

Channis did not resist while Nix, after taking a length of line from his satchel, secured Channis with a double-square knot, hands behind his back, and legs at the ankle. They sat him on his arse on the floor.

"Not even a chair?" Channis said with a sneer.

"How about a punch in the mouth?" Egil said.

"And if you shout to your girls out there, I'll stab you in the face," Nix said. "Clear?"

A knock – a knock! – sounded on the door.

Egil and Nix shared a look of bewilderment.

"Uh, who is it?" Nix called.

A voice from the other side said, "Ain't no way out of that room. We know it and you know it. This can go hard for you boys, or it can go harder. But it only ends one way. You clear? You hurt the Upright Man and it goes hardest for you."

Channis looked smug.

Egil said, "We already left more than a dozen of you girls bleeding on the floor. You try to come in and it'll be a dozen more plus your Upright Man. *You* clear?"

Murmurs from the hall outside.

"Don't hurt yourselves thinking things through, now," Nix called. He walked to the window and checked the bars. No give in them at all, like a fakkin' gaol. Shite. Minnear, fat and full in the velvet of night, cast the grounds in viridian light.

"Let me ask you fakkers a question," Nix called over his shoulder. "Do you have to be ugly to be a guild man?"

Angry murmurs.

"It's a serious question. Every one of you slubbers looks like you could scare children and couldn't pay your way into a woman's favor. What say you? Aster only likes 'em ugly, maybe?"

"Fak you!" someone shouted.

"Let us hear Channis," said the first voice from the other side of the door. "Eighth Blade, you hear us?"

Channis looked to Nix for permission to speak. Nix nodded.

"I'm all right," Channis called. "And I'm gonna be all right." He glared at Egil and Nix and spoke in a lower tone. "Can't say the same for these two, though."

Dark chuckles from the hall outside.

"Hells, man," Nix said to him. "You're the ugliest of them all. Lord of the Bungholes and King of the Repulsives, as it were."

Channis snarled. "I'm looking at dead men. But not fast, no. You came up through the sewers, no? You see that torture chamber–"

A backhand from Egil split Channis's lip and sent blood and spit flying.

"Shut your hole, slubber. I left the fat man who ran that show hanging from his own chains. And if we're going to die here, you're going to die first."

Channis spit and grinned up at the priest. "Don't matter none to me. Long as you get what's coming."

"Nix?" Egil said, still staring at Channis. "You got any miracle in that satchel?"

The priest took out his dice, rattled them in his hand. Nix found the sound reassuring. He licked his lips, rubbed his forefinger and thumb.

He feared he was all out of miracles. He had only one smokeball and his key and his amulet and his light and...

He looked up when an idea struck him, an ugly idea, a desperate idea.

"What?" Egil said, reading his expression.

Nix did a quick calculation in his head. He hadn't been able to hear Ool's clock while they'd been underground, but they couldn't have been more than an hour since leaving the Tunnel.

It could work.

Channis must have seen him eyeing the window. "You ain't getting out through that window. All the bars in the house were made special. Graduate of the Conclave even enspelled them."

"Graduates of the Conclave are bungholes," Nix said absently, and rifled his satchel. He quickly found the tallow sticks and the scribing wand and pulled them out. He also anticipated Egil's jest and cut if off. "I didn't graduate, priest, as you know."

"Possibly still a bunghole, though."

"Conceded," Nix said, with a tilt of his head. He held up the grease sticks for Egil to see.

The priest's eyes widened in disbelief. "You aren't...?"

"I am," Nix said.

"You don't come out," said a shout from the other side. "And we're coming in."

"You come in and the Upright Man dies first!" Egil shouted back, then to Channis, "And you best believe that."

Nix drew fat lines down either side of the large window.

"How can that even work?" Egil asked in a hissed whisper.

Nix spoke over his shoulder. "Might not, but I'm ever an optimist. Minnear's full and the time's right. Or *maybe* the time's right."

"Maybe?"

"Unless you're going to pull a door out of your arse, 'maybe' is the best we've got."

Nix whispered a word in the Language of Creation to activate the wand. The green flame ignited in the wand's mouth and Nix used it to scribe summoning sigils in the air.

"What're you doing?" Channis asked, his cocksure tone fading. He shouted, "There's sorcery in here! Get in here, men!"

Egil shut him up with a knock to the head, but he'd been heard. The men in the hall attacked the door with renewed effort. The jambs and even the wall vibrated under the impact. A painting fell from the wall. Nix ignored the tumult and stayed focused on his task.

"It's not an alley," Egil said. "I don't see–"

"It doesn't have to be," Nix said, completing the sigils. "An alley is just easiest. But all it needs is an aperture of some kind. A doorway or window will do. What's with all the questions?"

Then Nix remembered what Egil had experienced in Blackalley, his sobbing calls for Hulda and Asa, reliving moments he'd spent most of his adulthood trying to forget. Nix had relived only a few dark moments from his past. Egil had faced the single experience that overwhelmed everything that came afterward.

While the guild men hacked at the door with their blades, Nix turned around to look at his friend. Egil, blood spattered and haunted, looked at him, past him, at the window, through it, at a hateful point in his past, at the wife and daughter he'd been unable to save.

"I don't see another way," Nix said softly. "Can you bear it?"

If Egil said he couldn't, Nix would stand in the room with his back to his friend and fight every guild man that came through the door. They'd die eventually, but they'd send a score of guild boys to the Hells before them.

Egil swallowed, blinked. He put his dice in his belt pouch, ran his hand over Ebenor's eye and came back to himself. He focused his heavy-lidded eyes on Nix.

"I'll bear it," the priest said, one of his huge hands opening and closing reflexively.

Nix nodded, turned, and lit the grease lines with the special matchsticks. They caught right away.

"Let's block the door better," he said.

Working together, they scooted the chairs and divan before the doors, even as the wood splintered and an axe head popped through.

"There's that axe at last," Nix said, and stabbed his falchion through the gash in the wood. He was rewarded with a scream and a curse. He backed off just as a crossbow bolt whistled through the hole and sank into the far wall.

"We're using your guild master for cover, you stupid fakkers!"

"Stop shooting!" Channis shouted. "Just get in here, round up these boys so we can send them down to the hooks."

"He's dead the moment you come through that door!" Nix shouted.

Curses and a long series of oaths.

"Your people have shite manners," Nix said to Channis, then at the door, "You have shite manners!"

"They're unforgiving, too," Channis said.

"So am I," Egil promised darkly.

"If it comes," Nix said to Egil, nodding at the sigils and burning lines, "try to think only of hopeful things. Remember how we got out last time? Same game. Should be easier this time. And it'll spit us out somewhere else in the city."

"You boys are fooling yourselves," Channis said. "The only thing coming in here is my men."

"And if it comes, what about him?" Egil asked, nodding at Channis, looming over him like a dark promise.

"Him?" Nix said. "Fak him. Him we kill. Hells, kill him now. One less bunghole in the world."

Channis licked his lips, looked from Nix to Egil. He must have seen their resolve for he paled, his facial scars livid lines.

"Get through that door!" he shouted to his men, veins and tendons visible on his neck and forehead. "Now!"

He struggled against his bonds, rocking back and forth, all to no avail. No one slipped Nix's knots.

The guild men beat and chopped frenetically on the door. A blade opened another slit in the thick wood, worried at it to make it wider.

"They're not coming through in time to save you," Nix said.

The guild men's onslaught against the door stopped for a moment and a few crossbow bolts whistled into the room, all of them off the mark.

Egil stepped before Channis, hammers in hand, and looked him in the face. "The people in that inn you ordered torched were people we care about. You try to hurt ours and we come at you. That's the game, yeah?"

Channis said nothing and the priest grabbed him by his collar, lifted him from the ground.

"That's the game, yeah?"

"Yeah," Channis said, and stuck out his jaw, apparently resigned to his fate. "I just wanted the faytor. That was all."

Nix grabbed him his hair. "You think that helps you? You'd be gettin' the same if you'd tried to harm only her. You hurt ours, we hurt you, but worse. That's the game." He loosed his grip on Channis's hair and shouted at the door, now starting to splinter. "You hurt ours, we hurt you worse! The first dozen of you fakkers through that door are dead men! Count on it!"

Dur Follin's guild house was as good a place as any to die, he figured. He was glad Egil had chalked their names on the street before they'd entered the sewers. They'd left some kind of mark, however transitory.

"Do it," he said to Egil. Then, to Channis, "See you in the hells, fakker."

Egil dropped Channis to the floor and raised his hammer for a killing blow.

Before it fell a sudden pain stabbed Nix behind the eyes. He exclaimed, cursed, rubbed his eyes, his temples. Egil did the same, backing a half step away from Channis, lowering his hammer. Something... opened in Nix's head and he recognized it even before Merelda's mental voice penetrated his mind.

Egil, Nix, please come back! Rose is worse! I think... she might die if we don't do something! Come back now!

Nix hadn't known Merelda could reach into his mind without seeing him. The fact she could left him vaguely disconcerted. He'd had his thoughts guided by the sisters before and though it had been justified, he still disliked it.

Channis, perhaps seeing an opportunity, struggled frantically against his bonds. His men opened a hand sized hole in the door.

"Get in here!" Channis shouted. "Or shoot them, gods dammit!"

Nix kicked Channis in the stomach, turning his shouts for aid into a wheezing, pained gasp.

Mere, I don't think we can get back, Nix projected.

No, you have to come back.

Listen to me, Mere. I have an idea about how to help her. Veraal can take you.

His idea for how to help Rose was no less desperate than his idea to resummon Blackalley.

No, you come back. Both of you. Egil, you make him come back.

The guildman were almost through the door. The furniture Egil and Nix had piled in front of it didn't give them much of a shooting angle.

Mere, I don't think we can. Listen now…

Nix, I can't keep the contact any longer. It hurts too much. Come back, damn it. Come back.

Mere–

The mental connection closed. Nix cursed, blinking away the pain behind his eyes. Nix's thoughts were racing. Channis saw them recover and knew what it meant for him.

"Get in here now!" Channis shouted to his men.

Nix glanced back at the burning lines and the glowing sigils. There was just the window, no Blackalley. He shook his head.

"Sorry about this, Egil."

Egil put the head of a hammer in one of his palms. "Bah! It was my idea. Besides, I didn't come here expecting to leave."

"I had some doubts, but I'm me, so…" He shrugged. "I figured we'd come through all right. I feel bad not being able to help Rose."

"That's the faytor, yeah?" Channis said with a sneer. "I heard she came back to you broken. You both see it now, eh? You ain't walking clear of here."

"Didn't we just say that?" Nix said to him absently. "Are you stupid or just not following along?"

"My coin's on stupid," Egil said.

"You yammer a lot, slubber," Channis said to Nix.

"I die as I lived," Nix said, with a little bow. "And you aren't walking clear of here, either."

"That's truth," Egil said to Channis, and raised his hammer.

A sudden, cold heaviness suffused the air. The torchlight in the room dimmed. Something blocked Minnear's viridian light. Channis stared past them, wide-eyed, his pupils huge. Even the guild men in the hall must have felt it, for they halted their assay on the door. Egil looked past Nix, his heavy lips set in a hard, straight line. Nix knew what he would see even before he turned.

A curtain of shimmering blackness hung in the air where the window had been, suspended between Nix's arcane lines and glowing sigils.

"What…?" Channis asked, fear rooted in his voice.

"That's a death sentence for you, slubber," Egil said.

"Wait," Nix said. "Wait, Egil!"

"For what?" the priest said. "We kill him and we go."

Channis seemed barely to hear him. His eyes didn't leave Blackalley. He looked mesmerized. "Go…?" he muttered.

"We'll need him," Nix said, hating the words as they left his mouth.

"For what? Shite, does this have to do with the idea you mentioned to Mere?"

"Aye."

"Explain."

"Now?" Nix asked, eyeing the shredded door, the eyes staring through the growing hole in the wood.

Egil waited, eyebrows raised.

"Odrhaal," Nix said.

Egil's brow furrowed. "The Maker? That's lunacy."

"Maybe," Nix conceded. "But it's all I have. If anyone can help Rose…"

"No one even knows if he exists, Nix."

"Not for certain, no." But Nix had been in the Deadmire once, seen some of the ruins. Felt something there. He believed the rumors. "If you have a better idea…"

Egil shook his head, cursing, staring at the back of Channis's head, no doubt eager to spill its contents. Nix pressed. They were almost out of time.

"Egil, we fakked up here. We both know it. We wanted blood and we got it. But these boys aren't going to stop. We'd have to put them all in the ground. We have to find some other way to make peace or we're going to have to the leave the city. But that's neither here nor there because right now we've got to get out of here and help Rose, yeah? Yeah?"

Egil's jaw tightened, chewing on Nix's logic.

"We take this one as a hostage. Then the guild won't take runs at us the whole time we're looking for Odrhaal."

More of the door splintered. Another huge impact that jarred the furniture before the door.

Egil cursed and jerked the Upright Man to his feet. "Let's visit the dark together, slubber. I imagine a bunghole that lived a life like yours is going to have a grand time inside."

Channis shook his head, still staring at the wall of Blackalley, nonplussed.

"No," he said softly, and tried to drag his feet. "No, no."

Egil pulled him along as he might a child. Nix slit the binding holding Channis's ankles and took him by the other arm.

Staring at the dark wall of Blackalley's promise, a panic seized Channis. He kicked and squirmed frenetically, more desperate with each step.

"No, don't! Don't!"

Nix struggled to keep his hold.

Finally Channis got enough wits about him to shout over his shoulder, "Shoot them! Shoot them!"

Instead there was another tremendous crash against the door and Nix heard it give way entirely. Wood splintered, furniture slid over the floor, men shouted and poured into the room. Nix hunched over as crossbow bolts hissed through the air, thumped into his mail.

"What is that?" several of the guild men shouted.

"Forget it! Stop them!"

"Aster's balls!" someone oathed.

Blackalley hung before Egil and Nix, a shroud of ink, of dark water, and within it was the thing men hated most to face – themselves.

"Stop, fakkers!"

But they didn't stop, and they had no time to brace themselves. Without breaking stride they lurched into the black. Silence fell. Nix could see nothing and he was glad of it. All that the light from his magic crystal had done last time was let him see the suggestion of dark things at the edge of his vision, hints of terror. And eventually the light had shown him Professor Drugal, with his dark eyes and his body merged part way with the stuff of Blackalley.

As before the darkness, cold and greasy, tried to seep into him. He felt it gliding over his skin, taking his measure, summoning his self-loathing.

"Just walk a bit," he said, his voice hollow and small in the darkness. "Doesn't matter where. We just want to change the spatial relationship so it throws us out somewhere away from the guild house. You hear me, Egil?"

"Aye."

The substance under his feet, giving and spongy, felt like flesh. His mind tried to fill the silence with imagined sounds, or were they imagined? The flutter of wings, the rasping breath of something huge, the slithering undulation of an enormous, unimaginable form. He pushed the thoughts from his mind, focused on the sound of his breathing, his footfalls.

He felt it when the regard fell on him, a weight on his shoulders, a tightness in his chest. He faltered, stopped walking.

"I feel it, too," Egil said.

They'd been noticed by... whatever lived in Blackalley. The hair on Nix's arms stood on end. The air thickened and he found it hard to breathe.

"What is that?" Channis said, panic in his voice.

Nix thought he heard distant shouting behind him, faint but terrified. He imagined some of the fool guild men following them in, getting lost, and... enduring what Drugal had endured. He put them out of his mind and focused.

"Think of Mamabird's stew," Nix said to Egil, as much to distract himself as to distract the priest. "Think of your smiling daughter, the day she was born, the day you married Hulda."

"Aye," Egil said, his voice steady.

Nix struggled not to drown in the dark pool of his past misdeeds. Those he'd killed flashed before his eyes, those he'd left to fates worse than death, those to whom he'd lied, those whom he'd cheated. He faced the reality that he'd accomplished nothing, lived a purposeless life that meant nothing to no-one, that he could die and his only mark on the world would be a chalk message on Broadstreet that the rain would soon wash away–

Egil's hand was on his shoulder, shaking him. "You're my friend, Nix. My brother. I'd be dead without you. You've saved me and many others, too many to count. Focus. Focus."

Nix grabbed onto Egil's words, rode them out of the darkness to thoughts of Mamabird, to the urchins he'd helped in the Warrens, the lives he'd saved. He'd made a mark, a real one that meant something to at least some people.

He patted Egil's hand to signal that he was all right. Egil gave him one final shake and squeeze.

"This is far enough," Nix said. "Time to leave."

A rush like rolling surf sounded out in the darkness, a deep thrum that pressured Nix's eardrums. It grew louder as it closed on them, some huge, dark wave that they couldn't see but could feel. A breeze went before it and carried on it the stink of ruined dreams and lost hope and something else… a dry reptilian pungence.

Nix thought of the good things he'd done with his life, none to grand purpose, but all heartfelt and true. He allowed nothing else to enter his mind. He thought of his friendship with Egil, their brotherhood, the trust they'd built over the years, the things they'd done, the things they'd chosen not to do. They left a dozen corpses behind them in the guild house, but not the boy. The boy they'd left alone and maybe, maybe, he'd find another life for himself.

Beside him, Channis shook as if with ague. He made small, frightened, animal sounds that reminded Nix of the sound earthbound nestlings made when kicked from the nest while still unable to fly.

"It's coming," Channis said. "I can feel it looking at me. I can hear it. It's coming. Its eyes! Its eyes!"

Nix heard it and felt it, but he focused on matters of love and hope. Blackalley dredged his mind for self-loathing and the regret, found plenty, but Nix refused to pay it heed. He wondered in passing what Blackalley forced a murderous slubber like Channis to see.

"Egil?" Nix said.

"I'm all right," the priest said, softly, steadily. "I'm all right."

The rushing sound grew louder, closer. The stink grew more intense. The wind stirred Nix's hair, tunic.

Free us, Nix heard in his head, the sound an uncomfortable rumble deep in his skull. *Free us.*

"I hear it!" Channis said. "It's speaking to me!"

Nix opened his eyes, faced the black, the dark, but allowed himself to see only the memories in his head – Mamabird, Rose and Mere, Tesha, Kiir.

"Focus, Egil!"

"I am!"

Beside him, Channis sagged. The guild master was weeping.

"It's coming!" Channis said through his sobs. "It's coming for me! It wants me!"

The weight of the darkness's regard fell away from Nix and he gasped, realized that he'd hardly been breathing. Channis went entirely slack in his grasp, laughing and crying by turns.

"I'm empty and it loves me and it's beautiful and I'll help and–"

"Shut him up, Egil!"

A heavy thud and Channis went silent.

Nix felt the eyes out in the dark fix on him once more, but with less intensity. The rushing sound filled his ears, the roll of a dark surf trying to catch them up in its currents. He resisted the lure of regret and stayed focused on the bright times in his life, the small moments of grace, the smiles, the people he loved and the people who loved him, and the rush grew to roar and the wind gusted over them, threatened to knock them from their feet, and the voices carried by the wind shouted in his head, as loud as Ool's clock, gonging, gonging...

The darkness abated to that of a normal night in Dur Follin and the rush of approaching doom faded to silence. Ool's clock gonged the hour.

Nix was shaking. His legs were weak.

"Fak," Egil said beside him.

They still held the guildmaster between them.

"Fak, aye," Nix echoed.

He blinked away tears – had he been crying? – and glanced around, half dazed. Decrepit buildings, sagging roofs, narrow packed earth streets, rusty, ancient street torches that hadn't seen a linkboy in years. They were in the Warrens.

He put a hand to the alley wall to keep from falling.

"That was well conceived," Egil said.

Nix smiled, nodded. "Luckily conceived, at least."

"You credit yourself too little," Egil said. "We should be dead. We're not – because of you."

Nix never received praise from his friend without embarrassment, so he changed the subject. He shook his arm to shake Channis, who hung limp between them, suspended on their arms like drying laundry. The Upright Man didn't so much as groan.

"He still alive?" Nix asked. "He's only useful to us alive."

Egil checked him. "He's alive. Cold as a warlock's heart, though. You still set on Odrhaal?"

"I don't see any other way."

"Me either," Egil said. "Fakking Deadmire, though."

"Aye, that."

Nix took a deep breath, cleared his lungs and thoughts of Blackalley's pollution.

"Right, then. The guild'll be on the move. They saw us go in and some of their boys might have followed. They won't be coming out, likely."

"Good," Egil said.

"They'll be looking for us, though," Nix said. "They may hit the Tunnel. We need to get there before they do."

Egil said, "There's probably another pair of guild boys with eyes on the Tunnel, or maybe that same pair, if they woke up by now. But they won't know what happened at the guild house."

"Not yet," Nix agreed. "We need to get Rose and Mere and get clear. Fast."

"Getting out of the Warrens is easy, but exiting the gates is a problem at this hour," Egil said.

Nix knew. "Let's solve one problem at a time, yeah?"

"Yeah. First thing I do when we get back to the Tunnel is strip off this fakking armor."

"Aye."

Bearing the unconscious guild master between them, they hustled through the dark streets.

CHAPTER TEN

Rusk pushed his way through the throng of muttering men in the hallway. Trelgin, wearing the Sixth Blade that Rusk had coveted, fell in beside him, cursing with every step. Both of them still wore their ceremonial robes.

At least a dozen dead guild men littered the floor of the guild house. They'd been hit, and hit hard.

"What in Aster's name happened here?" Trelgin snapped, spraying spittle. A palsy had afflicted Trelgin at some point in his life and caused half his face to droop like an old ma'am's tits. Every fourth or fifth word exited his mouth wet and sloppy. It aggravated Rusk no end, but that didn't keep Trelgin from yapping.

"The night after Channis gets the Eighth Blade the guild house gets hit? Feels like inside work, I'd say."

Rusk stopped, turned, and stared Trelgin in his droopy face. They stood about the same height, but where Rusk was lean gristle, Trelgin was a thick layer of fat over bulky muscles. The Sixth Blade would've had an almost boyish face if it weren't for the droop. His skin was as pale as candlewax except where a bruise was rising on one cheek; his long hair as dark as a crow.

"You implying something?" Rusk said to him.

"I'm merely observing." "Observing" came out in the company of some drool.

"That big fakker nearly killed me, too," Rusk said.

Trelgin made a point with a long pause. "Didn't though, did he?"

Rusk made his own point with a long stare. "No. But then I'm hard to kill, ain't I?"

"I wouldn't know."

With that, they walked on.

"Make way for the Sixth and Seventh," shouted some of the men, and the crowd parted for them.

They walked through a shattered door, bits of it still hanging from the hinges, and entered one of the Committeemen lounges. Furniture, some of it toppled, stood massed near the door. A dozen sets of eyes turned to face Rusk and Trelgin, and beyond the crowd of men...

"What the fak is that?" Trelgin asked.

A curtain of black, somehow shimmering but reflecting no light, hung in the air where the window should be. Two guild men stood near it, poking at it with their blades.

"Stop!" Rusk commanded. "Don't touch it! Don't go near it!"

One of the guild men said, "Nim, Gorse, and Deenis went in already, Seventh Blade. They was chasing them two that pinched the Upright Man."

Them two. The men from the Tunnel, Egil and Nix. Probably they wanted revenge for the botched arson, and maybe for breaking that faytor. Rusk decided to keep that information to himself for the moment.

"It was them boys from the Slick Tunnel," Trelgin said, making sure everyone heard, his words a wet mess. "Can't miss the big one with the eye tat on his head."

Rusk cursed inwardly, but outwardly said, "You're sure?"

"Had to be," said another man. "I seen that tat and that fakker was *big*. No mistaking him. They came up through the sewers. Left a bunch of good men dusty down there." He named off a few, including Zren the Blade, which caused murmurs of disbelief.

Several men threw prays at Aster on behalf of the fallen men.

"And then those slubbers came up here and attacked the Committee while it was in session," Trelgin said. "That's blasphemy and then some."

Nods around, lots of men touching the charms of Aster they wore as signs of their faith. Trelgin continued:

"For that we make 'em both dustmen, yeah?"

Angry murmurs, nods.

Rusk had seen almost nothing of the attack after the small one, Nix, had put on his show to distract them. The grand room had filled with smoke and fire so quickly that he'd not gotten a clean look at the big priest, who'd thumped him from behind while pinching Channis. Rusk had an egg-sized lump on his skull to show for it. By the time he'd regained consciousness, everything had already gone down.

"Thought you boys had 'em pinned in here," said one of the men to another.

"We did," said the other, and pointed at the black wall. "They went through there as we broke through. Took Channis, too. I saw it. Just stepped in and poof, they was gone. The three of ours that went hard after them are gone, too."

A third man said to Rusk, "We can't just leave 'em, Seventh Blade. We should be going through, too."

Nods around.

"Them're good men went through," said another man.

"Went through to where?" Rusk said, eyeing the dark wall. He'd seen some sorcery in his life, but nothing like this. "Eh? Where? Where does it go? What is it even?"

His words got through. Eyes found the floor. The mutters died down.

"Let's not be fakkin' idiots," he said. "I want them men and Channis back, too, but that don't mean we all jump off the Archbridge now, does it?"

"What then, Seventh Blade?"

Before Rusk could answer, the black curtain started to pull back in on itself, a dark blanket being drawn back through a hole in the world that none of them could see. The men near it backed away, exclamations of surprise and fear running through them like the trots. In moments the black curtain disappeared entirely, revealing the window, the green glow of a low slung but full Mage's Moon.

Soft curses all around the room. Wide eyes.

Rusk glanced surreptitiously at his tattoo, hoping to see it announce Channis's death by sprouting an eighth blade. He'd aimed for Sixth Blade, with the wealth that it brought, but he'd do even better as Eighth.

But seven it remained. He sniffed, kept the disappointment from his face. If he could just waste enough time–

Trelgin was looking at him sidelong, a knowing look in his pig eyes. Rusk stared him down until Trelgin looked away. Rusk realized that everyone was looking at him, waiting for him to give an order. He cleared his throat, said, "What we do is we get the Upright Man back and we click those two slubbers who dared defile Aster's house."

Ayes and nods around.

Rusk decided to get out in front of the men's thinking with some lies. Best if they thought he wanted Channis to survive.

"Some of you may be thinking that Rusky sees this as an opportunity to grow an eighth blade. I don't. I didn't want a seventh but I'm content with it. I don't want the arse aches that come with the eighth."

Some chuckles at that.

He held up his hand, showing the men his tat, its seven blades.

"The Upright Man is still alive or this tat would have an eighth, yeah? So we'll get him back. And we'll get payback from those slubbers."

"Turn them dusty," said one man.

"Eternity crates for the both," said another, and so on with the men, most of whom seemed to credit Rusk's words.

But not Trelgin. The Sixth Blade wore a false smile, an *I know better* in his eyes.

"We got eyes on the inn," Rusk said. "Trelgin, let them know what happened. Get another pair of eyes out there, too, just to be double sure. And get eyes on the gates and reach out to our bought men in the Watch. Those boys get no safe haven anywhere in Dur Follin, yeah?"

"Yeah!" answered the men.

Rusk allowed that he enjoyed giving orders. Wearing an eighth blade would suit him, he thought.

The men milled out of the room until only Trelgin and Rusk remained. Trelgin regarded him with his droopy eyed gaze.

"Those boys would have to be crazed to go back to that inn," Trelgin said.

"They attacked the guild house," Rusk said. He turned and stared out the window, thinking, planning, giving Trelgin his back as Channis had given Rusk his. "They are crazed. And they're fond of that faytor and she's still there, last we heard."

"Maybe," Trelgin said. "Could be they already took her and piked off."

"We'll see."

A long pause and still Trelgin lingered. Rusk turned and regarded him across the expanse of the room.

"Something else?"

"Not so much. I was just thinking how it was shite luck when you jumped fifth to seventh direct."

"Aster's hard to figure."

Trelgin nodded. "Aye. But some things ain't quite as hard to figure."

Rusk walked up to him. "Something you want to say clear?"

"I think I just did," Trelgin said.

"Which tells me you're stupid," Rusk said. "Cause if this were inside work, Channis would already be dead, wouldn't he?" Rusk held up his tat for Trelgin to see. "But he ain't, is he?"

Trelgin's lips did their best to form a sneer. "Not yet. Maybe things just need to look right first. Then he'll die."

Rusk tapped Trelgin's head with a finger. Trelgin jerked back with a snarl, hand going to his blade hilt.

"You got a lot of thoughts in that skull, Trelgin. The lot of them are shite."

"Don't ever touch me again!" Trelgin hissed, spraying spit.

Rusk stepped to him, nose to nose. "Then keep your accusations to yourself, you bunghole, droop-eyed cunt. Next time it won't be my finger I touch you with."

Trelgin licked his lips, his breathing coming hard. "You threatening another member of the Committee, Seventh Blade?"

"Just us here, Sixth Blade," Rusk said softly. "You take it as you wish. Accidents sometimes happen."

"Don't they, though?" Trelgin said. "And I thought you and I was going to be friends, Rusky."

"I don't need friends, Trelgin. And we're done here."

"Everybody needs friends," Trelgin said. "But yeah, we're done. I'll help with the Upright Man, though, me and my men." He put a finger to his droopy eye. "Keep an eye on things, like. Make sure no accidents happen, yeah? Can't hurt. We both want him back safe, yeah?"

Rusk just stared.

"Right, then," Trelgin said, and turned to leave. Over his shoulder, he said, "Seventh Blade suits you, Rusky. Wouldn't fit me, though. I heard it's a shite job."

With that, he exited the room, Rusk making an obscene gesture at his back as he walked out.

Trelgin wouldn't be the only one who thought Rusk might have arranged for Channis to be taken. He had to walk softly for a time. He had to at least look like he was *trying* to get Channis back alive. If anyone could pin a half-assed rescue effort on him, he'd be as good as dusty. So he had to look like he was trying to get Channis back, all while hoping that Channis croaked and Rusk grew an eighth blade. And they still had that bitch faytor to kill. That was just business.

It would be complicated, but Rusk could handle complicated. He had a few lads he could trust. He'd lead them himself. They'd have to navigate around Trelgin's eyes, because the last thing a Sixth Blade like Trelgin wanted was to become a Seventh.

But then again: Fak Trelgin. Rusk would find a way to manage him, too. He had no intention of handing back the opportunity Aster had just placed in his lap. Channis's tenure as Upright Man would be short and bloody and Rusk would be the new Upright Man and that was that.

He threw a pray at Aster and went to gather his men. They'd scour the city until they found Egil and Nix and Channis and that faytor. And if all four died in a scrum, well, that's just how these things went sometimes.

Egil and Nix didn't bother with one of the gates out of the Warrens. They didn't want any questions from the Watch about the unconscious man they were carrying, so instead they picked a likely spot to scale the Poor Wall, a regular pastime among the Warren's urchins. Minnear had set and the thin silver crescent of Kulven cast little light. The hour was so small even the city's rats were sleeping.

The wall, cracked and pitted, rose half again Egil's height.

"How do you want to do this?" Egil asked softly.

"What I want to do is throw him over," Nix said, only half-jesting. "What say you?"

Egil pursed his lips, nodded. "Probably wouldn't break him. Much."

"What the Hells happened to him anyway?" Nix said. He lifted the guild master's cold hand, the one with the eight-bladed tat. "He's as limp as a corpse."

"Blackalley happened to him," Egil said.

Nix remembered the guild master's words.

It's beautiful and I'll help it.

Nix also remembered the plea he'd heard the first time they'd escaped Blackalley.

Free us.

Whatever was in there certainly shouldn't be freed, if freeing it were possible.

I'll help it.

Nix resisted the urge to slap the guild master in the face for being stupid. He reminded himself to check over the guild master when they reached the Tunnel.

"You go up," Egil said. "I'll pass him along."

"Aye," Nix said. "Up I go."

The Poor Wall was more symbol than barrier. Nix had climbed it hundreds of times in his youth and it presented no more problem for him as an adult. He straddled the top.

"Pass him."

Grunting, Egil passed the limp, floppy body of the guild master up to Nix. Nix didn't worry over it when Channis's head hit the wall a time or two or three during the exchange.

While Nix held the guild master at the top of the wall with him, Egil climbed the wall and descended the other side. Nix handed Channis down to the priest and joined Egil on the street. They hurried toward the Tunnel.

Keeping to the shadows, senses sharp, they walked streets as quiet and dark as the tombs they often robbed. A few blocks from Shoddy Way and the Tunnel, they stopped. Both of them knew what came next.

"You or me?" Nix said.

"You."

"I've done it the last couple times."

Egil snorted. "That's because you're the sneaky one."

"Sneaky? Me?"

"You. Sneaky. Yes."

Channis groaned.

"Shut up," Egil said, and shook him.

"At least we know he's alive," Nix said. "But let's return to the matter at hand. Sneaky you said? I think maybe you meant stealthy and dexterous."

"Stealthy and dexterous, aye. But also sneaky."

Nix sighed. "Fine, then. I go. *Again*. Being the stealthy and dexterous one."

"And sneaky."

Nix pretended not to hear. "If this slubber wakes up and says something stupid, try not to kill him. We need him alive."

"I could just hit him on the head now. Then he won't wake up."

Nix chuckled. "My hands are clean of it. Just make sure you don't kill him."

Nix stripped off his mail shirt and satchel and handed both to Egil. "How many you think?" he asked Egil, checking his blades and axe.

"Two," Egil said. "Same two, I'd wager."

"Aye. Nobody would want to eat that shite sausage."

If the two thieves they'd ambushed and left in the alley earlier had regained consciousness, they wouldn't have dared report their failure to the guild. Too embarrassing. They'd just return to the inn and sit on it, hoping for Egil and Nix to return. "I guess I'm off to see those boys again, then. Give me a half hour then head down Shoddy Way."

"Aye."

Nix sped off into the darkness. When he reached the muddy mess of Shoddy Way, he stayed out of the light of the dying street lamps and surveyed the street. The Tunnel was dark, as were all the other buildings on the street. He didn't see Veraal's men at the Tunnel's door, nor anyone on the balcony, though Nix wouldn't have trusted that balcony to hold more weight than a cat's. Probably Veraal had pulled everyone inside.

Using barrels, walls, and untended carts for cover, he worked his way down the street to a narrow alley near the Tunnel. From there, he eyed the rooftops and alley mouths, trying to imagine where the guild boys might settle in to eyeball things.

He saw several likely places, but didn't need to scout any. A breeze carried the whiff of smokeleaf to him. He shook his head in disbelief. One of those dumb fakkers was smoking. Not a problem on a busy street in the day, but smoking while doing an eye job on a dead street in the small hours? He had no idea how the guild had gotten as much power as it had, given the quality of its people.

Following his nose, he soon located the men. They were in the abandoned cooper's shop across and diagonal from the Tunnel. The roof of the shop had long ago rotted and collapsed, exposing most of the second floor to the sky. The walls still stood in places, but leaned inward or outward as their decay had led them. Through gaps in the leaning walls, Nix could see that piles of debris lay heaped on the floor. A few support beams still stood here and there, the bared bones of the structure. The lower floor was sealed tight: door barred, shutters nailed closed. The vantage from the second floor offered a clear view of the block, and the debris and leaning walls offered good cover.

Nix watched for a moment, trying to spot the men, but they'd at least hidden themselves well. Once he thought he caught the soft, small glow of a pipe, but wasn't sure.

Egil would be coming so he needed to hurry. Hugging the nearside buildings, he dashed along Shoddy Way. He circled around to the back of the building and looked for the rope ladder the men must have somewhere. Not seeing one, he shrugged, put a throwing dagger between his teeth, and climbed the wooden walls. He moved slowly, silently, using shutters, irregular edges, and a window jamb to get him up to the second story. A gap in the wall would get him inside quickly. He was about to heave himself up when a sound froze him, a footfall from right above.

He flattened himself against the wall, sweating, holding his breath, and glanced up. The tip of two boots extended over the lip of the edge. For a moment Nix thought he'd been heard, but then the man grunted and started to piss over the edge.

The man hummed while he worked, which made it worse. It went on and on, wearing on Nix's patience, the stream missing Nix by a hand's width. He had no intention of waiting for the shake. Drops would go everywhere.

He braced himself, reached up, grabbed the man by the shirt, and pulled him over the edge. The man shouted as he fell, but the shout died as the man did. Nix hoped he fell in his own puddle of piss. Would serve him right.

Nix quickly pulled himself up over the edge of the roof. Two guild men were in the middle of standing up from near one of the windows, one of them with a pipe dangling from his lips, both of them looking with surprise at Nix.

Nix recognized them as the two he and Egil had brained in the alley earlier.

"You!" the one with the pipe said, and fumbled to bring up a slung crossbow, while the other hastily drew his blade.

"None of that, now," Nix said, hurling the dagger he'd had in his teeth. The blade ended its whistling tumble by sinking hilt deep into the crossbowman's throat. He fell backward, choking on his own blood, his crossbow discharging into the night sky, as if he'd taken aim at the stars. He toppled backward into a decrepit section of wall, which gave way immediately. Man and planks of wall went over the edge and hit the ground below with a dull thud.

His comrade snarled and charged Nix.

"I could use one of you alive–" Nix tried to say as he drew his falchion, but the man was upon him, blade slashing and stabbing.

Nix parried, ducked, spun and dodged, the two of them dancing through the debris on the sagging floor.

With his boot, Nix flicked a small piece of lumber at the man and followed it up with a flurry of strikes from his falchion. The onslaught drove the man, wide-eyed and breathing heavy, back toward the edge of the building where the wall had given way. Nix bounded back.

"Listen, you stupid slubber. If I wanted you dead, you'd be dead. I need you take a message back to the guild–"

The man, his face twisted up in anger, lunged at Nix. His short blade slashed for Nix's throat. Nix leaned back, avoided the steel, parried a second blow with his falchion, and ducked under a third.

"You don't have to die here," Nix said. His footwork had turned him around. He was aware of the edge at his back, two strides. Possibly the man saw that as an opportunity.

"Fak you!" the man said, and bounded forward. He stabbed for Nix's abdomen, no doubt trying to force him to leap backward and fall, but Nix held his ground and slapped the smaller blade out wide. The parry knocked the man off balance, and his lunge carried him past Nix and to the edge of the roof. He pulled up, dropped his blade, tottered there for a moment, arms waving.

"Shite," he said.

"Shite," Nix echoed, and grabbed for him. He got a fistful of tunic but it ripped as the man fell, leaving nothing in Nix's hand but a swatch of torn fabric. The man's shout lasted only a beat, ending in a meaty thud as he slammed face down on Shoddy Way. Nix leaned over the edge and looked down, hoping the muddy road would cushion the fall enough that–

"Shite."

The man lay not far from his dead comrade and the fallen section of wall, his limbs at a grotesque angle.

"That was your own damned fault," Nix called down to him. "I tried to tell you."

Nix looked up and down Shoddy Way, wondering if any more guild men would emerge from other hidey holes. He saw none and presently he spotted Egil moving along the sides of buildings as stealthily as he could while bearing the Upright Man.

"I really am the sneaky one," Nix muttered. He lowered himself over the side and descended the building. He glanced at the bodies as he passed, then gave Egil an all-clear whistle. The priest hustled forward out of the darkness of an eave, bearing the still-limp form of the guild master.

"Find them?" Egil asked.

"Aye," Nix said.

"Chat with one and send him back to the guild?"

Nix pointed with his chin up the street to the bodies, a shapeless mound in the dim light of the streetlamps. "They weren't much in a talking mood. What about you? Kill Channis?"

"At some point," Egil said. "But not yet. You just gonna leave the bodies there?"

"Let the dung sweepers strip their coin." Nix looked up and down Shoddy Way. "Best get out of the street now. The rest of the guild'll be along before long."

Bearing Channis, they hurried to the Tunnel's double doors. Tables had been laid on their sides to block windows. Egil rapped on the barred door.

"It's us!" Nix hissed. "Egil and Nix!"

A long pause before movement sounded from within and the bar was lifted. The door opened and Egil and Nix found themselves staring down the points of three loaded crossbows in the hands of Veraal's men. One of them pushed past Nix and Egil, glanced around outside, and pulled the door closed behind. Another thumped Egil and Nix on their shoulders and replaced the bar.

"I never get the greeting I expect when I walk through that door," Nix said.

"We heard a tumult outside," one of Veraal's men said. "We thought it was the guild."

Nix turned to Egil. "Did he say 'tumult'?"

"I believe he did."

"Light," Veraal's voice said, and Gadd opened the shutter on a lantern set on the bar. The soft orange glow filtered through the common room.

Veraal and Tesha stood at the bar, both holding pipes. Gadd stood behind the bar, grinning with his filed teeth, a huge tulwar hanging from his belt. Veraal's men took station around the common room, cocked crossbows at the ready. Kiir and Lis sat at another table, heads on their hands, eyes closed, sleeping.

"I'm glad to see you lads," Veraal said, and planted his pipe in his mouth. "Bit surprised, too, I'll admit."

"Is that a body?" Tesha asked.

"A drink, Gadd," Egil said. "And no need to kill it first with that length of steel you're wearing."

The easterner grinned, nodded, and turned to his cups and the hogshead.

"Nothing went down here?" Nix asked Veraal.

"Quiet as a cloister," Veraal said.

"Isn't gonna stay that way," Nix said.

Their voices awakened Kiir. She opened her eyes, raised her head, blinked sleepily, and focused on Nix. "You're back!"

"I'm like bad luck," he said to her. "I always turn up eventually."

Smiling, she pushed back her chair, ran to him, and caught him up in an embrace.

"Ugh," she said, pushing back. "You stink."

"Walking the sewers will do that to you."

She looked at Egil and her eyes widened at the body he carried, at the blood and bits of gore that spattered his face and arms. Nix did not bother explaining.

"Go gather your things. You and Lis."

"Why?" she asked, still agawp at Egil.

"Just do it. I'll explain. Hurry."

Nix and Egil walked for the bar and Gadd's ale. Egil tossed Channis to the floor.

"Merelda's safe?" Egil asked, stripping out of his mail shirt. "Rose, too?"

Veraal nodded. His eyes lingered on Channis, on the blood all over Egil, but he said nothing of either. "They're both upstairs still. Sleeping probably."

"We'll need to get them up," Nix said.

Gadd placed foaming tankards on the bar. Both of them drank deep.

Tesha tapped her pipe on the bar. "I'll ask again. Why are you carrying a body?"

"Unfortunately," Nix said, and slammed back the rest of his ale, which Gadd set to refill, "that's not a body."

"Yet," Egil added.

"Yet," Nix echoed.

Tesha cocked her head sidewise and kneeled down to look at Channis's face. "Who is it? And why'd you bring him here?"

Nix reached into his satchel, found a match, struck it, and offered it to Tesha.

She put the pipe in her mouth and leaned in. Nix lit the bowl and she took a long draw.

"That's the Upright Man," Nix said, extinguishing the match.

Appreciative curses from Veraal's men.

"You're serious?" Tesha asked, her words punctuated with smoke.

"Aye," Egil said. He seemed to notice the gore covering his arms for the first time. Before the priest could ask, Gadd tossed him one of the rags he used to clean cups. Egil did the best he could to wipe his arms clean, but mostly just smeared the blood around.

Veraal took his pipe from his mouth. "You telling me you two took the Upright Man *captive*?"

"Sounds crazy when you say it out loud," Nix said.

"Why in the fak did you do that?" Veraal asked.

"Yes," Tesha said. "Why?"

Nix made light of it. "Seemed like a good idea at the time."

"A good idea?" Veraal said. "Gadd, I'll take one of those ales, too."

While Gadd drew him an ale, Veraal kneeled down, took Channis by the hand and examined his tat.

"Eight blades and no mistake. Shite, boys. You are a pair of crazy gits."

"If I told you Nix's idea about how to help Rose," Egil said. "You'd think we were crazier still." He signaled to Gadd for a refill.

Veraal let Channis's hand drop. "Do tell."

"Best no one knows but us, yeah?" Nix said.

"Of course," Veraal said. "Right."

Nix looked at Tesha. "We pinched the Upright Man for leverage. If you knew the whole story it'd make sense. Maybe."

She seemed to accept that.

"So," Nix said to the room. "Since we have the Upright Man and had, uh, harsh words for many other members of Dur Follin's esteemed guild of rogues, sneaks, and general bungholes, I suspect they'll be hard on our heels. And that means everybody's got to get out. Now."

Veraal nodded and signaled his men, all of whom immediately started gathering up their gear.

"Leave? Where are we supposed to go?" Tesha asked.

"Anywhere that's not here," Nix said to her. "You've got a quarter hour."

"And no one comes back here until we say so," Egil added, and finished off his ale. Gadd reached to refill it and Egil did not protest.

Mere appeared at the top of the stairs, still dressed, and called down.

"Thank the gods you've come back. Egil, Rose is—"

"Get her ready to travel," Nix called up. "We leave in a quarter hour."

"What? A quarter— Nix she can't travel," Mere said.

"She has to," Egil said softly. "Do your best, Mere. We leave soon. The guild's coming."

"Coming here?"

"Quickly now," Nix said. "Tell Kiir and Lis to be quick, too."

Tesha said something to Gadd in a language Nix didn't understand. Gadd nodded, eyed Egil and Nix, and retreated to his cellar and out the back. Tesha took a draw on her pipe, exhaled, and regarded Nix with the hard expression he'd come to know well. He held up a hand to cut off whatever she might say and donned his most disarming smile.

"You don't need to say it. Could be that we took a bigger bite than we could chew."

She frowned. "There's nothing amusing about this, Nix. These are people's lives."

Nix knew. He looked her in the face. "And I'm trying to save them, Tesha. You... sometimes. Argh! Listen, I jest all the time, yeah? That's just my way. But never, *never*, let that make you think that I don't understand the stakes. I understand them quite well, better than you, I expect. I've been running crosswise of bad people most of my life and some of things I've seen and done... well, I doubt you'd believe half of them. I know what people like these guild men are capable of and I *know* these are people's lives. Yours included. So do as I say."

She started to speak and he cut her off.

"No one fakked up here, if that's what you're thinking."

"It's not," she said, but Nix kept going.

"Certainly not me and Egil. We're just trying to fix it. It was just bad luck that they clicked the old Upright Man in Rusilla's tent while she was in his head. But now we are where we are. All of us caught up in it. So we deal with that bad luck and make the best of it, yeah?"

She stared at him a long moment. "You done?"

He blinked. "What? Yes."

"Then stop talking for once and listen. I agree with you. Apologies for misreading your humor."

"Uh. Right, then."

She pointed at his chest with her pipe. "But remember who you're speaking to, Nix Fall. I see through your shite. Now, you said you've got something in mind for Rose?"

He nodded.

"You don't want to tell me?"

"Should I?"

"No, you shouldn't. Not in detail. In the city or out?"

"Out," he said.

"And this one," she nodded at the Upright Man, whom Egil had placed on the floor near his stool. "He's key to that? Otherwise…"

Nix nodded. "Otherwise we'd have killed him already. He's just to ensure the guild doesn't harass us as we… go where we're going."

She nodded. "Good enough, then. I sent Gadd around back to prep the cart. You can use that to move Rose and the Upright Man. Meanwhile I've got some people I can rely on, a place for our workers to stay. That's where I sent the rest of them. We'll be fine for a while. It'll cost though, so that comes out of our profits when we reopen."

"Assuming the guild doesn't burn the Tunnel down."

She looked genuinely alarmed, her beautiful eyes wide with concern. "You think they will?"

He shrugged. "No telling with these slubbers. But if they do, the main thing is that no one's in it at the time, yeah?"

She recovered herself. "Yeah. I'll keep everyone away from the Tunnel until you two send word that things are squared with the guild."

"*If* they're squared."

"Don't say *if*. Get Rose better and get them squared then come back."

Nix looked at Tesha, at Egil, who smiled and looked away, then back at Tesha.

"Is now the appropriate time for me to tell you that I love you?"

"That I already know," she said, turned, and walked away.

Nix watched her go.

Veraal leaned in close. "Tesha's an interesting lass, I'd say."

Egil guffawed. "Hate to be the man that crossed her."

"Aye, that," Nix said, and watched her ascend the stairs. "Like to be the man who made her smile, though."

Egil grunted.

Tesha's voice carried from the upstairs hall as she barked orders. "Only necessities and small valuables. Don't bring anything else. Hurry now."

Veraal gulped his ale. "That's a damned fine ale."

"Gadd's a holy man when it comes to brewing," Egil said.

"You've been sitting here this whole time and didn't try Gadd's ale?" Nix said. "You missed out."

"So I see."

The three men tapped tankards, finished their ales, and stood.

Veraal regarded Egil and the smeared gore that covered him. "How many'd you end?"

Egil shrugged, so Nix filled in.

"Somewhere between a dozen and a score, all told."

"And this one," Egil added, nudging Channis with his toe. The guildmaster groaned.

Veraal whistled. "You hit 'em hard. But still they're coming?"

"We've got the Upright Man, now," Nix said. "They have to."

Egil ran a hand over his tattoo. "They'd be coming anyway. Zealous fakkers."

"We underestimated that," Nix allowed. "Going to be hard to square this up without it ending with either us dead or all of them dead. And I'm rather fond of me. Egil I could take or leave."

The priest smiled, as did Veraal.

"You boys manage to step in shite no matter where you walk," Veraal said.

"Now and again scraping it off gets old," Nix said.

"Aye, that," Egil said.

"If it matters, I think you were in the right, here," Veraal said. "They were going to keep coming for Rose until they got reason enough not to. You made your play and bloodied their nose and pinched their Man. They don't learn a lesson from that…"

"We cut their fakking throats," Nix finished.

"And that's why you two are my boys," Veraal said, and thumped the bar with a fist. "And look here, me and my men will escort your people to wherever they're going. I'll check on them, too."

"We'll owe you for all this when we come back," Nix said. "We already owe you for the mail. Those things saved us more than once."

"Owe me you do and will," Veraal said with a smile. "Feels right to be deeper in the game a bit, though."

"Doesn't it?" Nix said with a smile.

Egil's dice appeared in his hand, rattled while everyone gathered their things. Gadd returned from the back of the inn.

"Cart set," he said.

"What's with that blade, man?" Nix said, nodding at the tulwar. "It's as long as your leg. I don't think the guild has any giants in its employ."

"Big steel," Gadd said, playing dumb.

Nix smiled. "We weren't going to play this game anymore, remember?"

Gadd's expression turned serious. He looked around to see that no one else was listening. "It was my father's. It's a special weapon."

"You know how to use it?"

Gadd smiled, his teeth making him look like a predator. "Yes."

"Good," Nix said, extending his arm. "Luck to you, Gadd."

"And you," Gadd said, taking Nix's arm.

"Help Tesha, yeah?"

Gadd nodded and headed upstairs. After he'd gone, Nix looked down on the Upright Man.

"I'm going to check this fakker."

"For what?" Egil asked.

Nix hopped off his stool, grabbed the Upright Man under the armpits, and heaved him atop a table. Veraal's man watched him curiously.

"I don't know," Nix said. He checked Channis's arms, feet, legs. He opened Channis's shirt – the man's torso was as scarred as his face – but saw nothing unusual. Throughout, Channis didn't make a sound.

"Check his eyes," Egil said.

"What?"

"Like with Drugal. Check his eyes."

Nix peeled back Channis's eyelid. The eye had vertical slits, like a snake's, and the whites were black as pitch.

Nix cursed and shared a look with the priest while holding Channis's eye open.

"See this?"

"I see it," Egil said.

"Thoughts?" Nix asked.

Egil shook his head. "It got to him somehow. Same as with Drugal. He's a dead man."

It's beautiful and it wants me and I'll help it.

Free us.

Nix pried open Channis's other eye. It was normal, the pupil dilated, and Nix swore he saw terror in it. He smacked the guild master on the cheeks.

"Can you hear me, Channis? Channis?"

The Upright Man's mouth opened wide, as if he would scream, but no sound emerged. It was all the more terrible for the silence.

"This isn't good," Nix said.

"This hasn't been good for about a day and a half," Egil said. He nodded at Channis. "But if he goes out ugly, I'm not going to feel bad about it."

"Nor I," Nix said, though going out filled with whatever was in Blackalley seemed a hard way to go for anyone. "But we still have to bring him. He's all we've got. He keeps the guild off us until we get Rose help. And if we're to get square with the guild, it's going to be through him."

Egil grunted.

"Why didn't it get us?" Nix said.

"It did," Egil said.

"That's not what I mean."

Struck by a sudden fear, he checked his hands, arms, chest, and legs. No sign of Blackalley's touch. Egil took his point and checked himself, too. No sign.

"Must have been something in them," Egil said.

"Must have," Nix said. "We have to get moving," Nix said. He hollered up the stairs. "We about ready?"

Presently Kiir, Lis, Tesha, and two of Veraal's men descended the wide staircase, each burdened with a sack or small chest filled with their things. Mere followed, with Rose leaning on one of Veraal's men.

Egil and Nix hurried forward and Nix took Rose from Veraal's man. She leaned against him, smelling of sweat and sick.

"Hello, Nix," Rose said with a wan smile. She looked as pale as marble, her sweat-dampened red hair pressed against her head. Mere fell into Egil's arms. He embraced her in return, putting guild men's blood on her cloak.

"We're going to take care of you," Nix said to Rose. "I have an idea."

"Nix with an idea. There's a frightening thing," she said, and winced at some pain.

"I'm going to get you fixed," he said.

"Applause," she said softly.

He kissed her on the brow and she closed her eyes.

"We ready?" he said, looking about.

Nods around.

"That's it, then. Everyone out the back. Right now."

CHAPTER ELEVEN

Rusk and Trelgin, each with four of their trusted, hardened men, hurried through the pre-dawn streets. All wore boiled leather jerkins and bore steel and crossbows.

The street torches had burned down to piles of charcoal embers and the moons had both set. The streets were quiet and dark. Guild men called them "killing streets", the hours when the streets were bare of Watchmen and civilians, when clicks went down in dark alleys or rival gangs met on empty streets to sort differences with knives and truncheons.

Rusk would've clicked the old Upright Man during the small hours if he'd been able, but the whoreson had been so careful that a click in the Low Bazaar had been Rusk's best chance. And that one decision had fakked up the works. Somehow the faytor had learned guild business, Channis had ordered a torch job on her that'd been botched, and Egil and Nix had hit the guild house and pinched Channis in return.

And now the guild had to hit them back, and in the process Rusk had to appear as though he wanted Channis back alive, all while praying to Aster that the tough whoreson died. What a cockup.

He considered sending a private word to Egil and Nix, suggesting they kill Channis, but then they'd have something over on Rusk. And Trelgin was watching, always watching. The Sixth Blade would figure it out if Rusk didn't play things square. So Rusk reasoned it was best just to let matters proceed, maybe drag his feet a little, and hope at the end of it that Channis ended up dusty. That'd solve a host of problems.

Rusk surreptitiously checked his tat as they crossed the city. No change.

To keep up appearances and deflect suspicion, Rusk had put a pair of men on every gate out of the city. They ought to have been in position by now. Pairs also scouted the streets, all eyes. Dur Follin was a big city, though, and a pair like Egil and Nix could go dark if they really wanted to.

"Why'd they pinch the Upright Man, you think?" asked Varn, a hulking man who'd lost two fingers on his right hand in a knife fight.

Mors, a small, twitchy man they called "the bald mouse" said, "Could've just killed 'im, yeah?"

"They want him for something," a third man said. "Torture, maybe. They was talking payback in the guild house."

"They'll get their own payback," said Varn, and the others nodded.

"They strike you as the torturing type?" Trelgin asked, his words punctuated by slobbery inhalations. He didn't wait for an answer. "They pinched the Man for leverage, probably to bargain for the faytor's life. If the torch job hadn't been botched, we'd all be sleeping right now."

Ayes around.

"We're past bargaining," Rusk said. "They attacked the guild house and left a score of our men dead. They're dust and the faytor's dust and that's that."

Not even Trelgin disputed with him over that.

"Dustmen," said Varn, nodding.

"But whatever happens," Trelgin said, speaking slowly to avoid drooling. "The Upright Man comes back alive. Ain't that right, Rusky?"

Rusk wanted exactly the opposite but the requirements of guild law severed thoughts from words. "Yeah. No careless shots if you see them. Channis comes back alive."

"No shots at all, I'd say," Trelgin countered, smiling through his droop. "Just to be safe."

Rusk had to walk with a light step, so he merely grunted noncommittally. Trelgin's eyes lingered on him, but he ignored the look.

"We hit the inn hard," Rusk said. "Anyone inside shows any fight, you put them down. Clear?"

"Clear," said the men.

"Make it a slaughter and the Watch'll have to look into it," Trelgin said.

"I didn't say make it a slaughter," Rusk said, irritated. "I said put down those that show fight. And fak the Watch anyway. We got enough of 'em bought. There won't be any blowback whatever we do."

"I want a go at that big fakker," Varn said, cracking his knuckles. "I heard he strung up Zren the Blade by the chain."

"I heard that, too," said Mors.

They drew blades as they turned onto Shoddy Way. Decrepit buildings lined both sides of the street. The Slick

Tunnel stood out among the smaller shacks and shops for its size and long-faded grandeur. Rusk assumed it had once been the manse of a nobleman, before the rich had moved to the west side of the Meander.

They kept to the darkness on one side of the street, but otherwise did little to mask their approach. This wasn't a click that required precision or surprise. It was a straight muscle job and Rusk and Trelgin had manned the team with some of the guild's best blade men. He also figured the eyes he'd stationed on the inn would fall in with them.

The Tunnel sat on a square parcel of land bounded by narrow alleys on two sides, Shoddy Way and Tannery Row on the other. The building was two stories of stone and wood, with once ornate windows on three sides, most of the panes cracked or missing. A poorly built wooden fence bordered the back of the parcel, the slats leaning this way and that between the posts. A balcony with a balustrade stuck out from the second floor, but the posts that held it up sagged under its weight. Like most of Dur Follin, the building gave the impression of imminent collapse.

No light glowed in any of windows.

"Maybe they're sleeping," Varn said.

"They ain't sleeping," Mors said, his voice low and dangerous.

"No," Rusk said, though he wondered if maybe Egil and Nix hadn't come back to the inn. "Do the front door. I need at least one person taken alive for a chat."

"Front door, aye," Varn echoed, his tone eager.

They picked up their pace.

●●●●

Egil, Nix, Tesha, Veraal, and all the rest poured out the back of the Tunnel. The fence gate around the back of the inn was thrown open, manned by Gadd and his tulwar. A covered wagon waited for them on Tannery Row, a threadbare mule harnessed to it.

"Wagon will serve?" Gadd asked Nix.

A thick layer of straw and two bales were inside the wagon. Gadd had stocked it with two hogsheads of beer, a few water skins, two bags with several loaves of bread each, and several bags of roots and tubers taken from his cellar.

"That's well done, Gadd," Nix said, once more shaking the easterner's hand. "Take care of Tesha like I said, yeah?"

"Tesha can take care of herself," said Tesha, gathering off to the side of the wagon with the rest of the group.

Egil and Nix placed Rose in the wagon, wrapped her in blankets. Nix smiled at her.

"Ain't much of a rattler, is it?" Rose said. She shook her head. "Wagon, I mean. It's not much of a wagon."

"We won't be in it long," Nix said.

Egil took Mere by the waist and lifted her onto the wagon.

"You and Rose will stay back here," the priest said.

He gave her a dagger he produced from somewhere.

"Nix and I will drive. Channis stays with us."

"Veraal," Nix called. "Can your men spare a pair of crossbows?"

Nix had his sling, of course, but a loaded crossbow on the bench beside him would be an easier thing to fire.

"Make it three," Mere said from inside the wagon.

Veraal nodded, gave the order, and Nix, Egil, and

Mere all armed themselves with borrowed crossbows. The men supplied them with wishes of good luck and ten bolts a piece.Egil tossed Channis onto the floorboard and he and Nix took their seats on the driver's bench, Egil driving, Nix beside him.

"Sorry looking mule," Egil said.

Nix eyed the points of the skinny mule's spine, its threadbare fur and bent head.

"If we have to make a run for it, I say I drive and we yoke you to the bridle."

"Aye," Egil said with a smile, but it faded right away. "Be nice if we could wait a day. They're likely to spot us. The streets are empty at this hour. They're going to have eyes everywhere."

Nix knew Egil was right. But he also knew they had no choice. They couldn't hole up at the Tunnel. And Rose needed aid as fast as they could get it. "There's nothing for it. We risk it."

"Thoughts on getting us through a gate?" Egil asked.

"Working on it."

Mere's voice sounded through the canvas from behind them. "A gate? We're leaving the city?"

"Aye," Nix said. "If we can. I'll explain as we go."

Mere was quiet for a moment, then said, "I can get us through the gate."

"How?" Egil asked, then, "Mindmagic? Won't that hurt you, Mere?"

"I'll be fine, Egil."

"There," Nix said, and grinned. "Problem solved."

"That's one solved, anyway," Egil said. "Take odds there won't be more?"

••••

A pile of debris in the street caught Rusk's eye, the flutter of loose material in the breeze.

"Wait," he said.

"Wait for what?" Trelgin said, irritated, but the men held up and followed his gaze. What Rusk had first taken for rubbish he now saw for what it was.

"Bodies," he said, and they all hustled over to the two corpses lying in the mud of the street. The shattered wooden remains of what looked like a wall lay under them.

Rusk recognized them right away – guild men. They'd been two of the three eyes on the Tunnel. One had a dagger still lodged in his throat. The other had a snapped neck and broken leg. Rusk looked up at the abandoned, dilapidated building from which they'd probably fallen. The men followed his gaze up to the second floor of the building, muttering angrily.

"I'll check the top of that building," Mors said in his high-pitched voice.

"They ain't up there," Rusk said. "They were just blinding the eyes."

Rusk turned to the Tunnel, windows dark, doors closed. He'd be surprised if it wasn't already abandoned.

"Just left 'em in the street," Varn said, shifting on his feet. "Whoresons."

"There were three men on this duty," Trelgin said.

Rusk nodded. "We'll look for him later. Could be they pinched him, too. Right now, get these two onto the walkway. The mud's no place for our brothers. We'll collect them on our way back and give them the rites later. Meanwhile, throw a pray for 'em."

"We're wasting time," Trelgin hissed.

"No we ain't," Rusk said.

The man quickly gathered their fallen comrades, lifted them out of the mud, and placed them on the walkways, removing the wooden symbols of Aster they wore on lanyards.

Once that was done, Rusk said, "Let's see to this business, yeah?"

"Yeah," all of them echoed.

They stormed up and across the street to the Slick Tunnel, all of them with a blade in one hand and a cocked crossbow in the other. Varn took the door, splintering the bar in two kicks. The rest poured in behind them.

A crash sounded from inside the Tunnel, the crack of splintering wood.

Everyone out back froze. Nix put a finger to his lips.

"That was a door," he whispered to Egil.

"Those slubbers move fast," Egil said. The priest hefted his crossbow, trained it on the back door of the Tunnel.

"What is it?" Mere asked through the canvas.

"They're here," Nix said.

Veraal hurried to the wagon. Tesha followed him.

"Cutting it close," Veraal said softly. "You good?"

"We're good."

"Then good luck," Veraal said. They shook his hand.

Tesha came around to the other side of the wagon where Kiir would not see.

"I want to tell you something," she said to Nix. "Come here."

Nix leaned down and she took his face in her hands and kissed him softly, fully, deeply on the mouth. She tasted of citrus and smoke leaf and Nix was so surprised he barely returned it.

She let him go and smiled. "That's for luck."

Stupefied, he said, "You've made me blush, milady."

"That must be a first," she said.

More crashes from inside. Shouts.

"Get going," he said to her, to all of them.

Veraal nodded and he and his men shepherded Tesha, Kiir, Lis, and Gadd down the street. His men covered their retreat and advance with crossbows. Kiir blew Nix kisses while they moved away, the wind tousling her red hair.

"I think I could die happy right now," Nix said, watching Kiir and Tesha move away from him.

From within the wagon, Rose moaned softly.

"That makes one of us then," Mere said through the canvas. "Now drive this fakkin' wagon."

"Aye," Egil said, and whickered at the mule.

It pricked up its ears, lifted its head, and started off. The wagon creaked and rattled and groaned and Nix figured it could be heard all the way to the Meander.

Tables lay on their sides, blocking the windows.

"They were ready for us," Trelgin said.

"Were," Rusk said, because the common room was now dark and empty. Varn and Mors darted up the stairs, kicked in doors, shouted for anyone there to come out. Varn's voice carried down the stairs.

"There's no one up here!"

"These boys ain't stupid," Trelgin said.

Rusk heard the roll of wagon wheels over the cobblestones of Tannery Row.

"Maybe a whisker slow, though," he said, and sprinted for the back door. "Come on!"

He bounded over the bar and through the back door and through a storage room, his men hard on his heels. He burst through a back door to the fenced grounds behind the inn. A gate was thrown open and he ran through it, out onto Tannery Row. A covered wagon rumbled down the street, heading west.

"That's them! Shoot the mule!"

"Shite," Nix said, standing on the driver's bench and watching behind them. The dying street torches of Tannery Row provided scant light, but they provided enough. Nix saw a half-dozen or more shadowy figures run through the Tunnel's gate and sprint down the street after them, closing the distance with the slow moving wagon. One of them stopped to take aim.

"Lay flat back there!" Nix said to Rose and Mere. "Crossbows!"

A bolt whistled wide of the wagon.

"How many?" Egil asked.

"Eight, I think," Nix said. "Maybe nine. They hit the mule and we're done."

With Rose and the Upright Man unable to move, they'd never escape on foot.

Egil slapped the reins on the mule. "Hyah!"

The wagon lurched, nearly dislodging Nix, as the mule picked up its pace.

"Hyah, mule! Hyah!"

Another bolt whistled past. The mule snorted. The wagon bounced and jostled over Dur Follin's streets.

Under Nix's feet, Channis groaned.

"Why does everything have to happen at once?" Nix muttered.

He balanced himself, took aim with the crossbow as best he could in the bouncing wagon, and let fly. He didn't drop any of the men, but he heard them shout in alarm, so he must have come close enough for them to hear the bolt.

He turned around and sat on the bench to recock the crossbow. Channis groaned again.

"Stick to the paved streets, yeah?" He said to Egil. "We don't want to get stuck in the slop."

"Aye," Egil said. "Hyah!"

The mule showed more grit than they'd expected. It was no cavalry charger, but it moved at a good trot and showed no signs of fatigue.

Channis hissed, the sound vaguely bestial. His hand twitched.

"Keep your eye on him," Nix said, nodding at the Upright Man.

Nix stood up on the bench, legs bent, looked back, and took aim. The men hadn't closed any more distance with the wagon. The mule was holding its own and the guild men would tire before the mule.

"A little more from that mule and we'll outrun them!" Nix said over his shoulder.

"Hyah!" Egil said, and slapped the reins. The mule snorted, put its head down, and picked up its gait. Nix feared the pace would cause them to throw a wheel or snap an axle but they had no choice.

The twang of a crossbow sounded from the back of the wagon – Mere firing out the back. The men responded with more shouts of alarm. Nix fired again, eliciting more curses but hitting nothing. The pursuers reloaded as best they could on the run, firing mid-sprint. For several blocks it went that way, the men sprinting after, firing when they could, Nix and Mere returning fire, Nix praying to gods he didn't trust that a bolt wouldn't find a home in the mule's hide.

"Stubborn fakkers, I'll give them that!" Nix said, reloading.

Egil had to slow the wagon to take a turn onto the Serpentine and the pursuers gained some ground. A crossbow bolt whistled past Nix's ear.

"You shooting at us or the damned mule," he muttered. He settled his aim, picked one of the closing figures, and released, grinning as his target stumbled and fell to the road. The pursuers shouted, cursed, slowed.

Having rounded the turn, Egil goaded the mule back up to speed and they started to outdistance their pursuers. The men slowed further and finally halted, several of them turning back to help their fallen man. Nix watched until they were out of sight, then turned and sat back on the bench.

"We lost them," Nix said to Mere and Egil.

"We're not out of the city yet," Egil said. "Mere, you all right?"

"I'm all right," she answered through the wagon's cover.

"I'm thinking one of the fish gates, Egil," Nix said. "Any of them. We get through, we steal a boat, we're off. Mere, you have to get us through the Night Watch."

"I know," she said.

"How's Rose?" Nix asked.

"The same."

••••

Rusk and Trelgin and the men stood in the street over Mors, hands on their knees, gasping. Mors clutched his shoulder where a crossbow bolt had winged him.

"Shallow," he said, pressing on the bleeding wound. "Nothing to it."

Trelgin glared at Rusk. "I thought we agreed no shots. We could hit the Upright Man by mistake."

Rusk could only hope. "We can't stop them with curses, Trelgin. If the Man's conscious, he'd know enough to lay low. And if he's not conscious, he's flat in that wagon. The shots were rightly taken. If we'd dropped that mule, we'd have them."

Trelgin and his men stood on one side of Mors, Rusk and his men on the other, both groups eyeing the other darkly, things unsaid hanging in the air between them.

"What now, then, *Seventh Blade*?" Trelgin asked, making the title an insult, spraying spit in the process.

"You notice the direction they're heading?" Rusk asked.

Trelgin's droopy expression fell further. Rusk delighted in making the man feel a fool.

"The docks," Rusk said. "The Meander. My guess, they're piking for a boat. We've got eyes out there, yeah? Then let's move." He looked at Mors. "You good to keep up?"

Varn lifted the bald mouse to his feet.

"I'm good," Mors said.

They'd lost their pursuers, but Egil didn't slow. The rickety wagon made more noise than a street festival, but speed seemed more important than stealth. The mule was lathered, chest heaving, but it kept up the pace.

The streets widened and smoothed as they moved west through the city. Of course, moving west brought them back toward the guild house, so Nix stayed on edge, crossbow at the ready. He expected dozens of guild men to stream out of every alley.

He glanced down at Channis. The guild master's eyes were open and now both were as black as the moonless night sky, split only by yellow, vertical slits. Channis stared unblinking up at the stars, his expression slack. He had a vacancy to him that Nix found unnerving. Nix nudged him with his toe but Channis made no response. Even so, Nix leaned down and showed Channis a dagger.

"Move or speak and you die. Hells, irritate me and you may die. I'm in a mood."

Channis made no sign he'd heard or understood.

"He's awake?" Egil asked, his eyes scanning the road ahead, the alleys, the rooftops. The Archbridge came into view as they moved west, its stone arch rising above the cityscape.

"Sort of," Nix said. He stripped off his cloak and covered Channis with it. "Not sure if he's much more than alive, though."

Egil slowed the wagon as they approached the short wall that blocked off the piers and docks from the rest of Dur Follin. The smell of fish and earth and organic decay thickened the air.

Three gates – the fish gates, as most of Dur Follin called them; the tax gates, as fishermen called them – dotted the wall at intervals, allowing passage into the rest of the city. Only one of them would be manned at this hour. The others would be locked shut. During the day fisherman who wanted to bring their catch to the

fish market on Mandin Way had to come through one
of the fish gates and pay their tax. The Lord Mayor was
nothing if not an excellent revenuer.

Beyond the wall and gates were piers and docks
and berths of all sizes, some new, most old and rickety,
and beyond them, the dark, slow, eternal waters of
the Meander. Barrels, sacks, crates, and other cargo sat
in stacks and piles here and there on the docks. Boats
bobbed in the water beside piers. Most were the small,
wide fishing boats common in Dur Follin, but a few one
and two-masted shallow-hulled sailing ships were tied off
here and there. Glowing lanterns hung on dock posts and
boat prows. To the left were the municipal docks, where
the city's meager navy tied-off. Two tall, two-masted
carracks creaked in the water there. Even at the late
hour, a few sailors staggered along the pier, arm in arm,
while others worked in the rigging or on the deck of their
ships. Normally the docks were thronged with sailors,
merchants, and fisherman, but the in-between hour had
caught the wharfs in a quiet moment. Nix was glad for it.

The road they rolled led toward the northernmost fish
gate, the only one lit with lanterns, and so the only one
currently manned with watchmen. The wooden gate
was closed and latched, of course, and two members
of the Watch, their orange tabards visible at a distance,
emerged from the small guard shelter built into the wall.
Both stretched and stifled yawns as they stepped onto
the street. Any guard posted to the Night Watch was
either new or had somehow run afoul of their sergeant.
The men looked young to Nix, so probably the former.
They stepped before the gate and awaited the wagon,
blades sheathed, questions in their tired eyes.

"Ready, Mere?" Nix said through the canvas.

"Yes."

Nix put on his best false smile as the wagon pulled to a halt. He put a boot on Channis.

"Goodeve," he said to the watchmen.

A watchman moved to either side of the wagon, hands on their blades. The one, tall and thin, had a receding chin and looked barely old enough to shave. The other, similarly young, wore an oversized helm, had a thin mustache and beard, and shifted nervously on his feet. Both had crossbows slung over their backs.

"Goodeve," the thin one said. His voice was nasal. "Odd hour to be driving the streets."

"Aye," said the other.

Mere's mental voice sounded in Nix's head.

They're delivering netting. The wagon is filled with netting.

"Aye, indeed. Apologies for the hour," Nix said. He jerked at thumb at the rear of the wagon. "We're delivering netting. Needed to get here well before dawn."

The watchmen near Nix opened his mouth but said nothing, merely stood there with his jaw open, waiting for words to fill it. He blinked and his arms went slack at his side. His gaze went vacant.

It's important that the netting gets through. The wagon is filled with netting.

"It's important that we get this through right now," Nix said. "For the morning launch. You understand."

The man blinked, closed his mouth, nodded slowly. Nix thought that would be that and the guards would let them pass but the young watchman's gaze cleared and fell to Nix's blades, the crossbow, Egil's hammers, the brown smears of blood covering Egil's arms. A question entered his eyes and his brow furrowed with it. He reached for his blade.

Not your concern, Nix heard from Mere. *Not your concern. Not your concern.*

"This?" Nix said, putting a hand on his falchion. "Hardly know how to use it, but you can't be too careful, yeah?"

Not your concern, Mere projected. Let them through. Not your concern. Let them through.

"We're really in a hurry," Nix said. "If you could just let us through…"

The vacancy in the man's eyes uncomfortably reminded Nix of the look in Channis's eyes. The watchmen slowly lifted a hand and put a finger to his nose. It came away bloody.

"Let them through," he said, his voice a monotone. "Let them through, Eston."

"Aye," said the other man in a similar monotone. "Not our concern."

A line of blood ran from his nose down to his thin mustache and into his mouth. He seemed not to notice. He turned, plodded to the gate, unlatched it, and swung it open.

"Obliged," Nix said with a nod, as they started forward.

The guard opened his mouth to speak but instead gave a surprised gasp, pitched sidewise, and fell flat on his face in the street. A crossbow bolt stuck from his back.

Nix cursed, followed its trajectory back to the direction from which it had come and saw two men running down the Serpentine toward them, both with crossbows in hand.

"Go, Egil!" Nix said, and leaped off the wagon.

"Where are you going?" Egil called.

"Just go!"

Egil snapped the reins and the wagon rumbled through the wooden gate. Merelda parted the cover in the rear of the wagon, leaned out and took aim. She, too, had a line of blood running down from her nose.

"You all right?" Nix asked her.

She ignored him and fired past him at the onrushing men. She hit neither, but they must have heard the shot streak past them, for they cursed and separated, but kept on charging. Nix grabbed a fistful of the young watchman's tabard and pulled him through the gate after the wagon.

"Come on, slubber!"

The man fumbled with his crossbow, his dull eyes on the guild men, his motions and thinking obviously still slowed by the aftereffects of Merelda's mind magic. Nix shoved him forward and he stumbled and fell. Meanwhile Nix pulled the gate shut behind them and latched it. There was a thunk as a bolt sank into the wood of the gate.

"Get out of here!" Nix said to the watchman and pushed him along. "Wait!"

The man turned and Nix snatched the whistle all watchmen wore on a lanyard around their neck.

"Sorry. Now go."

Nix didn't wait to see if he obeyed. He sprinted after the still-moving wagon and leaped back onto it.

"That'll delay them a moment."

"What is that?" Egil asked.

"This? A whistle."

"Why do you have a whistle?"

"Why do you ask these questions?"

Egil shrugged.

Nix said, "We need a decent boat."

"Where are we even going?" Mere called from the rear.

Nix hesitated only a moment. "The Deadmire."

Egil shook his head and muttered.

Mere had the good sense not to dispute with him, but she also had the good sense to unleash a string of curses. The Deadmire had a dark reputation.

Nix scanned the piers and docks for a likely boat. The needed something wide, with a shallow draw, oared not sailed, ideally something with some gear stowed aboard.

Mere's shout sounded from behind. "They're through the gate! More than just the two now!"

Several fishermen's boats were tied off on a long, solidly-built pier to their left. He pointed.

"There, Egil! We take one of those!"

Egil pulled on the reins, turned the sweating mule. Nix was aware of eyes on them from various places along the pier, sailors up early or late tending to rigging or cleaning decks, some returning from a night of drinking, others sitting on a pier or dock. He hoped the watchman from the fish gate didn't have time to gather any of his fellows.

Nix stood up on the bench and looked back. He counted eight guild men running through the gate, all with blades or crossbows in their fists. Merelda's crossbow twanged and one of the guild men in the front stumbled and fell.

A couple "huzzahs" sounded from the watching sailors.

"Nice shot, Mere!" Nix said.

The mule balked at traversing the pier and its sudden stop almost knocked Nix off the bench.

"Hyah!" Egil said. "Hyah!"

Still the mule didn't move.

"Shite!" Nix said.

"They're closing," Mere said, and her crossbow sang again.

Cursing, Egil jumped off the bench, went around to the front of the mule, grabbed it by the bridle, and dragged it forward.

"Move, you stubborn fakking thing!"

Nix stood, turned, and fired. He didn't hit anyone that he could see. He should've just used his damned sling. He was no good with a crossbow.

The mule snorted and tried to pull back but Egil held fast, the veins and sinew standing out on his arm, and finally the creature relented and started down the pier. Egil hustled back to the bench, hopped up, and slapped the reins. The mule picked up its pace, the wagon's wheels thumping and bouncing and vibrating as they ran over the wooden beams of the long pier.

"Right next to that boat there!" Nix said, cocking his crossbow and laying a bolt in its groove. He rose and shot back at the onrushing men.

"Thrice damned thing," he said, and threw the crossbow into the drink.

He drew a dagger and slit the cover of the wagon behind the driver's bench.

Rose lay under her blankets, nestled between the hay bales, eyes closed, body bouncing with each bump of the wagon. A pained furrow linked her eyes, as if she were dreaming of pain. Mere crouched in the rear of the wagon, reloading her crossbow.

"Forget that!" Nix called to her. "Get ready to move!"

She ignored him, took her final shot at the onrushing crowd of men, and crawled back up to the front of the wagon.

"Help me get Rose," Nix said. "And get the bags of food Gadd left us. Leave the barrels."

Seemed a shame to leave Gadd's ale behind, but there was nothing for it. Together, he and Mere lifted Rose from the wagon. They turned her and Nix got her under the armpits. Once Nix had a good grip, Mere grabbed the bags of bread and foodstuffs Gadd had provided them.

Rose moaned in Nix's arms, then chuckled and said, "Him? I played dice with him. Easy chub to cog."

"What did she say?" Mere said

"She doesn't know what she's saying," Nix said.

"Almost there," Egil said, his voice tense.

"You get Channis," Nix said to him.

"Get him? We don't need him anymore," Egil said.

"Yes we do," Nix said. "At least till we get totally clear of the wharfs. Why do you think they're not firing?"

"They have been firing!"

"Strays," Nix said. "Or they were aiming for the mule. Trust me, Egil. Bring him!"

Egil pulled up the reins to stop the wagon.

"Quickly now!" Nix said, and he and Mere hefted Rose out of the wagon. Egil heaved Channis up, slung him over his shoulder, and leaped down from the wagon.

Shouting from behind drew Nix's attention. The guild men were sprinting toward them, almost to the pier.

"Stop!" one of them shouted.

An idea occurred to Nix.

"Egil, take Rose, too! That boat there. Go." He gave Mere one of his many daggers. "Mere, cut it free and go."

"What?"

"Go. I'm right behind you."

Egil maneuvered himself into position and slid Rose onto his other shoulder then plodded toward the boat Nix had indicated. Meanwhile, Nix grabbed the mule's bridle and hurriedly turned the wagon around as best he could on the narrow pier.

The guild men had reached the pier. They stormed down it, a long-haired fakker almost as big as Egil – the droopy faced Committeeman – in the lead, blade bare.

"Stop and it'll go easier on you!" one of those in the second rank said.

"Fak you, you bunch of ugly bungholes," Nix muttered, and slapped the mule on the hindquarters, hard. "Hyah!"

The mule snorted and lurched forward.

"Hyah! Hyah!"

The mule's lurch turned into a trot, the wagon bouncing and jostling back along the pier. The guild men saw it coming, saw their danger, went wide-eyed and pulled up.

Nix didn't bother to watch. He turned, ran, and leaped into the boat, which was starting to pull away from the dock. Egil caught him while the wide boat bobbed from the sudden weight.

Nix glanced back to see a few of the guild men driven into the drink by the wagon, though most managed to slip aside and narrowly avoid getting knocked off the pier. Those who hadn't fallen ran for the boat, shouting and cursing, but they were too late. The boat was away. Nix stood and gave them a fak-you-finger.

Applause, whistles, and a few cheers went up from the dozen or so sailors and dockworkers who'd watched the entire affair. Nix offered them a small bow.

"A bit early for bows, isn't it?" Egil said.

"You think?"

Egil had the rower's bench and set to in earnest, his powerful arms pulling at the oars and causing the shallow boat to move quickly through the water. Channis lay in the center of the boat on his back, his dark, vacant eyes staring up at the dark sky. Mere sat on the bow bench cradling Rose.

The guild men stood on the edge of the pier, shouting. Those who hadn't been driven into the drink, that is.

CHAPTER TWELVE

"Shoot them," Rusk ordered, and managed not to make himself sound eager. The boat with Egil and Nix was already well out into the river.

"Seventh Blade?" one of Trelgin's men asked.

"Don't!" Trelgin said, fumbling for something in an inner pocket of his cloak. "You'll hit the Upright Man!"

"He's down in the boat," Rusk said, not knowing if that was true. "Those slubbers have been using him as cover long enough. Shoot them and do it fakking now! Who knows where they're going or what they intend." He looked at the men, his face twisted in anger. "I said *shoot them*."

The men took knees, cocked, loaded, and took aim.

Trelgin cursed but did not gainsay the order. He did, however, remove one of the guild's small dowsing rods from his cloak. The forked stick of ivory was inlaid with silver glyphs.

Now it was Rusk's turn to curse, though he kept it in his head and not on his lips.

Nix cursed as the guild men fell to their knees and took aim.

"These slubbers can't make up their minds. Shoot, don't shoot." He cupped his hands over his mouth and shouted, "Stick with something, you bungholes!"

One of them pointed something that looked like a stick or wand at them. Nix recognized it.

"Shite. Faster, Egil!"

The priest set to with a purpose and the boat fairly skipped over the water.

A bolt sizzled over Nix's head. Another hit and stuck into the rear of the boat.

Over his shoulder, he said to Mere, "Lay flat with Rose! Flat in the bottom, Mere!"

Merelda slid off the bench and lay flat with her sister in the shallow bottom of the wide boat. She wrapped her arms around her Rose, protecting her with her body.

Egil ducked his head low but could hardly take cover and still row. Nix positioned himself in the boat's aft, shielding his friend as best he could with his body. Another bolt hit his satchel and stuck there.

"That's my satchel, you fakkers! You don't shoot a man's gear!"

He tore it loose and cast it into the Meander. Some of the sailors watching hooted and whistled.

A beam of sickly yellow light spiraled from the wand and snaked over the water at them. Nix recognized it the moment he saw it and cursed, but the beam fell short of the boat and fizzled.

Over his shoulder he said, "Fast would be good, Egil."

"That was a dowsing rod, yeah?" the priest asked.

"Yeah."

"A what?" Mere asked.

"The guild buys enchanted items from the wizards of the Conclave."

"Wizards," Egil said with a contemptuous grunt, then to Nix, "Why don't you buy your damned gewgaws from the Conclave instead of the bazaar?"

"Because the one is filled with lowlife, thieves, backbiters, and murderers. The other is the Bazaar."

Egil chuckled, but another bolt whistled overhead, narrowly missing him, and cut his laughter short.

"Damn it! Use the Upright Man!" Egil barked.

Nix should've thought of that.

"I'm using the Upright Man for cover!" Nix shouted back at the pier, then maneuvered himself past Egil, rocking the entire boat in the process. He grabbed the Upright Man by the shoulders. "We're using the Upright Man for cover, you stupid faks! And you're all bad shots! And ugly, too!"

Channis felt cold in his grasp, limp, and with his glassy black eyes he reminded Nix of a dead fish. His skin felt odd, rough. Nix feared he might have died but had no time to check. Grunting, he dragged him back across the rower's bench, nearly flipping the boat again, and took position on the rear bench, between the guild men and Egil. He positioned the limp form of the Upright Man as best he could, wearing the fakker like a bad cloak.

"Let's see if your men are interested in giving you a few new holes," he said to Channis, then, to the guild men, "Here he is, fakkers! Fire away!"

"Hold," Rusk said, and tried to keep disappointment from his voice.

They'd all heard the smaller slubber, Nix, claim to be using the Upright Man for cover. Rusk couldn't keep up the fire after that.

"You get him?" he asked Trelgin, who held one of the guild's dowsing rods at his side.

Trelgin's droopy face drooped further. "No. Too far out."

"Can any of you handle a boat?" Rusk asked the men. Heads shook and Rusk feigned disappointment. "They're away, then."

He'd just let them go and hope they killed Channis. Meanwhile, as Seventh Blade, he'd be the highest-ranking member of the Committee in Dur Follin. No one could say he hadn't done all he could have done and–"

"I can hit them with the rod from the bridge," Trelgin said. "Attune it there. Hells, I would've thought you'd have brought one of these yourself, Rusk. Just an oversight, I'm sure."

Rusk cursed inwardly but kept his face expressionless. "There's an idea, Trelgin."

He glanced out over the river. The small boat was nearly lost in the darkness, heading for the Archbridge.

"Let's go," Rusk said and started back down the pier at a run. Trelgin and the men followed him at a sprint.

"Come on!" Trelgin said, shouting at Varn and the handful of men who'd been driven into the river by the wagon. They were even then crawling up the rocks to the shore. "Run, you bunghole slubbers! To the bridge!"

The soaking men fell in and all of them pelted along the wharf. Sailors jeered and taunted them as they ran. Ahead rose the huge arc of the Archbridge. Rusk might have been the fastest of them, but he did not set the

pace. He merely kept up, hoping they'd be too late, that
Egil and Nix would be out of range of the dowsing rod.

Each stride summoned a grunt of pain from Mors and
his wounded shoulder, but he kept pace. Those who had
fallen into the river sloshed in wet boots and shed wet
tunics and shirts as they ran.

The guild's dowsing rods – one type of many enchanted
items the Committee'd had made for them by sorcerers
of the Conclave – could track a person or item more or
less unerringly, but first it had to be attuned to them.

"Faster!" Trelgin said, his gasps wet and sloppy
through his floppy mouth. "Faster!"

They eyed the water as they ran, but the docked boats
and darkness kept Egil and Nix from view. Rusk kept
hoping maybe they'd just cross to the other side of the
river and hole up in west Dur Follin, but he doubted
it. His luck didn't seem to be running that way. They'd
make for the bridge, Trelgin would get the wand attuned
to them, and Rusk would be obliged to continue the
game still longer.

He considered simply getting square with Trelgin,
making a deal in which they abandoned Channis, Rusk
took over as de facto Upright Man and Trelgin stepped in
as a well-treated and well-compensated Seventh Blade.
But looking at the intensity on Trelgin's face, he knew an
offer like that would just get Rusk killed. Trelgin would
do every damned thing he could to avoid becoming
Seventh, and if Rusk made a compromising offer, Trelgin
would betray him, spill the offer to the others, get Rusk
killed, and take the Eighth Blade for himself.

Rusk saw nothing to do but what he was doing – sprint
along Dur Follin's wharves in the small, dark hours, and

pretend that he wanted to rescue a man he desperately wanted dead.

By the time they reached the Archbridge, they'd left Mors and his wounded shoulder behind. The bridge, wider than any of Dur Follin's streets save the Promenade, extended before them, reaching across the Meander, connecting eastern and western Dur Follin, linking poor and rich, old and new. Low walls and ancient custom divided the bridge into narrow walkways on the left and right sides, with a wider, central way. By tradition wagons and carts and horses used the center way, while pedestrians used the southern walkway.

The northern walkway, meanwhile, was covered in a swirl of tents and makeshift shrines along the entire length of the Archbridge, all of them belonging to squatter cults too small or obscure to fill a proper temple. Even at the odd hour the smell of incense filled the air, as did the occasional ring of chimes and bells and gongs and chants.

Rusk and Trelgin and the men, already gasping and sweating, assayed the bridge. The wind fought them and Varn fell away, unable to keep up.

Cultists of various godlings and religious movements, perhaps preparing for the dawn, eyed them in surprise as they passed. Rusk caught blurry images of tonsured heads, tattooed arms, colorful robes and vestments.

A third of the way up, Trelgin veered right and darted between two tents, in the process knocking down a wrinkled, bald cultist in yellow pantaloons and a blousy shirt who tended a kettle of something on a small brazier. The tiny man cursed Trelgin in a language Rusk didn't understand. Trelgin ignored him and leaned over the side of the bridge, peering down at the river, the dowsing rod clutched in one fist.

"See them?" Rusk called, dreading the answer.

Trelgin didn't shout back but ducked down, his back to the ledge. He wore a grin, half droop, half teeth.

"Here they come,' he said, and the rest of them ducked low and crept up to the edge.

Nix watched the guild men run back down the pier toward the Archbridge. He stood in the boat and tried to keep his eyes on them, but the boat sat so low in the water that his line of sight was blocked by piers, docked boats, and stacks of cargo.

"Can't see them," he said.

"They'll head for the bridge," Egil said.

"Beat them there, then," Nix said.

Egil nodded, maneuvered them out to the middle of the Meander then turned the small boat downriver, pulling at the oars with long, powerful strokes. Nix let Channis's body slouch in the rear of the boat – trying not to stare at the man's dark, open eyes – and took stock of the gear they'd managed to bring.

Other than their weapons and a fraction of the rations Gadd had prepared for them, they had little. The boat contained a coil of line, a net, and a large canvas tarp. Nix could turn the tarp into shelter once they reached the Deadmire, but on the whole they were ill-equipped for any kind of expedition, much less one into a haunted swamp.

Egil read his thoughts. "We're short the usual gear."

"Aye," Nix said. "We'll have to manage, though."

In truth he and Egil had survived on minimal gear in many different situations. The priest in particular was a skilled outdoorsman.

"Can't stop now, though," Mere said. "We started, we finish."

"Aye," Nix said.

Rose suddenly sat up, her eyes distant, and said, "What am I doing on this bum boat?"

Mere put a hand on Rose's back. "Rose, sit back. We're going for help."

Rose sneered, the expression unfamiliar to her face. She pointed with her chin at Egil and Nix. "From these two slubbers?"

"Rose…" Mere said.

Rose's eyes cleared and her expression returned to normal. "Mere?" She glanced around. "Where are we?"

"We're on the Meander. We're going to the… to get you help."

"I've heard of a mindmage who lives in the Deadmire," Nix said. "Mere said a true mindmage could help you."

"Maybe," Rose said. She put her palm on her brow. "Maybe. There's a mindmage in the Deadmire?"

"Maybe," Egil said.

"Maybe?" Mere said, appalled. "What do you mean, 'maybe'?"

"Maybe's all we have unless you think Rose can withstand a month's journey to Oremal. Odrhaal's a legend, Mere, a rumor, but… I believe he's there."

Mere cursed. Rose groaned and took Mere's attention from Nix, for which Nix was grateful.

"Legend or no, it won't matter if we don't get clear," Egil said, heaving at the oars. "No boats in pursuit. But here comes the bridge."

Nix had already cocked Egil's crossbow, but he unloaded it and set it aside for his sling. At least with the sling he'd have a shot at hitting something.

"They won't shoot," Nix said, hoping to make it true by saying it.

"Maybe not with crossbows, but they will with that rod."

Nix didn't dispute that point. He sat in the bow, his sling and a few lead bullets ready to hand, as they neared the Archbridge. He scanned the wharf, as much as he could see, the edge of the bridge, but saw nothing. He eyed the water around them for boats. Still none.

They all fell silent as Egil pulled them closer to the monumental rise of the Archbridge. Nix had spent his entire life in Dur Follin and the scale of the bridge still awed him. It looked as though it had fallen out of the Three Heavens, like a holdover from another world, a world too large and well-made and – he admitted it to himself – too beautiful, for the otherwise small, dirty, ramshackle world of Ellerth.

At its apex, the arch soared a long bowshot above the smooth waters of the Meander. Many people had leaped from the apex over the years, the despondent or sick, perhaps wanting to fly for a few moments from the largest thing they'd ever seen before the Meander shattered their bodies and ended their pain.

Makeshift shrines and tents covered the walkway on the near side of the bridge – the whole of it sarcastically named the Road to the Heavenly Spheres. The colorful lanterns and paper lamps that hung from the bridge's edge looked like a line of will o' the wisps. The street of shrines was gaudy by day, but had a certain loveliness to it when seen from the water under cover of night.

Nix thanked all those ridiculous gods for the lanterns and lights. If he had any chance to spot the guild men, he'd owe it to the lanterns. He slipped a lead ball into the pouch of his sling, let it dangle loose in his hand.

Chimes rang in the night breeze, the soft sounds drifting down from above like ethereal music. Massive stone posts jutted from the waters to support the arch, the thick beams like the arms of a submerged god determined, even in death, to keep the bridge from sinking into the water. Graffiti covered the posts above the water line. Rumor had the posts hollow, filled with ancient rooms and treasure and devices secreted there by the ancient race who'd left the Archbridge as their legacy. Nix figured he'd test that rumor one day.

Nix caught a suggestion of movement along the stone rail of the bridge, a head popping up to peer over and then back down again. He couldn't be sure it was the guild men.

"I think I see them," he said. He loaded a lead ball into the pouch on his sling, swung it loosely at his side. Egil drew harder on the oars. The bridge loomed over them, painting the sky with its stone arc.

The head popped up again, lingered for a time. Another joined it. Another. Then they all went down out of sight.

"That's them," Nix said. He whirled the sling over his head, the weapon humming in his grasp. He waited, waited...

Three figures rose up over the edge. The distance and the darkness prevented Nix from seeing which of them was holding the wand, so he picked one at random and let fly. The lead ball flew true and one of the heads snapped back and disappeared. The other two disappeared for a moment but returned quickly, standing up fully, one of them leveling the wand at Nix.

"Shite!" Nix said, dropping another ball into his sling pouch and spinning it up to speed. "'Ware!"

The yellow beam from the wand forked down from the bridge like a bolt of lightning, straight at Nix. Nix dove forward, landing in Egil's lap, and the bolt missed him, striking the bottom of the boat. He pushed himself off Egil so the priest could renew rowing. He'd lost his sling bullet in the scrum, so he reloaded the pouch, but before he could fire, Egil had them under the bridge and out of sight of the guild men.

"Shite," Nix said. "Mere, you all right? Rose?"

"I'm fine," Mere said. "Rose is all right, too."

Nix said, "They're going to try to hit us with that wand when we clear the bridge on the other side."

"Aye," Egil said. "We could fight the current, go back, debark on the western bank. Get out of the city during the day, when the river's crowded."

Nix looked across the river to the western bank, with its finished stone buildings, municipal towers, the manses of the nobility, the temples. Rose spoke from the front of the boat, her voice small, but the tone and cadence her own.

"I don't know how much longer I have."

"That seals it then," said Nix.

"Aye," Egil agreed. "We'd probably run afoul of the Watch on the west bank anyway. We go, then. Ready?"

"Ready," Nix and Mere said.

••••

"Other side," Trelgin said. "Not you," he said to one of the men. "Keep an eye and make sure they don't try to sneak back out the way they came. Current would lose a fight with that priest."

"Aye," the man said, still rubbing his shoulder from where he'd taken a sling bullet.

Rusk, Trelgin, and the rest of the men dashed across the bridge, leaping the low walls that divided its sections. When they reached the other side, all of them leaned over the waist-high rail and looked out and down on smooth waters that looked like black glass.

"I don't see 'em," one of the men said softly.

"Me either," said another.

"Not out yet," said Trelgin.

A Watch whistle sounded from back on the wharves. Another sounded from elsewhere along the piers. A third.

"Orangies comin'," said Varn, who'd finally caught back up with them.

The wharf would be thick with Watch soon. They'd bought off plenty of Watch sergeants, but Rusk would just as soon avoid the hassle if he could. They'd have to head to the west side of Dur Follin and make their way back to the east with the day's traffic.

"We need to move," Rusk said.

"Not yet," Trelgin said, eyeing the water and holding the wand.

The whistles sounded again and Rusk grabbed Trelgin by the arm and whirled him around.

"We're leaving," Rusk said.

Trelgin's lazy mouth twisted up in a snarl but before he could speak one of the other men hissed, "There they are."

PAUL S KEMP   259

Rusk could not hide his frown and Trelgin could not
hide his smile. The Sixth Blade turned back to the edge,
rod pointed.

"Mere, I need you to shoot at them, too" Nix said. "Aim
for the one with the rod. Just try to keep him down. If
we can get out of range of that rod, he won't be able to
attune it. Then we're clear."

Egil fought the slow moving current and kept them
under the span of the Archbridge while Mere took up
her crossbow, cocked, and loaded.

"Ready?" Nix asked her. She nodded. "As fast as you
can, Egil. Go."

The priest grunted as he pulled at the oars and the
boat rapidly picked up speed. Nix started to spin his sling
over his head as the underside of the Archbridge passed
over them. Mere crouched in the front of the boat.

As they cleared the edge of the Archbridge, Nix spun
his sling rapidly over his head, ready to loose a shot.
Egil worked the oars hard and the boat cut through the
water. Nix looked up along the edge of the bridge but
without the lanterns and lamps of the cultists to light it,
he could see very little.

"See anything?" he asked Mere.

"No," she said softly.

The yellow, jagged beam of the rod cut through the air
between the bridge and the boat. Nix didn't have time
to curse before it struck the front part of the boat. He
loosed his sling bullet in answer, heard Mere's crossbow
twang, but had no idea if either of them hit anything.
Egil kept at the oars, opening the space between them
and the bridge.

"Did it hit you?" Nix shouted at Mere.

"No," she said, and Nix breathed a short-lived sigh of relief. "But I think it hit Rose."

Nix crawled over the Upright Man, past Egil on the bench, and to the front of the boat. Rose lay on her side, curled up in the bottom of the boat, eyes closed. Her hands and face were wan, as pale as a spirit. Mere hovered over her, her short, dark hair wet on her head, the crossbow still in her hand.

Nix held his hands over Rose's skin, palms down.

"What are you doing?" Mere asked.

Nix had the ability to feel lingering enchantments. He wasn't unique but he knew from his time at the Conclave that the gift was rare.

His skin warmed and the hair on his arms stood on end. He put his hand on Rose's cheek. She murmured something in slurred cant.

"Shite," he said softly.

"They got her?" Mere said.

"They got her," Nix said.

"What did it do to her?" Mere asked, alarm in her tone. "What does it mean?"

"It didn't hurt her," Nix said. "But she's attuned to the rod."

"It means they can follow us," Egil said.

Nix glanced back at the bridge, up at the rail. He could see nothing in the darkness, but he knew the guild men were there, and he knew they'd be coming.

"Got 'em," Trelgin said. The sigils carved into the rod glowed with a soft yellow glow. "Got 'em, boys."

The men nodded and grinned.

A headache lodged in Rusk's right temple and each beat of his heart sent a stab of pain through his head. He fought down a nearly overwhelming impulse to grab Trelgin and pitch him over the side of the Archbridge.

"You look displeased, Seventh Blade," Trelgin said to him, his eyes sly in the running wax of his droopy face. "We'll be able to follow them now, get the Man back unharmed."

"Aye," Rusk said, though it came out half-snarl.

Trelgin turned toward the water, holding the dowsing rod by each end of its fork. He spoke a word of power – taught to the guild by one of the Conclave's wizards – to activate it. The sigils pulsed as he held it and even Rusk could see the rod pull against his hold, following the direction the boat had taken.

"Which one did you get?" Varn asked. "The Upright Man?"

Trelgin shrugged and slipped the rod back into his tunic. "Don't know, but we've got a way to track at least the one. Unless they split, that means we can track them all. We need a team and a boat. We'll have the Upright Man back quicklike. He'll be generous to everyone who worked the job, don't you think Rusky?"

"Yeah," Rusk lied. He tried to sabotage the pursuit as best he could. "We can't spare many men for this. Just a few good blades."

"I plan to see it through all the way," Trelgin said. "So me, Mors, and Varn. You ain't gotta come, Rusky. Maybe you got work to do in town, yeah?"

Earlier in the day Rusk had been Seventh Blade to a vicious bunghole of an Eighth Blade and he'd seen no way out of the situation. But now he did see a way out, and he had no intention of letting it get away.

"No, I'm in," Rusk said. "With Kherne and Dool."

Trelgin's eyes widened at that. Kherne and Dool were men loyal to Channis from way back and Rusk knew that quite well. But he figured however things landed, they'd look better if he hadn't manned the group half with his own people.

"We'll have to take boats," Rusk said.

"Boats?" Mors asked.

Rusk nodded. "They're in a boat, and we can't get caught flat. We may need to cross the river. Could be they'll just drift down current a bit then cross over and run east. Then it's a foot race."

"I'll see to the boats, then," Mors said. "I know some smugglers work with the guild. They've got those small riverboats. I'll make them tithe two."

"Good," Rusk said, then to Varn, "Get some gear and rations and get it in the boats. A week's worth anyway."

"A week?" Trelgin asked, an accusation behind the question. "Could take longer than that."

"A week," Rusk said, squaring up to him. "We ain't chasing them all over Ellerth. We run them down within a few days or we turn the dowsing rod over to some blades-for-hire and let them get it done."

Trelgin puffed out his chest. "And I say we keep after until it's done."

"Then you'll keep it up on your own," Rusk snapped. "I've got a guild to run until Channis returns."

"*If* he returns," Trelgin said, his tone that of a man who thought he'd made a point.

"That's right. If."

Trelgin slurped to keep from drooling. "Hoping that tat grows an eighth blade, Rusky?"

"If it does," Rusk said. "Aster's likely to call you to be my Seventh Blade. Remember that, yeah?"

Trelgin tried to sneer but it came out a grimace.

Rusk had made his point. "Leg it, men. We need to get on the water as soon as we can."

Egil kept at the oars for a long while. Nix remained tense until they'd left the Archbridge and Dur Follin's crumbling stone walls in the darkness behind them.

"I think we're clear," Nix said.

"Of the city," Egil said, resting on the rower's bench, breath coming hard. The slow current of the river pulled the boat down the river. "But not the guild."

"You think they'll follow us into the Deadmire?"

"You already know the answer," Egil said. "They hit us with a dowsing rod, didn't they? They'll follow. And soon."

"Shite, shite, shite," Nix said. He nudged Channis with his boot. The Upright Man just stared out of the black globes of his eyes. "We keep this bunghole for a while, then. He could be useful to us if they catch up."

"Let's not let them catch up, yeah? How long's that rod keep its hooks in?"

Nix shrugged. He could check Rose from time to time see if the rod's enchantment on her remained, but he had no idea how long it might stick.

"So we're chasing a mythical mindmage while being chased by Dur Follin's thieves' guild. That about the size of it?"

"Sounds bad when you say it."

Egil ran his hand over Ebenor's eye and set back to oaring.

"You want me to take over?" Nix said.

Egil shook his head. "Keeps my head clear."

Rose whimpered, curled up in the bottom of the boat, her brow wrinkled with pain. Mere put her hand protectively on her sister.

"Tell me more about this mindmage," Mere said, her tone firm.

"Do you know anything about the Deadmire?" Nix asked.

"Just what people say."

Nix saw the swamp in his mind's eye. He'd been there before he'd first met Egil, on an expedition with his mentor, Hinse the Knife.

"Most of what they say is true, at least partially. It's vast and there are sunken ruins everywhere. It like... it's like the earth is slowly swallowing a city ten times the size of Dur Follin."

"You've been there, then?" Mere asked. "When?"

Nix hesitated. "Over fifteen years ago."

"Fifteen years!" Mere said. "You saw this mindmage fifteen years ago? He could be dead or gone or..."

She trailed off as Rose moaned.

Nix squared up to the rest of the story. He owed it to her to be honest.

"I never actually saw him, Mere," he said.

"No one has," Egil said. He racked the oars and sat sideways on the bench so he could see both Mere and Nix.

Mere eyed them, one then the other, her eyes filled with disbelief. To her credit, she didn't shout.

"No one has?" She gripped the gunwale, her knuckles white. "No one has? What have you done here, Nix?"

"Mere–" Egil started.

"No, Egil. This is... too much."

Nix felt himself color. "I'm trying to help her."

Mere glared at him but kept her voice low, which made it worse. "By dragging her to the Deadmire to chase a rumor? That's your plan?"

"Our plan," Egil said in his deep voice. "I was with Nix on this."

Mere looked at Egil as if he'd sprouted a second head.

"I think Odrhaal is real," Nix said. "I wouldn't have done this otherwise. You know that, Mere."

"You think lots of things, Nix Fall."

To that he said nothing. Egil stepped into the silence.

"We wouldn't have done it if we'd had another option," Egil said. "We love you two. You know *that*, too."

Mere colored, blinked. She looked as if she might cry but she fought it back. She ran her hands over her face as if to wipe away the emotion there. She looked down at her hands.

"I know you do. I'm just..." She made a helpless gesture. "I'm worried."

"Us, too," Egil said.

Mere looked up at Nix, her eyes glistening. "Tell me why do you think he's real?"

Nix wasn't sure his explanation would give her any comfort, but he had nothing else to tell her.

"Well, we set out for the Deadmire to... well, it doesn't matter why. But it went bad and they had to carry me out and I was feverish by then. We got lost and..." He hesitated to say it because it sounded ridiculous. "It was like I dreamed it but it was more than a dream." He looked at Egil, at Ebenor's eye. "It was like Blackalley, Egil. That feeling that something else is out there in the dark, watching you, reaching out to you. I didn't imagine it. I'm certain of that. I think it was Odrhaal."

He didn't like the pleading tone in his voice, but there it was.

Egil grunted but otherwise held his peace.

Mere spoke in a measured tone. "But you don't *know* it was Odrhaal?"

"No," Nix said. "I didn't have a name for it then, but the way it feels when you're in my head... it felt a bit like that."

She inhaled, stared out at the water, looked back at him. "All right."

"What does that mean, all right?" Nix asked.

"It means I know you're trying to help. And you're right. There was nothing else to be done. Rose's only hope," her expression fell, her face vibrating with withheld tears, "is that Odrhaal is real and that he'll help."

To that, Nix said nothing.

"I could use that break, now," Egil said.

"What? Right," Nix said.

Egil moved to the front of the boat, near Mere and Rose. He held out his huge hands. Mere took them, hers lost in his, then fell into his arms, weeping. Nix turned his back on it and set to rowing, hoping that he wasn't half the fool he felt he was.

CHAPTER THIRTEEN

Nix awoke not long after dawn, stiff and achy, to the sound of Mere and Rose softly talking. He was still in the boat and so were they. Rose winced now and again as she whispered, vexed by some pain in her bifurcated mind. Egil lay flat on his back on the grass just up from the muddy beach where he'd landed the boat, his arms thrown out wide as if to embrace the sky, his snores soft and regular.

Nix glanced down at Channis, who lay in the boat's bottom, legs bent at an uncomfortable angle, black, slit eyes open and staring and vacant. Nix nudged him with a toe – no response. Channis might not have been dead, but he certainly seemed absent. Rose had two minds in her head, but Channis had none.

"Rose," he said, and smiled at her.

She brushed her hair out of her eyes, a gesture so her that he knew she was of sound mind, at least at that moment. "Thank you, Nix. I want you to hear that from me, whatever happens."

Nix stood, though his legs protested. "Starting the morning that way, are we? Let's eat before we get all maudlin, yeah?"

He moved through the boat and extended a hand to Rose. "Milady."

She took his hand but did not try to stand. Something was in her eyes, a secret thought. Mere would not look him in the face.

"What?" he asked.

"Mere told me your plan," she said.

She winced, her right eye blinking uncontrollably for a moment. Mere's lips pursed.

He kneeled down, took her hand between his. "Are you all right? Egil, get up!"

She forced a smile, her right eye still blinking. "I'm as all right as I can be. Listen…"

She grimaced, her face bunching up with pain. Mere put a hand on her back, concern in her face.

"What is it?" Egil called, staggering to his feet, his hands filled with the hafts of his hammers.

"It's Rose," Nix said.

Egil hurried over to the boat. Rose moaned with pain and Nix looked from Mere to Egil for help, but they both looked on as helpless as him.

Rose opened her eyes, looked at Mere, and nodded.

"What?" Nix said. "What?"

"Nix," Mere said. "If Odrhaal exists–"

"He does."

"And if he will help."

"We'll pay whatever we have to."

"Do you ever stop talking?" Mere asked him.

He almost replied but caught himself and kept his mouth closed. Mere went on.

"Fixing this means… cutting things out. A mindmage can do that, we think. But that's what it means."

"The imprint of the dead man, yeah?" Nix said.

"Yes," Mere said. She looked at Rose, who leaned back against the gunwale, her pale face pained. "But it's been in Rose's head a while. Things are getting mixed up. Cutting it out is getting more complicated all the time."

Rose nodded. "It's a cockup," she said.

Nix looked from one to the other and thought he understood. "Are you saying it could accidentally cut some of her out?"

"That's what I'm saying," Mere said.

Rose groaned, held her head in her palm. Nix squeezed her other hand and she squeezed his back, hard, as if trying to hold on to something slipping from her grasp.

"Then we need to get moving," Nix said. "The longer it's in her, the worse it is."

Egil put one hand on Nix's back to keep him from standing. To Mere, he said, "What do you mean 'cut some of her out'? You mean memories?"

Mere nodded. "Memories, ways of thinking, emotions."

"Does she want to do that?" Egil asked.

"What the fak are you asking?" Nix said. He swatted Egil's arm from his back and turned to glare at the priest. Egil had eyes only for Mere. "There's no choice here, Egil. Mere. We don't have anything else. There are no miracles to pull. If we don't do this…"

Nix trailed off, eyeing Rose. Egil said nothing. Mere said, "No. There is a choice."

Nix looked her in the face, looked at Rose, back at Mere. "Dying's not much of a choice. You can't mean–"

"I do and it is," Mere said. Her dark eyes welled and her lips quivered while she spoke, but her tone was certain. "We talked about it last night. She's thought about it. If she's not going to be herself, she'd rather–"

"She'd still be herself!" Nix said. "Look at her. She's the same, she'd–"

Mere was shaking her head. "That body isn't her. Nix." She put a finger to her head. "That's her. That's all of us. Change it and we're... someone else."

Nix couldn't speak for a long moment. "Shite, Mere," he finally managed

"I know."

Rose moaned again, rolled onto her side. Nix put his hand on her hip. He looked to Egil.

"Priest? You want to help here?"

"I can't," Egil said, shaking his head. "She's right. She would be someone else. But maybe becoming someone else isn't that terrible."

"There," Nix said to Mere. "She can't just... quit."

"It's Rose's choice," Egil said.

"It is," Mere said with a firm nod, a single tear running down her face. "She hasn't decided anything. She just wanted me to know her thinking in case... it gets clouded later on."

Nix didn't press. He stared out at the Meander, its waters constantly moving, changing, no spot the same for any length of time. He knew what he wanted Rose to choose, but he also knew he couldn't choose for her. To no one in particular, he said,

"I wish we'd killed every one of those guild men. Every one. Their sloppy shite put her here."

Egil put a hand on his back, gently this time. Nix sniffed, looked up at Mere.

"We're already almost to the Deadmire," he said. "We keep going until you tell me we shouldn't. Well enough?"

"Well enough."

Rose shouted a series of curses interspersed with guild cant.

"Let's move," he said to the priest.

Egil pushed the boat back into the Meander's ever-changing waters. They were hours from the edge of the Deadmire.

Rusk delayed as long as he could. He set matters in order at the guild, though the house was still in an uproar. He had two dozen guild men volunteering to join the pursuit. Every guild man worth his symbol wanted payback from Egil and Nix. Rusk promised that payback would be coming.

Despite Trelgin's eagerness to strike out before dawn, Rusk insisted on waiting for watch activity to die down on the wharves. Meanwhile he regularly checked his tat, but it stayed stuck on seven. Egil and Nix had croaked eighteen guild men in the guild house but hung onto Channis like he was made of gold.

By dawn, Rusk and the men were on the river. Trelgin insisted on riding with Rusk, so the two of them manned one boat and put Kherne on the oars. Mors, Varn, and Dool took the other, with Dool on the oars.

As soon as they left the city behind, Trelgin pointed the dowsing rod south and spoke the word that activated it. Rusk held out hope that it would go wrong somehow – he didn't trust sorcery – but instead it visibly pulled on Trelgin in the direction they were heading.

"They're still on the river," Trelgin said. "Half a day ahead."

"Half a day," Rusk said. "Either they didn't stop to rest or that big fakker can row."

"But we're on 'em," Kherne said, pulling at the oars.

"Just keep rowing," Trelgin said to him. "We're on 'em, aye."

"That big fakker's mine," Kherne said.

"You'll have to fight Varn for him," Trelgin said with a sloppy chuckle.

The water of the Meander muddied as they neared the estuary. Smaller streams fed the river from the left and right. The churn in the shallow water filled the air with a rich, organic smell. The vegetation on the left bank thickened, with cypresses and willows leaning out from the muddy bank like drowsy sentinels. A western wind carried the thick stink of the Deadmire to them – the smell of decay, of old rot best left undisturbed. Nix checked behind them often, looking for any sign of pursuit by the guild men, but he saw nothing but the shimmering, dark ribbon of the Meander. He took the oars for much of the morning to give Egil a rest.

Twice they passed other boats heading upriver, one manned by a leathery fishermen and his sons, the second a large scow loaded with Narascenes, the boat a swirl of colored robes and chimes and drums and songs sung in their rich, complicated language. The Narascenes, riding high enough in the water, saw Rose and Channis lying in the bottom of the boat. They chattered among themselves and drew protective symbols in the air with their fingers.

Mere sat with Rose's head on her lap, singing to her softly. Rose moaned and whimpered and babbled guild cant. In her lucid moments, she simply lay still and stared up at the sky. Nix wanted to speak to her, to make her smile or laugh, but he couldn't muster the words and she seemed to want quiet.

At his feet, Channis was changing further. His skin had coarsened, darkened, and under it there were odd lumps and bulges. Nix hardly cared. Rose filled his thoughts, and Odrhaal, and the nagging fear that Nix had brought them all on a fool's errand.

A dark, viscous fluid leaked from the corner of Channis's mouth and his teeth had grown, sharpened. Nix considered tossing him overboard – the man was as good as dead – but kept him aboard only against the possibility that they'd need him should the guild catch them up. Egil shared a look with Nix and Nix could see that the priest, his face red and sweaty with prolonged exertion, was thinking the same thing.

"It's not going to be worth carrying him when we have to abandon the boat," Nix said.

"Agreed," Egil said.

Though cypress and willow and a thick wall of brush blanketed the eastern bank, Nix knew they were roughly parallel with the center of the Deadmire. It had been raining the day he had come this way with Hinse.

"There's going to be a fork up here to the east," he said. "We take that and head in. If things are as they were, we'll stay in the boat until tomorrow. Sometime after that, we'll have to abandon it and go on foot."

"You know where we're going?" Egil asked.

"More or less," Nix said. Assuming the spire hadn't fallen, he'd be able use it as a landmark to guide them in. And if it had fallen, then there was no Odrhaal and Rose was lost.

Within the hour they'd reached the fork Nix remembered and Egil rowed them in. The narrower waterway brought the trees and brush closer. A canopy of willows and cypress roofed them and the boat advanced into the Deadmire in the shade. Dead logs stuck out of the waterline here and there like unearthed bones. Insects and birds called and buzzed and chirped and sang.

Rose burst out in a long series of expletives and cant. At the sound a score or more of startled birds burst from the trees and took flight. Mere rubbed her sister's head and looked worried.

"How far?" Egil asked. "Maybe I can go faster than you did before, make up some time."

Nix wasn't sure exactly. He was working from ten year-old memories. He figured – he *hoped* – he'd know it when he saw it.

The breeze picked up, carrying the stink of something long dead.

"Just keep rowing," he said. "Follow your nose."

Rusk and the men passed a few other boats on their way downstream. A fisherman and his sons admitted to seeing a boat that fit the description of their quarry, but no one else had seen them, or would admit to seeing them. Trelgin checked every half hour with the dowsing rod, to keep them on Egil and Nix's trail.

"We're gaining," he said. "Faster," he said to Kherne, and shouted the same order to Varn in the other boat.

Kherne and Varn, already puffing and sweating from hours at the oars, cursed him, the sky, the water, the boats, the oars, and anything that caught their eye. Hours passed and as they headed south the bush and trees thickened on the east bank. The air got thick with the stink of the Deadmire.

Rusk could not understand where Egil and Nix thought they'd go. Dun Dorrigan, maybe, deep in the Meander's delta, near the shore of the southern sea. Nothing else made sense.

He got his answer a bit later when Trelgin activated the dowsing rod and cursed softly.

"What is it?" Rusk asked.

"They've turned east."

Rusk looked east. Trees, bush, and behind that, swamp.

"The Deadmire?"

Trelgin nodded.

Kherne racked the oars and took a long drink from his waterskin. "Why in the fak would anyone go to the Deadmire?"

"Because they don't think we'll follow," Trelgin said. "But we will." He looked at Rusk, his droopy face screwed up on a challenge. "Won't we, Seventh Blade?"

"For now," Rusk said with a nod. "But we're not going in deep. Too easy to get lost."

"Aye," Kherne said, and retook the oars. He called over to the trailing boat. "Those fakkers are running to ground in the Deadmire."

Heads shook.

"Scared rabbits, is what," Varn said.

"Crazy fakkers, more like," Kherne said.

Rusk sat in the rear of the boat. He eyed his tat, and, as he suspected, it was unchanged. Channis was alive, at least for the moment. Rusk had to figure a way to make sure the Upright Man went dusty in the Deadmire.

The water grew choked with roots and pads and rushes and dead wood. Egil navigated them through it as best he could, and Nix and Mere pushed them away from hazards. Still, time and again the bottom of the boat rubbed up against the rocks and mud of the bottom.

Twisted, droopy trees bordered the waterway, which sometimes expanded to the size of a small lake, sometimes shrank down to a thin stream. Nix was determined to stay in the boat as long as possible.

Grassy hillocks rose from the landscape here and there, topped with trees and brush. Birds and their songs filled the air, the buzz of bugs, the croaks of frogs. Splashes sounded in the water now and again, fish or frogs jumping. Snakes prowled the shoreline. They heard animals in the thick undergrowth from time to time, but didn't actually see any.

As the day waned, the trees cast long shadows on the water. The pungent air cooled and the swamp felt ever more ominous. The sunset cast the sky in red. Nix pointed to a distant hillock, upon which stood the crumbling ruins of a tower. Soon thereafter cut stone appeared in the waterway, chunks of timeworn obelisks, broken pieces of statuary. A huge sculpture of a snake head, half buried in the mud, looked upon them from the stream bank as they passed.

The water grew shallower, the stink of decay worsened. Nix imagined vast numbers of corpses decaying under the veneer of mud and shallow water.

More and more crumbling buildings and tall columns of dark stone loomed out of the vegetation, half covered in vines and filth. Nix and Mere and Egil watched them as they rowed past, witnesses to a lost civilization.

"This is the right way," Nix said.

Egil and Mere nodded, but said nothing.

As night fell, the birds and their songs disappeared, leaving only the buzz and croaks and chirping of frogs and insects. A column of bats rose from the roof of some ruins and stained the air black as they wheeled into the sky. The air cooled. They shared bread and cheese and water, did their best to feed Rose, who groaned and sometimes shouted in cant.

"We should rest soon," Egil said. "How much farther, you think?"

Nix wasn't entirely sure. "Tomorrow, should be. It's in the middle of the swamp, a tall spire, like the ones we've seen, but intact."

"And you think that's where Odrhaal is?" Egil asked.

"I do," Nix said, with a confidence he didn't feel. Hinse, his old mentor, had said that Odrhaal laired in the spire, and it was in sight of that spire that Nix had... dreamed odd things. "We'll need to go on foot, though."

Nix tied off to the root of a cypress and they slept in the boat. Rose muttered guild cant for hours on end, and Channis stared blankly at the sky, an eerie half-smile on his face. His eyeteeth had turned to fangs and Nix found the smile more disconcerting than his previously vacant expression.

Nix and Egil were on alternate watches, but Nix let the priest sleep rather than waking him. Working the oars all day would have drained even Egil. Nix leaned back against the gunwale and settled in for a long night.

He swatted at mosquitoes and bugs, listened to the lap of water, Egil's snores, Rose's murmurings, the buzz of insects and croak of frogs. He looked back in the direction they'd come, wondering if the guild men were still on their trail. Kulven rose, a ragged silver half-circle. Mist rose off the water.

In the moonlight the swamp felt surreal, dreamlike. The rhythmic monotony of the night made Nix's eyes grow heavy. He fought it, fought it, and finally lost.

A splash awakened him with a start. The boat was rocking. He sat up, his hand on his blade. Egil, too, sat up quickly, his fist around the haft of a hammer.

It was still the deep of night. Kulven had set and Minnear had risen, painting the swamp with its green brush.

"What was that?" Egil said.

"Shite," Nix said, when he saw that Channis was gone.

"What is it?" Mere said, and Rose whimpered.

"Channis is gone," Nix said, and looked out in the direction from which he'd heard splash.

Egil grabbed for Mere's crossbow, cocked it, loaded, and scanned the water behind its sight. Nix held up a hand for silence, listening for the splashing of a swimmer, but he heard nothing.

"We can't chase him in the dark," Mere whispered.

"No," Nix agreed. "He's gone. Shite."

"He'll die out there," Egil said.

"He was already dead," Nix said, thinking of the black veins growing under Channis's skin, his dark eyes, the weird bulges and ridges forming under his skin. Still, the memory of Channis's frozen smile troubled Nix.

"He could find his way back to the guild men following us," Egil said.

"If they're still following," said Mere. "Do you think they are?"

Nix looked out into the darkness behind, to the still water and the stands of rushes and trees turned ghostly in Minnear's light. "Best to assume so."

Nix and Egil both stayed awake afterward, against the possibility that Channis would return and try to attack. He didn't, but in the hours before dawn they heard screams out in the darkness, terrible, pained roars and angry hisses, but not those of a beast, those of a man.

Nix and Egil stared out into the black, the stink of the dead in the air, the skeletal ruins of a lost civilization all around them, and wondered what had happened to Channis out in the swamp.

"Sounds like he got what was coming," Egil said.

"Aye," Nix agreed.

Rusk, Trelgin, and the rest of the guild men came awake with a start.

"What the fak was that?" Varn asked.

"A dying beast," Trelgin said, his diction even worse than usual for having been just awakened.

"Didn't sound like no beast," Mors said in his high-pitched voice.

They'd camped after dark by pulling up on a small islet in the middle of a shallow pond. Tall cypress and willow bordered the pond, the limbs whispering all night. Ruins stuck from the water, the gravestones of a fallen realm. A toppled statue of a robed man who looked vaguely reptilian lay on the islet, most of the features worn away by the elements.

"Double watch the rest of the night," Rusk said. "All eyes, all ears."

Trelgin hocked and spit. "We start right at day break. We gained on 'em today. We can catch 'em tomorrow."

Ayes around, and all but Varn and Mors, both on watch, lay back in the boats to sleep.

Rusk held his arm before his eyes, staring at the unchanging tat and its seven blades. He soon fell asleep and dreamed of snakes.

As soon as the false dawn started to eat the stars, Egil shoved them off and started rowing. Mere soon awakened, blinking, yawning, softly coughing. Rose sat up and looked around, her eyes focused with clarity on her surroundings.

"Where are we?" she asked, her voice hoarse.

"In the Deadmire," Mere said. "We're looking for someone to help you. Do you remember?"

Rose looked at Mere in confusion, at Egil, at Nix. "I don't... know."

For a moment Nix had hoped that perhaps Rose had finally cleared her mind of the dead man's imprint, but even as he thought it her right eye began to blink uncontrollably. Mere eased her back down in the boat and she began to talk about torch jobs and clicks and jingles and members of the council on the guild's payroll. She spoke so quickly Nix could not follow it all, but he didn't need to. Rose was no better. Odrhaal was their only hope.

Egil rowed for hours through winding channels and narrow streams. Islets and thickets forked the waterway again and again. Ruins clogged everything. The trees, thick and overhanging the water, made it like rowing through a tunnel.

"Those fakkers are going to have a hard go following us through this," Egil said.

Nix nodded. The dowsing rod would give them direction and rough distance to Rose, but given the number of forks, it would be impossible for them to track Rose perfectly. Hopefully the guild men would have to double back a few times and lose some ground.

"You think they're still following?" Egil asked again

"I'm starting to wonder," Nix said. He figured he'd have seen a sign of them by now. Maybe they'd given up. Maybe now that Channis was dead, they didn't think chasing Rose was worth it. In any event, they had no other course than to keep going, and so they did.

Twice Nix and Egil had to portage the boat across short stretches of muddy tangles before they could put it back in enough water to float it. By mid-day Nix was covered in insect bites and mud up to his waist. The rushes thickened and grew taller, such that they could not see far ahead. But always they maneuvered around and past the broken bones of the realm that had existed there once – dark stone, monumental architecture, and snakes. Lots and lots of snakes in the sculpture, on the columns, in friezes.

Nix stood in the boat from time to time to look behind them, but the circuitous route and the height of the rushes prevented him from seeing much more than a spear cast back. Nix winced each time Rose had an outburst and shouted guild cant, fearing it could be heard for a league. But there was nothing for it.

By late afternoon, the choked, tree-lined waterway they moved through gave way to a series of shallow lakes. In the distance, maybe a third of a league, rose the majestic ruins of a bridge. Much smaller than the Archbridge, it nevertheless caused all of them to fall silent at the sight of it. Stone foundation posts jutted from the mud, straddling the lake but no longer linked by the bridge, which had collapsed into the water. Vines and creepers veined the dark stone, and bird shite painted it in streaks of white, but still it looked majestic.

"Shite," Nix said softly. "I don't remember this."

He looked left, right, behind, trying to see something that would jog his memory, but in truth he didn't see how he could have forgotten the ruined bridge.

"We went the wrong way?" Egil asked. There was no accusation in the question.

"I don't know," Nix said. "I don't know how I could have…"

He trailed off.

"Nix?" Mere asked, and Rose groaned.

Nix could barely make eye contact with her. "I don't know, Mere. I thought… I'll get us there. We'll be able to see the spire for miles if we can get to some high ground. Even if we took a wrong turn, we'll see it."

"We can't go back at any event," Egil said. "The guild men could be behind us."

Nix agreed and let his gaze linger on Rose. "Just keep going. When we see one of those tall hillocks again, I need to get to the top of it."

"Aye."

Egil steered them around an islet covered in vines and cypress and closed on the ruined bridge.

Nix stared ahead, preoccupied, searching his memories, until movement atop the bridge post on the right drew his eye.

A large animal in the shadows.

No, something else.

He leaned forward, having caught the movement for only for moment before whatever it was bounded off the ruins and into the treeline. He lurched up in the boat, trying to spot it in the trees, his sudden movement causing the boat to rock. Egil cursed and Rose groaned.

"You see that?" Nix said, pointing.

"See what?" Egil said.

"I didn't see anything," Mere said. "But I was tending to Rose."

A hiss, deep and wet, sounded from the thick tangle of cypress near the bridge, the same hiss they'd heard the night Channis had fled. Suspicion about the identity of the creature took root in Nix's mind.

Mere took up a crossbow and Nix did the same and both of them held the weapons ready as Egil rowed them toward the huge stone towers that once had supported the span. Ruins stuck up from the mud on either bank, dark stone bones being slowly overwhelmed by the swamp's vegetation. Nix imagined the ruins extending out into the lake, imagined an entire lost city below them, hidden under the murky water.

He watched for movement in the brambles and trees and bush, but saw nothing of the creature he'd seen atop the bridge. Still, it put him on edge.

In the bottom of the boat, Rose groaned. Blood leaked in a thin rivulet from her nose. Mere looked up from her sister at Nix, her expression plaintive. Nix took her meaning.

They were running out of time.

And somewhere along the way Nix had led them astray.

The distant roar they'd heard from somewhere out in the swamp had coiled all the guild men. Everyone except Trelgin and the men on the oars had crossbows at the ready, scanning the banks. Rusk thought the sound was the same one they'd heard the night before, and it wasn't the sound of any animal he'd ever heard before.

Towering cypresses and dense undergrowth rose like walls to either side of the narrow waterway, green curtains that blocked out most of the daylight. But now and again Rusk could see far enough into the vegetation to spot ruined structures between the tree trunks and roots: toppled stones and obelisks, pieces of sculpture half-buried in the humus or sticking out of pools of stagnant water. A serpent motif appeared in one way or another on most of it.

A crash and splash from deep in the underbrush to their right brought the crossbows up and Mors loosed a shot at nothing Rusk could see.

"There!" Mors shouted.

"Where?" shouted another man.

"Close your holes," Rusk barked.

The sound faded and there was nothing more.

An animal, Rusk supposed.

"You saw something?" Rusk called.

"Thought I did," Mors said, his high-pitched voice chagrined. "Must have just been a shadow or something."

"Eyes sharp," Rusk said. "Don't be edgy, though."

"Aye," said the men.

Trelgin leaned forward in the bow of the boat, the dowsing rod in his hands, its glyphs shining as it worked. He looked to Rusk like some kind of droop-faced figurehead and Rusk had to resist the impulse to crawl across the boat and push him headfirst into the dark, shite-stink water. He could see the magic of the dowsing rod pulling Trelgin in the direction they were going.

"Still on 'em?" Kherne asked Trelgin over his shoulder. The big man, sweating with exertion, stank almost as much as the swamp.

Trelgin's receding chin vanished into his neck for the moment it took him to nod.

"Still on them," he said. "And they're not far."

All of the men, and not just Trelgin, had taken the bit for the chase. They wouldn't have stopped pursuit even if Rusk ordered it. Not now. He'd just have to play things out. He still held out hope that Channis would end up dead, but for the moment, the seven blades on his tat said otherwise.

The water deepened and the two boats maneuvered through a series of jagged dark stones that jutted above the waterline, Kherne and Varn cursing throughout. They broke through the undergrowth, and emerged into a wide lake, almost a league long and dotted with treed islets here and there, stands or rushes. Rusk blinked in the late afternoon light.

Lilypads and weeds covered much of the surface of the lake but the structure at its far end drew his eye. What must once have been a grand bridge stood in ruins on the far side. Chunks of it had fallen into the shallow water and lay there still, like half-toppled grave markers. But the thick support posts that once had supported the span straddled the lake at even intervals, like the severed legs of giants.

Trelgin still held the dowsing rod, its glyphs still glowing.

"That way," he said, nodding at the broken bridge and sucking at some wayward drool. "They're that way."

CHAPTER FOURTEEN

A distant shout, faint but unmistakable, turned Nix around and spiked his heart rate. A man's voice, not a beast's growl – the guild men.

"I heard it," Egil said, still rowing.

Nix wanted to shout, "We don't even have Channis anymore! He's dead!" but that would have done no good. The guild owed Egil and Nix payback and they wanted Rose dead. If they'd come this far, they'd keep coming.

"Stubborn bunch," Egil said.

Nix nodded. "We should ambush them. Can't be that many of them."

"We get Rose what she needs first," Mere said, and her tone brooked no contradiction.

"Aye," Egil said.

"Aye," Nix agreed. "But then they die."

To that, Mere said nothing, but returned to ministering to her sister.

Nix looked back across the lake, but the distance and trees and islets blocked his view. A shadow fell on the boat as Egil rowed them between the bridge posts, steering them around the remnants of the span that had fallen into the lake. Nix examined them as the boat passed by, noted the repeated appearance of serpents and snakes.

As they passed out of the shadow of the bridge, Mere gasped, grabbed her head, and exclaimed in pain. Rose whimpered, loosed an outburst of nonsensical guild cant.

Egil dropped the oars and crawled forward to Mere's side.

"What is it?" the priest asked.

Nix snatched the oars before they fell off the boat. "Mere…"

Mere looked up, blinking, her eye watering.

"I… something," she said.

"Your nose," Nix said.

"What? Oh." She touched her nose with a finger, held it before her to examine the blood.

"Mere?" Egil asked. He drew her close.

"I think… he's near or…" Mere trailed off and looked at Nix across the boat.

"Who?" Nix asked.

"Odrhaal, maybe. He's near."

Nix sat up straight. "Why do you say that?"

She closed her eyes for a moment and waved a hand. "There's a… regard in the air. It's hard to explain. But it's a mindmage. It has to be."

Rose moaned and a trickle of blood leaked from her nose. Mere opened her eyes and dabbed it.

"Are you all right, though?" Egil asked her. She looked tiny beside him.

She patted his muscular forearm. "I'm all right. And this is a good thing, Egil. It means Nix was right. Now we just have to find him."

"Wait," Nix said. "Can you… contact him?"

"She's bleeding, Nix," Egil snapped.

"It's all right," Mere said, and patted his arm again. "It's hard to explain but the mental regard is… diffuse. It's like it's here but it's sleeping or not aware or…"

Nix didn't pretend to understand. He knew only that they must find Odrhaal and find him soon. But Mere's words had given him hope.

Egil kissed the top of Mere's head, gently touched Rose's pale face, and retook his place on the rower's bench.

The priest set to the oars with renewed vigor and Nix felt lighter by half. They kept moving the rest of the day, Nix kept an eye behind them for the guild men but saw no sign, though he couldn't see very far. The lake narrowed and grew shallower as the sun started to set, became more choked with trees, rushes, and ruins, and finally ended altogether. Egil pulled them up on the muddy shore as darkness started to fall. The priest ascended to the top of a rise and hurriedly came back down.

"The water picks back up just the other side of this rise," Egil said. "We drag it over and camp for the night."

"Aye," Nix said.

Behind them in the distance, another hissing roar sounded. Birds burst from trees at the sound and the incessant croaking of the frogs temporarily abated.

"Following us," Nix said.

"What is?" Egil asked, and Nix could only shrug.

Nix and Egil each took an end of the boat and lifted, leaving Rose in it, and pushed and pulled it over the muddy rise. They used broken statues for stepping-stones as they ascended. On the other side, the gentle slope of the rise descended to another lake, much larger than the other. Treed hillocks walled it in. Islets and fields of rushes dotted it here and there. The water looked black in the twilight. Nix figured if they could get across the lake and atop the far hillock, he could climb a tree and look around for the spire he remembered. They had to be close. Had to be.

"The guild men will have to camp, too," Nix said. "They can't travel the swamp in the dark any more than we can. We should be all right here."

They couldn't risk a fire so they huddled in the boat. Stars glittered faintly in the vault above them, but the darkness was deep. Ordinary growls, howls, and slitherings sounded out in the darkness, an occasional splash of water from the lake, a shriek of a creature caught by a predator. The air was alive with buzzing and the insects bit and poked constantly. Inspired, Nix took one of the blocks of incense he kept in his satchel and lit it with a match. The smell granted them relief from the reek of the mire and the swarms of insects.

Merelda sat beside Rose with her arms wrapped around knees. She turned sharply at this sound or that out in the darkness, obviously uncomfortable. It occurred to Nix that he and Egil had spent the last decade sleeping in tombs and other dark places. They were accustomed to it. Mere was not.

He reached into his satchel and took out the magical crystal eye he always kept to hand. He crawled over to Merelda, took her hand, and put it in her palm.

"Take this, Mere."

"What is it?" she whispered.

The Deadmire seemed to demand whispers of those who would speak at night.

"A light," he said. "A gewgaw, Egil would call it."

"I'm fine," she said.

"I know that." He tapped the crystal and spoke a word in the Language of Creation. The etched eye opened, casting a beam of light. It glared at Nix, as if irritated to be awakened. Insects, attracted by the light, started to swarm it.

"Dim," Nix said to the crystal, and the light dimmed.

"It's going draw bugs," he said to Mere. "It'll stay alight for a while."

"How long?"

He shrugged and smiled. "It's temperamental so it's hard to say. Keep it close so the beam doesn't attract attention from anything but bugs. Try to rest."

"All right."

Egil nodded appreciatively at him. "I'll take first watch," the priest said and rose from the boat.

"No argument," Nix said, and used his satchel as a pillow. He slept fitfully. Rose murmured restlessly through the night, occasionally blurting out a curse or name or cry of pain. When Nix took his watch, he climbed to the top of the rise and looked out on the swamp behind them. In the deep of night it looked like nothing more than a blanket of ink. The guild men, too, must have opted against a fire. Nix had no idea how much distance separated them from their pursuers, but he thought not a lot.

Cracking branches and a serpentine hiss from his right brought him to his feet, falchion and axe in hand. He saw nothing and heard nothing more. He descended the rise and took the remainder of his watch near the boat, near Rose and Mere and Egil.

"Are you sleeping?" he whispered to Mere.

"No."

"How is she?" Nix asked. He could not see Mere or Rose in the pitch of the night.

"I think she's failing," Mere said.

Nix did not reply, but the words stayed with him through the rest of the night.

Nix was on his feet the moment dawn lightened the sky. A mist rose from the lake and crowded the shoreline. Birds called; insects chirped. The wind rustled the trees.

They needed to get started before the guild men. He moved to Egil, snoring as always, and was about to shake him when he realized that Rose was awake and looking at him. Mere was asleep beside her.

Rose smiled at him. He smiled back.

She swallowed and whispered, "I feel like I'm disappearing."

"I'm not going to let you," he returned in a whisper.

"I know," she said.

Egil grunted, stirred, and broke the moment's spell.

"Time to go," Nix said to him.

"Aye," Egil said. He cleared his throat, spit, and slapped his face a couple times.

Mere opened her eyes, saw that Rose was awake and hugged her. She asked a question with her eyes, or maybe her mind, and Rose shook her head. Nix read the substance of the conversation in Mere's expression: Rose wasn't better. She'd just had reprieve.

Egil slid the boat into the lake, leaped in behind it, and took his place by the oars.

"You still feel Odrhaal?" Nix asked Mere.

She nodded.

"I feel him, too," Rose said.

"We have to be close," Mere said.

Rose's face bunched with sudden pain. "I need to lay down."

She lay back on her sister's lap, closed her eyes, and soon was asleep or lost in the swirl of her splintering mind.

Mere, her jaw set, stared out at the water.

Egil rowed them over the lake. He used the islets and rushes to block line of sight from the shore, in case the guild men came over the rise. The mist lingered, cloaking the boat, and it was like Egil was rowing them through clouds.

Within an hour the sun had risen fully, dispelling the mist. Its light dappled the water and Nix saw that where most of the Deadmire's ponds and pools and streams had been stagnant and murky, the lake was unusually clear and deep. Nix leaned over the back of the boat as Egil pulled them quickly through the water. He could see fish swimming in the depths, long green fronds swaying in unseen currents, and stone obelisks, lots of them. The frequency with which the obelisks and other large, cut stones appeared increased until finally Nix could see entire structures sitting on the bottom of the lake. The water distorted his view, but he made them as tombs, mausoleums, hundreds of them. Topiary featuring snakes and serpents appeared here and there.

"Look at this!" he said.

"What is it?" Egil said, leaning over the side.

"No, look at *that*," Mere said.

Nix looked up and saw what Mere was looking at. "Shite."

He'd been so preoccupied looking under the water that he'd missed the dome of a metallic tower, the view of it partially obscured by a small islet, poking out above the waterline. The body of the tower reached to the lake's bottom, a silver cylinder that descended thirty or forty paces down. A stairway made of the same metal spiraled around the exterior of the tower. Like a serpent, Nix thought.

Egil steered the boat around the smooth dome.

On the other side of it the stairway terminated in a landing and a smooth metal door. There was no handle on the outside, though there was a round keyhole.

"Enspelled," Egil said.

Nix nodded. "The whole tower, probably. I've never seen metal like this."

"You didn't see this last time through?" Egil said.

"No."

Egil kept rowing and they left the drowned graveyard and its unplumbed riches behind them. When they reached the far side of the lake, they pulled the boat onto the muddy shore and prepared to trek up the tall hillock. Egil prepared a makeshift sling to bear Rose, a satchel almost, from the canvas cover that had come with the boat. When it was done, he carried her as one might a child.

"Your gewgaw is prettier than the ones I carry in my satchel," Nix said. He touched Rose's face and she turned her cheek into his hand. She was burning up.

Frowning with concern, Nix started up the hillock.

With Egil huffing and sweating under the weight of his burden, the three of them picked their way through the undergrowth and cypress. The sodden landscape was choked with creepers, brush, and willow. Swarms of bugs were everywhere. Toppled and rotting trees blocked their way constantly. The air felt close, pungent with the Deadmire's reek. But the ground firmed as they ascended, and when they reached the top, Nix picked the tallest willow he could find and climbed it as high as he dared. From there, he looked out and down on the center of the Deadmire.

A verdant swath of rolling land stretched out before him, as much jungle as swamp. A green blanket of trees covered a rolling, rough landscape of ponds and lakes and streams. Hillocks rose here and there like boils in the terrain. The whole of the land looked broken, scoured, the streams and lakes and ponds old scars covered in a veneer of water. Even from a distance he could see the countless ruins that dotted the landscape, scattered buildings, a plaza, huge toppled columns, monumental sculptures. The verdure had grown over much of it, as if the thick vegetation were trying to hide a shameful secret, but then Nix saw scores of sites scattered across the terrain. And he also saw what he'd sought since entering the swamp.

The upper half of a thin dark tower rose above the treeline in the rough center of the terrain, a quarrel of dark stone aimed at the sky. He'd seen it from afar once before, when he'd assayed the Deadmire with Hinse, when the dreams had come. The tower was the only intact structure he'd seen then and it was the one he saw now.

That had to be important. It had to mean that's where they would find Odrhaal.

He realized he was hanging a lot of hope on unknowns, but hopes and unknowns were all he had. Besides, Mere had sensed the mindmage. They were on the right path.

He maneuvered himself across the tree to a limb that allowed a view behind them. The terrain looked much the same, but he did not see their pursuers. Of course the trees and undergrowth and rough terrain could hide an army. He descended.

"Well?" Egil said.

"I spotted the tower," Nix said and Mere and Egil both looked relieved. Mere touched his arm. Nix looked at Rose. She looked so pale. "It's not too far."

"That's where we'll find Odrhaal," Mere said, her tone hopeful.

"That's where we'll find Odrhaal," Nix said.

They started off right away, moving as quickly as possible through terrain choked with ruins and fallen trees and enormous willows. When the vegetation allowed them to see ahead, they sometimes caught a tantalizing glimpse of the tower, looming ever larger as they closed the distance. The sun slid across the sky as they sweated and cursed their way through the mud and undergrowth and bugs.

Nix's burgeoning hopes began to falter as they neared the tower and he saw it more clearly. Egil did him the courtesy of saying nothing, but Nix's eyes told a story he did not want to hear. From afar, the tower looked intact but, through the occasional breaks in the trees, Nix saw that was an illusion, a trick of distance and false hopes. Mere seemed not to have realized it yet, and Nix did not have the mettle to tell her. As they broke through the treeline, Mere's doubts manifested.

"This is it?" she asked. "Are you certain, Nix?"

The tower *was* more intact than most of the other ruined structures, but cracks lined its crumbling façade, and chunks of facing stone had fallen over the years to collect in dark piles at the tower's base. The spike of stone rose from what once would have been a grand plaza, but which was now a scattering of cracked stones overgrown with creepers and trees and undergrowth. A few toppled, half buried statues of serpents and serpent men littered the ground around the tower. One statue alone remained standing, though only because it leaned against the side of the tower: a robed serpent man, arms upraised, mouth open, tongue extended in a hiss. The statue stood next to the doorway at the base of the tower. The double doors were long gone, the hole of the doorway like a missing tooth.

"I'm not certain of anything," Nix said softly. He walked for the double doors, jogged for them, ran for them.

"Nix," Egil called, but Nix would have none of it.

He sprinted across the plaza, nearly tripping on a loose stone. He took the stone stairs two and time and ran past the statue.

"Nix!" Egil called.

Nix stopped cold two steps into the tower, chest heaving, hopes failing. He'd wanted a miracle; he'd gotten shite.

Loose stone lay in a few scattered piles and the remnants of what once had been a ramp or circular staircase clung here and there to the crumbling walls. Undergrowth grew out of the foundation, shrubs and trees. Mud had leaked in over the years, coating the floor in grime. Vines veined the walls. Birds cooed in the heights.

"No," Nix said. "Come on. No."

He was standing in a cylinder as hollow as his hopes. Rays of light from the setting sun reached through the open top – it had collapsed long ago – and filtered down the tower's length.

He'd failed Rose and his failure stripped away his mask. He pretended to feel things or to not feel things so often that he'd almost forgotten what it was like to genuinely feel something.

And what he felt was empty.

He'd failed her. She'd die in the thrice-damned Deadmire because Nix the Quick, Nix the Lucky, had thought himself so damned clever.

Tears tried to fall but he kept them in. He would not grant his grief the relief of release. He'd carry it, as he should, as penance for his failure. He stood there for a long while with nothing but his mistake for company.

At length Egil and Mere came in to stand beside him. Their presence made everything worse. They'd believed in him and they shouldn't have. At first no one said anything. Mere finally put the situation into words. "He's not here," she said. "Odrhaal. And we don't know how to find him."

Nix opened his mouth to speak, closed it, and just shook his head.

Rose whimpered in her sling and Nix could only clench his jaw and chew on his failure.

"You're not at fault," Egil said and put a hand on Nix's shoulder.

"No, you're not. We had to try," Mere said, then, "Oh, Rose."

She turned away, covering her face, weeping.

Nix looked at Mere's shaking back, at Rose's pale, fever blotched face, and his anger escaped his control.

"Fak all this!" Nix said, and stalked outside. "Fak it all!"

"Nix?" Egil asked.

"What are you doing?" Mere called. "Nix, what are you doing?"

Nix didn't bother with an answer. He knew he was being careless, foolish even, because the guild men might hear him, but he didn't care. He needed to give voice to his anger, anger at himself, at the guild, at Odrhaal. He paced around the goddamned tower, shouting.

"Odrhaal! We know you're here! We need your help! You fakkin' answer us or I promise by all the gods…"

He left the rest of the threat unvoiced. The sounds of the swamp had fallen silent at his outburst.

"Odrhaal!"

Light filtered down through the canopy. Bird wings fluttered among the treetops.

"Odrhaal!"

Nothing.

Mere and Egil walked out of the ruined tower, the priest bearing the unconscious Rose, the Rose they were soon to lose.

"Nix…" Egil said.

"No!" Nix snapped, waving the priest off. "Mere can sense him. He's here somewhere. He has to be. Odrhaal!"

"Nix," Mere said softly. "It could be some… residuum of this dead civilization that I'm perceiving. I can't be sure."

Nix whirled on her. "You can't be sure? *You can't be sure?*"

She recoiled, eyes wide, and Egil stepped protectively in front of her. His frown and narrowed eyes told Nix what his mouth did not: *Back off.*

A growl and hiss sounded from out in the trees, the growl and hiss that had plagued them since Channis had fled into the night. Nix drew his falchion and handaxe and stalked toward the trees. He wanted to kill something; he *needed* to kill something.

"Show yourself!" he shouted. "Come on! *Come on!*"

He walked along the treeline, staring into the shadowed foliage, the muddy earth sucking at his boots, but the creature answered him no more than had Odrhaal.

"Fak! Fak! Fak!"

He gathered himself as best he could and walked back to his friends. He could not look them in the face. He stared at his boots, his weapons limp and useless in his grasp.

"I... fakked this up, Mere. I thought... I thought it would go like everything always goes for me, like it would work out. I thought I could save her."

He looked up to see Mere looking at him, tears in her eyes.

"You're not at fault," she said.

"You're not," Egil said.

Mere looked at her sister, at Egil, at Nix. "But what do we do now?"

Egil spared Nix the need to answer. "We camp here and then try to go back..."

He trailed off and no one filled the silence for him. There was nothing to be said.

They'd have to face the guild men and Rose would die on the way back.

••••

Even Trelgin fell silent as the boats carried them over what looked like a submerged necropolis. A metallic spire poked out of the water in the center of the lake, like the hand of a drowning man reaching up above the waterline to grasp at air he'd never breathe again.

"Has to be a lot of swag down there," Mors said, leaning over the side of the boat.

Aye's around.

"Unless you're a fish, that's just where it'll stay, too," Varn said.

"Keep your voices down," Rusk said.

When they reached the far end of the lake, they found Egil and Nix's boat, pulled up on a muddy beach at the base of one of the hillocks that ringed the lake. They pulled their boats up beside it and hopped out. Quickly, Trelgin activated the dowsing rod and took a sense.

"That way," he said, nodding up the rise. "I think–"

He stopped and inhaled sharply, the sound wet with drool. Rusk followed his eyes and saw at the top of the rise a tall figure standing in the shadows of the cypresses, partially hidden by the undergrowth. It was bipedal, with dark, scaled skin and overlong, muscular arms and legs. It was hairless, its eyes set in ridged sockets, and the whole of its features gave it a reptilian cast.

Rusk cursed and fumbled for his weapon. Varn and Mors unslung their crossbows but by the time they had them to hand, the figure was gone.

"What in the Eleven Hells was that?" Mors asked, his voice even more high-pitched than usual.

"Looked like a…" Varn said, and shook his head. "I don't know what it looked like."

"Swamp's got all kinds of secrets," Rusk said, feigning confidence. "Just stay sharp."

"We leaving the boats?" Trelgin asked.

"You said they went that way," Rusk said, nodding up the rise. "Unless we plan to turn back now, we have to leave the boats."

"We could leave a guard," Trelgin said.

"I ain't staying at the boats with that thing out there and a drowned graveyard behind me," Varn said, and the other men nodded.

Rusk looked a question at Trelgin. Trelgin's eyes went to Rusk's tattoo, its seven blades.

"We can't turn back, now," the Sixth Blade said, resigned. "Come too far."

"Get the gear out of the boats," Rusk said. Night was falling. They'd have to camp at the top of the rise. Rusk did not welcome another night in the swamp, especially with an unknown creature out there in the dark.

"What do you think these boys are even doing out here, Rusk?" Varn asked.

Rusk could only shrug. The Deadmire was no place for a man, and if guild law hadn't put him in such a bind, he'd never have come at all.

Egil set up their camp inside the empty spire.

"It's shelter," he said over Nix's protests. "Fewer bugs, no wind. It'll be better for Rose."

Nix had let the matter go, but better for Rose seemed almost a moot consideration.

Night soon shrouded the swamp. Nix knew he'd be unable to sleep, so he stood watch. For hours he stared at the inky air inside the ruined tower of a lost civilization, listening to Rose moan and thrash, listening to Mere fret and weep.

Nix and Egil sat in silence and did nothing, for there was nothing they could do. After a few hours Rose quieted and slept. Mere and Egil soon dozed off, too.

Nix sat alone with his thoughts, his regrets, the darkness of the tower his own personal Blackalley. He clenched his fists, his jaw, cursing himself for letting it all go so wrong. Maybe they could have gotten Rose to Oremal in time, or maybe they'd have encountered a mindmage en route. Instead Nix had led them into the stinking, sodden sewer of the Deadmire, where Rose would die, another ghost haunting the swamp.

He stood and paced because he had to, because he couldn't sit still, because he despised himself for his arrogance. He treated everything like it was a game, like no matter how the pieces moved, it'd always turn out all right for Nix the Quick, for Nix the Clever.

"Nix the stupid fakker," he whispered.

He walked to the doors and slouched down in the doorway, staring out at the swamp. Insects sang, the cadence rising and falling. Fireflies winked on and off out in the darkness, a constantly changing constellation. Kulven's silver light leaked dimly through the canopy. The breeze whispered among the vines and leaves, carrying the stink of decay.

Nix felt like he was standing on the grave of an old world, a secret world buried under the stink and filth. He'd tried to dig up Odrhaal for Rose and all he'd ended up with were hands covered in mud and stinking of shite.

"Fak," he whispered.

He loved Rose the way he'd have loved an older sister. And he'd failed her.

"Fak, fak."

He stared out into the darkness, spent. He still refused tears. He'd carry it, bear the grief because he deserved to bear it.

His eyes grew heavy as the day's events weighed down on him. He knew he'd soon fall asleep. He tried to rise, to go rouse Egil to take a watch, but he could not move his body. Alarm spiked his adrenaline but still he could not move. He opened his mouth to call out but couldn't summon a sound.

Fak. Fak.

He felt a tickling behind his eye, a pressure against his skull. He turned his head – he could at least turn his head – and found himself eye to eye with the face of a serpent.

No, a serpent *man*.

His heart leaped against his ribs. Sweat formed on his brow when he looked into the vertically-slitted, yellow reptilian eyes, filled as they were with an alien intelligence. Deep green and black scales and bone ridges formed a sloped, sleek head with deep eye sockets. Two ridged gashes formed a nose and the mouth.

The alienness of the creature shook Nix. His thoughts went jumbled. He wanted to move, to cry out, but he could still do neither. He could simply sit there and shiver.

The serpent man wore green robes made from a fabric that glistened in the moonlight as though it were slick. Triangles within triangles were sewn into the sleeves and collars.

Nix had seen the creature and the robes before and in a flash realized that it had been the statue. The statue of the serpent man had come to life.

But the statue was still there, looming beside him. But it had spawned the serpentman somehow.

Or Nix was dreaming.

Was he dreaming?

The serpent man reached up and placed his clawed, scaled hand on Nix's head, the touch cold and dry.

The pressure in Nix's skull grew. His eyes went wide and he opened his mouth in a silent scream. A presence nested in his thoughts, ancient and alien. He felt it probing at his thought processes, flipping pages to read the book of his mind. Nix's stomach fluttered and he tasted bile. For some reason he thought of Blackalley.

He gritted his teeth as the serpentman dug deeper into his thoughts. His heart was going to burst. He had to try something, anything.

Are… you… Odrhaal? Nix asked, daring to hope.

His thoughts seemed to echo through his own consciousness, as if the serpent man's violation had left Nix's mind as empty as the tower.

Need… your… help, Nix projected. *We need… to see… Odrhaal.*

Ssseee, said a voice in his head, the power of its projection much stronger than Mere or Rose's, strong enough to make Nix wince. He felt something pop behind his faceplate, felt blood trickle from his nose.

Yesss. Ssseee. Seee.

And Nix did see, things he could not have imagined.

Images formed in his mind, rapidly shifting, images of Ellerth when it was young, when an empire of serpentmen built basalt towers that soared to twice the height of the Archbridge, when flying cities floated through Ellerth's skies, when creatures of myth prowled primeval forests and grassy, windswept plains, and mountains that reached the roof of the sky.

He saw a great war between that empire and another, the latter an island empire ruled by pointed-eared human wizards in red robes, wizards who rode dragons and brought fire and ruin and commanded soldiers who carried weapons of sharp steel that glowed with magic. And Nix saw the serpent men answer with weapons that infected the mind, that trapped the thinking. He saw cities fall, saw men and serpent die on great battlefields by the tens of thousands.

Stop, Nix said. *Please stop*.

He saw the human wizards respond with an army of constructs, animated men of stone and metal who marched on the soaring cities of the serpent men and left heaps of cracked stone in their wake. He saw the serpent men answer with tubes of strange metal that vibrated in a way that destroyed the wizard's magical constructs, that shattered their flesh.

Nix's mind was swelling with the knowledge. He could feel his heart pounding against his eardrums. He thought his skull must soon burst. Surely it would burst.

He saw the war go on for decades, saw mountains of corpses, the enormity of the conflict changing the face of Ellerth, drying lakes, destroying mountains, diverting rivers. And he saw it end, finally, in the defeat of the serpent men. Most were killed, but some fled and some were imprisoned.

Imprisoned.

Imprisoned, the serpent man said.

The images vanished, leaving Nix gasping.

Free me, projected the serpentman, and Nix heard in the mental voice an echo of the same plea he'd heard while leaving Blackalley.

You're Odrhaal?

I'm Odrhaal, yes. Free me. I know what you seek. I can help the girl. Free me, Nix Fall.

How? Free you from what?

The chime is in the tower, the serpent man said. *Get it and bring it here. Free me.*

What chime? Nix asked. *This tower? The one that's here?*

Not this tower, Odrhaal said, and showed him, and Nix understood.

There is a guardian, Odrhaal said, and showed Nix a sleeping horror of eyes and toothy mouths and grotesque, trembling mounds of flesh.

Nix awoke in the deep of night, gasping. He lay at the base of the statue of the serpent man, the statue of Odrhaal. He was freezing and had a headache worse than any hangover headache he'd ever had. But that didn't matter. He also had hope. He climbed to his feet, dizzy for a moment, Odrhaal's mental voice echoing in his head.

Get the chime, bring it here. It's in the tower.

He ran into the tower, stumbling in his excitement. "Egil! Wake up!"

The priest sat up in a flash, hand on a hammer. Seeing no danger, he rubbing his head and eyes. "What is it? I dreamed–"

"I know what we need to do," Nix said.

"The tower in the water," Egil said distantly. He looked at Nix sharply. "That fakking tower."

"Get the chime," Mere said, also awakened by Nix's call.

"Bring it here," Nix said, almost jumping up and down.

They'd all had the same dream or vision or whatever the Hells it had been.

"Odrhaal, he's here," Nix said. "You were right, Mere."

"No, you were right," she said.

"He's trapped in that statue," Nix said.

"They froze him in stone, to imprison him forever," Mere said. "The men with pointed ears."

"And we need to free him," Nix said. "And then he can help Rose."

"Then let's get him the fak out of there," Egil said, standing.

"Aye," Nix said, grinning. "Gear the fak up."

"It's the middle of the night," Mere said.

Egil was already loading up his gear.

"We've got to backtrack," Nix said. "Which will take us toward the guild men."

"We can sneak past them at night," Mere said, understanding.

"Aye. And they won't be checking that dowsing rod at this hour. Egil and I get into the tower, get the chime, and come back here. We free Odrhaal, he helps Rose, then we deal with the guild men."

Egil dropped his hammers into their loops on his belt. "And if we have to deal with them before that…"

Nix nodded. "They get between us and that tower and they get a hard go."

"Aye, that," Egil said. "Though we could just ambush them now."

Nix considered it. "We don't know how many they are and we can be sure there are good blade men among them. Won't be like in the guild house. We get Rose fixed first, yeah?"

"Yeah," Egil said, grudgingly.

"We can't find our way in the dark," Mere said.

She was right. The moons were down and the darkness was like tar. They'd have to risk a light. Nix took his magical eye from Mere, spoke in the Language of Creation, and awakened it. It opened and its beam split the night. Nix tapped the eye with his forefinger.

"Dimmer," he said.

The etched eye bunched up in a glower but did as Nix commanded. Nix would keep it pointed at the ground and shielded with his hand. The guild men wouldn't see it unless they were looking for it.

"Let's move," Nix said. "And be as quiet as possible."

They started off and every damned sound they made seemed amplified by the night's relative quiet. Even Egil's breathing sounded loud in Nix's ears. Even so, Nix couldn't stop smiling.

CHAPTER FIFTEEN

Sleep eluded Rusk. Wrapped in his bedroll, he listened to Varn and Kherne's snoring, listened to the sounds of the swamp. He searched his thinking for some play to get the situation to work in his favor, but other than something obvious and risky – killing Trelgin, for example – nothing came to mind. He found himself circling back to the same conclusion again and again. Rusk would have to rescue Channis unless Egil and Nix killed Channis for him. Hells, maybe Channis would be less of a bunghole if he owed Rusk his life. Doubtful, though.

He heard a sharp, wet intake of breath from Trelgin, saw the flabby faker tense and lean forward, as if hearing or seeing something out in the night. Rusk thought of the scaled creature they'd seen earlier and sat up himself, his hand on his blade hilt. He followed Trelgin's gaze out into the darkness. At first he saw nothing more than the ink of the undergrowth, but then he saw it, too.

A light, far out in the swamp. It appeared and disappeared now and again, probably blocked by the undergrowth or shielded with a hand. But it was definitely someone bearing a light.

Rusk eased up beside Trelgin.

"You see it, too, yeah?" Trelgin asked.

Rusk nodded.

Trelgin pulled the dowsing rod from his inner pocket, activated it with a word, and let it pull in the direction of their quarry. Its pointer settled in the direction of the light.

"That's them," Trelgin said, sucking drool.

"They're heading for the boats," Rusk said.

"Probably," Trelgin said. "Must have spotted us. They'll sink our boats, go rabbit in theirs, and leave us to die in the swamp."

"Let's move," Rusk said. He moved through the camp, rousing the men. Trelgin did the same.

"Back to the boats," Trelgin said softly. "Those fakkers are going there now. We go quiet and fast and end this right now. They're walking right into it.

The men were awake, on their feet, and armed in moments.

"No lights," Rusk said.

"And no stray shots," Trelgin said. "Remember that they still have the guild master."

They set out in the dark, heading back to the lake and the boats, to Egil and Nix and Channis.

Even before they reached the lake, Nix said to Mere, "We'll all row out to the tower, but when Egil and I get out and take our run at the place, I want you to row back to shore."

"No, I can wait for you there."

"Row back to shore," Egil said to her.

"Odrhaal said there's a guardian," Nix said.

"I had the same vision, Nix," she said.

"Then you know what it looks like. I don't want you nearby if... something happens."

Mere said nothing so Nix took her silence as agreement.

When they reached the lake, they instead found three boats.

"We ought to sink these fakkers' boats," Egil said. He pulled a hammer and moved toward the first. Nix grabbed his arm and halted them

"Too loud," Nix said. "Just flip them and let them fill."

"Aye," Egil said. The burly priest stepped into the water and flipped the guild men's boats. The water pulled them down. It'd take a long while to pull them out and get them drained.

Afterward, they placed Rose in their boat, Mere took her place, and Egil shoved them off. They moved quickly over the dark water. Nix imagined the graves below them, hidden by the dark. The metal dome of the tower rose out of the water before them.

Rose whimpered, thrashed, cursed, finally screamed, the sound loud and cutting like a knife through the still air.

"We have to hurry," Mere said, a trickle of blood leaking from her nose. "I'm doing what I can but..."

"We know," Egil said, and touched her hand. "Once we're off, row back. We'll be along."

Nix and Egil stripped down to their trousers and boots. Both kept their weapons and Nix kept his satchel. Egil gave his dice a single shake and handed them to Mere. He let his pack and its crowbar – his tool of choice – go only with reluctance.

"You could go shirtless in winter with that pelt," Nix said to Egil.

The priest's powerfully built shoulders, chest, and back were covered in dark hair.

"I have," Egil said with a chuckle. "Ready?"

Nix leaned over the side and touched the water with his hand. "Warm at least."

Both of them leaped off the boat and onto the top of the stairs that led to the door in the tower's dome.

"Go on now, Mere," Egil said.

"Be careful," she said, and took position on the rower's bench. She struggled to work the oars, but managed them well enough to get the boat turned and heading back to shore. The darkness soon swallowed the boat, leaving Egil and Nix alone on the lake, standing on a submerged tower, twenty paces above an ancient graveyard.

"Strangely, this doesn't feel unusual to me," Nix said. "You?"

"If the tower's filled with water?" Egil asked.

"Then we go swimming," Nix said.

Egil eyed the door. "Open it."

Holding the glowing, etched-eye crystal in his palm, Nix took out the magical key he'd purchased in the Low Bazaar.

"Give us a fish," the key said.

Nix felt around in his satchel, pulled out the first thing he found, a browning apple.

"You get an apple," Nix said. "Later, I give you whatever you want."

"A fish," the key said.

"Gewgaws," Egil breathed.

"You get a fakkin' apple and you'll like it," Nix said. "Otherwise, I'll drop you in this damned lake where you can rust away for a thousand years."

A long pause then, "Give us an apple."

Nix gave the key a bite of the apple, let it chew, then stuck it in the round keyhole. As always, the key warmed and squirmed in his hand as it changed shape to fit the mechanism. It shifted several times, struggling with the lock, but at last it stopped moving and Nix gave it a turn. The lock clicked open and the smooth, metallic door slid aside as if on rollers. The stink that emerged on the stale air, like corpses ten days dead, made both of them gag.

Wincing at the stink, Nix stepped onto the small landing just inside the tower and aimed the beam from his light crystal into the tower. Metal walls glittered, their surface covered in complicated strings of glyphs and sigils, all of them etched deeply into the metal. Nix had never seen anything like them, not even at the Conclave. He could discern no method to their placement, either. The spirals and whorls and serifs and sharp angles twisted and turned this way and that, a disjointed, chaotic script that reminded Nix of nothing so much as the thinking of a madman. Or an alien mind, like the serpent men. Staring at the writing overlong made him uneasy. It was of another time, another world, and men weren't meant to see it.

A spiral staircase snaked down and around the interior of the tower, the stairs seemingly forged out of the wall. He swallowed and stepped farther in, Egil following. The door slid closed behind them before the priest could stop it.

"Fak," Egil cursed.

"Hsst," Nix said, but too late. A wet hiss sounded from down in the tower's depths, causing the hairs on Nix's arms to stand on end. He covered the crystal with his hand and he and Egil froze on the landing, listening.

Nothing more.

The etched eye of the crystal squirmed against Nix's palm. He lifted it to his lips and whispered, "Very dim."

More agitated squirming against his palm, but the crystal did as he commanded.

He slowly released his palm from the crystal. The dim light it shed was similar to that cast by a full moon. He and Egil took another step into the tower, to the edge of the landing, and let the glow shine down into the tower's depths.

Their breath caught when they saw the grotesque form attached to the wall a third of the way down the tower. The dream had not communicated its horror. The shapeless mound of grayish-blue flesh was three or four times Egil's size. Lines and ridges and boils and puss filled abscesses and thick blue veins covered its form. A glistening substance that looked like phlegm coated its skin and caked to a crust in its creases. As they watched, one of the ridges opened to reveal a rictus filled with a handful of sharp teeth as long as a dagger. Strings of yellow spit stretched between the fangs. The mouth snapped shut. Another opened elsewhere on the fleshy mound, another, another. The creature was covered in mouths of all sizes, all filled with sharp teeth. The horror they were looking at belonged to the world no more than did the alien sigils. Fortunately it looked like it might be sleeping, or perhaps it was just insensate.

Queasy at the sight of the thing, Egil and Nix backed away from the ledge. They put their heads close together and spoke in tiny whispers.

"Fak," Egil said.

"Aye," Nix said. "That's about the size of it."

"What's the plan?"

Nix glared at him in the faint light of the crystal. "I always come up with the plan. You come up with the plan this time."

Egil was already shaking his head, the eye of Ebenor wagging at Nix. "I smash things and make pithy yet profound observations. You make plans and then things go wrong."

"Did you say 'pithy'?"

"And we always have this kind of conversation before risking our lives. See? Pithy and profound is what that was."

Nix was nonplussed. "Who *are* you?"

Egil ignored the question. "I also said 'then things go wrong'."

"I won't argue that," Nix said. "Fak. I wish you had your lucky dice."

"Aye. Now plan, small man. Rose needs us and that thing looks unfriendly."

Nix crept back to the edge of the landing and shined the light along the tower's walls, down into the depths, taking it all in.

The glyphs and sigils carved onto the walls stopped just above the point where the creature was attached to the wall. He pondered over that for a time, deducing purpose.

The staircase descended all the way down, though the creature's enormous bulk blocked it a third of the way down. The stairs ended before a door very much like the one they'd entered through. There was a metal chest near the door. Nix estimated rough distances then backed away from the ledge to regroup with Egil.

"The tower's watertight, so there's that," he said in a whisper. "Nothing else good though."

Egil waited so Nix went on.

"I think the sigils are to keep the creature from crawling up to the top. Probably they fed it or tortured it or… whatever they did to it, from the top."

Egil ran a hand over Ebenor's eye. "They drew it up the wall, maybe fed it from the top, and while they did that, they put their treasures in the bottom."

"Maybe makes sense," Nix whispered. "Maybe also makes us fakked. The stairway goes all the way down and ends at a door like the one behind us. There's a metal chest at the bottom." He consulted the dream-vision he'd had of Odrhaal. "I think the chime is in it."

"Fakkin' chime," Egil said. "Why'd they put them here? What's the point?"

"Secreted them here at some point during the war?" Nix speculated. "To keep them from the wizards? I don't know. When do sorcerers or mindmages or anyone who trucks in magic do things that make sense? Add to that the fact that we're talking about serpent men and this shite makes even less sense than usual."

Egil tiled his head to concede point. "So?"

"So… I have a plan. It's a very bad one."

Egil waved him on. "That's assumed. Continue."

"The only way to get past those sigils is fast. We have to leap down the tower."

"Too far," Egil said, frowning.

"That's why we go fishing first."

Nix stared at Egil until the priest's eyes widened in realization. "As bad plans go, this may be your worst ever."

"Agreed. I have nothing else."

"Seems like we've been saying that a lot this time through."

"Aye, that."

Nix let Egil digest matters.

"Even if we get down there and don't break legs or skulls, then what? We still have the thing above us."

"We go through that door."

"And then?"

Nix raised his eyebrows and shrugged. "Fun's in finding out?"

Egil grunted.

"I told you it wasn't a good plan."

"You said it was a bad plan and you were exactly right." He ran a hand over Ebenor's eye. "You have enough line in that satchel?"

"Pfft. Enough line? Who're you talking to, Egil? Enough line. Besides, I only need half the length of the tower. Not even that, as I've got to err short. Meat, too. Had it for the key."

Egil blew out a breath. "Line will probably snap."

"Could," Nix said, nodded. "But I always buy the finest. And I had this enspelled for extra strength."

Egil nodded, considered, finally said, "Fak it. We go."

Nix tapped him on the shoulder. "No one will ever believe us if this works."

"No one would believe half of what we've done," Egil said.

Nix unslung his satchel and started working on his lines, one ear on the creature below. He wound two lines together to make a single, stronger line, then measured it off in armspans, estimating the length.

Egil sat beside him, eyes closed, praying.

"One for me, too, yeah?" Nix whispered.

Egil nodded without opening his eyes.

Nix took a small piece of now rotting meat from his satchel, frayed one end of the line, and used the freed fibers to tie up the morsel of meat. He tied himself into the line, a full-on harness that ran under his legs just under his arse and up through his crotch. He left lots of slack after him so he could do the same harness for Egil.

"Like a chair, see?" he said to the priest. He pulled at the line. "Though if this line slips up into the crotch, I'm likely to never have children."

"I wouldn't worry," Egil said. "With the small bits you've got hanging in there, I'd wager you could fit a couple ropes between your legs and hit nothing vital. Me, now…"

Nix grinned. "Neither pithy nor profound, priest."

"No?"

"No."

Nix harnessed Egil to the end of rope, both of them grinning the while. When he was done, Nix checked the length of the rope once more.

"Going to be a little short. I'll cut it the moment we're down. We'll fall the last bit."

Egil nodded, the grins disappeared, and they shared a look.

"I didn't mean it when I said your plans always go wrong," Egil said.

"I know that."

"I did mean what I said about your crotch, though."

"Not the first time you've been wrong about something," Nix said. "Here we go."

They crept to the landing and shone the dim light from the crystal down the tower onto the quivering mound of stinking flesh. They positioned themselves for a clear fall and Nix lowered the meat over the edge toward the creature. When it was low enough, he swung it toward the creature.

It thunked into the creature and Nix tensed, ready.

Nothing.

"Shite," he hissed. It occurred to him that the creature might not even eat meat. It probably didn't need to eat at all. Still, with nothing for it, he swung the rope again and hit the creature once more.

Still nothing.

"Wake it up," Egil said.

Nix nodded; shouted, "Open your fakking mouth, beast!"

A great tremor shook the mound of flesh. Two score sets of eyes opened all over the creature, all of them bloodshot and swinging wetly in their sockets. A dozen of them looked up at Egil and Nix, focused on them, and then a score of fanged mouths opened, hissed and growled and roared.

"Good morn to you, too, fakker," Nix said. "Breakfast time."

"It could spit it out or chew through the rope," Egil said.

"Little late for that, priest. Time to roll your fakkin' dice."

Nix swung the rope at one of the medium sized mouths and the creature snapped at the morsel. The moment its mouth closed, Egil and Nix leaped of the ledge, both of them shouting, intent on dying defiant if die they did.

Nix's stomach hit the back of his throat. He was aware of the glyphs and sigils in the wall flashing as they fell past them, each arcane character shooting lines of green or red or yellow energy across the length of the tower, but their fall carried them past so quickly that they outran the magic.

He caught a flash of eyes and mouths snapping at them as they fell past the creature. The floor rushed up fast, too fast, but the moments stretched slow, too slow, and Nix imagined himself hitting the bottom at speed, lying there dead and broken, or worse, broken but alive and unable to move as the horror crept down the wall for him.

The rope jerked taut, held on one end by the creature's mouth, and the sudden stop was so jarring that it cut short Nix's shout and made him feel like he'd run into a wall. The immediate stop pulled all the air from his lungs, cinched the rope so tight on his legs and arse that they went numb, and caused him to bite his tongue. The rope bounced him back up, but only for a half-beat before the rope between him and Egil snapped taut and jerked him down again. Egil grunted from the impact and bounced up while Nix fell back down. They bumped against one another, causing Nix to see sparks for a moment.

Above them, the creature's mouths roared and slobbered. Egil and Nix hung there suspended three or four paces above the floor, gasping, pained.

"Cut it, Nix," Egil said through gritted teeth.

Unable to breathe, his entire body aching or numb, Nix fumbled for the dagger at his belt.

Another series of wet rumblings and roars sounded from above, a sickening sloshing sound as the creature started to move. But instead of the creature's downward motion lowering them closer to the floor of the tower, they started to rise.

Nix glanced up at the quivering mound of flesh, its dozens of eyes fixed on him, its huge body undulating wetly down the wall. Three of its mouths were working in unison to reel in the rope.

Shite and shite.

"Nix!" Egil said. "Cut the damned rope!"

Nix finally got his dagger drawn and sawed at the rope. The magic that made it extra-strong also made it extra-resistant to Nix's blade.

"Damned gewgaws!" Nix shouted, sparing Egil the need.

They rose another pace or two, another, and the creature oozed down at them.

He sawed more frenetically, finally cutting through the first of the two ropes he'd twined together.

They rose another pace. The creature came down another.

"Shite, shite," Nix said. He finally cut through the second rope and he and Egil plummeted the short distance to the floor, hitting it in a tangle of limbs and gear. They wasted no time, despite their pain. Both of them staggered to their feet and over to the chest.

Above them, the creature wormed its bulk down the wall, teeth snapping, slobber falling like rain.

Nix took his key from his satchel, dreading what the fakking thing would demand.

"Give us a carrot."

Nix could hardly believe it. "Finally got some luck."

"Hurry, Nix."

Nix gave the key a bit of carrot and shoved it into the chest. It warmed while it did its work.

The creature was getting closer.

"Nix?"

"Hit that fakkin' creature with a hammer or something," Nix snapped. "Come on, key!"

The key cooled and Nix turned it. Inside the chest were pages of thin metallic plates inscribed with an alphabet Nix had never seen. On top of them, in a leather harness, were six hollow tubes, all marked with magic sigils. Nix grabbed the harness and, unable to resist, three of the metallic pages. He shoved the lot into his satchel.

"Nix…" Egil said, the tension in his voice as sharp as a blade.

"I know," Nix said.

He looked up to the see the bulging form of the creature nearly down. Mouths extended from its form, almost like short arms, and snapped at the air.

"Move," Nix said, and ran to the door near the chest. To his relief, he saw a keyhole like the one they'd seen on the door above. Nix still had the key in hand.

"Open it," he said. "Now!"

"Give us a pomegranate," the key said.

"Fak you and your pomegranate!" Nix said. "Open this lock!"

The creature let itself fall from the wall and hit the floor in a huge, stinking, wet heap to the floor. Scores of eyes fixed on Egil and Nix and the creature rolled and squirmed and bulged toward them.

"Fakking gewgaw!" Egil said, cursing not at Nix but at the key. He threw a hammer at the creature and the huge weapon hit the mound of flesh with a sickly thwack. The creature roared but did not slow.

"Give us a pear, then," said the key.

Nix held the key up before his face. "You're going to end up in the gut of that thing behind me where you'll eat nothing ever again unless you open this fakking door! You hear me?"

Egil backed into Nix, trying to keep his distance from the snapping mouths.

"Nix," the priest said.

The key was quiet for a moment. "You owe us a pomegranate."

Nix shoved the key into the lock, felt it warm, the bit fitting itself to the complicated, enchanted mechanism.

"Hurry!" Egil said.

The key did its work, Nix turned it, the door slid open, and he and Egil piled through. The door slid closed behind them, cutting off the frustrated growls and roars and hisses of the horror.

"Fak," Egil said, breathing heavily.

"Seconded," Nix said, his heart a hammer on his ribs.

They stood in small square room, perhaps three paces on a side, their backs to the door. Another metal door was opposite them. The glyphs and sigils etched into its surface made Nix dizzy. He saw it had a keyhole like the others.

"Is that another lock?" Egil said.

The creature slammed into the door behind them. The wall shook, and the metal groaned. The creature slammed into it, again, again. The metal bent and veined under the stress.

"Time to go," Nix said.

He moved to the door, studied the glyphs as best he could. Likely they were some kind of triggering spell if the door were not opened with the proper words or items.

"Those glyphs?" Egil asked.

"Some kind of trigger, I'd wager," Nix said.

The creature hit the door behind them again, its frustrated roars and growls gaining ferocity. The metal squealed and a line appeared in, a slight buckling.

"What will it trigger?" Egil asked.

"Nothing good," Nix said. To the key, he said, "Open the lock. Try not to trigger the magic."

"Give us a pear."

Nix and Egil cursed in unison.

"Why does everything have to be so damned complicated with you?" Nix said to the key. "Fine. I owe you a pear, too, to go with the pomegranate."

He didn't wait for a reply, just shoved the key into the lock. It fitted itself to the mechanism, grumbling the while, and he gave it a turn.

The glyphs on the door flared and acrid smoke filled the room. The door didn't open.

"What happened?" Egil said.

Nix shrugged. "Maybe the glyphs fizzled? I don't know. It's unlocked, though. Let's pry it open."

Nix gave Egil one of his daggers and, while the fleshy horror tried to beat open the door behind them, the two of them worried at the seam between the door and the wall. They got it open a hair's width and water started streaming in, warm and stinking.

"Shite," Nix said, seeing their danger. "Hurry. Hurry."

The more they pried it open, the faster the water poured in, filling the small room. Egil jerked it open a hand's width and the water started to rise rapidly.

"By fakkin' drowning?" Nix said, pulling at the door. "Really? Really?"

"On two," Egil said.

Both of them grabbed the edge of the door.

"One, two."

They pulled, both of them grunting with exertion.

The water rose to their waists, their stomachs.

"Come on, Egil! Fak!"

The sinews and veins and muscles in the priest's arms looked carved out of stone. His face and head reddened with exertion, turning Ebenor's eye bloodshot. With a final heave he jerked the door open enough for them to fit through. Water rose to their necks.

Nix held the light crystal before his face. "Bright," he said, and the eye opened fully, casting a bright beam of white light.

"Get a breath," Nix said, tilted his head upward to keep it out of the water. He shed his falchion, keeping only his daggers and his satchel, the latter with his the metal plates and the leather sling of chimes he'd taken from the chest.

"And leave your hammer."

"Aye," Egil said, then, "Don't drop your satchel. Those chimes came dear. One, two, three."

They went under. The moment they cleared the doorway they were in open water. The submerged mausoleums and crypts and tombs of the necropolis loomed darkly around them. Nix flashed the light from his crystal around to get his bearings and watched in horror as the bottom of the lake rolled and boiled, throwing up a fog of mud.

But even through the mud he could see the grasping, bony hands and decayed forms of dead serpent men clawing their way out of the bottom. He understood immediately what had happened. The glyphs he'd triggered on the door hadn't fizzled. They had awakened the dead.

Nix grabbed Egil by the arm, spitting bubbles, and pointed through the murk at the rising dead. Clouds of mud and dirt polluted the water. Corpses were clawing their way up all over the lake bottom. Nix pointed up toward the surface, shined his light that way. Egil nodded, but before Nix could start for the surface, a bony hand emerged from the lake bottom under his feet and grabbed him by the ankle.

He exclaimed in surprise, expelling a cloud of bubbles. He lurched upward, pulling the dead thing with him. A torso emerged, scaled skin sloughing from the boncs. A reptilian skull capped the sinewy neck. The mouth opened wide, as if to bite him, but he kicked it in the face, knocking its jaw clean off. But he could not dislodge the undead's grip.

Egil swam down, bubbles pouring from his nose, grabbed the corpse by the arm and chest, and tore the arm off at the shoulder. Nix was free and swimming, catching sight of countless undead lurching and swimming toward them through the murk. He shook the severed arm free as he swam.

They pulled at the water for all they were worth, following the path of Nix's light, legs kicking, arms wheeling. Nix's lungs already burned and the churn from the bottom had turned the water dark. He had no idea how far they were from the surface. He imagined the dead right behind him, lipless mouths revealing rotting fangs, their decayed bodies sloughing skin and organs as they tore through the water after them. His heart pounded his ribs. His chest ached, screamed for air, and it was all he could do not to gasp a lungful of fouled water. All it would take is one of the dead to get an ankle and pull him down. He'd drown in–

They broke the surface at last.

"Go, go!"

Both of them gulped air but neither of them slowed. Side by side they swam like the Hells themselves were at their heels, legs kicking, arms wheeling. The air reeked of decay. The release of the dead had turned the lake into a charnel house.

They reached the shallows. Nix could see the shore line ahead. He was relieved that Mere had gotten clear of the lake, but wasn't sure he would. His arms and legs were numb from exhaustion. He was failing. After two more strokes he could not lift his arms. He stood in the shallows and tried wading, but even that was too much.

A hand closed on him, pulled him along: Egil, always Egil.

"Move!" the priest shouted at him.

Nix did his best, but Egil did most of the work, towing Nix along through the waist deep water. Nix looked behind, where the smooth surface of the water gave no hint of the horrors rising out of the murk. The water came to thigh, knee, and Egil let him go. Nix stumbled along beside his indefatigable friend. Behind them, the water started to churn as the dead rose.

"Mere!" Egil called, as he and Nix staggered onto the beach. Nix fell to all fours, but Egil pulled him up.

"Where is she?" Nix said, weak-legged and gasping. "Mere!"

Figures emerged from the treeline, six of them, and Nix knew they'd stepped out of one pile of shite to plant their foot firmly in another.

CHAPTER SIXTEEN

The two guild men in front held Mere between them. One was a droopy-faced, heavy set man with his long hair pulled back in a top knot, and his face still showing the bruise Nix had given him back in the guild house, while the other was just as tall, but more compact looking, with sharp features and intelligent eyes. Nix could not see it but he imagined a blade at Mere's back. Her eyes were not frightened. They were fixed intently on Egil and Nix.

"We have her," said the compactly built man.

"And her bitch sister, that faytor," said the droopy faced one. "Now, you spill where Channis is and maybe someone lives through this, or at least dies easy."

The other four guild men moved up. They must have had Rose back in the treeline.

Mere's voice sounded in Nix's head.

You tell me when.

"We don't have Channis," Nix said.

"That's a fakkin' lie," said the droopy one.

The other one checked something on his hand, a tattoo.

"We know he's alive," the man said.

"He slipped us a day and half ago," Nix said. Suspicions started to form in his thinking, but the sound of soft splashes from behind pushed them away. He shared a look with Egil and the priest gave an almost imperceptible nod.

Get ready, Nix said to Mere.

Nix glanced back to see heads breaking the surface, grinning, reptilian skulls, first just a handful, then a dozen, then several score. The dead rose in their stinking dozens, rising as they walked through the shallows. They moaned wetly.

"Gods, what are those!" Nix said, feigning terror.

He beamed the light from his magic crystal out into the lake. The guild men exclaimed in fear, cursed, and – as Nix had known he would – Egil burst into motion while they were momentarily distracted.

The two men near Mere gave sudden gasps and grabbed their heads. Mere had done her work.

And Egil, unarmed, simply charged, covering in only a few strides the space between him and the man holding Mere. The man recovered from Mere's mental assault enough to throw Mere aside and slash awkwardly at Egil, but the priest simply caught the man's forearm in one hand, stopping the slash, then loosed a punch with his other hand that caught the man squarely in the side of the head. Nix had never seen anyone remain standing after taking one of Egil's punches flush and the droopy faced man was no exception. He hit the ground like a brained pig.

The man who'd checked his tattoo – the Seventh Blade, Nix presumed – backed off and took a fighting stance while the other four men charged out of the treeline, but before the four could close another form burst out of the trees from the side, tall and dark and scaled and fanged and clawed – the creature that had harried their steps since Channis had fled.

And all at once Nix's suspicions – suspicions he'd held since he'd first seen the creature on the ruined bridge – hardened into certainty. Channis's transforming body, the ridges on his face, the fangs, the sloughing skin and hard, scaly skin beneath. Channis hadn't been killed by the creature. Channis *was* the creature.

Channis roared and hissed, bounding forward on overlong legs, and tore out the throat of one of the guild men with a clawed slash. The others turned to face it but they were too slow. It leaped atop one and they fell to the ground in a heap. It opened its mouth wide and sank fangs into the man's throat. The man screamed and writhed, but only for a moment before he went quiet and still. The others stabbed the creature with their short blades and it hissed in rage and pain. A backhand claw turned the face of one man into a bloody flap dangling from the exposed faceplate, but the other managed to drive his blade deep into the creature's hide. It hissed, its tongue sticking far out, and bounded back, bleeding profusely.

Egil, meanwhile, used the distraction of the creature to charge the compact man. He hit him in the side and they fell to the ground. The man tried to bring his short sword to bear, but Egil held it out wide and slammed Ebenor's eye into the man's face. He went still, dead or unconscious.

Channis loped off into the treeline, and the last guild man, a mousy looking slubber with a protuberant nose, took in the situation. His expression fell and he backed off a step, another.

"You can stay with them dead things," he said in a high-pitched voice, nodding at the lake. "I'll just go my way."

Nix drew and threw one of his throwing daggers before the man took another step. It slipped into his neck and the man fell, gagging, dying.

"The fak you will," Nix said.

"We have to go!" Mere said, pointing at the dozens of corpses shambling out of the water.

"Aye, that," Nix said. "Where's Rose?"

"They didn't hurt her," Mere said, and led them to where they'd left her in the trees.

She opened her eyes as Egil started to lift her.

"I think I can walk," she said. "You click them guild slubbers?"

"Clicked them," Nix said, with a nod. "And we're going to go fix you right now."

He glanced back at the lake. The dead had stopped at the water's edge, standing in the shallows, hundreds of them, empty eye sockets staring out at them, fanged mouths open in frustrated anger.

"Let's get back to Odrhaal," Nix said.

"What about those two?" Mere asked, indicating the two unconscious guild men.

Nix spat. "Throw them to the dead, Egil."

The priest nodded and walked toward them.

"You can't do that," Mere protested.

"Why can't we? They were going to kill you."

"But they didn't," Mere said.

"Then what?" Nix said.

"Bring them," Mere said. "I have an idea."

Nix didn't like it, but he trusted Mere. "You get the big one, Egil."

Nix searched both men, disarmed them, found the dowsing rod on the droop faced one. He snapped it in half. He recovered his and Egil's clothes and other gear from the boat, got dressed, and they set off. Egil armed himself with a sword from one of the dead guild men. Nix collected his daggers.

"Eyes and ears," he said. "Watch for that creature."

There was nothing more dangerous than a wounded animal.

They made their way back through the dark toward the tower. When they reached it, Nix stepped before the statue of Odrhaal, his pants soaked, his body battered, one of the metal chimes cold in his palm, but the magic in it sending a warm tingle up his arm. Egil stood beside him. Both of them eyed the image before them, the reptilian face, the clawed hands. The voice in his head, in all of their heads, was silent, as if in pensive waiting

Behind them, Rose whimpered.

"Do it," Egil said.

Nix nodded and struck the chime on the sculpture's pedestal. The high-pitched note it rang caused him to wince and recoil. Egil and Mere cried out. The tone rang only one time that was audible to their ears, but it nested in Nix's mind and continued to sound in his head, like a prolonged scream of agony. He shook his head and staggered back a step, his own shout matching the scream in his head.

The tube warmed in his hands, pulsed as though it

had a heartbeat. Waves of magical energy, like expanding smoke rings, poured from its end. He pointed the chime at the statue and the energy from its tones, perhaps from their collective screaming, put a latticework of cracks in the stone.

The ringing in his head was going to split his skull but still he kept the chime aimed at the statue. A piece of stone the size of a gold royal fell away, revealing scaled flesh beneath. Another fell away, another, the bits of polished white stone falling like snow, Odrhaal molting his prison.

Nix's eyes watered, his head throbbed, his mouth formed screams, and the shriek of the chime reverberated around in his skull. He thought he must soon pass out but he clung to consciousness and kept the chime pointed at Odrhaal.

More stone fell away, revealing the finely scaled, shiny black-green skin beneath, the deep eye sockets, the shallow nose ridges, the sleek head, the three-fingered hands, the long fangs poking out from under the lip ridges. Odrhaal wore thick, layered robes of green cloth. Triangles within triangles were sewn in gold thread on the sleeves.

By the time the time the ringing in his mind began to diminish, Nix was on his knees. The chime, now brittle, cracked in his hand, crumbled to bits. He looked up at Odrhaal, his vision blurry. A clawed hand flexed, the long fingers graceful even in that small movement. Odrhaal's eyes opened and the vertical slits looked down on Nix.

Nix began to scream anew.

●●●●

Odrhaal's slit-eyed gaze had weight and it took all Nix had to stay on all fours rather than lie flat and grovel. Nix felt as if he'd awakened a demon, or maybe a god, but he'd done it for Rose and he'd have done it all again.

He twisted his head to the right and saw that Egil too was on all fours. The priest's head was down, the eye of Ebenor staring at Odrhaal, and a string of drool hung from his mouth. Mere alone remained on her feet, standing between Odrhaal and Rose, her eyes wide. Twin streams of blood leaked from her nostrils. Nix wondered if they were communicating mentally.

We are, said Odrhaal, his soft voice like a hammer blow in Nix's head. *We all are now.*

Nix's vision blurred and his head felt... full, swollen. An irrational terror seized him, caused his body to tremble, his thoughts to churn. He couldn't understand it and didn't want to. He only wanted to curl up in a ball and weep, but his body would not answer his commands.

Without warning, blood gushed from his nose and he retched. He was vaguely aware of Egil experiencing the same thing near him. The priest, however, managed to utter a few curses between retches.

You're hurting them, Mere projected, then said aloud, "You're hurting them. Stop. Please."

"I needed to feed," Odrhaal said, as if that somehow explained what had occurred. "But I'm sated. For now."

The pressure in Nix's head relented. The terror subsided. He spit blood, raised his head.

"I'm not hurting you, though," Odrhaal said to Mere, his sibilant voice measured, as smooth as a polished stone. He stood right before Nix. The serpent man reached down and took the leather sling holding the remaining chimes.

"You're hurting me some," Mere said, dabbing at the blood leaking from her nose. "But not like with them."

"You're strong," Odrhaal said, his tongue flickering forth as if tasting the air between him and Mere.

"Help… Rose," Nix managed.

Odrhaal waved a scaled hand dismissively. Bands of polished stone wrapped several of his fingers. "I already have. She is, once more, herself, and only herself. I keep my promises, Nix Fall of Dur Follin."

Nix exhaled with relief. At least they'd saved Rose. That made it all worth it. Whatever might come from freeing Odrhaal, at least they'd saved Rose.

The mindmage stepped forward, kneeled, and put his clawed hand on Rose's head, a possessive gesture that Nix disliked. Rose groaned, rolled over, blinked open her eyes. They showed surprise upon seeing the serpent man, but only for only a moment. Mental communication must have passed between them for a drip of blood leaked from her nose.

"Merelda and Rusilla," Odrhaal said, as if trying out the names.

Nix didn't like the way he spoke their names. It suggested a familiarity the serpent man hadn't earned.

Odrhaal helped Rose sit up. She glanced around, as if awakening from a dream.

"Both of you show considerable strength," the mindmage said to the sisters. "Rusilla was able to keep herself mostly untangled from the psychic imprint, and what was tangled presented an uncomplicated knot."

He cocked his head to the side, as if he'd just heard something interesting. He looked at Mere, at Rusilla, his slit-eyes narrowing.

"You and she are sisters. Both of you born of devils."

Mere said nothing, at least nothing Nix could hear, though she and Rose shared a nervous look.

A blur of motion behind and to the side of Odrhaal drew Nix's eyes and caused his heart to thump against his ribs. Channis, or whatever Channis had become, bound out of the treeline, his long strides devouring the distance between them. Nix opened his mouth to speak but no sound emerged. He tried to point but his body would not function.

Channis ran with his mouth open, gulping air, revealing long reptilian fangs. Black scales covered his muscular body and he loped with a silent, terrible grace, a man transformed into an instrument of bloodletting. Nix struggled to make his mouth work, to force words from between his lips. Channis was closing and no one seemed to notice.

Mere noticed his pained expression and her voice sounded in his head.

What is it?

Behind you! Behind you!

Odrhaal, Rose, and Mere turned as one to look. Rose gasped, put her hand to her mouth. Mere took a half-step toward Egil. Odrhaal merely stared. Nix expected the mindmage to smite Channis somehow, expected to see blood pour from the former guild master's nose and eyes, but nothing of the kind happened.

Channis drew closer, closer, and then slowed. Rose and Mere nodded, as if they'd heard something sensible and both visibly relaxed.

When Channis reached Odrhaal, he bowed his head and sank to one knee, as if he were in audience with a king. Odrhaal put his hand on Channis's snakelike head and Channis's nostril ridges flared. Before Nix could ask, Odrhaal said,

"I saw what happened to him in your memories, Nix. What you call 'Blackalley' was a weapon used in a war fought long ago, the war I showed you. It fed on the energy of those captured."

Nix thought of his dream, of the wizard war that had swept Ellerth, that had brought down entire civilizations and remade the face of the world. The pressure in his head suddenly relented, as if a cork had been pulled from him, and he was able to speak. His voice sounded hoarse. "It was your weapon? You made it?"

"I was involved in its making," Odrhaal said with a nod of his scaled head. "It's a psychic drain. It traps weak minds within it, feeds on their energy.

Nix disliked the way Odrhaal spoke so casually of making playthings of a person's emotions and innermost thoughts. He imagined that Odrhaal could empty his mind, strip him of him, tear out everything that mattered and leave him a shell, a veneer of a man. He thought of Channis as he'd been after Blackalley, the vacant look he'd had in his black eyes, now replaced with the eyes of something... else.

"It fed on regret somehow," Nix said, meaning Blackalley.

Odrhaal turned to look down on Nix and under the serpentine gaze Nix once more felt cold fear bubble up from his gut, irrational, profound, overwhelming. He could not keep his head up. He dropped it, ashamed of himself but unable to stop.

"Nix?" Egil asked.

And in that moment Nix realized that Odrhaal made and fed on fear the same way Blackalley – or the creatures in it, or Channis or whatever he'd become – fed on regret. Odrhaal fed on fear. Perhaps all mindmages fed on emotion. What did the sisters feed on? Did they even know it?

"You use fear for fuel," Nix said.

"Let him go," Egil said, clenching his fists and standing.

"But not your fear," Odrhaal said. "At least not anymore. As I said, I'm sated."

Once more the pressure eased, and the fear subsided to something manageable. Nix spit, stood.

Odrhaal said, "The weapon, Blackalley, evolved into something else over time, something new. Your Channis let what it had become nest inside him and now... he's this."

Nix looked at the malformed, dark creature on its knee before Odrhaal. "Is he... still alive?"

"Channis? Barely, and not for very much longer. Soon he'll be gone altogether. Does that displease you?"

Nix considered asking if Odrhaal could help Channis as he had Rose, but pushed the thought back down. Channis deserved no consideration. He'd tried to murder Rose and Mere.

"No," Nix said.

You see? Odrhaal's voice sounded in Nix's head. *Emotions are weapons for you, too.*

Nix did not try to chase down the mindmage's meaning. He suspected he wouldn't like what he learned, and he'd already learned too much.

"Why did he come back to me?" Odrhaal asked, staring down at Channis. "I don't know. A weapon returning to its maker? A child to its parent? It will be interesting to find out."

He made a dismissive gesture at Channis and the creature rose, turned, and sprinted off into the swamp. Watching Channis's dark form disappear into the brush, surrounded by the ruins of a civilization that had used Blackalley as a weapon, Nix felt... trivial. He wished he hadn't learned what he'd learned, about the world, about himself.

"We're going to leave now," he said to Odrhaal, and tried not to make it sound like a question.

He wasn't quite sure where they'd go, probably New Dineen, but he knew he wanted out of the Deadmire, away from Odrhaal.

"Are you?" Odrhaal said.

"We are," Egil said, the words almost a growl.

Mere helped Rose to her feet then said, "I'd ask something, Odrhaal."

Odrhaal's lips ridges curled in a smile. "I know," he said, and turned from Nix to face Mere."

"We should just go, Mere," Egil said, but she didn't listen to him. She drew herself up and nodded at the two unconscious guild Committeemen. Nix had forgotten they were even there.

"Make them forget," Mere said. "Give them false memories so that we can return to Dur Follin."

Odrhaal's tongue flicked and he stared at her a long moment, his snake eyes unblinking. "You request this for your friends." Not a question.

"We don't need it," Nix said, unwilling to go into debt to the serpent man.

Mere nodded. "I know you can do it."

Channis licked his lips with his long, forked tongue, tapped his claws one against the other.

"I can do it," Odrhaal said. He regarded the guild men. "What would you like them to think happened?"

The question seemed to take Mere by surprise. She looked to Nix, back to Odrhaal.

"I'm not certain. I thought—"

Odrhaal smiled and Nix liked the look of it not at all.

"We don't need this," Egil said, echoing Nix. "Let's just go. Now."

Odrhaal ignored him, as did Mere and Rose.

"I do have an idea," the mindmage said. "But since you ask a favor of me, I'd ask one of you."

Nix could only imagine what a being like Odrhaal might request. He liked matters less and less with each passing moment. His hand would've fallen to the hilt of his falchion but he'd left it at the bottom of the lake.

Mere stared back at the serpent man. Nix thought she looked braced for a punch. He could see that thoughts were passing between Mere and Odrhaal. And whatever those thoughts were, they caused Mere to pale, her lips to tighten. Rose's, too. The sisters clasped hands. As one they looked at Egil, at Nix, back at Odrhaal. They seemed to share some kind of communication and both their expressions hardened. They stuck out their chins and nodded.

Odrhaal let out a slow, satisfied hiss.

"Say it aloud," Mere said.

"So they can hear," Rose added.

Odrhaal turned to face Egil and Nix.

"I agreed to do what she asked if she agreed to become my apprentice."

"And I stay if she stays," said Rose.

A pit formed in Nix's stomach. "Mere, no."

"No," Egil said, his word as a final as a dirge.

"Your opinions on this matter are irrelevant," Odrhaal said.

Mere looked to them. "This is my choice to make. Our choice, Rose and me."

Nix had heard enough about choices in the last day to last him a lifetime. He realized he was sweating.

"It's not just yours, Mere. You're making it for us. That gives us a say."

"No it doesn't," she said.

Nix shifted on his feet, antsy, wanting to do something but unable to figure out what.

"It's just a town, Mere," he said. "We can go somewhere else. All four of us."

"Aye," Egil said.

"New Dineen," Nix continued. "We can start over. It'll be good. The guild will never find us. We don't need… him."

Odrhaal's eyes narrowed but he said nothing, or at least nothing Nix could hear.

"It's not just a town," Mere said, and Nix knew she was right.

"Mere," Egil said. "Please don't… I just…"

She smiled and her eyes filled with tears. "You don't have to say it, Egil. I know you can't. But I know what you want to say. I love you, too, in the way you can't say. I have for months."

Now Egil's eyes filled with tears. Mere went on:

"That's why I'm doing it, don't you see? Dur Follin is your home, you and Nix. Without it, you two would be almost as lost as you would without each other."

"It's just a town," Egil said softly, but there was little fight in his tone. "Just a town."

His weakness seemed to give Mere strength. She spoke in a confident tone. "You know it's not. You saved me and Rose, once. Now I'm going to save you. My choice."

"No, Mere," Egil said, shaking his head. "No."

"I've been in your head, Egil," she said. "I know the pain you're carrying. I don't know how you bear it, how you manage to be so gentle when you're… so hurt. But you're not ready, Egil. You and I… can't happen, not now. Maybe someday."

Egil sniffed and looked up sharply, not at Mere but Odrhaal. He wiped snot and tears and blood from his face with the back of his hand. "Then take it out, Odrhaal. Cut it out of me."

"Egil! No!" Mere said.

Nix was appalled. "Don't be an idiot!"

"My choice," Egil said, turning her own words against her.

Mere looked as if he'd slapped her.

"Take it out, snakeman. I've earned that, at least. Do it."

Odrhaal regarded the priest with his unblinking slit eyes.

Egil stared back then bowed his head, the eye of Ebenor on Odrhaal.

"Don't, Egil," Nix said, and tears formed in his eyes. "Egil. Don't."

Odrhaal stepped forward, reached up, and put a clawed hand on Egil's bald pate.

Nix took a step toward them but Odrhaal's gaze froze him.

"Moments, Egil," Nix said, his hands pleading. "We're the sum of our past moments. Those are your words. Yours."

Odrhaal, clasping Egil's head, stared down at the priest. Egil's body began to shake.

Nix imagined Odrhaal cutting memories out of Egil's mind, leaving him something other than Nix's Egil, remaking him into something he was not, making his eyes as vacant as Channis's.

"Don't, Egil! Don't!"

He tried to draw his blade but his arm wouldn't respond. He was sweating, straining, but couldn't move.

"Stop, Odrhaal!"

Mere had a hand to her mouth, her eyes wide and pained. Rose looked away.

Spit flew from Egil's mouth, blood from his nose.

Odrhaal suddenly released his hold, blinking his slit eyes, and Egil sighed and sagged to the ground.

"Damn it, damn it," Nix softly cursed.

Odrhaal released whatever he'd done to hold Nix in place and Nix ran to Egil's side, shoving Odrhaal out of the way. He kneeled and took his friend in his arms.

"What have you done," Nix murmured, not sure if he was talking to Egil or Odrhaal. "What have you done?"

It was too much. He'd sought out Odrhaal to save Rose and in the process he'd lost both sisters and his best friend. He cursed himself and could not hold back another round of tears.

"I can take the pain out of you," Odrhaal said to Nix.

Nix laid Egil aside and jumped to his feet. He drew a dagger and pointed it at Odrhall's throat.

"Fak you! Fak you, Odrhaal!"

Odrhaal's lip ridges curled in a smile. He seemed untroubled by Nix's weapon. He turned and looked at the two guild men, prone on the ground, then at Mere and Rose.

"Now I'll honor our agreement. As I said, I keep my promises."

The mindmage went to the fallen guild men and touched the heads of first one and then the other. Both of them murmured, trembled, sighed, and went slack.

Odrhaal stood, his own sigh half a hiss.

"Their names are Rusk and Trelgin," Odrhaal said, reciting the story he'd planted in the guild men's minds. "The Seventh and Sixth Blades of their guild. They've learned that Rusilla and Merelda were witches who enspelled the two of you to protect them. They tracked all four of you to the swamp, where they killed the witches, but not before the witches killed Channis. The death of the witches freed you and Egil of their spell and you requested mercy of these two, Rusk and Trelgin, which they granted in exchange for agreement to compensate the guild in gold for the men you killed. These two are rivals. Their concurrence in this story will make it still more credible. You can return to your city. I'll see to it these guild men get back to their boat. Go now, and go alone."

"Fak you," Nix said. He turned to Rose and Mere. "Are you sure?"

They nodded.

He walked past Odrhaal to embrace Rose and Mere. He breathed in the smell of Rose's hair, the feel of her in his arms.

"Thank you," he said, and she hugged him harder.

Egil rose, his eyes distant. He, too, hugged Rose, then took Mere in his arms and held onto her for a long time. He kissed her gently, the only one they'd ever shared so far as Nix knew.

"Thank you," he said to her.

She touched his cheek and stared into his eyes. Maybe she said something in his mind. Nix hoped so.

Nix cleared his throat, tapped his temple. "You call if you need us."

"We will," Mere said.

Egil and Nix turned to face Odrhaal, who regarded them with his reptilian eyes.

"You hurt them and we'll come back," Egil said. "That's a promise. And I keep mine, too."

"And if we come back for that," Nix said, tapping the hilt of his blade. "There's no amount of fear or regret or mindmagic shite that will save you from us. I'll make those pointy-eared fakkers you fought before seem like gentlemen."

Odrhaal's eyes narrowed a bit but he said nothing.

Nix and Egil took one last look at Rose and Mere, turned, and headed back to the boat, back to Dur Follin.

Egil rowed them upriver at almost a leisurely pace. Nix sat in the back of the boat, staring at the mountainous back of the priest as he worked the oars. They spoke little. Each lived in his own head for much of the journey.

"Could be none of that happened," Nix said. "You know that, right?"

"Aye," Egil said.

"Everything we think we know. Odrhaal could have put there, just as we think he did with the guild men."

Nix searched his memory for their names: Rusk and Trelgin.

"Why bother?" Egil said.

"Can't say," Nix said. "Could be a reason, though. We just wouldn't know it because whatever it is was replaced with what we're meant to think."

"I think you should stop," Egil said over his shoulder. "It happened. Hurts too much to not have happened."

"Fair point," Nix said.

The river rolled past. Nix had the question on his tongue for a long time before he could finally bring himself to ask it.

"Assuming everything that happened, happened... Did you do it?"

Egil's back muscles tensed. He pulled up the oars for a moment and looked out on the waters of the Meander. For a while Nix didn't think he'd answer, but finally the priest spoke.

"Most religions are about expiating transgressions, giving the faithful a way to live with their faults, to forgive themselves for those faults. You know what I mean?"

"I suppose."

"But if you could just," – Egil made a cutting gesture with his hand, and his voice cracked – "cut your failings out, be made to forget they ever happened, then you'd remake yourself as a better you. Wouldn't you do that if you could, Nix?"

Nix, with his many and sundry faults and regrets, hesitated only a moment. "No. And I mean that. No."

"You've never been a religious man, Nix."

"No, but I'm around one sometimes."

Egil said nothing, so Nix continued:

"I think that if you cut it out then you're not remaking a better you. You cut it out then you're not you at all. A priest I know once taught me that over ales."

Egil's body shook with a short chuckle or maybe a shudder. "Maybe you're more religious than you realize."

"Maybe," Nix said. He stared at the back of his friend's head. "You didn't answer my question. Did you do it?"

Egil inhaled deeply and shook his head. "I didn't do it. I came close, but I couldn't leave them again. Hulda and Asa. I can't leave them ever again."

Nix closed his eyes, thanked gods he didn't believe in, and reached up to put a hand on his friend's shoulder. He left it there for a time then left Egil to himself.

The priest took up the oars again and rowed them back upriver to Dur Follin, their city, their home. Nix pretended not to notice when Egil wept.

"You row," Rusk ordered Trelgin.

The droop faced Seventh Blade did not even grumble. He pushed them off, took a seat on the rower's bench, and started back toward the Meander. They'd had to leave the bodies of Varn, Mors, and the others in the swamp, though Rusk had collected the symbols of Aster each wore. They'd throw a pray to the God of Stealth in the name of their fallen guild men. The witches had been vicious, had turned Varn and Mors against their fellows, the same way they'd forced Egil and Nix to attack the guild house.

Rusk still didn't understand why the witches had arranged an attack on the guild. He supposed the red-haired witch had been hurt somehow when Rusk had murdered the old Upright Man in her tent. So she and her sister had enspelled Egil and Nix to take their vengeance, and things had escalated from there.

Rusk eyed the tat on his hand, the new eighth blade it had grown.

"Bitter taste to let Egil and Nix live over this, Eighth Blade," Trelgin said. "They killed a lot of good guild men."

"They did, but they were as enspelled by both those witches as were Varn and Mors. And they're going to pay compensation to make good. They'll be grateful we treated them square and that'll be useful to us someday."

"As you say, Eighth Blade," Trelgin said, sucking drool, and Rusk liked the way the title sounded on another's lips. When they cleared the swamp and broke out into the Meander-proper, Trelgin spoke over his shoulder, his diction sloppy with palsy.

"My loyalties are always to the guild and whoever wears the eighth blade. I know we had some words on this deal, but I hope you can respect that."

Rusk didn't bother to respond, instead letting Trelgin stew.

After a time he smiled and said, "Seventh Blade's a shite job, Trelgin. Get used to it."

ACKNOWLEDGMENTS

My thanks to Mr. Leiber, for *Fafhrd and the Mouser*, and to Mr. Howard, for the Cimmerian.